Paying Back Jack

Paying Back Jack

A Vincent Calvino Novel

Christopher G. Moore

W F HOWES LTD

This large print edition published in 2010 by
W F Howes Ltd
Unit 4, Rearsby Business Park, Gaddesby Lane,
Rearsby, Leicester LE7 4YH

1 3 5 7 9 10 8 6 4 2

First published in the United Kingdom in 2009
by Atlantic Books

A CIP catalogue record for this book is available
from the British Library

ISBN 978 1 40745 789 5

Typeset by Palimpsest Book Production Limited,
Falkirk, Stirlingshire
Printed and bound in Great Britain
by MPG Books Ltd, Bodmin, Cornwall

For Busakorn Suriyasarn

CHAPTER 1

Calvino's last sports jacket was ruined when Nicky 'the Toad' Marras's blood splattered over the lapel and down the pocket. A couple of things to bear in mind about Nicky the Toad: he didn't die, as Calvino only punched him in the nose after the Toad had reached a knife hidden inside his boot. One of those fake Gurka knives sold by street-side vendors. The Toad had an affinity for blades. He pulled it when he got drunk and argumentative, or started getting mad over some contested World Series statistic. The year Joe DiMaggio was eligible for the Baseball Hall of Fame and half a bottle of whiskey had set him off. It was the kind of thing the Toad could kill someone over.

Calvino's maid had sent the bloodied Gucci knockoff to the dry cleaner, and the dry cleaner had sent it back with a note. It seemed that Nicky the Toad's blood was as obstinate and mean as the man himself. Nothing could be done to remove the stain. They could sew on some patches, but it wouldn't look like an original Gucci anymore but more like a counterfeit tailored inside a Bangkok sweatshop. And that blurring of the distinction between an original and a counterfeit pretty much summed up Nicky the Toad, who'd watched too many gangster movies.

Calvino had moved on from that night in Bangkok, as had Nicky, back in New York. Calvino's law: After thirty years without any contact, an old school friend surprises you with a trip to Bangkok, gets loaded, starts coughing up old grievances, and reaches for a gun to settle scores; you may have to hit him hard and sacrifice a perfectly good sports jacket. Life was a series of blowbacks but blood is one that sticks to the clothes and to the memory.

A light drizzle outside cast a mid-afternoon gloom over the interior of Venice Tailors, a hole-in-the-wall Sukhumvit shop-house tucked underneath the broad concrete arch of the Skytrain. Everyone said it was climate change that had made the weather weird, out of sync. Vincent Calvino stood in front of a floor-to-ceiling mirror at the far end of the shop. He was the only customer. With an election up in the air, no one had been spending. People held tight to their money, planning to use it for an emergency escape – except for Calvino, who had nowhere to escape to. Arms stretched out, eyes closed, he meditated and let his mind float. Circling around him was Tony, the Thai-Chinese tailor, a measuring tape draped around his neck, a piece of blue chalk in one hand. Slowly Tony removed the jacket from the wooden hanger, pulled it onto Calvino's left arm, swung it around, and then threaded Calvino's right arm inside. Grinning and bobbing his head, he admired the final work in the mirror. Only the name of the shop and the Italian posters had any real connection to Italy. Customers played along, pretending that Tony was actually a Tony and that he channeled a line of Italian tailors back to Leonardo Da Vinci.

Tony's assistant, an elderly Thai called Uncle, sat at the cutting table on a high stool, smoking a hand-rolled cigarette. Uncle had liver spots sprayed on his neck and hands like he'd been hit by a double-barrel blast of buckshot. He drank green tea for energy and flashed nicotine-stained teeth. In front of Uncle were stacks of well-thumbed fashion magazines bought secondhand from service staff at five-star hotels. Zegna, Brioni, Kiton, and about every other highend brand were in the glossy ads and editorial features. Tony studied these images the way a counterfeiter examined a hundred-dollar bill. Sadly, imitation was dismissed as second-rate. Tony had turned it into high art.

Tony signaled his assistant to switch on the lights. The overhead neon fixtures flickered, the light danced off the faded posters of Grand Canal, the Coliseum, and Palazzo Vecchio. Tony had never been to Italy, but that didn't matter much. He was a brilliant copyist. He'd mastered the ability to copy the fine detail from the silhouettes, using similar fabrics, and that was enough to come up with a replica that would have fooled the hardcore fashion-conscious New Yorker. Tony's reputation had drawn many customers.

'Don't look, boss,' said Tony, who had slicked-back hair and a diamond pinky ring. Tony adjusted the shoulders and buttoned the middle button of the jacket. In the back of the shop Tony's wife sat on the floor with a couple of kids, watching a game show on TV.

Calvino opened his eyes and looked in the mirror. It had been Colonel Pratt who'd suggested it was time to up his game. Calvino was half-Italian, and convincing him to buy a stylish sports coat had taken no arm-twisting. Tony had made a perfect Brioni knock-off. It looked like a five-grand jacket – powdery blue with cream windowpane, a cashmere-and-silk blend, with dual back vents and hand stitching. Tony had worked his magic.

'Do you like?' asked Tony.

Calvino raised his arm, watching the sleeve rise slightly. 'I fixed the sleeve from last time,' said Tony. This had been the third fitting.

'It's okay.'

Tony yanked down on the back and the jacket tapered at the waist.

The assistant made a grunting laugh and gave the thumbs-up sign. 'Very beautiful, Khun Winee.' Then the wife looked around the corner, tearing herself away from the game show to pipe in with her two cents: 'You look like young man, very handsome.

You now high-society man. Women like you too, too much.'

Calvino unbuttoned the jacket and shot her a look in the mirror. The last thing Calvino wanted to hear was that he looked like some overdressed Chinese merchant who couldn't tell a Merlot from a Shiraz. He liked the jacket. It had exceeded his expectations and his budget. Even unbuttoned, there was no sign that he was holstering a handgun.

'Tony, it's good work.'

For a second he thought Tony was going to hug him and kiss him on each cheek. But there were limits to how far down the Italian turnpike Tony was prepared to go. Instead he put his fingers together in a wai and gave a little bow toward Calvino. All that Tony knew about Italians came from fashion magazines and American gangster films. He understood the essence of tailoring: a man's jacket made a statement about him. The perfect man's sports jacket occupied a middle zone between 'back off' and 'fuck off,' and Brioni had figured out the dress formula for a man who walked in that no man's land.

Tony had a special feel for fabrics and a gift with needle and thread, and he took pride in recreating the best of Italy. High style on a backpacker's budget had always been one of Bangkok's draws for visitors. A bit of self-delusion was all that was required; the rest could be pure Thai. Tony understood suits could be a problem in Bangkok temperatures. The heat, searing and raw, gave the impression that the universe was dragging you through a vapor trail of a supernova. Calvino had said, 'I gotta be able to breathe.' Walking around the city in a jacket could be like wheeling around in a portable sauna. So Tony had gone inventive making a jacket without lining in the body except for a few secret pockets. He read that farangs liked creativity, so he got creative.

Calvino turned to look at himself in profile. Semi-badass, he thought. Tony had taken extra care to tailor the jacket so his leather holster and .38 police special wouldn't bulge. A real badass didn't need to advertise that he was packing. He glanced at the large clock on the wall. He had an appointment with a new client, General Yosaporn. The General had been retired for many years, and Vincent Calvino had been the first private eye he'd ever hired. The General had been glad to pay the fee. And Colonel Pratt, a member in good standing of the Royal Thai police, who had introduced Calvino to the General, had suggested using part of the money for the new jacket. It was a jacket for impressing a new client. On the job, the upscale tailoring might draw too much attention. 'Time to go, Tony.'

Calvino paid the freight and stepped outside onto Sukhumvit Road. He opened his umbrella and walked to the crosswalk. The new jacket made him feel good. He had put on a light blue shirt and a yellow necktie with gray stripes. They matched his soft black leather Italian shoes.

Walking down the street, he told himself the rain didn't matter. The rain adds something – a pinch of mystery, a teaspoon of intrigue, he thought. My wet hair gives off a noir posture – or I could be just another guy fresh from the gym.

In a lot of big cities, a good pair of brass knuckles was worth more than a bucketful of gold rings. As he walked along, he thought about the pocket Tony had made for a pair of brass knuckles. 'That was thoughtful of him,' Calvino said to himself. He'd reached the crosswalk, what the English called a zebra crossing, a term that fit well in Bangkok. Only a wild animal would cross at the designated place.

Drivers of cars, motorcycles, taxis, trucks, and buses saw a crosswalk and stepped on the gas. He watched the traffic. Colonel Pratt had told him that gold was all anyone needed in Bangkok. That's why skinny, brainy men went for the gold. They could buy muscle. A bus rumbled past, blowing out a glacier-melting belch of black fumes. Calvino, hands in his pockets, feeling on top of the world, asked himself, So what came first? The chicken or the egg? The brass knuckles or the gold rings? It was the kind of dilemma his mother had loved. What do you want with knowledge? It only drives you to know how little you can ever know. What's the point of that?

A clearing appeared in the traffic. Calvino edged onto the crosswalk and was halfway into Sukhumvit Road when a gray Benz – one of the upper-end models with tinted windows that cost the same as a village upcountry – came straight at him. He saw the driver inside, a woman on a cell phone eating satay chicken (it might have been pork), but she didn't see him. The car brushed his side – a grazing blow that felt like the bare tip of a bull's horn passing just inside the bullfighter's red cape. It spun him around and he lost his balance, falling on one hand in the street. A group of schoolgirls who might have taken him for an aging NBA star started laughing. Falling down, better yet coming up bloody, was always good for bystander laughter. Slowly he rose to his feet. The Benz was long gone. He wiped his hands together and found his umbrella. It had been run over and ruined. Clutching the naked spines, he nodded his head, eyes half-closed, and meditated for a moment, trying to find that quiet space within. Not finding it, he opened his eyes and saw the schoolgirls waiting for his next move.

He stopped in front of the 7-Eleven at the top of Soi 33 and examined his jacket and tie in the window. Finding himself in one piece, he figured he'd won. One more time he'd crossed Sukhumvit Road on foot, leaving him wide-eyed, with his heart racing – all the necessary elements for post-traumatic flashbacks. Colonel Pratt would like the story. Calvino walked tall, head up, shoulders back, as he turned into Soi 33. The General had had two influences on him. He'd provided the cash for the jacket. And he had introduced Calvino to meditation. Inside Venice Tailors, he had practiced his meditation as Tony hovered around him. It had cleared his mind, opened it to every possibility as Tony had asked him what he thought. He'd had no thoughts.

Calvino stopped beside a street vendor who was cooking a long, tight coil of dead-liver-colored sausages over a charcoal fire in a large clay pot. Closing his eyes, he told himself that he wanted to see the soi as if for the first time, as if looking through the eyes of someone straight off the plane. It had been Colonel Pratt who had warned him that, after so many years inside the country, he would forget what had startled him at first.

He considered the possibility. After thousands of days, Calvino didn't really see the street anymore. That had been Colonel Pratt's point, and the General had agreed. They'd suggested that he try looking at things as if they were fresh, new, and of another time and place.

I've just arrived, and this is the first street in Asia I've ever seen. A smile crossed Calvino's face as he moved down the soi. Each step was a foot deeper into the freak show, starting with the huge banyan tree. Its large, twisted trunk wrapped with dozens of thin, colored nylon scarves, the tree had long, stringy veins that hung like gnarled tentacles over the soi. A dwarf stood on the broken sidewalk in front of a bar, dressed in a vest, a white shirt, and a bow tie. Holding up a sign for happy hour beer, he tagged along after each passing tourist for a few steps. Then, exhausted, he'd stop and retrace his steps to the bar and wait to strike again. 'Come inside!' he shouted. 'Many pretty girls!' The dwarf was right. There were dozens of girls in their late teens wearing too much makeup, decked out in short skirts, smoking, flirting, eyeing customers, throwing them smiles, then frowns, then another frown. It was early afternoon and there were few customers.

A tuk-tuk, the high pitch of its engine pushed to the limit, made Calvino step back on the sidewalk. A couple of drunken farang tourists sat in the back seat, laughing and screaming, rocking and rolling, as if their future had arrived and they liked what they saw. Calvino waved as they passed. He stopped in front of another street vendor's cart bearing fried grasshoppers, scorpions, and water bugs in separate trays, stacked high under a fluorescent light. The vendor was set up in the street in front of a Japanese karaoke place with a sign that said no non-Japanese allowed. The sign was in Thai. A couple of yings dressed like Japanese geisha called out to him. They liked his jacket. They smelled money.

'I'm not Japanese. I can't go inside,' he called back in Thai.

'No problem. You not come in. We go out. Sure.'

If he had just arrived in the country, he'd have gawked at the lifeless carcasses of the bug massacre, so he stopped now to take a look. The vendor asked, 'You try. You like, buy. You no like, no problem.'

The bug vendor held out a water bug and Calvino took it. She made a point of showing the yings. They applauded. A bug-eating farang was about as close to heaven as they'd get on a rainy Tuesday afternoon on the soi with the dead artists bars. While the city was short on museums, Calvino's soi was rich with bars named Renoir, Degas, Monet, or Cézanne, filled with people who had no idea who those painters were.

There was an attitude in the thick, grayish air – of the vendor and of the yings – that Calvino liked. He looked at the water bug in the palm of his hand as though it was a multivitamin and popped it in his mouth. His teeth got traction on the soft outer shell. As he chewed, he saw the General's car approach on the wet pavement, slowing as it reached a space in front of Mona Lisa. Calvino stood beside the vendor's cart, watching the General park his car. He was a kind old man who'd been the perfect client: he'd paid for Calvino's services, and he'd used the payment for his new jacket. It was an awkward social moment, an old man holding out money. Calvino had asked the General to keep the money and to accept his services as a favor. That was the Thai way, but the General shook his head and insisted that he pay. When the General had phoned Calvino and asked to meet him mid-afternoon for a coffee, he'd decided to look presentable. The new jacket would send a message of proper respect to the General. The lunchtime trade had gone back to the offices,

11

shops, and apartments until dinnertime. It was as quiet as it ever got on Soi 33 this side of mid-afternoon.

A short distance behind the General's black Camry a motorcycle had been tailing the car. It slowed as the General's car slowed, and the rider flashed a red laser penlight on the General's car. The General had come to a stop between Goya and Papa's. Calvino looked over his shoulder and saw a second motorcycle, a blue and silver Honda, with a driver and a passenger turn into the soi from Sukhumvit. Both riders on the Honda wore wraparound sunglasses and black clothes. The rear passenger's face was covered with a ski mask. This wasn't the time to act like a newbie fresh from the airport, seeing things for the first time. The hand of the fast-approaching rider had reached inside a nylon jacket and emerged holding a handgun. The gun, the laser: it added up to a certainty that the motorcycle riders were working together. The laser beam pinpointed the man inside.

The time from the moment a gun is drawn to when it's used is calibrated in seconds. Glancing up and down the street, Calvino counted one, and before he got to two, pushed the deep-fried insect vendor to the side, and using his body, shoved her cart into the path of the oncoming motorcycle. Both driver and passenger had been concentrating on the target and hadn't seen the cart coming. When it hit the motorcycle's midsection, it knocked the driver off balance, and he had no chance to recover. Rider, passenger, and bike skidded hard, tipping over on the rain-slick road. The Thai driver had tried to brake at the last second but lost control. His machine spiraled, shooting out a trail of sparks as it struck from behind, engine still running, a parked motorbike that had four torpedo-shaped metal cylinders strapped to the back. Rider and passenger held on, thinking that against the odds they'd somehow come out of the spill, shoot the General, and escape down Soi 33. If they'd seen the soi the way a foreigner saw it for the first time, they wouldn't have made that mistake. The gas delivery boy, who did a nice business selling gas cylinder refills to the roadside vendors, stood in the street a few feet away, rolling away an empty and attaching a new one in its place. Wiping the sweat from his brow when he heard the crash, he looked up and saw the bike spinning toward his bike where it was parked in front of the banyan tree.

The impact of the two bikes occurred with maximum force. In the collision, the first cylinder exploded, setting off a chain reaction that burst the other three, each adding more fuel to the large orange ball of flame shooting up the banyan tree. The vendor looked at what remained of her cart, bugs strewed over the road, and then at the fire leaping up the banyan tree, catching the dry and brittle veins on fire until the umbrella of branches and veins ignited a virtual New Year's fireworks display. The wrecked bikes and riders were enveloped in the ball of flames. The helmeted head of the driver shattered, sending fragments of plastic and skull across the road, splattering the dwarf and the tree, and coated the legs of half a dozen girls.

The yings from the Japanese karaoke place backed away in horror and fear. The vendor stared, hands clutched into a ball. There were tears in her eyes. Her livelihood had just been destroyed. Calvino reached inside his new jacket, unholstered his .38 caliber police service revolver, and ran down the street. Sidestepping the flames, he came up level to the General's car. The General waved at him. But Calvino was looking past the General at the motorcycle rider who had tagged the old man using a laser light. He had managed to stop a short distance behind the General's car and remained a threat. With the point bike out of action, was the hit still in play? Calvino had no way of knowing. It was possible that the rider of the second bike was also armed, but he showed no sign of pulling a weapon. When the biker saw Calvino running at him then kneeling with a handgun pointed at his head, he wheeled his bike around and fled in the direction from which he had come. Calvino holstered his .38 and opened the General's door.

'Did you see that accident?' asked the General.

Half out of breath, Calvino nodded. 'Yeah that was something.'

'Doesn't look like they survived. What a tragedy!'

'General, let me buy you a cup of tea.'

The General stood beside his car, looking out at the burning remains.

'We should phone the police.'

Calvino took out his cell phone and called Colonel Pratt.

'The General's had a problem,' he said. 'He's parked on Soi 33 outside Goya.'

'Crazy driver,' said the General.

Calvino ended his call with Colonel Pratt. He knew that it would take Pratt a while to arrive at the scene in front of the dead artists bars. Meanwhile, it was just the two of them, the General and Calvino, standing downwind, waiting as they watched the smoke and flames shooting out of the wreckage. There was the pop of ammo exploding. Calvino figured it must have been spare rounds one of the men had squirreled away for a rainy day that would never come.

'Driver's training,' the General continued. 'That's what we could use.'

The fire brigade drove up at about the same time as the police. They sprayed foam on the wreck, and the body snatchers (they were one of the voluntary Chinese benevolent societies who raced to crash sites and collected the dead and injured) arrived to sort through the remains – bone in this container, metal in that container. 'Colonel Pratt will be joining us,' Calvino said, walking the General toward a restaurant between the closed bars and nightclubs.

'I didn't want to bother him,' said the General. 'He's in the area.'

'Well, in that case, that's my good fortune.'

'Good fortune' is one way of putting it, thought Calvino.

The General pointed his remote at his car and it automatically locked. He hadn't seen the second black motorcycle, or the guys with their heads covered coming at him at high speed.

Calvino walked back to the vendor and gave her five thousand baht. 'Buy a new cart,' he said.

'You bad man, you kill those boys,' she said, taking the money.

A witness to the slaughter, he thought. Not the line he wanted her taking before the police, at least not until Colonel Pratt arrived. The ball of orange flame had climbed down the side of the banyan tree, burning through the dozens of old nylon ribbons. That should piss off the spirit, thought Calvino.

He found the General again, open-mouthed, standing beside his car. 'We'll need to make a statement,' said the General.

Calvino's new jacket had a slight tear near the front pocket. He sighed, pissed off, as this meant a return trip to Venice Tailors and Tony shaking his head in disapproval over the damage to the masterpiece. Walking toward the burning bike, Calvino knelt down and picked up a nine-millimeter gun from the street and showed it to the General. 'Driving and shooting should be against the law.' Calvino slipped the gun into his jacket pocket.

'I could use a cup of tea,' said the General.

Calvino had the feeling the General said that every time he saw something blow up.

Thais, in the presence of a stranger or someone with authority over them, fall into a default of stone silence. They clam up. What few words they muster fall into the category of nondescript pleasantries. Have you eaten? Where are you going? These two questions are the staples of a Thai inquiry. A stranger could be forgiven for thinking that given the long silences in these official circumstances that words were exchanged with the same reluctance as a woman pawning her mother's gold necklace. But the reality is that they've figured out it's usually better to smile and say nothing of substance.

As the police, the body snatchers, and the fire brigade appeared at the scene of the wreck, Calvino reached down and picked up a piece of chrome. Colonel had arrived and circled the crash as General stood in the shade. It had been decided, after consultation with Colonel Pratt, the ranking officer at the scene, to rule what had happened a tragic accident. Only a miracle had prevented a larger loss of life. And no one said a word about an attempted hit on the General.

'That's it? What about the gun?' Calvino found himself asking awkward questions about evidence that didn't fit Colonel Pratt's report.

Colonel Pratt smiled at his American friend, nodding. Sometimes a farang friend could be amusing at the strangest of times. 'It's been bagged and will go to the lab.'

Such a statement might have on the surface suggested that the police investigation would focus on the ownership of the gun and the identities of the two men who'd been burnt beyond recognition.

As the three of them walked to Calvino's office, Calvino asked the Colonel about the carefulness of Thais when drawn into a conversation. The Colonel thought long and hard and then simply smiled at the General.

Ratana, who hadn't expected Calvino to be back so soon from his appointment with the General, was at the park across the street with her baby. Calvino led the General and the Colonel upstairs to his office. Once inside, the three men sat down. It was the first chance they'd had to talk openly, without others around.

'I saw the guy riding pillion pull a gun. The rider on a second motorcycle coming from the opposite direction had pointed the laser beam at the General.'

The old man with his short bristle of white hair raised his hand.

'There's a Thai saying, Pla moh taay praw pak,' said the General, a veteran of the Department of Special Investigations.

'The fish is dead because of its own mouth,' said Calvino.

'He knows this one, General,' said Colonel Pratt.

A few months ago Calvino hadn't fully understood the proverb. On that occasion, the Colonel had sketched a sea bass for him with a large mouth and bulging eyes. The mouth of the fish brushed against the surface of the water. Colonel Pratt, an artist at heart who had secretly studied art in New York, had taken pleasure in his drawing. It wasn't an elegant rendition, but that hadn't stopped Calvino from having it framed and hung on his office wall. But the line of bubbles that rose from the open mouth of the fish served now to illustrate the General's point.

The General looked at the drawing.

'Pratt drew that one,' said Calvino.

Pratt had signed his name at the bottom and given the sketch to Calvino. It wasn't a Picasso – more like Warhol: Marilyn Monroe as a fish.

'And you framed it and put it on your wall,' said the General, as if not believing his eyes.

Pratt's drawing stared down from the wall, reminding Calvino that a man who was careless about what he said sooner or later got himself hooked, pulled out of the water, gutted, and cooked. That was a Thai way of referring to trouble. Two men had been gas-fried in the street, and pieces of a vendor's cart and a small forest's worth of dead bugs had been strewed about the wreckage, but the General didn't want to talk about what had happened on the street. Colonel Pratt sat back in his chair, arms folded, asking no questions of the General or Calvino. The three men sat in silence.

Calvino found himself studying the sketch. People had this fishlike nature. They couldn't help but float to the surface and blow bubbles, even though it gave away their position to the fisherman on the riverbank, and put them one step away from a dinner plate.

Calvino turned his attention to the large box wrapped in silver foil paper with red ribbon. It had been delivered that morning. General Yosaporn had signed the card in classic, refined handwriting, curls and swirls that only a fountain pen could make. It was a thank-you note. Before he'd gone to Venice Tailors, Calvino had read and reread the card and stared at the bottles in the open box. The General beamed with pride as he watched Calvino pull out a bottle of whiskey. Calvino asked himself what to do with the windfall. Altogether there were a dozen bottles of single-malt whiskey, the upscale stuff that sold for two hundred dollars a bottle at the airport duty-free.

'I hope you like whiskey,' said the General.

Calvino thought the single malt went well with his new jacket. 'One bottle would have been enough,' he said.

'Share it with your friends,' said the General, glancing over at Colonel Pratt.

'Vincent, you did the right thing,' said Colonel Pratt. It was the first time he'd acknowledged what had happened earlier in the soi.

'I almost shot him,' said Calvino. 'It crossed my mind. But they were moving fast and I didn't have time.'

'That was a good thing, Vincent. It avoided a problem.'

Someone being cooked to a dark leathery brown like a rice-field rat in a bonfire could be explained as another example of reckless driving. A gunshot could not be ruled out as the dead artists bars had been known to draw armed patrons.

Calvino nodded. A crooked smile flashed across his face as he handed the Colonel a bottle of whiskey. 'Now that's doing the right thing,' he said. 'Isn't that right, General?'

The General agreed. Colonel Pratt accepted the bottle, turned it around, read the label, and nodded to the General. The two had spent a few minutes alone before they walked over to Calvino's office. Whatever they'd said to each other, Calvino hadn't been briefed on. It stayed between the General and the Colonel; they'd closed ranks for whatever reason. Cautious, security-minded men, they were distrustful of anyone not on the inside. This wasn't like Colonel Pratt. It took some getting used to – Pratt's show of total deference to the General. In addition to the case of single-malt whiskey, the General had also sent a large stuffed bear for Ratana's baby and a dozen long-stemmed red roses for the mother. All bases in the gratitude department had been neatly covered. Like Pratt,

Ratana had shown more than the usual respect to the old man.

'It was Apichart,' said Calvino out of the blue.

Calvino guessed that this was what the General and Colonel had been talking about. Coldness crossed the General's face as swiftly as an arctic wind. His upper teeth bit gently down on his lower lip as he caught himself stooping in his chair. He sat erect like a soldier at a mission briefing. 'That business is finished.'

'In New York,' said Calvino, 'there's an old lesson that business is never finished with a wise guy. And that's how I make Apichart. He put a hit on you. We're alone. We can say it the way it is. You'll run a check on the two dead punks, find the link, and then what?'

'Not another empty coffin,' said Colonel Pratt.

The General's translucent paper-thin skin revealed hundreds of veins snaking up his wrists to his forearms and disappearing inside his shirt. Of medium height with slightly stooped shoulders, he was an unassuming white-haired man in his seventies who could have been someone's grandfather. Years before, the General had been Pratt's mentor in the police force; that was the personal connection that had brought the General into Calvino's life.

The General had recently had a problem with a tenant named Apichart, the owner of an advertising agency, who had an office on the ground floor of a building the General owned on Sathorn

Road. The office was in an excellent location but Apichart had neglected to pay rent and refused to leave the premises. Colonel Pratt had sent General Yosaporn to Calvino's office. That was, of course, not the usual way of handling things. Five minutes into the case, Calvino was convinced that Apichart was an asshole, and there were Thai ways of dealing with assholes. Going to a private eye wasn't usually one of them. The General, given his rank and social status, was quite capable of taking all necessary measures to recover his rent. But at the same time, he was a good Buddhist who followed the five precepts, including the ban on cheating and lying. Of course, not killing was on that list, too. He'd spent twenty minutes talking about meditation that day and had even gotten Calvino to try out the technique, showing him how to sit, where to put his hands, how to breathe, and most importantly, how to clear the mind.

Calvino had said he'd clear his mind properly after he'd collected the rent from the General's tenant. Five days later, Apichart, a Chinese-Thai who always traveled with two bodyguards, had seen the light and did what he was forced to do. But seeing the light had given Apichart some dark thoughts. As a man who made a living hawking skin-whitening cream, instant noodles, cheap flights on a budget airline with a terrible safety record, and shampoo that promised every ying the atten-tion of men, Apichart had no trouble creating a cruel, damaging campaign.

Apichart could've learned something from Colonel Pratt's drawing of the fish. But he'd gotten rich with easy money and thought he had nothing more to learn. It had come as no surprise when he opened his mouth and blew out one large bubble after another. Apichart had told everyone in the building that General Yosaporn owed him money and that he was withholding the rent to offset the debt. It was cheaper than taking the General to court, he'd told anyone who would listen. Sheepishly, the General had admitted to Calvino that he had once received money from Apichart but had assumed it was a donation to his meditation center. They had constructed a pavilion using Apichart's money. Whether the money was a loan or a donation was a matter of who was telling the story. In any event, the General had no way to repay Apichart. And it wasn't the debt but the interest that had been murderous. Apichart had pulled the figure of twenty percent a month out of the air, and at that rate it wouldn't be long until Apichart owned the building.

Calvino had told the old General he'd do what he could.

On that morning a couple of months ago, Calvino had waited until the General had left and found a crawl space between the baby crib and the toys, diapers, formula, and baby bottles. Ratana sat behind her desk reading an online article about infant nutrition. There had been a lull in the baby's crying, an expanse of time that threatened to exceed the previous record of twenty-eight minutes. It was like a cease-fire as both sides reloaded and cleaned up the wounded. Calvino cleared his throat and, getting no reaction, leaned over her desk and tapped Ratana on the shoulder. Jumping as if from a bolt of electricity, she looked up with startled eyes.

'Order a Chinese coffin,' he whispered. 'I want one that's cheesy.'

'Cheesy?' She tilted her head, trying to figure out how cheese could factor into coffin buying.

He saw her confusion. 'A tacky coffin that is butt ugly, a disgrace. One that no self-respecting Chinese family would buy. I want the coffin that the coffin maker's wife predicted wouldn't sell until the late afternoon of his next life.'

She understood 'next life, late afternoon.' In Thailand, that meant something that would likely never occur. He'd caught her attention. It wasn't every day her boss asked for a coffin. 'Who died?'

'No one died,' said Calvino. He handed her a slip of paper on which he had drawn the floor plan of General Yosaporn's building.

'Why do you want a coffin?'

'For a deadbeat.'

'You said no one died.'

The conversation had turned into a cross-cultural nightmare.

'Have the coffin delivered to this address. Tell them to put the coffin exactly where I've marked with an X. Then I want you to arrange for three monks to go to the building for the next three days Tell them to chant beside the coffin.'

Ratana's eyes grew large as she looked at the paper and then up at her boss. Working for a farang was always a bundle of surprises. She had told her mother and her friends that after a few years, though, you became shockproof. Nothing ever surprises you about a farang. Now she told herself that she'd been wrong.

'That's the General's building,' she said.

Calvino nodded, thinking what a relief to actually get his message through.

'I think this is a mistake. You shouldn't do this.'

'Better yet, see if we could just rent the coffin for a few days. Buying it isn't necessary,' he said.

She had never heard of anyone renting a coffin. 'Khun Vinny, have you talked to the General about this?'

'Okay, if they won't rent a coffin, then order the cheapest, most stripped-down basic model. And I'd like it delivered tomorrow. Monks tomorrow would be good, too.'

After he explained the purpose of the coffin, Ratana shivered. 'You don't understand the problems this could cause.'

Sometimes he forgot that his secretary was half-Chinese.

'It's a superstition that you should never walk past a coffin, right?'

'It's bad luck.'

26

'When reason fails, then superstition is a good backup.'

Accepting that this was a battle she couldn't win, Ratana phoned several shops. There was a long pause each time after she asked about renting a coffin. In the end, she found a shop past Soi 101 on Sukhumvit Road that seemed to be going through a slow period. The owner agreed to sell a coffin for five thousand baht and to refund one thousand if it was returned undamaged. Even in the coffin trade, there was a middle path to doing business.

Later that day, a coffin was delivered to the location Calvino had marked: a space in the corridor outside Apichart's office. The wooden coffin was painted white. Red and orange rosettes festooned the sides and the lid. Squinting hard at a distance, one might take the rosettes for a drug-addled artist's idea of exotic aboriginal flowers. Closer examination suggested they might pass for blood clots or lepers' boils. People walking down the corridor averted their eyes. The coffin maker also brought a small shrine to hold candles and incense and set it at the head of the coffin. Three monks arrived the following day and chanted for twenty minutes. The coffin, the shrine, and the monks provoked a considerable amount of attention – not the good kind, but horrified stares like those of passersby who stopped to look at the carnage of a car accident.

Bangkok is a large Chinese city. As Colonel Pratt

had once said, the whole population has Chinese DNA. The borderline between Chinese and Thai-Chinese is a matter for debate, but eventually most people become plain, unadorned Thais without a Chinese modifier. Their Chinese blood is like that of minor royalty – diluted over the generations to the point where it has been drained of most meaning.

Calvino figured General Yosaporn's tenant, who was second-generation Thai on his mother's side, had enough residual Chinese identity to register the shock of seeing a coffin beside his office. As Ratana had pointed out, coffins are not just a symbol of death but also bad luck for the living. The Chinese will walk two blocks out of their way not to pass a coffin. Office workers who used the corridor of the General's building had no choice but to pass it. Customers and clients, though, who were mainly Chinese, did have a choice.

From the day the coffin appeared outside Apichart's office, his business went into a stall, then a nosedive. If his business had been free peanuts, there wouldn't have been a single monkey willing to take one.

Apichart begged, threatened, shed tears – tears of rage, tears of shame, and most improbably of all, tears of helplessness. The General said the situation was out of his hands, meaning Apichart had had his chance and having crossed the threshold of socially acceptable behavior, he'd lost his right to appeal to the General for help. Apichart was all alone staring down the farang over a coffin that wouldn't be moved. A couple of days later, one of Apichart's bodyguards delivered the back rent and a year's payment in advance. All in cash. He also signed a document saying the earlier money given to the General had been a donation and not a loan. The company that had delivered the coffin had it removed that day. They returned one thousand baht to Ratana, who gave them a tax receipt. She was informed that any time her farang boss or his friends wished to rent a coffin, they'd be happy to throw in free delivery and give her a 10 percent commission.

Once Colonel Pratt had news of Calvino's success in collecting the rent, the Colonel phoned to thank him. Calvino's scheme had been crazy but it had worked. Thais rarely fought against anything that proved effective. The General's influence had gradually dissolved over the years except among the community of devout meditators, where his star had never been higher. Like the unwritten rules that governed who was Chinese and who was Thai, each year past retirement at age sixty had washed away another level of power and influence. By age seventy-five, for General Yosaporn, only Colonel Pratt remained his steadfast friend. There were one or two other old-timers, but most of the powerful people he knew were dead. Newspapers sometimes profiled his meditation work. The reality was he was a relic from a time when decency and compassion had value.

As Colonel Pratt sat in Calvino's office, holding the bottle of single-malt whiskey, he turned to his old mentor. 'I would recommend that Vincent leave town for a few days.'

The General nodded. 'My good friend has a hotel in Pattaya. He can stay there.'

'Hold on,' said Calvino. 'I'm being exiled to Pattaya?'

'It will take a few days to clear up the problem,' said Colonel Pratt. 'Look at it as a vacation, Vincent. You deserve some time away from the office. Kids, clients . . .'

'Two fried thugs.'

'Repeat to yourself: I am going on a holiday.'

'Do I have a choice?'

Calvino looked at Colonel Pratt and then at General Yosaporn and saw that he didn't have any choice. Every one had already agreed he had to go away. The problem was that Calvino had been too successful. He hadn't just won the battle with Apichart; he had vanquished him, left him naked and humiliated. Apichart had paid the rent money and signed the letter, but with such a loss of face that some blood would have to be spilled to get it back again. Apichart's clients were laughing at him. That was intolerable for a Thai-Chinese. The coffin story had become legendary, whispered between the wives among his circle of friends.

'I could use a holiday,' said Calvino. 'A few days away from Bangkok might be a good thing.'

A faint smile crossed the General's lips. 'We hope it will be only a few days.'

Calvino rolled his eyes. 'It could be longer? I've got ongoing cases to handle.'

'Remember what I taught you about meditation,' said General Yosaporn.

'Let go, don't get attached,' Calvino replied. 'And I can do that until I start thinking about how I'm going to cover the rent and Ratana's salary.'

The General was on his feet and Colonel Pratt rose and followed him out. There hadn't been anything else to say. Colonel Pratt would settle the problem with Apichart – doing what had to be done in order to repair the damage. With guys like Apichart, the five precepts were never a good place to start.

After they'd left, Calvino sat alone in his office, thinking about a client named Casey. He owed Calvino money. He made a note to have Ratana phone him and let him know that he'd been called away by a client in Pattaya.

He pulled out another bottle of the single-malt and studied the label. He knew a bar owner in Pattaya who might buy it from him. He smiled and glanced a final time at Colonel Pratt's drawing, lifted the whiskey from his desk, and walked out to his car. He convinced himself this wasn't an exile; he was instead doing something he'd not done for a long time: he was taking a vacation. The whiskey was his passport, a way to escape from Bangkok for a week and to kick back and relax by the sea. Calvino drummed his fingers on the box, a smile on his lips. Passing the baby crib and holding his breath against the smell of freshly soiled diapers, he said his goodbyes to Ratana and little John-John, and to the tiny limbs of the other infants in the crib with John-John, whose names he couldn't remember.

CHAPTER 2

Twenty-four hours after Colonel Pratt and General Yosaporn had left his office, Calvino arrived at his hotel in Pattaya. He'd tied up a few loose ends and left Ratana in charge of the office – meaning the nursery wouldn't have to cope with his interruptions or those of the clients: grifters, gamblers, drunks, suspicious spouses; mainly men bruised and worn down from their swim in the gutter end of the Thai business world. Calvino was going upstream to where the big fish stayed submerged, blowing no bubbles.

The road curved around the bay. Large umbrellas and beach chairs were lined up in rows by the sea; baht taxis patrolled the perimeter. And tourists in shorts, bodies glistening with sunblock, and displaying faded tattoos, walked along the quay. Calvino turned into the hotel driveway. A doorman opened his car door and an assistant offered to take his luggage and park his car in the lot below the hotel. He figured the General had phoned ahead. The staff was too attentive, the wais too much for a farang. The hotel was all chrome and glass, modern, imposing, catching the light from the sea. Modern only went so far, though; in front of the hotel was a traditional spirit house. Peel back the latest European design, and underneath probably lurked an ancient tradition to appease the spirits of the land, angry spirits that bring misfortune, bad health, and business failure. Placed on a pedestal, the spirit house looked more like a dollhouse managed by a mentally disturbed child. Tiny ceramic figures were placed on the small terrace that surrounded it – painted warriors, demons, giants, and angels staring with blank black eyes at Beach Road.

Spirit houses were a dime a dozen in any Thai city, and Pattaya was no exception. If Calvino were to stop to examine each one, he couldn't have covered half a mile in a day, so he was selective in his appreciation. When he first saw a young woman making an offering to the spirit, she had a cold, graceful elegance. She gave the impression of being carved out of ice, one of those fancy ice sculptures that hotels set out in the lobby for weddings. Her eyes were closed, hands folded in prayer, her head bowed. Unaware of his presence, she caught and held his attention. Seeing a woman pay homage made a man remember that in the spirit world, a woman had a chance of evening the odds.

Great-looking hotel, beautiful ying in front of the spirit house . . . what's not to like? Calvino thought as he worked himself down the list of possibilities: A ying could be good or bad, young or old, educated or illiterate, ugly or beautiful, kind or mean, available or unavailable. He gave this ying a high score. It was the start of a perfect exile – or vacation, depending on a man's point of view. It doesn't much matter which, he thought, as a smile crossed his lips. He started to approach the woman but stopped short. Some basic instinct told him to pull back, wait a little longer before making his move.

Looking as if transported from the Wailing Wall in Jerusalem, the woman moved her lips in prayer. Below the ice Calvino sensed trouble, and the feeling had been strong enough for him to abort his approach. He reminded himself of Calvino's law: Act on impulse when betting on a horse, but never with a woman. A horse never drags a man into its life. It either wins or loses the race. A man can spend an afternoon at the track and, eight races later, count his money and know whether he has won or not. With a woman it's never that simple. With a woman the numbers never add up.

A seagull landed on top of the spirit house. Its belly fluted with gray feathers, it walked along the roof and dropped down beside a plate of oranges. Opening her eyes, the woman saw the seagull and smiled. The bird flew off with a wedge of orange in its beak. After the seagull had flown away, she sensed someone watching her and, turning around, had seen Calvino. For a brief moment, their eyes had locked, and she had smiled. It had been the most human of connections, fleeting, without demand, without flirtation, and it had lasted only an instant.

Don't be a fish blowing bubbles close to the surface, he told himself. Besides, vacations are about leaving problems behind. Who had caused that woman's great expectations about life to dissolve into a cocktail of anxiety with a super-stitious chaser? He didn't really want to know. Why spoil the rare opportunity to be free of other people's problems, aches, pains, disappointments, and regrets?

At the front desk the receptionist looked up his name and pulled out a couple of pieces of paper. Reading through them, he nodded and told Calvino he'd been upgraded. Bless General Yosaporn, Calvino thought. He'd pulled the strings to put him in a suite.

Upstairs, Calvino slipped the keycard into the door and walked into a large suite with a sepa-rate sitting room and bedroom, a flat-screen TV in both rooms, and a bathroom the size of his bedroom in Bangkok. This is what a vacation is supposed to be, he thought. A temporary escape from reality. He'd rarely been in such a large hotel room except to meet a client. Outside the door he'd noticed a bronze plaque declaring his new digs the 'Regency Suite.' If he had to lie low, this was definitely the way to do it.

Calvino had the bellhop set the case of whiskey on the table and pull back the curtains. Then he tipped him a hundred baht. Looking out at the blue sky, the ribbon of white sand, and the dolphin-gray sea dotted with Jet Skiers, fishing and pleasure boats and, on the horizon, cargo ships, he felt like a high roller at Atlantic City who'd been put up in style by management. All that was missing was a high stack of chips and some playing cards.

Calvino's good mood lingered like a familiar song as he sat alone on his balcony overlooking the sea. There were a lot of fish out there – but he had in mind the two-legged variety who strolled along Beach Road as the sun came down over the water. Pattaya was stretching, arms out, waking up and getting ready for the night, putting the line out for those hungry mouths moving in the far distance.

Now was the time to catch up on doing nothing. Sit back and read a good book or two. He'd packed Graham Greene's *The Quiet American* – on the basis that he'd never met such an American – and a battered copy of George Orwell's *Burmese Days*. The authors were a couple of guys who had established reputations for knowing a thing or two about Southeast Asia. There might be another coffin-like trick he could pick up from their books.

More than a year had passed since Calvino had taken his last real holiday. This was his first forced exile. Either way, it was a milestone to be in the suite overlooking Beach Road in Pattaya. No stakeout, no phone calls to clients, no security detail, phone bugging, or tailing assholes at three in the morning. He pushed back in the chair and poured himself a drink, telling himself that life was good. The hotel hugged the rim of the beach. It was a dream location, a dream room, and on the lucky ninth floor. The Chinese thought highly of the number nine. But they were also big on eight and thirteen. They had number madness that could leave them in a shrill and dazed place.

Colonel Pratt had said the hotel owner was an old friend of General Yosaporn's. The General had made the arrangements, and by paying for the suite he'd given Calvino a lot of face. He figured that the General's name had been linked with his own, and that fact had been passed down the chain of command. A Thai receptionist seeing a farang being taken care of by a Thai general saw a face the size of a full moon. The social network of names and ranks coiled itself around lives like ivy. Once it started, there was no way to fight the foliage; it simply consumed everyone.

Calvino opened a bottle of Johnnie Walker – having promised himself not to touch the expensive stuff from the General – and poured himself three fingers of scotch. He sipped it and thought about going out for dinner. He also considered whether Apichart might send someone to shoot him. That was an easy thing to arrange in Pattaya. Colonel Pratt had been less concerned about Apichart than about the cops. A couple of people had seen him push the vendor's cart into the path of the motor-cycle, and Thailand was a place where, in the not so distant past, over a hundred people had seen someone shoot a cop in the head but afterwards no one could remember a thing. Colonel Pratt had the experience on the ground. He had convinced the police at the scene to write it up as an accident. Just in case someone from the department came around to ask more questions, it was better for Calvino to be out of town.

Calvino looked over at the case of whiskey and smiled. The guy who wanted to buy the whiskey also ran a restaurant where the steaks were thick, the mushroom sauce was perfectly seasoned, and the women were smiling and available. The restaurant was located at the far end of South Pattaya Road; it was squeezed between a dive where the Russian mob drank vodka and plotted crimes, and an Italian joint where old criminals had retired, having beat the system and set up a restaurant. Removing the lid from the ice bucket, Calvino breathed in deeply, closed his eyes, and tried to remember what the General had taught him about meditation. When he opened his eyes, he stared at the sea and felt calm and alive. He even allowed himself to feel happy.

He lowered his glass, sucked in the air, and admired the view. Had it been possible to hold a moment for eternity, this one would have been high on his short list. The problem with such a moment is that it never lasts.

The spell broke when Calvino saw a naked woman in a freefall, directly in front of his balcony.

Long black hair flowing, lips parted in a silent scream – the look of someone who knew she was already dead. He stared straight into her face, and it hit him like a jolt of electrical current. The hair on the back of his neck stood on end. He rose to his feet, grabbed the railing and looked down. 'What the fuck?'

He backed away, shaking his head. Then, moving forward, he stuck his head out, looking above and then down below. His heart raced. He couldn't think straight. Blood was pumping hard and fast. He steadied himself at the railing, looked down again, and shook his head. 'What the . . .' was all he could manage to get out. What the fuck do I do now? Again he leaned over the railing, looking at the people who gathered around the body on the pavement. Some of them looked up. He stood back from the railing. This was the last thing he wanted to get involved in.

It had happened so fast that there hadn't been time to comprehend much of anything about the young woman. Then her face registered in his mind; she was the ice goddess at the spirit house.

From the ninth floor the woman's body looked tiny, unreal, as if a doll had been thrown over the side, sprawled arms and legs at unnatural angles, partly on the sidewalk and partly in the road. A car braked hard and stopped. Another car slammed into the back of the first car. Soon the street filled with people circling the body. Calvino stood staring at them all. It had been a dead drop. One hand on the railing, the other hand cupping his whiskey glass, Calvino looked at the concrete bottom of the balcony above his head. She'd fallen from above, but how far above he had no way of determining. It seemed that the spirit hadn't been at home when she'd planted the incense sticks in the tiny bowls filled with beach sand.

He dropped heavily into the balcony chair. Finishing his whiskey, he put the glass on the table. Then he went inside the suite and phoned the reception. A woman's voice came on the line. 'Someone just fell from this hotel,' he said. 'Phone an ambulance and the police.'

'Yes, sir,' she said. The police had already been called.

'I saw her.'

'Yes, sir.'

'She's dead.'

'Let us notify the police.'

He put down the phone and went back onto the balcony and looked down.

It had been as if she'd briefly stopped her long swan dive to say a short goodbye to a stranger, a final silent farewell. It made him a witness to death for the second time in two days. He'd done the right thing by reporting it, he told himself. Colonel Pratt would have to be notified. But not right away. He needed to think through what had happened.

She had plunged head-first, and that bothered him. When someone jumps off a building, it's

41

almost always feet first. This is a basic human instinct. People are hardwired to fear heights. High off the ground, looking down, a ying who is determined to kill herself will calculate where to go over the edge, and even then some inner voice will still tell her to land on her feet. A murder victim is a different story. Most of the time there is a struggle. Even if the victim is surprised from behind, the result is the same: the victim is pushed over the edge, and the force throws her off balance. There's no time for her instinct to kick in and override the natural fear. Calvino wrapped his fist around his glass and pressed it to his lips, forgetting it was empty. Realizing his mistake, he put it down hard on the table and sank into the chair, head in his hands.

This isn't good, but it's okay, he told himself. Shit like this happens. Pratt knows that. It just happens more frequently to some people. I wasn't doing anything, just having a drink. People get themselves murdered all the time. He shouldn't take it personally. He had nothing to do with it. He knew what he had to do. He had to go downstairs and tell the police what he'd seen.

He remembered her smile as the seagull had flown away. There had been some heat behind the ice.

Calvino left a message for Pratt, and took the lift to the lobby. When he walked out, he saw the police were talking with the receptionist and the bellhop. With clarity, Calvino saw his future, and having a holiday wasn't part of it. He saw himself filling out endless police reports, attending interrogations, and inevitably, viewing the dead body. He'd be asked, 'Was that the woman you saw dropping past your balcony, Mr. Calvino?'

He'd lost his appetite for the steak dinner and revised his dining plans. He'd talk with the cops and then go back to his room and watch what little was left of the setting sun. A few minutes later when his cell phone rang, he didn't answer it. He saw Pratt's number in the missed call window. Calvino told himself he needed to handle this his way.

CHAPTER 3

For private security contractors like Alan Jarrett, dawn was not just the start of a new day; it was a favorite time for executions, torture, or confessions. Interrogators, ambush point men, dictators who worked along the edge of the dark side of truth, they watched their targets illuminated by the first light on the horizon. Old military habits tend to graft onto a life, and after some years in the service no one can tell the grafted bits from the original. Dawn work detail was one of those grafts. Civilians slept through the dawn. Soldiers and ex-soldiers doing a soldier's job were up and already at work, checking weapons and the perimeter, heading out for that place no one wants to go, with no choice in the matter. Dawn was the time for a hanging or an ambush. Jarrett and his buddy Tracer, both five days in from Kabul, had an appointment here in Bangkok, a job to do. Then they'd fly back to Afghanistan.

At five in the morning the new day's light was no more than a fragile crack at the edge of the sky, running like a fissure of gold in a deep shaft.

Within fifteen minutes daybreak would spread into a full-blown dawn. As if programmed, Jarrett's eyes opened. He reached above his head and pulled back the curtain to look out. Letting the curtain fall, he laid his head back on the pillow and relaxed his muscles against the sheets. He felt the chill in the air and listened to the background buzz of the short time hotel room's air-conditioning. It was always good to wake up in a safe civilian zone, an environment removed from the danger that lay just ahead. Jarrett raised his left arm slowly and glanced at his Rolex. It was 5:27 a.m.

His head slowly pivoted on the pillow. A ying in her early twenties, naked, back turned toward him, slept with one fist clasping the sheet waist-high. She moaned as she turned over, as if responding to someone in her dreamscape. She was an upcountry beekeeper's daughter, and he wondered if in her dreams she was out in the fields tending the hives. Or was she just back in the bar, fleeing from a drunk who was pawing her? Rivulets of long black hair fell over her pillow. Her breathing was slow, regular, the kind that accompanies the deepest sleep. Jarrett told himself she was dreaming of tending hives somewhere in Surin province, the sun on her face and buckets of honey at her feet. At least he wanted to believe that. She introduced herself as Wan, which meant 'sweet' – as in honey sweet. He had known her eight hours, long enough to learn her life story, or at least the edited version bar yings learn to tell. Her charm and body were enough to cause him to feel the excitement that comes with an unexpected close encounter with a young woman.

He smiled, thinking of an old blues song: 'A man always has a price to pay/A woman knows her value/But she sells it for what she can/ There's always a price/always a price/but you don't always know how much/'til you break it/always a price/and it ain't always money.'

Jarrett slipped out of bed without disturbing Wan. He moved like a shadow with its own life and purpose. The hotel room was smaller than he remembered from the night before. From the edge of the bed he crept over to the chair and slipped on his jeans and T-shirt. He froze as she curled on her side, moved her leg, and pulled the sheet up to her chin. He waited until she settled back down and her breathing became more regular; then he kept an eye on her as he dressed. He thought about how civilians slept in a different way. They could sleep through their own deaths, he thought. He reached over to her handbag, a fake Prada bag bought from a Sukhumvit street vendor, and tucked ten thousand baht into the front pocket.

At the bar the night before, Jarrett had asked if her father's bees were dying, like the ones in America. She'd blinked, shrugged. She didn't know. Her father had abandoned the family and taken the bees with him. They'd been alive when he loaded them into two trucks.

'Where you from?' she'd asked.

'America, but I'm working in Afghanistan.'

'You on holiday?'

He smiled. 'Working holiday.'

'I need the money to get back into the bee business.' It was a clever variation on the handicapped-mother and water-buffalo-with-a-heat-stroke stories.

'How much do you need?' His question hadn't been serious.

'Ten thousand baht.'

'That's a lot.'

Wan had shrugged. 'I just started working. I haven't saved anything. Not yet.'

She'd left her lady's drink untouched. The mamasan who'd been eyeing her progress with the customer swept in from the shadows and ordered her to drink up. Wan had sipped her drink until the mamasan drifted away and flopped onto her stool in the corner.

'My father come at night with his friends and take away all of the hives. He left us nothing. He loved those bees more than he loved us.'

Jarrett had automatically divided the hotel room into coordinates. He moved from space to space, checking the curtains, the windows, the bathroom door, and going through the ying's clothes and handbag. He found her ID card and tried to read it, but the Thai script defeated him. Her cell phone was turned off. He examined her makeup, lipstick, and brush, along with an inhaler, wrapped hard candy, and a box cutter. He slid open the blade and let dawn sun touch the sharp edge. Closing the blade again, he slipped the box cutter into his pocket.

His movements had a purpose. Jarrett wasn't just being sensitive; he was putting himself through a training exercise. The beekeeper's daughter – number thirty-eight, Wan – was young, alert, in top physical condition. Exactly the type of person Jarrett liked to test his stealth skills against, sharpening them for use in the field. Moving around a room without waking someone was a specialized skill in his line of work. Not everyone could do it – go unnoticed, unheard.

Using his training to anticipate another person's reaction required regular practice. Working yings were a good challenge. They had street smarts and basic night-time survival training. They worked in a world where they had to calculate each move in advance. They practiced the art of deception, set up emotional ambushes, and orchestrated side plays to defend their position and throw their customers' counter-attacks into disarray.

Jarrett studied her on the bed. In the bar she had clung to him. She'd carried out the role of the playful ying, and her catlike purring and brushing of her body against his leg, side, and arm were precursors. Only cats and humans toy with their victims before killing them. She was playing with him, finding the vulnerable center before striking. A working ying acquired the unique ability to convince her customer that their roles

48

were reversed, that she was the target. And she needs him for protection. The only magic in the relationship was this sleight of hand.

Once inside the back-alley hotel room, she'd whispered to him that the bees had started dying in Thailand, too. Whole colonies had collapsed. Her eyes had grown large, as if she could see the horror unfolding as she spoke.

She had smiled when he'd asked her about what she wanted out of life.

Jarrett stood at the room door and took a last look at her. He thought about the empty beehive with only the queen bee and the royal jelly inside. The workers had gone walkabout, as the Australians say. 'Abandoned' is the right word. Bees, like people, have been known to disappear. Buddhists say everything is impermanent. They understand the world of bees. It's nature, just not human nature. Wan's father had been swallowed up into the distant hills, finding sanctuary on the slopes where the Khmer Rouge had once laid down land-mines. He'd returned home but only to get his bees. No one had seen him or heard from him. He'd timed his mission to avoid confronting his family. Abandonment of a losing position was an essential skill Jarrett had been taught in the service. Of all the skills he'd learned, he felt this one might be the most underestimated. Like something from an old blues song about how it's too late to say you're sorry.

CHAPTER 4

Six foot three, New Orleans born and raised, Trace LeLand, who early on acquired the nickname Tracer, had played high school football and been all-state running back for three years. 'Fast' didn't cover Tracer with the ball on an open field; he outran the wind, the rain, his own shadow. He could also catch a football like no one else – he had magic hands, a great sense of timing, and perfect eyesight – from all those carrots his mother fed him when he was young, he liked to tell people. Tracer had had a scholarship to play football at Michigan but had gotten himself into some trouble when a guy from Rhode Island insulted his girlfriend.

Tracer had been onstage playing saxophone in a honky-tonk bar when the guy, who turned out to be a banker one generation removed from Ireland, just wouldn't take no for an answer and grabbed his girlfriend by the arm. That was a bad thing to see from the platform, blowing on the tenor sax and watching his girlfriend squirming, some jerk holding her by the wrist. He flew off the stage like a man heading for the end zone, and instead of catching a pass, he found himself standing between his lady and the banker. With the authorities, it didn't seem to matter much that the banker had thrown the first punch, because after that, Tracer had hit him half-a-dozen times and was still hitting him as he collapsed on the floor. The bouncers had to drag Tracer off, his fists spinning like windmills, his girlfriend bawling her eyes out.

The police came and arrested Tracer. The prosecutor filed a felony assault count, and in the plea-bargaining that followed, the trial judge made some comments that suggested that if Tracer had signed with LSU the way the boy's mother had told him to, he would have been more lenient. Perhaps the charges would have been dropped. Louisiana is a serious football state and Tracer's taking an offer from Michigan was something of an insult to LSU. But Tracer had figured the national spotlight of playing for a Big Ten powerhouse would get him closer to one of those hundred-million-dollar pro-football contracts.

The trial judge made it clear to Tracer that his options had narrowed down to only two: a state correctional facility or the military. The marines suited Tracer, and by volunteering to serve, he could prove to everyone he was a loyal American even though he hadn't signed to play for LSU. By the time he'd finished basic training, the past – with its potential trial, the lawyers, the judge with owl eyes and jagged, sharp teeth – had blurred.

The jail cell where he'd been kept, the interrogation room, the courtroom, and tears falling down his mama's face: all of it had fallen away like water under a distant bridge.

Tracer hummed to himself as he drove. Singing was the way he passed the time, that and thinking about the words as he sang. 'Women,' he said under his breath, smiling. There was no defending them. No predicting them. The blues were all about women doing crazy shit – only, until this experience, he hadn't thought the words in the songs could apply to him. He'd thought, like most people, that he was the exception to the rule.

As he drove into Pattaya, the traffic thickened up like water turning to ice. The car in front slowed, then stopped. After ten minutes, he was edging along Beach Road. Through the window, Tracer saw a number of uniformed police, a body snatcher's van, and hordes of onlookers. A body under a white sheet was half in the road and half on the sidewalk. A man in a security guard's uniform leaned down and pulled back the sheet, and a TV camera crew moved in to film the dead woman. What was your big sorrow, little lady? he thought. What team didn't you make?

The traffic picked up, and in a few minutes Tracer turned into the Royal Garden Plaza and parked in the shopping mall's basement garage. He climbed out of the Mercedes and dragged an orange plastic traffic cone over to the side. Wiping his hands, he climbed back into the car and pulled into the spot. He locked the car and then put the traffic cone behind it, crossed the parking lot, and pushed the elevator button for the first floor. When he emerged from the elevator, he hadn't walked more than twenty feet when he ran straight into two men in civilian dress who he knew from the look of were military; they were loitering outside an all-you-can-eat restaurant, studying the menu. They looked nineteen, twenty years old. About the same age he'd been when he'd enlisted, just in time to see action in the first Gulf War.

'You boys with Cobra Gold?' asked Tracer.

'Yes, sir,' they said at the same time. Just looking at Tracer they could see military written all over him.

Tracer smiled. 'Thought so. Watch yourself in Pattaya.'

'We've been briefed about the situation, sir.'

'Then you'll be all right. Don't forget that when push comes to shove, lady boys are more boy than lady.'

'There's not a lot of lady in that boy,' said one of the marines, breaking into a smile. 'We're here to assist you, sir.'

Whoever had come up with that password exchange knew a lot about Thailand. That would have been Mooney's doing. Tracer was no prophet, but like he always said, the blues gives a man insight into the human condition. Working with a guy like Mooney, it paid to know something about the human capacity for bending the rules. The men shook hands with him and, seeing Tracer's Marine Corps ring, exchanged a knowing glance. He wondered what Mooney had told them. His bet would be next to nothing. 'A jarhead's head ain't a place to store knowledge,' Mooney had once said. 'It's a place to store orders, one at a time.'

'Why don't I take you boys to dinner?' Tracer turned up the amps on his hundred-watt smile. 'I know a place where they bring you a steak that just about defeats any man.'

On the walk to the restaurant one of the jarheads whispered into his cell phone, letting Mooney know everything was going according to plan.

They walked a couple hundred meters along Beach Road to a small rèstaurant. Once they were seated at the booth, one of the jarheads asked Tracer about the first Gulf War. Bar girls talk about sex, bond traders about the market, soldiers about war.

'You boys done your tour in Iraq?'

They nodded, smiles coming off their faces.

'Then you know that no one who's been there wants to talk about it. But if you wanna talk about football, I'd put money on Michigan taking the conference this year. They got a quarterback who shifts downfield like Spider-Man.'

His companions looked disappointed, shifting their knives and forks around.

'Okay, I saw some shit, did some shit,' Tracer said. 'Some I was proud of, other stuff I'd just as soon forget. You know what I'm saying?'

The two marines knew what Tracer was trying to

say; they'd seen and done some shit themselves. When the steaks were delivered to the table, the meat was hanging over both sides of the plate. The conversation eased into college football, women, and bars. He told them about the dead woman he'd seen in the street. The jarheads listened as Tracer described the scene. 'Shit happens,' said one of the men. 'Civilians don't get it,' said the other.

Tracer paid the bill and left the two marines to find their own path to the yings. Not so much a path as a super highway with tollbooths as far as the eye could see. They'd learn that civilians in Pattaya have their own roadside ambushes.

The marines had arrived along with a couple of thousand American military personnel who were joining hands with the Thais and a handful of Singaporeans, Malaysians, and Indonesians to squeeze some discipline and toughness into the Cobra Gold exercise, the annual military training exercise run by the Thais and Americans. Live-fire exercises, find-the-terrorist exercises, training exercises; all designed to keep men in condition for their mission. Tracer and Jarrett had driven to Pattaya and hooked up with some lifters, Tracer's old friends from his time in the service, guys senior enough to come into town as part of the advance detail. There were other private security contractors like them mixing in, looking for recruits, talking about the situation in Baghdad and the bad old days of Desert Storm. That storm had left the desert and pretty much spread everywhere.

That much everyone agreed on as they bought each other rounds of drinks and waited to crank up one more Cobra Gold exercise.

Jarrett had bowed out of the festivities because he had stuff to do on the job in Bangkok. That was Jarrett code that meant some woman had got his attention. Tracer knew exactly who the woman was, some beekeeper's daughter. And the other reason had to do with securing a couple of weapons, including a .308 sniper's rifle – lightweight, good range, reliable, and efficient for work in a big city. There wasn't a better companion for a sniper in Bangkok. Jarrett had asked for that sniper rifle because he knew Mooney could deliver. He'd take the rifle out of inventory and not leave any record that it was gone.

Tracer checked the time. He'd bought his Rolex at the duty-free shop in Dubai on the way to Bangkok. He was proud of that watch. It made clocking the time a pleasure. Two hours had passed since he'd parked his car in the basement of the shopping mall. He walked along Beach Road. Crowds pushed down the narrow corridor, negotiating rows of parked motorcycles and vendor tables spilling onto the road, stacked with bikinis, brass knuckles, and switchblade knives. Tracer worked his way through the knots of tourists in sandals and shorts, picking at their sunburns and getting grabbed by Indian tailors moving as fast as sand-trap spiders.

He turned down a small soi rimmed with food

stalls and restaurants, parked motorcycles, sleeping dogs, and yings squatting on plastic stools, using their hands to eat som tam and smoking cigarettes. He ignored a couple of young touts who stood in front of the go-go bars. They had short hair and sunglasses and looked like they worked out, playing the part of tough guy from some pirated movie they'd seen. Finally he reached the end of the narrow lane. He stopped in front of the bar with a red and green neon dragon breathing fire and walked in. It was one of those lonely bars that didn't bring in enough money to pay for a door tout and not much cash for the yings, either, who danced for drinks and the hope of an early bar fine. The ramshackle door and concrete step in front had all the indications of the kind of place Mooney would choose. That fact was soon enough established as Tracer pushed back the beaded curtain and glanced around.

Two yings leaned against chrome poles, looking at their nails and yawning. Over in the corner, Mooney sat erect, hands on the table, staring at the stage. Tracer shook his head, thinking the career sergeant looked more edgy than the last time he'd seen him under fire. He gave it a couple of minutes until Mooney saw him leaning against the back wall. It was no good sneaking up on a man like Mooney. They'd done business before, during the Gulf War and afterwards, as if they were doomed to keep a fire alive that Mooney, if he had his way, would have doused a long time ago.

Sometimes there's no choice in life, thought Tracer, and you keep on dealing with people you knew a long time ago because those are the only people you can trust. They both knew that Mooney was looking to take retirement from the army and be hired by Colonel Waters's private security company. That would have made them coworkers. Mooney caught his eye and waved him over.

Tracer sat down and ordered fresh orange juice in a tall glass with no ice. Mooney had been drinking Singha beer. A black man in a tailored shirt and trousers with expensive Italian shoes who drank fresh orange juice at the deadest bar in Pattaya was definitely a man who had some kind of official business. Still, Tracer played it cool with Mooney. History had taught him there was no other way, unless you wanted trouble.

'You look like a live-bait shop owner who just heard they're gonna dam the creek ten miles upriver,' said Tracer.

'It's the bullshit I don't like,' said Mooney. He lifted the Singha bottle and took a long swig, wiping his mouth with the back of his hand.

'Who does?'

'No one's cut an order on this thing. It's all verbal. They say, "Mooney, this is a stealth exercise. You're team leader." Only they leave out the part that there ain't anyone else on the team. Unless it's you, and brother, you don't count as a player on my team. And Jarrett, he didn't even bother to show up. What the fuck is that?'

'You'll be coming over to the company soon enough. Think about the future.'

'You're talking to me like I talk to a bar girl,' said Mooney.

'We're all playing ball, Mooney. Jarrett, me, you. You are part of the team.'

'I've had Blackwater talking to me, too. Waters ain't the only game out there.'

'I know that. But you work with people you know. Whom do you know at Blackwater?'

Mooney drank again, draining the bottle. He waved the empty at a dek-serve, the Thai name for a ying who served customer drinks but didn't dance, and she scurried away for a fresh beer. 'I ask myself, "How is this building up any expertise if I'm working alone?" But I don't come up with any answer. You got one, Tracer?'

Tracer smiled, sipped the orange juice, knowing there was no point taking Mooney's bitching to heart. 'Waters says it's because you're good. You're the man. You get the job done. No complications.'

Mooney shrugged. 'Something like that.' Really, Mooney liked to hear that. He did get things done. Finding out how to move weapons, ammo, supplies, and men without paperwork was a lost art. Mooney was a craftsman.

'It's what you do.'

'Exactly what is it that I do?'

They both looked at the yings on the stage, who were practicing for a zombie audition.

'Hide stuff without anyone seeing you. I'd say that's a skill.'

'Not much of a skill around my wife.' Mooney had that married-to-the-Corps, married-to-the-old-lady-for-life look about him.

'Ain't any man who's any good at hiding shit from his wife. You know what I'm saying.'

Tracer got out his wallet to pay for his drink. Mooney took away his chit cup and waved off the money. 'Take care of yourself. Don't forget one thing?'

Trace gave him a what-could-that-possibly-be look.

'Kate comes back undamaged in three days. Otherwise . . .'

'Man, there is no otherwise. We're gonna bring her back. Promise.'

Even in the dark bar, Tracer saw Mooney's eyes roll. Why do white boys always come up with names like Kate for their boats and airplanes? He didn't begin to have an answer.

A week earlier, Mooney had gotten a phone call from his old commanding officer, who'd given no details about the counter-intelligence operation Mooney was being asked to assist. Not that he expected any information about the mission; in fact, he didn't want to know. Knowledge was highly overrated in the military. Colonel Waters had called in a favor with a man still working inside and gotten Mooney assigned to the Cobra

Gold exercise as a weapons specialist. Waters had been shuttling on the company's expense account that covered Algeria to Zimbabwe and any other hot spot up or down the alphabet. If someone decided there was a place of interest vital to America, sooner or later Colonel Waters showed up to take a risk survey. That was what Logistic Risk Assessment Services, which everyone called LRAS, was on the books to do; the extra services provided were off the books. Waters worked on the extra services side of LRAS where, among other duties, he assembled his boots on the ground, recruited the right team of experts and briefed them on their off-the-book assignments.

Two years ago, a couple of MBAs, IT, and logistics specialists at LRAS had been brought in to manage, and the old team was put out to pasture. It was a purge passed off as a generational change. Waters had survived at LRAS but in the first few months after the internal coup, the new team had buried him under paperwork. It didn't take long for the new management to figure out that they needed Waters. By that time, Waters smiled and returned to his paperwork. He'd already put in place an inside group for the special operations assignments that were independent from the suits. Creating a secret team within the company had been his one small victory in the corporate wars.

A month before Cobra Gold, Tracer had been in Kabul when he'd gotten a call in the middle of the night. 'I might have something for you and

Jarrett. It's in Bangkok,' said Colonel Waters over a secure line. 'You want it?' He'd given Tracer a name and hung up.

The next morning Tracer had told Jarrett about the phone call, but Jarrett had just shrugged. They were in a Humvee on the way to the airport, working a security detail for an assistant secretary of state who was seated in the back wearing a vest and helmet. He was going home.

'Bangkok,' Tracer said. 'Our deal is we get ten days' leave. No pay deduction. We split forty grand. I told him I liked it but I'd ask you.'

'What's the job?'

'A bad guy needs taking down.'

Jarrett nodded his head. 'That's what we do.'

Three days later they were in Bangkok inside a bar, yings dancing. Jarrett had blinked as he looked at the naked bodies. Every so often a flash of their position at the airport in Kabul cross-wired through his consciousness. Tracer shook his head, let out a low whistle, and slapped his big hand against his thigh as one of the skinny yings smiled at Jarrett.

'You need a fat mama with some shakin' going on. That's what you need, Jarrett. A woman needs some meat stickin' to her bones.'

'Tracer, you ought to be living in Samoa.'

'I want a .308 for city work.' Tracer hadn't discussed a backup rifle as part of the shopping list with Waters. The fine details were left to him and Jarrett to work out with Mooney.

62

Jarrett looked away from the stage. The ex-football player might have passed for a Samoan in the half-darkness of the bar. 'How do we get the weapon?'

Tracer smiled, shaking his head. 'He's got it worked out with Mooney.'

'Cobra Gold Mooney.'

'Mooney is Waters's man. Six months and he'll be working for LRAS.'

'Tell Waters I want a night scope, too.'

Tracer nodded. 'I already did that. And a silencer. And a tripod. Twenty rounds should do it.'

'One shot, one kill,' said Jarrett.

Jarrett stared straight ahead, his eyes no longer focusing on the yings. He said nothing through two songs. This was Jarrett's way of thinking through his options and deciding there weren't any real ones on the table – or on the stage, for that matter, or just about anywhere one looked in the world. Tracer understood this about his partner. The man was giving himself some thinking time. Staring at the yings without looking at them, as if some Zen answer could be found in the way they moved onstage.

'He can find one, for sure?'

'They've come as part of Cobra Gold. Mooney delivers the rifle, and then three days later we do the job, return the rifle, and go back to Kabul. And everyone's happy.'

Jarrett nodded. 'Who's the target?'

Tracer shrugged. 'The asshole who murdered Casey's son a couple of years back.'

63

'I thought Casey'd taken care of that himself,' said Jarrett.

'Casey's working in Bangkok. He can't do something where he works.'

'We do that all the time,' said Jarrett.

'That's different. What we do in Baghdad, Kabul, or the other shitholes doesn't necessarily work in places like Bangkok. There are political considerations.'

'That sounds like Waters talking.'

Jarrett had nailed it straight through. Those had been Colonel Waters's words. Casey had been transferred to Bangkok a couple of years earlier. Everyone in Baghdad who knew Casey thought he'd kill the man who'd murdered his son. When the weeks drifted into months and the months into a year, it looked like Casey had gone soft and had become meek, Christian-like in his forgiveness. Casey had been assigned along with six other private security contractors to work in a prison in Baghdad. The transfer was a promotion and more money. Everyone who knew him, including Jarrett and Tracer, thought Casey had thrown himself into his work and was working his way through his son's death.

'Waters couldn't say much on the phone. He was in Bogotá.'

Jarrett shot him a frown.

'Hand on my heart,' said Tracer.

'Man, you ain't got no heart. Everyone who knows you knows that. And I thought he hated Colombia.'

'It ain't written anywhere they send you to the place you wanna go.'

That much Jarrett agreed with. Even legends like the Colonel had bosses who cut them orders on the basis of certain skills in the field. Waters once said he'd rather be surrounded by Taliban than a squad of MBAs. He worked for LRAS, but he wasn't the typical company man; he was a holdover from the old corporate culture, when veterans had run the management. Waters blamed himself for not having the right business skills to make the transition as a corporate team player. He said he'd wasted his time learning to speak fluent Spanish rather than balance sheets. It made him an asset in Latin America but a liability to the bottom line. Once during the Gulf War, Colonel Waters, then a captain, had told Tracer that his one regret was that he hadn't studied Swedish. Six-foot blue-eyed blondes with legs as long as the New Jersey Turnpike had a powerful pull on him.

CHAPTER 5

Who was the woman who fell to her death from the hotel? What was your relationship with her? How long have you known her? Why did she come to your room? Did you have a fight?

That was the string of questions asked by a couple of cops, though one officer did most of the talking. The interrogation started at the front desk of the hotel. It continued in the lobby, out into the street where they showed him the body, and back in his room. Maybe they thought they could find an inconsistency in his answers. They pounded away as if he were guilty of a crime. The main policeman interrogating Calvino spoke good English. He wrote notes as Calvino gave the same answers to the same questions he'd been asked over and over until his phone rang again. Colonel Pratt was on the line. It was his turn to ask the questions.

'Who was she, Vincent?' asked Colonel Pratt.

'She didn't tell me her name.'

'But you knew her?'

'She was lighting incense sticks in front of the spirit house outside the hotel when I arrived.

66

A seagull startled her and she looked around and smiled. I smiled back. Does that sound like an intimate relationship?'

'Vincent, what happened, is disturbing.'

'I'm not real happy about it either. I'm supposed to be relaxing, having fun. The idea was to keep away from Apichart's backup team.'

The thought had crossed Colonel Pratt's mind that Apichart might have had something to do with the woman falling off a balcony, but as hard as he tried, he couldn't make the connection work. Apichart would have had no idea where Calvino had gone. Only the General and Ratana had known the name of the hotel.

'I'll drive to Pattaya tomorrow morning.'

'Pratt, the cops are talking about putting me in jail. Someone whispered fifty thousand baht would keep me out.'

There was a moment of silence. Someone had put the squeeze on Calvino, and the Colonel took that as a direct slap in his face and in the General's as well. 'Don't pay anyone anything,' he said.

'What happened has got nothing to do with Apichart and nothing to do with me,' Calvino said. 'People fall off balconies all the time in Pattaya. You read the newspapers.' He looked around the room filled with uniformed cops.

'Those are depressed farangs, Vincent. Not young Thai women.'

The Colonel had a point. The ying Calvino had

seen at the spirit house had been in her prime. She'd had everything to live for.

'I don't want to spend the night in jail. I wanna pay the fifty grand.'

Colonel Pratt hadn't had time to phone General Yosaporn about what had happened in Pattaya. The General's friend, after all, owned the hotel. He'd have to tell him before the owner phoned.

Ratana had warned Calvino about the danger of using a coffin to collect the rent, and now her words rang in his ears: This is bad luck. With the body count already at three, he was starting to doubt himself.

'You're not going to jail. Let me work on it,' said Pratt, ending the call. He had sounded weary, upset, and yet resigned to figuring out how to keep Calvino out of jail and in his room. It couldn't be the farang way; that never worked. It had to be a middle path, a compromise. Fifty thousand was a starting position, leaving room for negotiations. After questioning Calvino, they'd think he would understand that the figure was the opening bid. It was now Pratt's turn to negotiate a reduction, closer to the price reserved for Thais. But a farang, now and again, given the right connections, had ways of approaching the same results.

In the hours after the woman's death, Calvino's Pattaya vacation had ended with all the warning of a sunburn on an overcast day. Sitting in his room, waiting for Pratt to make a deal, he was stuck between the world of freedom and the world of jail. None of the police had been able to decide what to do with him. That was a good sign; they were cautious, firm, and suspicious. After they'd found out General Yosaporn had personally paid for Calvino's room, their mood changed. The thermostat of their belligerence toward a farang started to drop. An hour later, one of the officers informed Calvino that he was to remain in his room, and a couple of police guards would be posted outside the door. 'I wanna go out for a walk on the beach. I need some fresh air, you know what I'm saying?'

The senior officer shot him an angry look. 'If I had my way you'd already be in jail.' He'd obviously heard that Calvino had turned down the request for 50,000 baht.

'No beach walk,' said Calvino, closing the door, resting his head against it, banging softly, once, twice, three times. Then he turned around and looked at the cops in his room. 'Careful with that jacket,' he said, moving across the room. One of them was going through the pockets of his new jacket. The cop put it to his nose and made a face. 'Smells of smoke.' He smelled it again. 'And gas.'

This wasn't the time to explain how the sports jacket had taken on those smells. It wouldn't help his situation. If anything, the fifty grand would suddenly rise to a hundred grand. Instead Calvino decided to go on the offensive.

'What you're doing isn't kosher,' he said. They

stared blankly at him. 'It's illegal. You can't keep me under house arrest. You know what I'm saying? So if you would leave my room now, I'd like to drink whiskey and read my book.'

The cops yawned and went back to their own conversation, passing Calvino's jacket around for a sniff. One of the cops took out a hanky and blew his nose. He said he had an allergy to gas fumes. They'll be laying other charges, Calvino thought. Interfering in a powerful way with the tiny follicles lining the policeman's nose. He sneezed a couple of times, his face flushing red. He cursed and handed the jacket to another cop. The last place to make a stink was in Thailand; the Thais hated any smell that fell within their expansive definition of 'bad,' and the constant tropical heat supplied a range of foul, decaying odors that often sent a Thai fainting or running. The last cop handed it to Calvino. He smelled his own jacket and then put it on. 'Smells okay to me. Maybe bad smells are a cultural thing,' he said. 'Have I told you guys that I'd like you to leave so I can start my vacation? I can translate that into Thai if you want. But I think you've got the basic idea.'

He understood that while he wasn't free to leave his room, this was no small concession. Some creative, face-saving, promotion-preserving compromise was being made. It took about forty minutes before the senior cop came back into the room, smiling. That smile is a good thing, or it could be a good thing, Calvino thought. It means they got the deal together – or else they're going to get the fifty grand off me or lock me up. It never came to that. The final deal bore the earmarks of Colonel Pratt's influence; he would have phoned General Yosaporn as well as the commanding officer in Pattaya, an old friend from the academy – or the friend of a friend from the academy – and they would have worked out the compromise. The hotel owner would have called the commanding officer, and General Yosaporn would also have phoned his remaining friends in the police force.

The phone on the desk of the commanding officer in Pattaya would have rung off the hook as he heard from three or four high-ranking officers, a politician, a military general, an admiral, and maybe influential figures in the province. If he had graphed the strands of influence, he would have seen a spider's web with Calvino caught in the center. After the second or third call, the commanding officer would have got the message: Calvino wasn't just another farang. The police had to be careful.

Calvino figured the press would be all over the lobby and hotel grounds, interviewing people as they walked out of the elevators. The nude body of a young woman was guaranteed to keep viewers glued to the TV. In the morning, images of her crumpled body would be splashed on the front pages of the Thai newspapers. The Pattaya police would want to duck any political problems that might arise if they just let Calvino go. There was no denying that Calvino was a material witness, and with an election coming up, a couple of veteran politicians had been banging away on the problem of farangs. How farangs were committing crimes. The image of farangs – never lofty at the best of times – had plummeted with the recent arrest of a crop of foreign pedophiles, con men, drunks, crazies, and dopeheads. Politicians sensed a chance to strike, an irresistible opportunity to pander to the worst instincts of voters. The cops had no stomach for crossing politicians this close to an election. Farangs were on a kind of probation, watched with suspicion, as if they might be secretly planning to skip out with containers of yings, corporate profits, rice, and gold. Many Thais assumed most farangs who lived in Thailand were up to no good; otherwise, why would they be in Thailand and not back in farangland?

Two witnesses on the ground – a motorcycle driver and a vendor on the beach – had said they'd seen Calvino at his railing as the woman had fallen from the building. That made him a suspect. After a few more questions the witnesses had convinced themselves that the farang on the balcony had had something to do with it. The cops told Calvino that there were witnesses who put him at the scene of the crime. Calvino told the cops once again that his room was below the scene of the crime. He'd looked over the balcony only after the woman had fallen from one of the rooms situated above his. They looked at him like they didn't believe him. He assumed that as the night wore on, the descriptions of the witnesses would become more and more detailed, and other witnesses would step forward and corroborate what the first two Thais had said.

It was a gathering storm. It's a good time, thought Calvino, for the fish to close his mouth, dive deep, and wait on the bottom until Colonel Pratt shows up in the morning. He sat in his chair, looking out at the sky and sea, thinking maybe it would have been better after all if he hadn't used the coffin to extract the rent money for General Yosaporn. The police stood in a semicircle around him. His back was to the balcony. If he wanted to do the right thing and join the woman below right then, he was being told, no one would stop him. A couple of the officers had spotted the case of whiskey and pulled out and examined the bottles.

'The whiskey is a gift from General Yosaporn,' said Calvino. He didn't say anything more.

The officer in charge told the two policemen to put the whiskey back.

'Metta,' said Calvino. It was Pali for compassion, and the General's signature word for saying goodbye.

The worst fears for a Thai were to end up on the wrong side of a power struggle or an argument, or to make a mistake. Whoever this farang was and however he got that whiskey from a Thai general,

73

his position had been buttressed by numerous phone calls from people who rarely phoned the police, and it made the policemen tense and fearful. The immediate aftermath of the death had brought a half-dozen cops to his room, but the numbers had dwindled as the phone calls had come in. After the last call, the senior officer and the other police had huddled and whispered, glancing back at Calvino, who'd been moved from the balcony and made to sit on the edge of the king-sized bed.

'You will stay in this room at all times,' said the senior officer, making it sound like a police victory.

'I can't leave the hotel?'

'Do not leave this room.'

'Metta,' said Calvino. The senior officer tried to decide whether the farang was mocking him. He weighed the options at his disposal and went back to consulting with his officers. A moment later he vanished.

The Thai way was an unofficial house arrest. It amounted to face-saving through babysitting. It could be worse, Calvino told himself. It could be jail. He sat back on the bed and resigned himself to the reality: a chain of events had started with the death of a woman, and no one, not even Colonel Pratt or his mentor, could fully control what would happen now. Pratt had said nothing about the duration. Thinking about the two cops left behind as a security detail, he felt depressed. They could hold him until after the election, or he could even be kept for years. The cops outside might grow

74

old and retire and gradually be replaced by fresh recruits from the academy: young policemen who would have only a vague idea why the farang inside the ninth floor wasn't authorized to leave his room. They would only know that his confinement had something to do with a woman who'd died a long time ago and that no one had ever decided how or why she died. No one would ever question the decision to keep Calvino in the room since it's easier for a rich man to enter the kingdom of heaven than for a Thai to step forward and reverse a decision.

CHAPTER 6

In Thailand, it didn't take long to figure out that you didn't have to outlive anyone to know you were alone. House arrest in Pattaya wasn't much different from a no-show funeral with a couple of attendants looking after the body.

The two cops left behind to guard Calvino were the same two officers who had taken an extraordinary interest in the case of whiskey. Having failed to score a bottle, they'd decided that their assignment had the hallmarks of a punishment detail. In other words, they'd been left behind because they'd been volunteered, until a further order was given allowing them to leave. Neither one showed any emotion: it was swallowed back like nasty medicine. But after the other police had gone, they made it clear to Calvino that he had caused them a big problem. When a Thai says you've caused him a big problem, he's using an English expression to signal that the time has arrived to collect your passport and take the first taxi to the airport. Asian problem-solving techniques have a certain finality to them. Calvino said nothing, knowing it wasn't a good time to be blowing bubbles their way. With no reaction from the farang, the anger slowly cooled. Calvino had been demoted to a pain in the ass with a smelly sports jacket. In private, they whispered that the farang had done it. The two cops who pulled guard detail glared at Calvino. He smiled; they frowned. Then one cop snarled and the other cursed. They were like a bad nightclub routine.

Calvino had decided he wanted information from the cops: Who else had they been talking to, which rooms besides his own had they searched, and what had they found?

From the bed, his hands still cuffed behind his back, Calvino watched his guards walk around the room. He sized them up. Each wore a brown uniform as tight as a scuba diver's wetsuit, holstered nines, handcuffs (minus the pair on Calvino's wrists), and radios on their hips. Vests covered their chests with POLICE written in illuminated white on fluorescent orange. Both had short-cropped black hair.

One of the cops had pockmarked skin carpeting his cheeks and neck, as if a massive acne glacier had once rumbled over his body. A couple of those old scars had left craters as deep as the dimples of a smile in full bloom. He was a dead ringer for the deposed Panama dictator Manuel Antonio Noriega. Calvino started thinking of this cop as Noriega. Though the officer was in his early thirties, he looked older and tougher; a no-nonsense veteran who could line up men against a wall, knee them in the balls, slap them around, and then order them shot. He stared at Calvino with a mixture of hostility and suspicion.

Noriega's partner, a few years younger, unsmiling and rigid, clutched his radio as it began to squawk and reported back to someone at the other end that the farang hadn't confessed. Not yet. He looked at Calvino as he said this in Thai. This cop's head had a shape similar to that of the Chinese leader Mao Zedong, with a bulb-like forehead swelling out from a receding hairline. This Mao, like his namesake, had a slightly superior curl of the lip, giving him the appearance of someone who knew dark secrets. He looked like a man well acquainted with the benefits of arrogance and the use of violence.

Calvino had been spared the usual arrest formalities. The cops left behind had a few ideas of their own. Before Calvino got what he wanted, he needed to establish a little good faith.

Mao had shown the most malice as he'd looked Calvino up and down, made him turn and put his hands against the wall, and frisked him. He'd pulled a .38 from Calvino's ankle holster and with a smirk showed it to his partner. Calvino had told them he had a license for the gun, but they weren't interested. Once they'd disarmed him, Noriega had unhooked a pair of handcuffs from his belt and ordered Calvino to turn around with his hands behind his back. Handcuffing had been their original duty.

After the cuffs were on, Noriega had gestured for Calvino to sit on the bed and told him to sit very still. The two officers had searched the room, pulling out every drawer, going through his suitcase. He'd heard one of them in the bathroom opening doors and drawers and drawing back the shower curtain.

After they'd finished the search, they'd returned and, standing shoulder to shoulder, confronted Calvino. He hadn't shifted position. He hadn't said a word. The two cops continued their conversation on the assumption that Calvino had no clue what they were saying.

'Ask him why he killed the girl,' Noriega said.

Mao wrinkled his nose. 'Why do farangs have a bad smell?'

'You think he pushed her off the balcony?'

Mao shrugged. 'Why don't we take him back and lock him up?'

'Because we have orders. He stays in the room. We stay with him.'

'What's he doing with a case of whiskey?' asked Mao. 'Maybe that's why he killed the girl. We should take it as evidence.'

Noriega shrugged. 'Later. Now we follow orders.'

'I'm hungry. How about you?' asked Calvino in Thai. 'What if I ordered some food?'

Mao shot Calvino a hard look. 'You speak Thai?'

Calvino smiled, asking him in Thai to remove the handcuffs. 'I'm not going anywhere. And technically I'm not under arrest.'

The two cops exchanged a glance and then looked at Calvino, nodding. That was true. But as far as they were concerned, his not being under arrest had nothing to do with keeping him handcuffed.

'Besides, how can I use the phone if my hands are cuffed? Why not get some food? I'm thinking about some big steaks, French fries, ice cream. But you guys probably don't like farang food.'

Noriega found the key for the handcuffs and gestured for Calvino to stand up. Standing at the foot of the bed, Calvino turned around and Noriega unlocked the handcuffs. Calvino rubbed his wrists and then slowly, with his hands in full sight, leaned over and picked up the phone.

'I'm ordering food.'

They had no instructions about allowing the farang access to the phone. They had to think for themselves, and fast. 'Only food,' said Nariega.

'Steaks and ice cream,' said Calvino.

Calvino phoned the steakhouse and ordered three large steaks, medium rare, with extra sauce on the side, a bucket of French fries, and half a liter of mocha ice cream. Next he dialed the number of the Russian restaurant and ordered a liter bottle of vodka, a dozen dumplings, and borscht. He then called the Italian restaurant and ordered veal and three plates of pasta. Mao and Noriega watched and listened. Each time he phoned another restaurant, they nodded with a flicker of a smile. Calvino wasn't certain what that meant, but he decided it was a signal to keep on ordering.

Mao walked over to the table and pulled out a bottle of the whiskey. 'How much does it cost?' he asked in Thai.

'Six thousand baht,' said Calvino, knowing this was about equal to a month's salary on the police force.

'What are you doing with eleven bottles? One's missing. You already drink it today?' asked Noriega. He was running a calculation in his head on the total value of the case. Eleven bottles was close to a year's pay.

'They're sold. I was delivering them tonight.'

Noriega thought about the possibilities. 'You don't want to open one?'

Calvino looked at the bottle of Johnnie Walker on the balcony table. Noriega got the message without exchanging a word. He went out on the balcony and grabbed the bottle. When he came back in with it, he was smiling.

While they waited for the food, Calvino called room service for glasses, ice, and soda, and a few minutes later he tipped the room service attendant a hundred baht. He poured three glasses of Johnnie Walker, handing Mao and Noriega each a glass.

'Chai yo,' said Calvino, the Thai salute, raising his glass. 'I didn't kill the woman.' The salute translated as 'victory' and the way he said it left open whose victory they were celebrating.

The cops drank. They sat in a semicircle, the cops on chairs and Calvino perched on the end of the bed holding his glass. 'Any idea who was staying in the suites above this one, from the tenth to the fifteenth floors?'

The cops shrugged and held out empty glasses, which Calvino refilled.

The Russian food and vodka arrived first, and the hotel concierge accompanied the delivery boy. Calvino borrowed the concierge's ballpoint pen, signed the bill, and handed it to the concierge. 'Put this on my bill,' he said.

The concierge looked at the bill, the two cops in the room, and then at the delivery boy. 'Impossible,' he said.

'I can't go to the ATM. Ask these two fine gentlemen. And I have no cash.'

The concierge, Noriega, and Mao exchanged a few words. The concierge sucked his teeth and shot Calvino a smug look of contempt. Calvino closed the door, leaving the concierge in the corridor. He carried the steaming dumplings to the table, opened the container, and the room filled with the smell of minced meat, spices, and mint.

Calvino grinned as he unscrewed the cap on the bottle of vodka and poured out three glasses. He didn't bother rinsing the glasses after the Johnnie Walker. He was amused by what they'd told the concierge: 'The farang is a VIP and we've been ordered to make certain he doesn't make any trouble. You don't want to cause a problem, do you?'

It all came back to the possibility of causing someone a problem. The aversion to problem causing was only exceeded by the desire to maintain face. Calvino raised his glass, touched the glasses of Mao and Noriega, and took a long swig. The cops stared at each other and then sipped the vodka with a strong hint of whiskey. Perhaps they believed the story they'd given to the concierge.

Mao held the glass of vodka in his fist, watching Calvino. He was wondering whether this farang was a VIP or a murderer. Or was he perhaps part of the recent trend of VIP murderers?

Noriega, the senior of the two officers, was half a step slower. He circled around the table, picked up the bottle of vodka, read the label, and then let his hand slip down to pick up the glass. Calvino refilled the glasses as the steaks arrived, and once again Calvino told the delivery boy to get the money from the concierge at the front desk. The delivery boy looked at the cops, who both nodded and told him to go downstairs for the cash. They'd fallen into a kind of routine by the time the Italian food arrived ten minutes later, and Noriega told the delivery boy to give the bill to the concierge. There was no room left on the table, so Calvino put the Italian food on the bed. Dumplings, pasta, steaks – the room smelled like an all-you-can-eat buffet in a redneck town somewhere in Missouri. Mao relaxed after finishing the second vodka and managed a smile.

'Any more food?' asked Mao.

Calvino shook his head. 'Let's eat this first. I can always order more.'

Noriega grinned, picking up the phone. He ordered plates and real silverware. The concierge sent a lackey with a trolley loaded with plates, silverware, pepper and salt, pepper sauce, and raw red chili, twisted and ugly, in a porcelain bowl. Neither he nor his partner was feeling punished anymore by guarding the farang detail. It was something every man at the bottom of the ladder could appreciate: a party with good Western food and drink, and an invitation to eat as much as you wanted and to drink until the empty bottles rattled against one another on the floor.

The Thais had a food-sharing culture; communal dining automatically overcame the circumstances of how the diners had been thrown together. Calvino poured the third round of vodka. Noriega asked about the United States. Calvino explained he was from New York and that it was a small island off the coast of the United States, no matter what anyone else said. It was no more America than Bangkok was Thailand. That explanation was accepted with knowing grunts by Noriega. Neither Noriega nor Mao was from Bangkok, and they bore the usual upcountry grudge against the big city.

'In Los Angeles, you are what you drive. In Washington, D.C., you are your job. And in New York you are how much money you've got.'

Calvino watched the cops chewing large slabs of steak, thinking about his description.

The cops thought about this for a couple of minutes, digging into the pasta. 'In Bangkok maybe we have all three American cities in one,' said Mao, the one who was fast on his feet.

Cars, money, status, and women were warehoused in places like New York and Bangkok. If you value those things, it makes sense to live there, thought Calvino. He scored the case of expensive whiskey because he was a farang who had understood the nature of the Thai way of paying obligations. Mao got the point immediately. But Noriega's brain sputtered and spat, trying to get out of neutral and into high gear.

'I want to go to America,' said Noriega.

'Why do you want to go?' asked Calvino.

'So I can be rich.'

'Any idea who was in the suite above me?' He pointed up at the ceiling.

'The dead girl,' said Noriega.

'Then you know she didn't go off my balcony. She was pushed off her own balcony.'

Mao frowned. 'How do you know she was pushed? Unless she came to your room and you pushed her.'

'Why would I want to do that?' asked Calvino.

Noriega pointed his finger at Calvino. 'You lose temper. Hot heart. You have a fight, she tries to hit you, you push her, and she falls. Not your fault. You don't worry if you tell me this is what happened. Everyone will understand.'

So much for the food and liquor. Neither Noriega nor Mao had let his dining and drinking pleasure interfere with what he'd already decided. Calvino lay back on the bed, an arm resting over his eyes. It was going to be a very long night.

'How are you so sure?' Calvino asked.

'She checked in yesterday and paid for your upgrade to this suite,' said Noriega.

He rose out of bed. 'She paid for what?'

'An upgrade.'

'You double-check with General Yosaporn. He paid for the room.'

Noriega nodded and smiled at his partner. They'd obviously talked about this before.

'The General paid for a room. Not for a suite. The dead woman paid to have you in the room below hers.'

His heart pounded his chest and neck. No wonder the cops had wanted to lock him up. If these two flat shoes had this information, it must have been passed on to Colonel Pratt. He hadn't said a thing about this on the phone. It was something Pratt would have wanted to think about long and hard. Pratt would want to look Calvino in the eye and ask him why a total stranger would upgrade him to a suite. How would she even have known that he was in that hotel? The situation was much worse than he had imagined. Somehow Apichart must have arranged it in the two days that had passed before he left for Pattaya. That was long enough if Apichart had known his plans.

There was no way short of a gun pointed at her baby son's head that Ratana would have divulged that information. His heart was still racing as he lay in bed, wishing he'd never rented the coffin. It had been a big mistake, and luck, bad or good, had nothing to do with it.

CHAPTER 7

Colonel Pratt had once told Calvino that he reminded him of the kind of guy who walked into a dynamite warehouse and lit a match to see where he was going. After he lit the first match and looked around at the stacks of dynamite, he'd wait until the match burned down to fingernail-igniting length, and then he'd strike another match. Pratt thought about that conversation as he drove to Pattaya.

Entering Pattaya, he used the siren to clear a path through the traffic. He pulled into a hotel guest spot and then spent half an hour talking with two senior police officers in the hotel. They'd gone over the paperwork for the suite, looking at handwritten notes setting out the arrangements for payment of the room. The suite upgrade had been paid in cash. Then he rode in the elevator with the concierge, the manager, the two senior police officers, and a bellhop to the ninth floor. They stood in front of Calvino's door, Pratt collecting his thoughts. He didn't knock, letting the concierge slip a plastic card into the slot. The manager pulled out the card and opened the door.

Colonel Pratt asked to talk with Calvino alone. The others waited in the corridor as the Colonel stepped inside and looked around, leaving the door open behind him. Noriega slept in a stuffed chair, his head resting against the sliding glass door. An empty vodka bottle lay at his feet. Mao slumped over the glass table, snoring, his face a couple of inches away from a plate of pasta. The room looked like it had been raided and pillaged by a band of Vikings. Bones, scraps of food, clothes, plastic bags, and Styrofoam containers were scattered across chairs, tables, the bed, and the floor. Ants, geckos, and cockroaches feasted on the leftovers. The jungle had begun to reclaim the building, starting from the ninth floor.

Colonel Pratt cleared his throat as he stood at the end of the bed.

The men jerked, and Noriega instinctively reached for his holstered sidearm. He looked groggy-eyed at Colonel Pratt, who stood with his hands on his waist, his nine in a holster on his right hip. Noriega thought he might be dreaming until he realized a superior officer had entered the room. He shook Mao, who sat up too quickly, knocking the plate of pasta to the floor. The two cops snapped to attention. Noriega's hair looked like a bad wig, and his skin, a slightly greenish color, looked ready to be harvested for high-end boots. He saluted Colonel Pratt while Mao, smoothing the wrinkles in his trousers, waited for the Colonel to say something. Calvino raised himself on one elbow in bed and stretched.

'What time is it?'

Pratt walked around the edge of the debris. 'Time to find out what happened yesterday afternoon. And you might start by explaining about this room.'

'We had a small party. Then these two gentlemen decided to spend the night.'

'Vincent, the police have two witnesses who claim they saw you push her off your balcony,' said Colonel Pratt.

'They can get a dozen witnesses. It was getting dark. A woman fell from a hotel balcony. It happened in a couple of seconds. They saw nothing. But that doesn't stop them thinking they saw what happened. Like I said on the phone, I was on my balcony and had just opened *The Quiet American*. I looked up and saw her falling. I leaned over the railing. A couple of seconds later she was on the ground.'

'There's something you should know. The dead woman paid to have you upgraded to a suite below her own suite. Why would she do that?'

Calvino shook his head. 'I heard about the upgrade from these two.' He nodded at the two cops. Then he stared at Colonel Pratt for a long moment, rolled off the bed, and walked over to the balcony. 'Pratt, I have no fucking idea who she was. That's the truth. The cops have been through my room and found nothing. Not a single print, hair, or fingernail clipping.'

'You didn't know her?'

Calvino swung his legs over the side of the bed. 'I have no idea who she was. Or why she'd do that. It's gotta be Apichart.'

'On the phone, you said you'd seen her earlier in the day.'

'I know it looks bad.'

The other police and hotel staff had slowly filtered back into the sitting room area. Calvino now had a complete audience, just as on the previous evening. He paced in front of the balcony window, filling his cheeks with air, looking at his feet. He threw up his hands, resting forward with two hands on the back of a chair. 'When I arrived at the hotel yesterday, I saw a woman at the hotel spirit house. A seagull flew up and startled her. She turned and saw me. We exchanged a smile. Does that amount to knowing someone? I saw her face for less than a minute. She didn't say anything. If she'd said, 'I just upgraded your room to a suite, big guy. This is your lucky day,' I'd have remembered. The woman who went over the side looked like the woman in front of the spirit house. I only had a second to see the woman who fell. I'm trying to match a stranger I saw for less than a minute with another stranger I saw for a second.'

'It was the same woman who paid for the upgrade, Vincent.'

'I'm not denying it was. I'm saying I didn't know who she was.'

It was a defining moment, one of those flashes

that make a man ask whether he really knows another person. Colonel Pratt had known Calvino for years, fought for him, defended him, and sent him work. He looked at Vincent as if trying to read something inside his own mind at the same time.

Noriega and Mao gave up pretending to follow the conversation in English. Mao lit a cigarette and went out on the balcony. Noriega joined him with two of the cops who had followed Colonel Pratt up in the elevator. One of the senior officers was on his radio reporting that a colonel from Bangkok was interrogating the suspect in English and he wasn't certain what was being said.

'I've done it this time. I'm in big trouble,' said Calvino.

'I've got someone checking to see if there is a connection between the woman and Apichart.'

'And if there isn't one?'

The Colonel's mouth firmed. 'Then you're right.'

'I should have stayed in Bangkok,' said Calvino.

'We're going to work this through, Vincent.'

Calvino nodded. 'Thanks, Pratt.'

When they stepped back inside the room, Noriega asked if Calvino had told him anything useful. Colonel Pratt stared at the policeman.

'You can go now,' said Colonel Pratt.

That wasn't much of an answer, and certainly not the one they'd expected. A colonel didn't have to answer to patrolmen who had spent a night drinking and eating. As far as Pratt was concerned, the two cops had done nothing more than average greedy babysitters, and now that the parents had come home, it was time to dismiss them. The two junior officers exchanged nervous glances. The two senior officers stared at Calvino. They made no effort to intervene.

'Check in with Colonel Pin if you feel that is necessary,' said Colonel Pratt. He was the big boss who made the final decision.

It was the kind of invitation that neither Mao nor Noriega would ever accept. To do so would violate a basic premise of Thai culture: one's senior is never questioned. And a superior's polite invitation to check him out is nothing more than politeness.

'That won't be necessary, sir,' said Noriega.

They saluted and walked across the room toward Calvino. He shook hands with Noriega and Mao and promised to keep in touch. He gave each of them a bottle from General Yosaporn's stash. Both men looked sheepish and waied Calvino. The gesture registered a hint of a smile on Colonel Pratt's lips. What had happened that night was a reversal of the Stockholm syndrome. The captors identified with the hostage.

'They have nothing. They should have let me go last night,' said Calvino.

'The system doesn't work perfectly, Vincent. It wasn't until late last night that the police found that the dead woman had registered in a room on the fifteenth floor and that she'd paid for your upgrade. The eyewitnesses said they saw you at the railing. No one saw her going over your railing. The police just made an assumption, connecting dots that shouldn't be connected, and that happens more than anyone would wish to admit.'

'Who was she?'

Pratt had the details from the Pattaya police. 'She was an assistant manager at an insurance company in Bangkok. Khun Nongluck. They found her ID in her handbag inside her room. She's from a good middle-class family. University-educated and single, but unhappy in her personal life.'

'So she killed herself?' She'd prayed at the spirit house, and people who were intent on killing themselves didn't interrupt their plans to light candles and incense sticks. Suicide didn't make sense.

'It looks that way.'

'I can go?'

Colonel Pratt nodded, took off his cap, and sat at the table. He looked around the room. 'Stay until I've got things under control in Bangkok.'

Calvino glanced over at his new friends Mao and Noriega, who were still lingering, and who would have liked to hang out for a couple more nights. 'Things aren't under control here.'

Colonel Pratt shrugged. 'Up to you. But General Yosaporn went to the trouble to arranging a room for you.'

'And a dead woman went to the added trouble to get me upgraded to this suite. Pratt, I can't stay here. And I'm not going to another hotel in Pattaya. I'm going home.'

Colonel Pratt had played the Thai social shame card. Only it was a card game that Calvino usually refused to play. What the Colonel was saying was that he'd lose face if his farang friend packed up and left after a long line of chits had been burned to get him the room. And Apichart's failed hit hadn't been resolved. He was still running around Bangkok pretending to be a victim.

'I came to Pattaya so I'd be out of the way until the General and you decided what to do with Apichart. I didn't want to come here in the first place. But I did what you asked. I knew it was important to you and the General. Now things are changed. Apichart's going to know I'm here. The newspapers will make certain of that. Besides, I've got another case waiting in Bangkok, a farang husband in love with someone other than his wife, and the wife says it's an emergency. The client has paid the fee in advance. Ratana has told me she's desperate. Would the General want me to lose business?'

The problem with a guilt card is that it can be trumped by another guilt card. 'The General will understand.'

Calvino started throwing clothes into his suit-case. He looked up as he held a Hawaiian shirt, black with vertical rows of yellow pig heads.

'Before we go, can we have a look at Nongluck's room?'

'Don't get involved, Vincent. Let's go back to Bangkok and let the local police finish their job.' Colonel Pratt knew that Calvino wasn't likely to follow his advice.

'I am involved. The local cops still think I killed her.'

'They've changed their minds.'

'Maybe they'll change them again.'

The Colonel said his goodbyes to the Pattaya police and watched them take the elevator down to the lobby. They'd seemed surprised when he hadn't gotten into the elevator with them. He waied them and waited until the door closed, then pushed the up button and waited with the hotel manager, whom he'd asked to stay behind.

The manager let them into Nongluck's suite. The first thing Calvino noticed inside room 1542 was the cloying smell: a mix of perfume, soap, and powder. The scent of a woman. On the table was a wine bottle. Beside it was a corkscrew with the cork screwed deep, the metal tip sticking out at the bottom. A glass with two fingers of wine was next to the bottle. Beside the French wine were some playing cards wrapped with a rubber band. 'Doesn't look like she was playing with a full deck,' said Calvino, reaching for the minideck on the table.

'Don't touch them,' said Colonel Pratt. The cards looked fairly new. Calvino was right; it was only a few cards. Pratt pulled off the rubber band and turned over the first card: the ace of hearts. He worked through the eight of diamonds, the six of clubs and the six of spades. The last four cards were the queen of hearts, the six of hearts, the five of hearts, and the nine of spades. He slipped the rubber band back on the cards, looked away and palmed the cards, slipping them in his pocket. Calvino pretended not to see Pratt take the playing cards.

'Any idea what happened to the rest of the deck?' asked Calvino, looking around as if they might be elsewhere in the room. He walked over to the closet and pulled back the door.

'They didn't evaporate,' said Pratt, kneeling down level to the wine glass on the table and examining the lipstick on the rim.

Calvino looked back from the closet. 'Cards don't evaporate, Pratt. That's not the right English word.'

Pratt raised his hands covered by surgical gloves. 'In Thailand many things can evaporate, Vincent. That includes money, reputation, and life. Subtracting a few cards from the list, I am certain you will agree, does no permanent harm to the English language.'

A suitcase had been slipped into the closet. A couple of dresses, some underwear, bras, T-shirts, jeans, and three pairs of shoes were also in the closet. Calvino remembered the blue dress. Nongluck had worn it when she'd made her offering at the spirit house.

'Looks like no one has tossed the room,' said Calvino as Colonel Pratt slid the balcony door open and stepped outside onto the tiled floor.

'That includes us. Housekeeping was told to not enter the room, but if they had to go in, then to not touch anything,' said Colonel Pratt, standing at the railing. It was the most Thai of instructions.

Calvino followed the Colonel outside, disappointed about the restrictions on inspecting the room. He looked straight ahead at the beach and sea, holding onto the railing. He glanced down at the street. Fifteen floors was a long way to fall. It was more likely an eighteen-story drop to the street by the time the lobby and mezzanine levels were factored in. She'd had a few final seconds of consciousness – what had gone through her mind, knowing that she was going to die, knowing that nothing she could do, say, or think could save her? His stomach churned, and he turned away. He hated heights and couldn't understand why people spent huge sums of money to climb mountains only to fall into a crevice or die of frostbite. How anyone could summon the courage to jump off a balcony fell in the same category of wonderment. He pulled away from the railing, feeling shaken. Turning his back to the ocean view, he tried to clear his mind of the flood of disturbances racing through it. Then he walked from the balcony into the sitting room. The suite was cookie-cutter identical to his own.

The sheets of the bed had been neatly pulled

back and the pillows bunched into a pile at the center with a book nearby. It was a self-help book on relationships with a smiling, confident woman on the cover who looked like a beauty-contest winner.

Colonel Pratt closed the balcony door and walked across the room. He took photographs of the table, the closet, and the bed. 'Early this morning. I went to the house where Nongluck's parents live. They were still asleep when I arrived. They invited me inside. I told them about their daughter's death. The mother broke down and cried, but the father didn't look surprised. He said she'd had problems in her personal life. Of course, what they meant was she had a problem with a boyfriend. The mother confirmed that a series of boyfriends had caused her nothing but anguish. She wailed that she'd killed herself over a man, but she didn't say who he was. That can wait for later.'

'Was there any connection between the family and Apichart?'

Colonel Pratt shook his head. 'They'd never heard of him.'

Calvino, frustrated by the answer, walked into the bathroom and examined, without touching, Nongluck's shampoo, soap, and cosmetics, neatly arranged in rows along with the standard hotel toiletry items. A bottle of Opium perfume was open. That seemed strange. A woman as tidy as Nongluck wouldn't be leaving her prized perfume

99

open to the elements. He called to Colonel Pratt, who'd been taking more photographs.

When the Colonel stepped inside the bathroom, Calvino was on his knees looking at the bathtub. 'You'll need to get the hairs out of the drain. Hairs and skin from the sink, too. And check the lid on the toilet. It was up when I came in. Women always keep the lid down. They shouldn't flush the toilet until lab guys have swabbed down the inside. And look at the perfume bottle. It's open. She doesn't strike me as someone who'd leave it like that.'

'Where did you come up with all of this?' asked Colonel Pratt.

Calvino smiled, looked over his shoulder. 'I study investigative techniques.'

'Sounds like you saw that program on National Geographic about bathtub murders.'

Calvino's cheeks flushed two shades short of a red light. 'It was a good show. Mao and Noriega watched it with me last night.'

A couple of seconds passed before Pratt registered that Calvino was talking about the two policemen who had stayed overnight in the room. He'd been joking about the TV forensic show; Calvino apparently hadn't taken it as such.

'You watched that bathtub murder investigation with the police?'

Calvino nodded as if it was the most natural way to spend time with two cops. 'During a commercial break, Mao went into my bathroom and swabbed it down.'

'In this case, a woman died. The police want to know why. The local politicians may try to make something of it.'

The election campaign had made Pratt cautious about what was possible. The daily cycle of mudslinging, lies, rumors, and vilification had exhausted him. Everyone was treading water, waiting to see who won.

'I'd like to have talked to her,' said Calvino.

Pratt had already gathered from the parents the background of the dead woman: her name, age, occupation, marital status, hometown, history of mental problems, and conflicts with family, neighbors, or friends. The police lab report said there were small traces of alcohol in her blood. But her blood tested negative for drugs. There was no evidence of a struggle in the room. And so far there was no evidence that anyone other than Nongluck had been in the room. Hotel rooms were like working girls; they had many customers, people with no connection to each other, coming and going over a short period of time, making it more difficult for investigators than a room in a house or an office.

It was only after they left room 1542 that Calvino began to enjoy his release from house arrest. When he turned up at the reception desk with the Colonel, they had his invoice prepared. The concierge in the far corner stared at him without a smile. As he checked out, everyone behind the reception desk seemed relieved to see him, with his suitcase and case of whiskey at his feet. The bill for room service ran to two pages. Calvino studied it, clicking his tongue like a Bantu warrior on the eve of battle. Colonel Pratt asked to see it. He glanced through the steaks, the fries, the ice cream, the pasta, the vodka, the Russian food with names he couldn't pronounce; he flipped the page and read through the various delivery charges and expenses. He did the sums in his head. Vincent had managed to run up about a week's worth of room service charges in one night. The owner would be satisfied; General Yosaporn would not lose face. Colonel Pratt handed the invoice back to the clerk and told him that the owner's friend, General Yosaporn, had arranged Calvino's stay.

The clerk stared at the desk. A colonel in full dress uniform had spoken.

'No problem, sir,' he said.

The hotel staff shuffled and looked at their hands. None of them were willing to push for cash in the circumstance of a colonel supporting a farang. If anything, they were relieved to see Calvino leaving, and the manager who had been hovering behind the desk slipped away into his office. The matter was settled. With the invoice cleared, Colonel Pratt asked who had been on duty at the front desk the day before. After talking with a couple of hotel staff, he found the receptionist, who remembered checking in Nongluck. She had checked in, alone, at 2:10 p.m. the day before her death. They had made a photocopy of her Thai ID card. She had gone to her room and only later returned downstairs to pay for her room and Calvino's upgrade. She had used fresh one-thousand-baht notes. She had said the upgrade was a gift, and no one should tell the farang. Let it be a surprise. There had been nothing out of the ordinary about her that afternoon. She had smiled and counted out the cash, slid it across the reception desk, and watched as the clerk counted it again.

On the day of Nongluck's death, the receptionist recalled, she had worn a blue dress and carried a Prada handbag and a plastic Siam Paragon shopping bag with a bottle of wine inside. A bellhop remembered watching her walk out the front entrance an hour later and stop in front of the spirit house, where she'd lit incense sticks. A few minutes later, she had returned to the lobby, waited for the elevator, and returned to her suite. No member of the staff remembered seeing her leave the hotel after that. Could someone have gotten past security and slipped into her room without even passing another guest? No one at reception admitted that this could have happened.

Calvino suggested checking the security down-stairs, on the way out of the hotel. The two of them found the garage security guy who'd been working the day shift on the day of the death. Lots of cars had come and gone during the day.

'Did you see anything unusual yesterday after-noon? Maybe a car that you remember?' asked Colonel Pratt.

The guard remembered a Thai arriving in a red sports car the previous afternoon. It had been a beauty, a European two-seater, polished, not a scratch on it, tinted windows. No, he didn't remember the license plate number; he was too busy looking at his own face reflected in the high sheen of the car. But he thought it might have been a Bangkok plate.

'Why do you think that?' asked Colonel Pratt.

The guard told him that if it had been a local car, he'd have recognized it. He'd have known who owned it. A car like that wouldn't be a secret for long in a small town like Pattaya. It was flashy like a car from the movies, a car built and sold to attract attention, the attention of women in particular. It wasn't a family car the guard described. And it wasn't the kind of car you'd drive to commit a murder, thought Calvino. A professional hit man would have driven a plain vanilla Honda.

Whomever the driver of the sports car was, Calvino had a good idea he hadn't planned to kill anyone. But maybe things turned out in a way he hadn't anticipated. Something unexpected might have come up – a surge of anger, the wrong word or look – and Nongluck could have found herself airborne.

CHAPTER 8

T racer realized that it felt good to be back in Bangkok. He stretched his arms and turned up the music as he glided through the early-morning traffic on Sukhumvit Road. The rain slanted against the windscreen, the wipers working overtime. The city roads were wet and slick, and traffic from the motorway had started to build. He passed the Emporium Shopping Mall and Benjasiri Park, then turned into Washington Square. Taking a parking ticket, he drove on until he eased the S-Class Mercedes in a parking space in front of the Bourbon Street Restaurant. He sat in the car, leaving the air conditioner on, listening to Muddy Waters's 'Got My Mojo Workin'' and keeping the beat on the steering wheel. He touched the small leather pouch he wore under his shirt. He didn't go anywhere without his mojo bag with the pinch of spices, herbs, a snake tooth, and the dead body of a mean motherfucker of a black widow spider.

He didn't object when his friend and fellow LRAS employee Alan Jarrett had suggested the restaurant in Washington Square because it was a good place to sit, wait, let the power rise up inside, get strong. And it was around the corner from a short-time hotel where Jarrett had planned to spend the night. Time stops when a man is in touch with his mojo. Six in the morning and Tracer was ready to go to work. Mooney's men had stored the .308 in the trunk. And Jarrett was all set, he thought.

He sat in the car as the security guard came around with an umbrella and opened his door. Tracer got out of the car, locked the door, ducked his head under the umbrella, and walked up the steps to the front door. The girls behind the counter gave him the early-in-the-morning once-over. A man at that time of the morning was in the neighborhood to order himself some coffee, bacon, and eggs. The security guard, who had folded up the umbrella, followed Tracer through the door and told the waitresses that the black man had arrived in a Benz with embassy plates. The yings looked at Tracer, thinking he was a diplomat, someone they had to treat real nice. Not many African diplomats rolled into Washington Square at six in the morning on a rainy day, or, for that matter, any time, any day, rain or shine. Tracer turned right, walked over to the bar, dropped the car keys on the counter, and ordered a coffee.

'Bring it black, bring it strong,' said Tracer.

The waitress stared long and hard, like she had some problem.

'The man wants a coffee,' said Jarrett. 'Is there any part of that message you don't understand?'

She turned away and walked over to the coffee pot.

'You're in a good mood.' Tracer slid onto the stool next to Jarrett. 'Rain got you down?'

'How was Waters?'

'He didn't make his flight.'

'You didn't expect him to,' said Jarrett.

'Mooney had all the details. There wasn't much for Waters to do. Shake hands and calm down Mooney.'

'And you could do that?'

'Got that right. Mooney had me meet him in a bar with two of the most movement-challenged dancers I've ever seen. Looked like they were made of stone. Mooney was their only customer. Apparently he owned the place, so he wasn't exactly a customer.'

'That's the point. You control the perimeter. An ideal place. I can see why Mooney chose it. No one coming in or out in the middle of your business. Just the two of you talking about the old times.'

The waitress delivered Tracer's mug of coffee.

'Mooney said we've got three days before he comes personally to get his weapons.'

'You scared, Tracer? I don't find myself in fear of Mooney.'

Tracer blew on his coffee before taking a sip.

Jarrett was in a work phase, and when he worked he avoided coffee, tea, and alcohol. Chemicals cause a reaction in the human body, change the reflexes, vision, depth perception. A drunk doesn't last long in combat. Jarrett's military training kicked in, and he told himself he didn't miss the coffee – until, of course, he saw Tracer enjoying a cup, smacking his lips. Jarrett promised himself a pot of fresh brew once the job was done. He liked giving himself a reward for completing a mission.

While waiting for Tracer, Jarrett had been watching a middle-aged farang with a young woman at a table in the back. The woman looked like an office worker. The farang had eaten wolfishly, downing his bacon and eggs in big gulps, soaking his toast in the egg yolk. The ying had slowly sipped Chinese tea. He wore a suit and a tie, and she wore a short skirt and a blouse with creases on the sleeve sharp enough to cut butter, and she showed a bit of style with a pair of pearl earrings large enough to indicate she had experience in prying open large oysters. Not too much makeup – but who wore makeup at 6:00 a.m.? – and she had that self-confident, determined way of sitting, listening to the farang rattle on but not committing her expression to one emotion or another. Jarrett glanced at the time.

'We've got lots of time,' said Tracer.

'Time is the one thing no one has lots of.'

Tracer nodded as if to concede the point. 'Just let me finish my coffee. I've had a long drive. Tell me, how did it go with Miss Honey Bee last night?'

'It was all milk and honey.' As they'd lain together in bed, Wan had told him how she'd sneak up on the hives, sit down, and watch the bees for hours. She watched them dance. In the darkness of the room she'd stroked his bare chest and said that when you understand the meaning of their dance, you learn something about nature. All the dancing was communicating important information: the distance to food, the direction, the force of the prevailing winds. At the bar, she'd watch the yings dance, looking for some pattern, some directional indicator toward the honey. She'd said there was a lot to learn from watching bees dance.

'She seemed different from the others,' said Tracer.

'I never met anyone in a bar like her.'

Tracer ordered him another orange juice. 'You have any idea how much orange juice I drank in Pattaya?'

Jarrett shrugged. The pained expression on Tracer's face made Jarrett smile.

'A gallon and a half at least,' said Tracer.

'Your eyeballs must be floating.'

'Don't worry. There's nothing wrong with either my bladder or my eyes.'

Jarrett needed to have his spotter's eyes sharp and focused, checking out the target and the perimeter around it. He needed Tracer at the top of his form, and Tracer was giving his usual reassurances. 'No problems in Pattaya?'

'The only hiccup was driving in yesterday on Beach Road – the traffic. If you'd have told me the cars were backed up to the Cambodian border,

I'd have not called you a liar. Nothing was moving. I edged along for half an hour until I finally saw the problem. There were cops and reporters and a dead Thai woman on the driveway in front of a hotel. They had a sheet over her. But people kept pulling it back for the TV cameras. I rolled down my window and asked someone what had happened. Young Thai guy says a woman's gone killed herself. I say to myself, baby, if I'd been there two hours earlier and we'd had a drink, listened to the blues, I could've talked you into living.'

'Life doesn't always let you choose your dance partners,' said Jarrett.

'Where'd you read that?'

Jarrett cracked a smile. 'Miss Honey Bee said that.'

Tracer raised an eyebrow. 'That girl's workin' her mojo on you.'

The smile on Jarrett's face widened. 'Yeah, that crossed my mind.'

More than once, Tracer's Louisiana gris-gris, a homegrown mojo, had shown some power to defeat an enemy or to entice a friend.

He glanced over at the ying at the table with her farang boyfriend. It occurred to him that if Wan had the tailoring and makeup, she wouldn't look much different. Where was the dividing line between the ying who watched bees dancing and an office worker sipping tea at six in the morning? Weren't they both harvesting as much honey as they could while the flowers bloomed?

CHAPTER 9

Aslick film of oil coated the wet street. A red and blue Honda 150cc came out of nowhere. The rider had a black helmet with flames along the sides and a tinted visor pushed back on his head. He wore the motorcycle taxi uniform – cheap plastic sandals, faded blue jeans, and an unbuttoned orange vest over a Liverpool football T-shirt. He steered with one hand and held a cell phone to his ear with the other. Calvino slammed on the brakes, made a hard left and clipped the rear left side of a Mercedes parked in front of Bourbon Street. The motor-cycle driver lost his cell phone, frantically pulled out of a freefall, regained control, and opened the throttle. He turned, drove back, picked up his cell phone, and cursed and spat at Calvino.

Calvino sat at the wheel for a full minute before he reversed and pulled into the empty parking spot next to the Mercedes. He closed his eyes and remembered the two men on the motorcycle spin-ning out of control, their bike slamming against the cargo of gas cylinders, the explosion, the burning bike cart wheeling into the base of the banyan tree. That hadn't been an accident. He'd caused them to die. Calvino's stomach churned, upset and angry. He'd just come close to killing another man on a motorcycle. He looked at his hands. They were shaking. He tried to steady himself by gripping down hard on the steering wheel. He told himself it wasn't his fault that the motorcycle had been going the wrong way, the driver not paying attention. On the bright side, maybe his luck had turned.

Getting out of the car, Calvino squatted down beside the Benz and examined the license plate. Diplomatic plates, he said to himself. He didn't recognize the country from the first two digits. He shook his head, running his hand over the dent along the rear left-hand side. Calvino sucked in a deep breath and told himself it was time to find out which embassy personnel were either just leaving the Square or had just arrived.

A Benz in front of Bourbon Street early in the morning looked out of place. Calvino rubbed his hands together thinking. The day before he had been in Pattaya – now a lifetime ago. Some flecks of scraped-off paint clung to his palms. He sighed, rubbed his hands on his trousers, and wished he were someplace else, like his own bed. This time of the morning was for the dead, not the living, he told himself. And he told himself no more playing around with customs and cultural beliefs that could come back to haunt him. He'd do the right thing; he'd go inside the restaurant, do his job, and when he was done he'd settle with the Benz owner. It was a rare morning in Washington Square that Calvino faced a dual threat of a punch-up.

As he walked in, he concentrated on his job: positioning himself and getting a couple of photographs of the client's husband and his Thai girlfriend. He looked around the room. The pair – the reason for his being in the Square – were seated at a far table. The ying perfectly fit the wife's description, pretty in a short dress, blinking eyelashes, and lipstick that matched the color of her fingernails. Like most women, this one seemed to possess the ability to coordinate a large inventory of color, gesture, makeup, and dress; no man could match that level of skill. The bar was empty except for a couple of guys sitting side by side, one drinking coffee and the other orange juice. He figured one of them owned the Benz. It wasn't the farang at the table in the corner; Calvino knew he was a stockbroker and not a diplomat.

Neither one of the men paid him much attention. The one with intense green eyes and the hint of a knowing smile had looked at him for a moment and turned away. The guy who had the build of a professional athlete kept looking straight ahead. He'd tried to remember the last time he'd seen men so fit in the Square, and shrugged when he drew a blank. That they had ignored him was just the way Calvino liked it. Jarrett sat with an empty glass on the counter in front of him and

Tracer cradled a cup of coffee with those hands that he could catch a football with in his sleep. Calvino was trying to decide if one of the men was an ambassador, or if they were a couple of third secretary types.

The Doors' 'L.A. Woman' played in the background, and when it ended, Jeff Buckley's 'Mojo Pin' picked up the beat. Tracer tapped out the rhythm on the side of his coffee mug. The music was another reason Tracer had chosen Bourbon Street as a place to meet before going off to do their mission. It was one of the agreements Jarrett and Tracer had made early on; whoever got to the restaurant first would request that they play the blues. Music was like a slice of bread; it soaked up all the anxiety that settled in a man's gut when time seemed to slow to a crawl. The blues entertained the first man to arrive, cooled him down until a little chill quivered up his spine. It was more than casual listening. The blues isn't casual; it's in your face, your heart, your groin. A good blues song has the power to sweep away stressful thoughts about things going wrong. Jarrett loved the blues. His favorite blues song was in the queue, and it was about the price people paid.

'There's a price to pay / always a price to pay / you don't know how much until you break it.' He thought there was more than a little piece of God's truth to shake out of those words. Hang those words out on the line to dry; watch them soak up the sun. Jarrett had been taught that most of the time what you broke fell into two pieces, and you could glue them back together; but other times it broke into a million pieces, and no amount of glue was going to put it back together again. Like death, some broken things just can't be fixed.

The farang at the far table had turned and was staring at Calvino. It was time to reverse order. Calvino needed a beard, and the owner of the Benz was the guy who'd supply it.

'One of you guys own the Benz out front?' Calvino still hadn't figured out the country code, and the appearance of the two men gave no real clue as to nationality.

Tracer cocked his head to the side. 'What's the problem?'

An American accent, thought Calvino. 'From the plates, you're with an embassy. Maybe a diplomat.' Each embassy plate had a distinctive number.

Tracer liked that, the thought of being a diplomat, and his mother would have been proud, so he shot a smile. 'And what are you selling?'

'I'm not selling anything. But I hit the back of your car.'

Tracer's eyebrow rose up. He smiled. 'You're shitting me. You ran into my car?'

'The damage is minor. I've got insurance.'

'Minor? That's okay. Don't worry about it.'

Tracer put money on the counter and started to stand up. 'If you will excuse us.'

But Calvino blocked his path Jarrett stopped a couple of inches away, looking straight at him.

'Don't worry about it,' said Jarrett. 'If it's broken, I'll get it fixed.'

Calvino made it clear that he insisted on dealing with the damage. 'Give me a couple of seconds. Then I can deal with it.'

The farang at the corner table had stopped looking over at the bar and scanning the room the way guilty men do. He felt he'd gotten away with his cake and now was the time to take a big bite. He held the girl's hand, stroking it, playing with it, kissing her knuckles, his lips against the high-gloss pink fingernails. They were the kind of pink that shades the sky early on a Bangkok morning. Calvino decided this farang was a real piece of work. Seeing the man slobbering over his girl-friend's hand early in the morning made Calvino wonder what kind of nightmare the man had escaped from under his own roof to push him into Washington Square that time of day. Anyway, that was his problem, and besides, his wife was paying the shipping and handling for photographs of his knuckle-licking antics.

Calvino reached inside his jacket pocket for his small digital camera. As he removed his hand, Jarrett with the speed of a sand-trap spider grabbed his wrist, tightened his grip. There was no question about the muscles behind the vice-like embrace. They exchanged a long, hard look.

'You're the bodyguard?'

His broad shoulders flexed. 'Bring your hand out of your jacket real slow,' said Jarrett.

Calvino showed him the black Nikon. 'It's a digital camera.'

Jarrett released Calvino's wrist. Calvino pointed the camera at the couple across the room, who weren't paying them any attention. He snapped a series of photos, capturing one hand kiss, then another, until he had enough to show that the farang was more than a little interested in the ying sitting at the table. A couple of lovers caught stealing a few moments from the start of the day. Calvino slipped the camera back into his jacket.

Neither Jarrett nor Tracer liked the idea of the camera. 'What the fuck are you doing with the camera?' asked Jarrett.

'I'm working.'

'Are you a photographer?' asked Jarrett.

'An investigator.' When a man slipped his leash in Bangkok, it never took long to pick up his trail; it was like tracking a furtive, not-too-smart burglar who dropped his driver's license at the scene of the heist. Catching such a creature was almost guaranteed. It was a crappy, mind-numbing, soul-destroying way to make a living.

'A private investigator.' Tracer pursed his lips, looking over at the farang and the Thai woman at the table.

Calvino nodded.

'We're outta here,' said Jarrett. 'The man's got his work. We've got ours.'

'I'll call my insurance company,' said Calvino, pulling out his cell phone. 'The company will send someone around.'

Tracer shook head and held up his hand. 'I'll take a pass. But thanks.'

'It's no problem. I hit your car.'

'You're right, it's no problem. So let's leave it at that,' said Tracer.

'What my friend is saying is just let it ride,' said Jarrett.

There wasn't any humor about either man. Young and fit, quiet, arriving in a Benz, huddling over orange juice, wanting to forget the damage to the car, the elements added up to a couple of men with something important on their minds and wanting to avoid anyone getting in their way. Calvino turned, walked over to the door, and held it open. 'At least have a look at your car.'

Jarrett and Tracer took a leisurely walk around the Benz. The impact of the collision had broken a taillight and left a dent as if a giant had punched his fist against the rear end. Calvino's car, an old Honda City, was parked beside the Benz. It had enough body damage to make it unclear exactly what part of the car had hit the Benz.

'It was an accident,' said Calvino, handing a business card to Tracer.

'Looks like it wasn't your first accident,' said Jarrett, looking over Calvino's car.

Tracer read the card, twisting his neck to the right and then the left, a neck-cracking exercise that was one of those defining mannerisms as individual as a fingerprint. When he felt a little too much stress, the kinks built up in his neck muscles, tightening them like a vice, making them bulge and throb, until the only way to get rid of the pressure was the quick left-right move. 'You're a good citizen to have reported what happened. A lesser man would have hit and run. If there is any problem, we have your card and will be in touch' – he looked down at the card – 'Mr Calvino.'

Calvino leaned against his Honda and watched as the two men got into the Mercedes. Jarrett climbed behind the wheel and Tracer slid into the passenger's seat and put on his seat-belt harness. Jarrett backed the Benz out in one sleek movement, changed gears, and headed toward the Soi 22 exit. Calvino stepped in the road and watched as Jarrett turned left, heading in the direction of Rama IV Road. He made a mental note of the license plate.

Calvino climbed into his Honda and started the engine. Waiting until the air-conditioning came on and the temperature was bearable, he twisted around and looked both ways before pulling out of the parking place. He pegged the slender green-eyed guy as someone who looked vaguely Middle Eastern. The Honda was a wreck, not a car, more like the debris left from a terrorist attack. But it had a bonus. His car was theft-proof. He drove slowly and braked when he passed the couple from the restaurant as they walked, holding hands.

Calvino held the camera against the window and clicked off a couple more shots of the lovebirds. He gave a final look, shaking his head. He couldn't help thinking that some guys knew they were being followed, that they wanted to get caught, have it over.

Reaching the exit, he turned right onto Soi 22, heading toward Sukhumvit Road and his office. Some husbands leave a trail to the den of soiled sheets that's so obvious a bloodhound with a head cold could follow. He glanced at them in his rearview mirror. As they were on foot, clearly they had no intention to head for Rama IV; more likely they were on an automatic glide path to the nearby Hotel 27, a sanctuary creating the illusion of privacy that came with a short-time room.

At the traffic light at Sukhumvit Road, he waited, thinking about the last twenty-four hours. It already seemed like a much longer stretch of time. He'd come back to the city to get lost in his work. But all he had for his efforts was an early-morning raging headache. It hadn't mattered to his temperament that he got the pictures of the husband on the make. He should have felt better. He told himself that he had every right to feel like part of the world had collapsed on him, and he was still digging himself out of the debris of a busted vacation, a ying falling out the sky, an evening with Mao and Noriega. He shuddered, feeling a sudden chill, as if the slipstream of evil had followed him out of the rubble.

The light changed and Calvino turned right onto Sukhumvit Road. As he drove, he glanced at Washington Square on his right – the shabby entrance, broken pavement, rats scurrying over the garbage. It was quiet on the street. Like Bangkok, the Square was never just one kind of place; its character depended on the time of day. The Square attracted a different crowd in the morning. People pretending to be diplomats; people pretending to be in relationships that had some meaning other than sex, drugs, and rock 'n' roll. It was a place of randomness, of accidents, of inexplicable encounters. A place for rats and rogues and people with pasts that cast shadows long enough to touch their futures.

CHAPTER 10

Tracer looked out the car window and watched the street vendors setting up stalls to sell noodles, socks, shirts, and pirated DVDs. Early-bird office workers, eager to return to the corporate hatchery, hurried along the pavement, breaking formation as they stepped into the canyon of high-rise buildings. Motorcycles threaded through the narrow passages between cars. A light at the intersection turned red. Three or four more cars shot through like explosive rounds. No one ever moved forward for the first couple of seconds of a green light.

When Jarrett's car had stopped as the light turned red, he'd nearly been rear-ended. The driver behind him hit the horn. In the rearview mirror he saw that the man had a murderous, hateful look. Everyone was on their way to work. Some had more important deadlines than others, but the default was speed, as if life and death depended on getting through the intersection.

'Let's run through the operation,' said Jarrett.

It was one of their rituals, something Jarrett and Tracer had put to good use as they rotated between

Kabul and Baghdad with stopovers in Fallujah. As a team, they went through the checklist until every angle, element and sequence became automatic. The procedure made them effective, tough, and reliable. They never cut corners in doing their homework. Tracer brushed his fingers against his mojo bag. He kept it low, out of sight, so Jarrett couldn't see him stroking the soft leather. Despite all the preparation, a team still needed luck.

They had checked out the condo two days before. Getting a feel for the location, locking it inside his head, kept Jarrett focused.

'I made the distance three hundred and fifty meters.'

'No obstructions. That's what I like,' said Jarrett.

The target would emerge from another high-rise as he stepped out onto the balcony sometime between 10:30 a.m. and noon.

'After we finish the job, I'm going for a workout,' said Tracer.

'I thought we'd planned on going for a massage. Get someone to work out those kinks in your neck.'

'I can always go for a workout tomorrow.' Tracer gave a thumbs-up sign as he caught Jarrett's eye. Tracer had a way of calming the situation, making Jarrett feel like everything was under control and it was just another mission. They'd been through the drill before, always coming out the other side, thinking, 'Glad that's over and done.'

Jarrett slipped the Benz back into the sluggish

stream of traffic. By the time they turned into Soi Thong Lo, Tracer had folded the newspaper and placed it on the seat. The car stereo played a bluesy rendition of 'Summertime,' and neither man spoke.

One day in Fallujah, Jarrett had killed an insurgent who'd been sitting with a rifle in a car. The insurgent had pointed it at a passing US military convoy. They'd been listening to 'Summertime' then, too. Jarrett had three confirmed kills that day. 'Ain't nothing gonna harm you.' The world just had a whole lot of harm standing by, ready, canned, and waiting to be opened. Bangkok was an urban nightmare jammed with cars and swarming with people fighting for space to move. Like doomed salmon swimming upstream to breed and die. But compared with Baghdad or Fallujah, it looked more like a pond in a fish farm.

Soi Thong Lo was an upscale farang ghetto in Sukhumvit, with enough high-rent Japanese residents to make a quorum at a Honda stockholders' meeting. Soi Thong Lo had once been a sleepy out-of-the-way soi in Sukhumvit with middle-class Thai family compounds, but it had become a trendy area, drawing in the rich and powerful foreigners who bought the high-end condos, joined the members-only clubs, dined at the hundreds of restaurants, and cut away from the office to one of the massage parlors.

Casey had done the advance legwork, renting a unit two months earlier under 'Melvin Taylor,' the name of a blues singer – a nod to Tracer, who liked Taylor's music. He'd prepaid the rent and security deposit in cash and said it was for a wealthy investor from abroad who would use it infrequently. No one had asked him for an ID. Cash was the only ID required on Soi Thong Lo. Jarrett, whose Turkish-born mother had passed along the permanent tan look, and Tracer, a lightskinned black, could have been from Cairo or Damascus.

Jarrett eased the Benz into the entrance of a twenty-five-story luxury condo building whose parking garage had all the personality of a high-security prison. He used a plastic card to activate the traffic-gate arm. As it slowly rose, on the opposite side a security guard took down their license registration number. The tinted windows prevented the guard from seeing who was inside. No guard making two hundred dollars a month with a family upcountry taking 30 percent of his takehome was going to ask someone in a Benz to roll down the window and show ID. He made do with a quick glance at Jarrett just as he powered up the window. Jarrett drove up the ramp to the fifth floor and parked next to the exit door and the elevators.

Tracer got out of the car, hands stuffed deep in his pockets, whistling Peeping Tom's 'Mojo' as he stood beside the trunk. Jarrett sprang the trunk lock from inside the Benz and stepped out of the car to watch the perimeter as Tracer removed a large rectangular Pelican case. Slamming the truck lid shut, Jarrett lifted the case and walked toward the exit door. It was better to use the stairs. On the ninth floor. Jarrett pushed open the emergency exit door and Tracer stepped out first, checking the corridor. It was empty. Tracer signaled to Jarrett, who stepped into the corridor with the case. He walked quickly, the case growing heavy, and stopped at one of the units. Tracer unlocked the door and held it open. Jarrett went inside and Tracer, after glancing once again up and down the corridor, followed him inside. Once in the condo, Jarrett swallowed his breath, closed his eyes, and eased the Pelican case to the floor.

Jarrett leaned against the wall in the entryway for a couple of seconds, catching his breath. Carrying the case up the stairs was heavy lifting. It was over thirty pounds. But it wasn't just the lugging of the dead weight. They were both on high alert; there was the possibility of a tenant coming up or down the stairs, but it was unlikely; rich people rode elevators. Guards patrolled the lobby and grounds, but inside the building they left people alone. That was one reason Casey had chosen the building. It had the right elements of lax security and very rich people who were rarely seen.

Tracer walked across the large sitting room. His heart hadn't stopped racing from the final stretch, taking two steps at a time on the staircase. Except for the brush with the private eye in Washington Square, it had been a flawless operation. Getting to this point was the result of a concerted effort of planning and coordination. Like any operation in the field, the battle was won or lost before the first shot was fired.

Jarrett lifted the case onto the dining room table and sprung open the side locks. Mounted inside the case was an M24 sniper weapon system – the bolt-action rifle, day-and-night telescopes, a silencer, a bipod, and two boxes of ammo. Like a woman, a sniper rifle was nothing without the right accessories. He pulled the rifle out, running fingers down the graphite and fiberglass stock. A hint of epoxy resin filled his nostrils. The rifle had the same Remington 700 action as the Marine M40A3 Jarrett had been using in Kabul and Baghdad. The company had made certain they had the best weapons taxpayers' money could buy, manually operated, air-cooled, and magazine-fed. Jarrett opened the box of ammo and pulled out one of the rounds, feeling the cold, hard casing against the palm of his hand. He squeezed the 175-gram round, slowly opened his hand, said a prayer, and began to fill the magazine.

'Everything's here,' he said. 'She's got all the right parts in the right places, and she's ready to go.'

'Mooney said the scopes alone cost over two grand each,' said Tracer.

'A good woman has her costs,' said Jarrett.

'Mooney sent M118s.'

'We don't want to be punching holes through walls,' said Tracer.

Jarrett shrugged. The round would go through the

opening they'd cut in the glass with enough forward velocity to keep on going through the target, fragmenting into slivers, and coming out the other side in a spray of red mist.

'It's good for city work,' said Jarrett. He fixed the bipod to the base of the rifle and set it up on the table in front of the balcony window. The hole they'd cut in the glass brought in a stream of warm, moist air. A couple of days earlier, they'd done the measurements and prepared the area for the weapons.

The condo was more than three hundred square meters, all of it with expensive teak wood, polished floors, modern glass tables with chrome legs, and wall-to-wall blinds. The artwork could have been in any large luxury hotel room – blotches of silver and gold foil with dabs of ochre on white and hazelish orange. There were half a dozen of the paintings. Each at first glance looked the same, but close examination showed that each had a significant difference from the others, leaving open the possibility of reading a message into it, or, at the same time, concluding that none of them had any meaning other than a riot of color and ragged lines and disjointed interfaces. The unit had been built for those grown fat with money. No one ever builds a unit for a sniper, thought Jarrett. If he'd had the cash for such a place, he'd have designed shooting positions from each room. That's the way castles had been built in the Middle Ages.

'We've forgotten how much our ancestors understood about the violence of the world.'

'Amen, brother,' Tracer replied.

Someone had sunk real money into outfitting the room. It was meant to impress, but Jarrett couldn't help feeling that the room had been designed by artificial intelligence rather than by a real human being who might live in the place. A full-sized pool table with the balls neatly racked had been set up in the middle of the living room.

'Nice place Casey rented,' said Tracer, rolling his eyes. He walked into the kitchen. 'The pool table's a nice touch.'

Jarrett followed him to the kitchen counter where provisions had been laid out. But his mind was elsewhere; the pool table in the living room made him think of Hua Hin. He'd played a few games with an Aussie engineer named Ian MacDonald. He'd had red hair just like Jack and was a good pool player. 'Yeah, I could see kicking back and spending time here.'

'Ain't that the usual short end of the stick? We do the job and miss out on this good living. Like being a plumber. Unclog the shit and then get pushed out the door.'

Tracer swung open the fridge and had a look inside. Casey had stocked it with jam, white bread, beer, and hot dogs. He looked over at the counter beside the fridge, where Casey had left out microwave popcorn, potato chips, pancake mix, a pound of butter, honey, burritos, Cheerios, hot dog buns, and mustard. A wad of Villa supermarket plastic bags was stuffed in one of the drawers.

'Would you look at this shit Casey bought for us?' asked Tracer.

Jarrett smiled. 'Looks like it was bought by someone who hasn't been to America for twenty-five years.'

'That's Casey. You want some popcorn?' asked Tracer.

'I'd rather wait alongside Kate.' They had over an hour, maybe two to pass before the target appeared on a balcony some three hundred meters away.

Jarrett walked back into the sitting room and pulled back a stainless steel chair with wine-colored cushions. He stored the rifle case under the table. He unzipped the first bag and, holding the day scope to his right eye, looked out the window along the perimeter. He fitted it to the top of the rifle, working carefully, each movement precise, controlled. He double-checked each stage like a pilot in the cockpit of a 747 waiting for tower clearance. A pilot didn't climb in and take off. There were procedures to follow, equipment to check and test, and possible problems to be discovered.

'Welcome home, Kate,' Jarrett said, feeding four rounds into the internal magazine. He ran his hand down the length of the weapon. 'You be good to me, baby, and I'll be real good to you.'

'That's what you say to all your women, Jarrett.'

'Kate knows I mean it.'

'Well, she's just gonna have to trust you.'

Tracer squatted down, looking through an opening in the curtains with a pair of high-power binoculars. 'I'd say that's three hundred meters. Not three-fifty.' Someone like Jarrett could use, with accuracy, any number of rifles inside five hundred meters. He had a 0.5 MOA rating – meaning that at five hundred yards he could put holes in one-inch groups between the eyes of a paper target. At three hundred or three hundred fifty meters, Kate was pure overkill, a sledge-hammer to smash an ant.

Tracer pulled the beaded drawcord, opening the vertical curtains about a hand's length. He slid back the balcony door and the small tunnel of air blowing through the hole cut into the window gushed into a torrent of hot air, sending the room temperature soaring. He felt it on his face and neck. Compared to the Gulf, though, the temperature hovered well within the comfort zone.

Jarrett positioned Kate on the dining room table. Finding a gap in the curtains, he smiled. He pulled up a chrome-backed chair, wrapped himself around the adjustable stock of the M24, and looked through the telescope sight. Had the impact of the car crash jiggled the sight? There was no way to know. He was like a paratrooper waiting for the jump light to be switched on, sweating out the downtime. If anyone else packed his chute, he could never be certain that that man hadn't gotten a little careless or cut a corner. A soldier's life depended on keeping to exacting calibrations, knowing even the slightest variation could be fatal in the field. Working as a private contractor, he was constantly fighting with the suits to maintain the military way, even when it hurt the bottom line. But suits weren't warriors, and bottom-line men had no problem using anyone off the street to pack a chute. He'd insisted on Mooney's being the one to line up the right weapon. Tracer had backed him up, and Casey had, too.

Tracer moved away from the window, circled the table with his rifle, squatted, looked through the sight, and then walked over and sat on a sofa a few feet to Jarrett's right. Tracer removed an envelope from his jacket and, from the envelope, an A4-size photograph of the target: a late-middle-aged Asian man, gray hair combed back, large teeth, eyes disappearing into slits, smiling one of those 'I'm on top of the world' smiles. The man in the photo was about to find out just how interconnected and dangerous that world had become. Tracer handed the photo to Jarrett, who studied the man's face. He looked like someone who'd had a good life. Looking at the face, Jarrett reminded himself that this was the man who'd had Casey's son murdered. The target had earned his destiny with Kate; he'd earned his fate.

The target's name, Somporn, translated as 'warrior from the magical golden land.' The golden land maybe. But the target was no warrior and whatever magic he clutched onto wasn't going to rescue him once he stepped onto the balcony.

'That's a picture of our target and his mojo around his neck,' said Tracer.

'Chinese?'

'Chinese, Thai, Japanese . . . don't know, don't care.'

'Isn't he running for some position?'

'He's a politician. One less won't be a bad thing.'

Tracer walked over and looked down at the picture. Somporn wore an oval amulet the size of a Softball hanging on a gold chain around his neck. The light from the camera's flash reflected off the amulet. The man thought he had some powerful mojo protecting him, but Tracer grinned, showing teeth, shaking his head. 'That is some sorry mojo he's got around his neck.'

Jarrett put the photograph on the coffee table. He'd seen the face before. Casey had shown him a photograph in Baghdad and said that this was the man who needed some killing. 'He killed my boy.' Casey had said.

Somporn had switched on his high-voltage smile in the photograph. It was a politician's false smile. Jarrett thought about his own company. He had known executives at LRAS who pulled that kind of smile at briefings. They looked friendly, like an uncle at graduation, the man with a warm heart and the compassion of a saint. It inspired confidence and trust. Only a few people ever saw the real face behind the smile. It never showed up in any photographs. Kate would help him look for that true face, and focus on it for a second before sending a final message straight through the amulet. They had another hour or two to go.

Tracer broke into a wide smile.

'What's so funny?' asked Jarrett.

'I was thinking about driving through Pattaya. I had the window open and sea air filled the car. I inhaled, held my breath, thinking how I love that smell.' The thought had transported Tracer to an enclosed space in his mind where that smell lingered.

Jarrett glanced over at the pool table, closed his eyes, and said a little prayer for Jack. He remembered the smell of the sea as he helped his father, Harry, break into a beach house on the Gulf of Thailand, under cover of soft waves slapping the wharf and the screams of a man in extreme pain.

Smoke drifted across the living room and down the corridor. The acrid cigarette smoke mixed with a familiar scent of the sea and something else. Burning flesh. They'd heard MacDonald's screams as they entered the house from the rear, working their way forward through the kitchen, following the sharp, shrill voice of pain, creeping down the long corridor until they reached where MacDonald was being held. They crawled into the room, split up – Harry going to his left and his son, crouching low, moving to the right.

Neither of the men inside must have had any training or one of them would have been watching the door. Instead, both men stood with their backs to the main corridor, as if no one in the world was expected to interrupt them. Also, it took only muscle, not training, to do what they were doing to MacDonald.

They'd stripped him to the waist, his white skin broken by a frost line of freckles that ran across his shoulders. He'd been tied to a chair, rope wrapped around his chest and waist. In front of MacDonald on an office table sat a computer, and on the terminal screen a young and rich-looking man smiled. Under his photograph, spaces were allotted for a log-in and password. Once logged in, they were in a bank computer system, one located in the Channel Islands. A wisp of smoke poured from Varley's nostrils. Jarrett recognized him from earlier at the pool hall, the one with the build of a quarterback and a gold earring in his right ear. Varley slapped MacDonald's face, the force whipped his head to the side, and his chin dropped.

The other guy was forty pounds heavier than Varley. Daws looked to be the size of a fat man's walk-in fridge, big, powerful hands ready to drive a fist into MacDonald's face. He had the face of a disappointed day laborer. Just like at the pool hall, Daws waited until Varley told him what to do. MacDonald whimpered, chest heaving in and out as he pleaded with them to stop. His speckled shoulders sported a row of small red festering craters burnt into his flesh.

'I already told you, I can't access the account on my computer,' said MacDonald.

'You fuckwit,' said Varley. 'Transfer the fucking money. Do it now.'

'But I can't.' MacDonald sobbed. 'I would if I could. Believe me.'

'Give me the password.'

'I gave it to you,' shouted MacDonald. His face twisted with fear and hatred, making him nearly unrecognizable as the man he'd played pool with earlier.

'But it doesn't fucking work.' He burned MacDonald with the cigarette.

An animal-like bellow came out of MacDonald's mouth – agony and hopelessness, the sound of pure grief. To one side of the computer was a bowl of red chili pepper mushed up into a fine liquid paste. Varley dipped his finger into the bowl and showed it to MacDonald.

'Please, please.' MacDonald had no other words left.

'I think you are fucking with us.' Varley drew his finger across the burns on MacDonald's back.

Daws became angry. 'We did a guy earlier. Looked just like you. We don't have time for your shit. Varley asked you nice. I asked you politely and you won't help. All the shit is on your computer. We can get someone to hack it and get the information. It's not going to be hard.'

Varley puffed on the cigarette until the end glowed and then slowly pushed it against MacDonald's back as Daws held him in the chair.

Harry pointed at a holstered handgun resting on Varley's hip. He then held up a second finger, pointing at Daws, who struck MacDonald on the chest with the barrel of a pocket-sized .38. Jarrett had seen it before in the pool hall; it was the .38 MacDonald carried in an ankle holster. He must've seen that on TV or in a movie and thought it was a smart move. Yes and no. In his case, he'd have been better off throwing it in a dumpster. The first thing Varley and Daws would have done was to frisk him, and his protection scheme had done nothing but add to their arsenal. They would've laughed at him.

Both Jarrett and his father had heard enough to know that these men had killed Jack. It didn't take any imagination for Jarrett to understand what his father intended to do about Jack Malone's disappearance. Daws and his big mouth had eliminated all the guesswork. All that was left was the timing, and that gave them an advantage.

Jarrett had taken cover behind a sofa to the right. Hovering on the other side, Harry signaled the countdown, holding up his hand, lowering one finger at a time, until his hand was a fist. He rolled out on the floor first.

'Stand back and drop your weapon,' Harry said, prone on the floor.

Daws came around holding the .38 and Harry

shot him twice in the chest. The big man's eyes blinked, rolled up in his head, and he crumpled. Varley ducked, pulling out his gun. Jarrett had time to circle around far enough but MacDonald blocked his shot.

'It's not looking good,' said Harry.

'Depends how you look at it.' Varley stepped forward and squeezed off two rounds in Harry's direction.

Jarrett's cluster was a tight three rounds into the side of Varley's head. He stood up and walked over to MacDonald, knelt down, and untied his arms. Tears spilled down MacDonald's cheeks; sobbing, he leaned forward, coughing up blood and spit. 'They were going to kill me.'

Harry checked the two bodies. 'They ain't gonna kill anyone now,' he said.

Jarrett sat on the sofa, shaking his head. 'You got a boat?'

MacDonald nodded.

'Goddammit, why'd they have to kill Jack?' asked Harry. He juggled a lot of death in his day, and each time, thought, 'You don't pick which tomorrow you are going to live, it picks you.' He'd invited Jack to Hua Hin and promised to take care of everything. He'd taken care of everything but it wasn't the way he wanted it.

CHAPTER 11

Waters had receding blond hair and the build of a middleweight fighter. A small pelt of trimmed beard worn under his lower lip drew the eyes, as if he were a stage actor. In a way, that wasn't too far from the truth. With pale skin and blue eyes with pupils like hollowed-out nine-millimeter rounds, Waters had the kind of face that never seemed to change. He looked pretty much like he had when he was twenty-five years old. And he had an odd talent for accents. Depending on his mood and the context, he would riff in Irish, East London, Cape Town, or Delhi English. On the phone, he could fool a native of these places. No one was ever certain what his real accent was – not that it mattered much in his line of work. His ability to take on any persona had given him an edge.

Several months before Jarrett and Tracer received the assignment, Waters and Casey scheduled a meeting in Bangkok. Naked except for a white towel wrapped around his waist, Waters sat in a sauna, sweating. Seated next to him with his back to the wall, Casey leaned over, took the scoop from a bucket, and threw water on the hot stones, sending a fresh spiral of steam through the small room. On the bench next to him Waters had a cell phone and another device that looked like a phone, but was a scanner for electronic listening devices. Waters was a cautious man. Even in a Bangkok massage parlor he assumed someone might be listening. Having witnessed firsthand the capabilities of those who issued orders, Waters understood that in their impersonal world there were never any hard feelings. There were never any genuine feelings at all, only objectives, road maps, and zones that needed to be made secure.

'Christ, aren't you hot enough?' asked Waters.

'Sweat gets rid of all those impurities.'

'A bit hotter and you can get a confession out of me.' Waters was hitting close to the bone. But that was his way of shadowboxing in the field.

Waters got up from the bench and pushed open the door. A few minutes later, Casey found him drinking a beer at the ground-floor restaurant, leaning forward, hands folded on the table. He'd changed into his green windbreaker with gray piping around the collar, a red sweater, black slacks, and a Rolex, his hair combed back, freshly shaved, a glint of mischief in his blue eyes. People in the company said Waters should have his own TV show.

Waters spoke French, German, Italian, and Spanish. His Spanish had been refined to pass for Argentinian, Mexican, and Colombian. Casey had known Waters long enough to wonder what his baseline was. Who was Waters when he closed the door and took off his stage makeup?

The massage parlor had been Rick Casey's idea, a place to relax, with no one with five words of English, six miles away from the farang ghetto on Sukhumvit Road. On his way to work each day, Casey passed the large neon sign with the sexy young woman in a low-cut evening gown, her red lips in a perfect O, and long black hair falling over her shoulders. Waters had made a special trip from Baghdad to meet with Casey, and the sauna in the massage parlor was Casey's revenge.

As they soaked in the sauna, Casey was thinking about the last time they'd met; Waters had chosen the location: a bookstore on Broadway in New York City.

'Ever get laid in a bookstore?' Casey had asked.

Casey saddled up to a chair at the table as Waters flipped through a photo album of the yings working at the massage parlor. Some looked Chinese and others had a Japanese appearance, but most were overly made-up Thai women.

'Find anything you like?' asked Casey.

Waters closed the album.

'The target's high-profile,' said Waters. He was in the mood to talk business.

'I'd look at it a different way. He's a high-value target.'

That had become a familiar term among the private contractors. Working in a secret prison, that kind of talk made a private contractor feel good about what he did at his day job and gave him a moral justification for the persuasion used to unlock a man's plans, secrets, and information about colleagues.

Casey explained the details of what had happened to his son, Joel – a thirty-four-year-old accountant with one of the major firms, a man on his way up, a man with a bright future. A man who had gotten himself killed. Waters knew the broad strokes of the story but not the specifics of the murder.

Rick Casey leaned forward over his coffee, his Lakers cap pulled down just above his eyes. He wore a pair of dark aviator glasses and a black leather jacket unzipped to the sternum. The same gear he'd worn for their meeting in New York, except in Bangkok it was blast-furnace hot; the jacket only worked inside heavily air-conditioned rooms. Rubbing his three-day-old salt-and-pepper stubble, Casey asked Waters if he'd read the *International Herald Tribune*. Waters said he hadn't. Besides, this was Bangkok, not New York, and didn't people in Thailand read the *The Bangkok Post*? This bounced off Casey like a bullet off Superman. He had a copy of the newspaper and turned the page as Waters sipped his coffee.

'Another nine soldiers killed by a suicide bomber in Baghdad. If we didn't have a facility in Bangkok like the one I work in, we'd never get these fanatics to cooperate. They truly hate us. There would be a hundred times that number if it weren't for the work we're doing,' said Rick Casey. He folded the newspaper and put it on the empty chair. 'But let me tell you a secret. It's just so many numbers unless one of them is your own son.'

Waters nodded, thinking about the old Stalin quote that a single death was a tragedy, while a million deaths was a statistic. Both Waters and Casey had jobs working inside the death industry. Early on they'd learned to distinguish between tragedy and statistic.

Casey removed the aviator glasses. His eyes were a web of tiny red veins, and the skin underneath puffy, loose, and dark. His were the eyes of a man who'd seen too much, felt too much, and suffered too many losses. Waters had seen such eyes before hundreds of times among men he had served with, and among the families of men who hadn't come back.

'I miss my boy,' Rick Casey said. 'He shouldn't have died the way he did.'

'What happened was a bad thing, Casey. It's not been easy to put this through channels. Leaning on people sends the wrong signal, Rick. People might get the idea that you are out to cause some damage. I tell them that that isn't the Rick Casey I know, that you're owed for what they did to your son.'

'Then it's approved?'

'One of the finance guys wasn't happy about it. But he's never happy. Yeah, we got the approval.'

Casey pulled a briefcase from the floor and set it on the table.

'I've brought along forty grand.'

Waters shook his head and in a New York accent said, 'It's not about cash.'

It was rare to hear that line in Bangkok, where almost everything was about cash, or the lack of it. Casey tried to think of a place where cash wasn't the driving force behind a yes. He couldn't think of one.

'I heard what you said,' said Casey with a lopsided grin.

'Then why did you bring the briefcase to a whorehouse?'

'A man agrees to do a job, then that man should get paid upfront.'

'My men like upfront payments. But the point isn't the money,' Waters said. 'Jarrett is who I have in mind. He once said that payback is the second best thing after sex. But there needs to be a good reason for payback, beyond the money.'

'A father has lost his son. His killer walks around a free man. If anyone has earned the right to payback, it's me,' said Casey.

Waters had heard several versions of Harry Jarrett's story about paying back Jack. Harry, who was Jarrett's father, had raised his son on the original Nepalese story that over years had taken on legendary proportions. Twenty-five years later, Harry fulfilled a promise to his son, Alan, and organized a reunion with Jack. Father, son, and Jack flew in from three separate places for the silver anniversary celebration in Bangkok. But things

144

went sideways and the celebration had been cancelled. What had been two stories, separated by an ocean of time, became stitched together into one and Jack's name had become a code word for special assignments, ones that fell outside the scope of normal contracts and were included in a miscellaneous category of work done for extra pay.

When such an assignment came through, Harry Jarrett's influence was clear in the first words spoken about it: 'I've got a new assignment. It's paying back Jack. You interested?'

After 1990, the code words 'Paying Back Jack' acquired a different spin on paying back, with interest, a moral obligation, especially a selfless debt of honor. But that was getting ahead of the original story of how Harry and Jack initially met.

In 1965, Harry had got himself into some serious trouble in Nepal. He was in his early twenties when he decided that Everest was God's personal challenge to him. What he hadn't counted on was the speed of his climb. Having gone up the mountain far too quickly, he came down with a serious case of altitude sickness. Harry needed immediate medical attention, and he was alone on the mountain. Another climber found him, carried him down the mountain, and took him to a doctor. Harry always credited this guy, named Jack, with saving his life. Jarrett liked telling Tracer 'Harry was unmarried at the time, so if he'd capped it in Nepal, I wouldn't be sitting next to you.'

From an early age, Jarrett knew one thing about

his father: he had a special place in his heart for Jack. It especially had to do with Jack sticking around the clinic for a week, waiting for Harry to recover fully. When he found Jack packing his gear for a return climb up the mountain, Harry stopped him. 'I owe you. Give me your address so I can send you some money when I get home.'

Jack smiled, lit a joint, and shook his head. 'No need, man,' he said.

'You saved my life,' said Harry. 'You gotta let me do something in return.'

A big grin crossed Jack's face as if something special had occurred to him. 'You can pay me back.'

Jack had taken off his gold wire-rimmed glasses and was cleaning them with the end of his shirt. He squinted as he stared at Harry (who wasn't that old then) and said, 'Whenever you find someone who has a serious problem, you stop and give them a hand, help them out. And you know what, Harry? That will be my payback. Do what you need to do, and when they want to give you something for your trouble, you just tell them, 'I'm paying back Jack.' You think you can do that for me?'

After that, the highest purpose of Harry's life was to find a person in desperate need, who had no way out, about to be dragged under by the forces of life, and then extend his hand. As he pulled such a person free from harm's way, the guy would have that same grateful look Harry had had. He'd ask Harry what he could do in return, and Harry would tell him, 'No need, I'm paying back Jack. And you can pay him back as well by helping the next guy.'

Then Jack got himself killed on Harry's watch. It would be more dramatic if I told you that Harry and Alan had rowed the bodies of two men who killed Jack a mile offshore and dumped them in the sea. But that's not exactly the way it happened. They loaded the two dead guys into a powerboat and set off in the dark. What did Harry know about the Gulf of Thailand? He didn't need to know much; he was a gifted sailor. He knew boats. So did Alan. They had revved up the four-stroke outboard engines and headed off. Harry said there'd been a million stars in that clear night sky. But Harry said that night there hadn't been any moon. The surface of the sea had been calm. In the distance Alan, spotted some lights on a freighter. It was too far off for the freighter to see them. They sailed ahead without any lights. Once Harry cut the engines, he said how quiet it had been sitting there in the dark with his son, feeling the forward motion of the speedboat slow. Once the boat stopped, he'd thought about saying something about Jack. But the words wouldn't come. So Harry and Alan wrapped chains around one body, dumped it over the starboard side. Harry paused for a cigarette, saying nothing before he helped Alan thread heavy links of chains around the waist of the second dead guy. After a nod, Harry held the legs and Alan lifted by the armpits, lowering the body over the side. There was a splash, bubbles, and after a few minutes the surface was as smooth as glass. They sat in the boat, both of them thinking about Jack. His body was somewhere in the sea. Now his killers had joined him. Alan said, 'Dad, it wasn't your fault.' Harry said he looked up at his son, trying to see his features in the dark. He knew that he was crying, and said, 'Son, it will only be my fault if we let Jack's memory die.'

Waters paused after telling Harry's story, waiting for Casey to react. It was a crucial moment. No commitment followed without an acceptance of the basic ground rule. Money couldn't override the debt to be paid back to Jack.

'They do the job, and the money goes to the foundation.'

'What's the foundation got to do with it?'

'You've heard of cyclones, tsunamis, earthquakes? Natural disasters happen all the time. The money goes to people caught in the eye of the storm. The kind of people Jack would have wanted to help. Are you with me?'

'I'm hearing you,' Casey said. 'The forty grand is in the briefcase.' He slid it across the table.

Joel Casey had been murdered in Thailand. His death had been in the newspapers for a couple of weeks, and then the story had disappeared completely. No follow-up, no mention of the investigation into the killing. It was as if the murder had never happened. The man who had masterminded

Joel's murder had never been charged with the crime. The police had said there was insufficient evidence to prosecute. Case closed. Joel had been killed just as he was about to disclose irregularities in the accounts of a company owned by Somporn and his friends and family. Joel had gone through all the company records and computer files. He'd unearthed a second set of books, confronted Somporn, and demanded (never a good idea in Thailand) that Somporn tell him what was going on.

The response from Somporn had been a smile and a wave of the hand. 'Don't think too much,' he'd been told. But Joel didn't get it. He was warned a couple of times to forget the issues when writing his audit report. That wasn't Joel's style. He believed that audit reports should reflect the true state of affairs of the company. Joel's murder was a lesson that respecting cultural differences translated to a different set of working principles for accounting. Joel had seen his duty in simple terms: an auditor's responsibility was to report what was found, not what the company big shots wanted found and reported. Somporn had seen the report as mindless paperwork for outsiders who should trust him, and so long as he made them money, why would they care if there was leakage here and there? He was running a commercial enterprise, and not some non-profit rescue-the-children project.

After a long struggle with the police, prosecutor,

and courts, Casey felt that there had been no justice. Nothing but a man dead because he tried to do what he thought was right. Joel was the kind of man Jack would have liked. They could have shot pool together, talked about walking with your head up high because you lived to honor your principles. To square the outstanding debt owed Casey for his son was something Jack would have understood.

'Are you in?' asked Casey.

Waters fingered the photo album. 'I'm in for the payback,' he said in Colonel Waters's New York accent.

Casey looked across the table at Waters, with his movie star looks and clothes.

'But there's going to be blowback,' Waters added. 'You're living here. You're the first person they'll look for.'

'I've already thought that one through,' said Casey.

Waters looked at him, thinking of course Casey would do that. He'd use his special skills to divert attention. Casey was good at the basics. Waters had talked with a couple of people who knew Casey from the prison system in Baghdad. They'd said Casey started with mild pressure before turning up the heat, stroking, beating, knocking heads, backing away – relentless, determined, and patient. He was a planner who never missed a detail. He'd have a plan to cover his back, his front, and his sides.

CHAPTER 12

Casey had hired Vincent Calvino to tail Somporn's minor wife, a Chiang Mai woman named Meow – Thai for 'Cat.' The investigation had lasted two weeks. Each day, Calvino shadowed her, keeping a detailed diary of Cat's movements, whom she saw, where she went, what she ate for lunch and dinner, where she had her hair and nails done. Somporn owned a fully furnished condo on Thong Lo – the unit was registered in the name of one of Somporn's companies. Cat occupied it. Twenty-three years old, tall, white-skinned, long-legged, Cat was Somporn's favorite side lady. She'd been a night-club singer and, during the day, a presenter – one of the beauties who appeared at shows selling new cars, high-tech gadgets, or the latest condo development in Phuket. She towered above the other yings in her hot pants and tank top. Her fingernails were painted like tiger claws on the day Somporn had met her, and she'd persuaded him to buy a Lexus. She had a smile that triggered a man's reflex to reach for his wallet. She'd sealed the deal by draping her body over the floor model of a red Lexus, licking her lips slowly with her tongue.

Before the deal was completed, Cat had talked him into buying every accessory available, including air bags, a high-end stereo system, and a GPS monitoring system. If there had been a mini-helicopter pad for the car's roof, he'd have bought it. He couldn't take his eyes off her for a minute.

Somporn finally found the courage to joke about whether Cat herself came with the car. She wondered why it had taken him so long to ask. She joked that she wasn't an accessory. To sweeten his proposition, the next day he invited her to the condo and handed her a set of keys to the front door along with a second set of keys for a new Camry parked downstairs. He was a businessman and she was a businesswoman. With the business out of the way, each pretty much got what they wanted.

Calvino's report also included dozens of photographs of Cat. There she was in her new car, parking at Siam Paragon, shopping for shoes, lunching with several of her presenter friends in an upscale restaurant on Silom Road. He had photos of Cat and Somporn together, but nothing compromising. No down-and-dirty shots of naked, sweaty bodies. Cat could have passed as his personal assistant or his daughter. They never held hands or showed affection in public. Cat was a professional, turning off in public, turning on in private; a combination that had seduced and hooked Somporn. He used the Lexus, which he neither wanted nor needed, each time he had an appointment to meet her. He showed no regret in buying the car. He had the ying who turned heads and moved cars from the showroom to the garage with the flicker of a smile.

Casey had passed copies of Calvino's report to Waters, who'd handed it down the chain of command until it reached Jarrett and Tracer. Now photographs of Cat and Somporn were laid out on a coffee table near the balcony window. Occasionally Tracer glanced at one, picking it up, studying the features of the woman and the man like a hangman measuring a prisoner for the noose. Tracer pulled the binoculars to his eyes and focused on Cat's balcony three hundred and twenty-five meters away. He stood just to the right and slightly behind Jarrett. Neither Jarrett nor Tracer had any idea that the foreigner who had hit the Benz was the same man who had done the report. That made it a level playing field, since Calvino was unaware that his report had ended up in their hands.

Somporn arrived in his new Lexus for an appointment with Cat every Wednesday. He arrived between ten and eleven in the morning, stayed through lunch, and left around two in the afternoon. His visits had become predictable, routine. As Calvino had noted in his report. Somporn's world was without surprises, and that made him vulnerable.

What Jarrett and Tracer were waiting for was

153

Somporn's weekly love-in with a ying who understood that, like her lover's new Lexus, sooner or later she'd be traded in for a new model. On the surface Cat appeared devoted to Somporn. Her habits were only slightly less predictable than his, and she was no more careful to cover her tracks than he was. Both of them were a private investigator's dream. They lived in worlds they thought they controlled – more than that for Somporn, who lived in a world he thought he owned.

Jarrett folded his hands behind his head and sat back in his chair. The Jack Malone Foundation in Hong Kong had confirmed that Casey's money had been received. Tracer had turned on his iPod, hooked up to two small speakers. The words poured out: 'Just get it done. Don't matter how you do it.'

Jarrett checked his watch. They had an hour to wait.

As Calvino climbed the stairs to his office, he heard someone calling his name from the street below. He leaned over the railing toward the massage yings sitting in front of the massage parlor. One of the yings called up, 'Tell Ratana – Noi come to office late.' Behind her was a customer. Evidently, she was going out for a short time. It wasn't the first time Noi had dumped her kid on Ratana for an additional hour to turn a trick. Strangely, Ratana no longer complained about working in an office above a massage parlor. The ying would eventually come into the office and collect her daughter. Which one of the babies was hers? He couldn't keep straight the shifting combination of babies who lurked along the edges of the playpen any more than he could identify fish in an aquarium. Little kids were like old people in that way; their features blurred into a generic rubbery face; hairless, jug-eared, wet-mouthed. It was difficult for him to remember how the office ran before Ratana had given birth to a dead man's child.

He hadn't been expected; as far as Ratana and everyone on the soi knew, Calvino had left town. As soon as he opened the door, the whiff of babies hit him like a wall of freshly fertilized soil. Then came the sound of their blubbering and incoherent babbling, their armor-piercing cries, their shaking of rattles, and their bouncing against the sides of their small, caged world.

The space had been transformed from an office into a community daycare center. Ratana's desk had been pushed aside to make space for a playpen with see-through nylon mesh for tiny little fists to grasp, squeeze, pull – the basic exercise program for a six-month-old. Mouth open, Calvino stood frozen on the spot, surveying the wreckage that the children had unleashed. Ratana sat behind her desk, earphones from an iPod on, sipping coffee, looking at her computer, and singing out of tune. On the screen, she read about how to be a perfect parent on a working mothers' website – actually a blog written by a Thai living in Los Angeles – adorned with teddy bear logos and pictures of two small snotty-nosed babies whose every movement was caught on the web cam.

He walked to her desk, reached over, and pulled out an earphone.

'Noi's going to be late picking up her kid,' he said.

She jumped. 'I wasn't expecting you until later.'

'She was just leaving with a customer.'

Ratana shrugged, turning away from the computer screen. She had dressed casually in a pair of black slacks and a white blouse stained with baby slobber and bits of baby food. Her hair fell across her face. She pushed it back, twisting around in her chair as she scanned Calvino from head to toe. She had already talked to Colonel Pratt the night of Calvino's detention, confirming that she'd never heard Calvino mention the woman who'd fallen to her death.

'I'm sorry about Pattaya. What a terrible thing!'

'Pratt told you?' He wasn't surprised.

She nodded. Calvino's best friend and his office assistant had long ago established a line of independent communication. 'I thought you'd be in this afternoon.'

'I wanted to finish up on Beckwith's case.' He showed her the pictures on his digital camera. The babies stirred in their sleep. Ratana put a finger to her lips. Sometimes he forgot the new rule of the office: talk in a whisper. 'I had a minor accident in Washington Square.'

'Anyone hurt?' Her hand instinctively touched her throat.

'The car I hit was parked. No one inside.'

She sighed. 'That's a relief. I'll handle the paper-work with the insurance company.'

'The owner's handling it.' The attitude of the two men irritated him, made him shake his head. But compared to the lockdown in Pattaya, the incident made little impression. As he stepped back, he brushed against a pram, which rolled into the playpen. The reception area had become a minefield of car seats, buggies, toys, piles of disposable diapers, bottles, and bottle warmers. Getting through to his office had become an ordeal.

One of the babies in the playpen started bawling. The others soon joined in. Ratana leaned over her desk and made some of those cooing noises inter-spersed with tongue clicking that mothers use to soothe infants. The language of comfort, an ancient, borderless language.

'Colonel Pratt asked you to phone,' she said.

Calvino had switched off his cell phone, but there was no way to avoid messages filtering through to his office. He didn't want to talk with Pratt or anyone else. He wanted to forget the dead ying falling past his balcony.

'They're hungry,' said Ratana, reaching out for the bottles. 'Let me know when you want me to phone Colonel Pratt.' Babies sucking on their bottles, their tiny legs in the air, had suddenly become individual forces to reckon with. 'Why don't I phone the Colonel now?'

'Not now. Later.'

He found a path into his office and collapsed at his desk. He had needed the vacation from the office, from the babies, from Ratana, from Colonel Pratt, from the clients and chaos of Bangkok. No one could handle Bangkok full blast very long without a break.

'You're upset,' she said. 'Tell me what's wrong.'

'Telling you what's right would take less time.'

The Pattaya police had put him through the chili-grinding machine, she thought. That accounted for his flushed face, hot temper.

'I'm curious about one thing,' he said.

That made her happy for a moment. 'What thing?'

'How many babies are out there?' He nodded in the direction of her office. 'I thought there were three.'

'Four,' she said.

'Some investigator,' he said. 'I can't even keep track of the number of babies in my reception area.' He thought he'd correctly counted the babies in the playpen – three, four, five? Perception sometimes failed to attach the right number. It was the same with time passing. How long had it taken the ying to fall to her death? Two, three, four seconds? The police had asked him. Time did strange things too, getting tangled up like a clump of babies, hampering judgment.

'Colonel Pratt said the Pattaya police don't consider you a suspect.'

'They told Pratt what he wanted to hear. It's the Thai way.'

'So there is no problem. That's good,' she said, confirming that the Thai way had followed him straight to his desk.

Snuggling a cooing baby against her chest, she returned to Calvino's office and sat in a chair opposite his desk.

'John-John's sleeping,' she whispered, swaying the child from side to side, making a clicking sound with her tongue.

Every time he looked at the baby, he asked himself whether the luk-krueng farang kid looked more like his father or mother.

The baby's father, John Lovell, had been murdered and cremated a year and a half earlier. Ratana's mother had counseled her to get an abortion; so had her friends. Until the baby was born, Ratana's mother had insisted that farangs in Thailand were all scam artists, con men, grifters, or dangerous criminals. Since John-John's birth, her mother phoned a half-a-dozen times a day with advice, worried that Ratana was giving the baby insufficient attention, telling her to quit her job and devote herself to the baby full-time, and instead of campaigning for an abortion, now campaigned for Ratana and John-John to move back to the shelter of the ancestral home. The old lady would have made a perfect Thai politician.

'Someone knew where I was staying in Pattaya. I need to know if you told anyone about the hotel.'

Ratana raised her hand and drew an imaginary line like a schoolteacher across the room and the playpen. 'Do you really think I'd ever let you down?'

She waited for the emotion to register in his face. It was one thing that Calvino was convinced wouldn't happen. 'Any other messages while I was away?'

'A few clients phoned. Mrs Beckwith phoned. Her husband's being transferred to Chicago and . . .'

'She wants to close the case,' said Calvino.

'There's no point in continuing. They're leaving Thailand. And Casey's messenger will deliver forty thousand baht this afternoon,' said Ratana with a radiant smile. She had saved the good news for just the right moment to lift her boss's shattered spirits.

'Did he call when I was away?'

'I told him you were out of town.'

'Did he say anything else?' asked Calvino.

'He said he was very happy with your work.' She snuffled John-John's cheek. He had seen her perform this ritual before. The sniffing of her baby appeared to intoxicate Ratana. It gave her a baby high. The gesture was one that Thais commonly performed on their loved ones. Her nose on John-John's neck, she breathed in, then gently exhaled. The smelling-ceremony style was a mixture of wine tasting and perfume sampling. She never tired of burying her nose into John-John as if she wished to breathe him into her lungs. It was feeding time, and Ratana unfastened her blouse.

Calvino looked away. 'Why don't you go back to your desk? You'll be more comfortable.'

Ratana smiled, shaking her head. 'You mean you'll be more comfortable.'

Life revolved around the edges of reality for most people. They saw and heard and felt what they wanted. Calvino had no reason to believe Ratana had dropped his travel arrangements with anyone. Alone at his desk once again, he checked his email, wondering who had passed on his Pattaya hotel arrangements. Of course it could have been Apichart, or one of the investigators sifting through the remains of two dead men in the Soi 33 carnage. Who else would have gone to the trouble of finding out where he'd gone?

CHAPTER 13

Jarrett pressed his eye against the daytime telescopic lens, his feet firm on the floor, one elbow positioned on the table. A two-foot silencer on the end of the barrel gave the weapon an otherworldly appearance. He stretched his arms and shook his hands loosely at his side as he waited for Tracer, standing to his right, to confirm the target. Tracer, his ears plugged and wired, stood a foot back from Jarrett's position, looking through a pair of binoculars at the buildings in the vicinity of the target.

Tracer and Jarrett had supplied each building within a ninety-degree arc of the target with a code name: Ripper, Papa Bear, Grizzly, Scorpion, Firebird, Rooks, and Black Sheep. The target building itself was code-named Zapper. The code names and locations had been written in large, careful blue lettering on a whiteboard. The whiteboard rested on a chair to Jarrett's left. All Jarrett had to do was look up from the telescopic site at the whiteboard if he needed a confirmation. That wouldn't be necessary because he had the information memorized. But there was comfort in having it there, knowing that memory sometimes failed. It was a lot of information to keep straight. Screwups more often than not were information screwups; communication gummed up as it worked its way down the chain of command.

Floors and units also had codes running left to right, such as one-eight for the first unit on the eighth floor. Tracer passed three-nine on Firebird, paused, looking for any activity before moving on. He'd studied the buildings and the line-of-fire floors of each one. Waters hadn't indicated any problem. But that wasn't the point. Training kicked in, and it had to be assumed that a force with hostile intention might be in one of the buildings. Only a rookie would focus just on the target on the balcony of three-nine Zapper, never letting it cross his mind that someone could be targeting him. As the blues teach, when anguish gets hung out to dry, it finds itself in a world wet with anger, rage, and revenge.

'Tracer, there isn't anything alive that I can't hit at three hundred and fifty meters.' This wasn't a boast, just a fact. Jarrett was talking to himself, giving himself a talking-to, knowing the time for liftoff was approaching.

'I know that for a fact.' Tracer didn't look away from his binoculars. It had just turned eleven when Tracer spotted movement at the sliding-glass door leading to the balcony. 'We got someone at three-nine Zapper. A woman,' said Tracer. 'She's with an Asian male.'

Jarrett embraced the rifle, staring through the daytime telescope. Kate's eye picked up the woman, as did Tracer's binoculars.

'Got her.' He watched her through the crosshairs.

'She's a looker,' said Tracer. She wore a dark short skirt and silk blouse, diamond earrings in both ears, and another larger diamond mounted in a gold pendant around her neck. A woman with a diamond at her throat was a woman not just displaying the number of carats she thought she was worth, but the real value a man had placed upon her. Her hair had been pulled back from her forehead and ears and tied with a clip.

'If you've got money, you don't buy ugly,' said Tracer.

'But it don't buy love.'

The binoculars scanned the distance. 'Got that right, but it can pay some rent.' He paused. 'The balcony door's sliding back. She's out. He's behind her. His right hand is on the small of her back like he's balancing her.'

The telescope picked out a man's head. Jarrett leaned into his embrace with Kate.

'Wait,' said Tracer. Two, three beats of silence. 'That's not him. That's not our target.' He reached down and picked up the photo of Somporn.

'You sure it's not him?' Jarrett had the man in the crosshairs, his finger on the trigger.

'Look at the photo.'

'I know what Somporn looks like.'

'Then you're seeing a guy thirty years younger

164

and half-a-foot taller than Somporn. If that's our target, then that boy's got himself a major face-lift and some elevator shoes.'

Jarrett looked again and then sat back in his chair, drumming his fingers on the edge of the table. He was wound up, pumped with adrenaline, and the race had been called off.

'Then who is he?'

'Does he look Thai to you?' asked Tracer.

Jarrett rested his right eye snug against the scope.

'He looks like a Japanese punk rapper. Look at that wild, thick kinky hair. Looks like an eagle's nest,' said Tracer, with a whoop of glee that dove into a valley of disappointment.

They both watched the young woman in the short skirt and silk blouse show her stuff. 'Either he's a boy toy, or she's double-dipping,' said Jarrett.

'The bitch is kissing him,' said Tracer. 'Like a bear licking honey.'

Jarrett shivered as he thought how close he'd come to killing the wrong man. A mistaken identity had been what had killed Jack. Jack's red hair had been a near perfect match for an Australian named MacDonald. He shook off the image of Jack, thinking instead back to the beekeeper sleeping in bed early in the morning. He wondered what time she'd woken up, found the money, put on her clothes, and left. He glanced at the photo of Somporn taped to the side of the whiteboard and looked back through the telescope sight. 'Tracer, you hear about the bees going AWOL? Dying everywhere?'

'We're finished here,' said Tracer. 'At least for today. I can't see Somporn joining this party. I'd bet the bank he's not coming around to make up a threesome.' Tracer reached over to a side table and cranked up the music. The empty, disappointed space of the sitting room filled with the voice of a wailing blues singer. She was singing about the moment of truth when a man satisfies a woman, makes her knees go weak. They both watched Somporn's mia noi and her boy toy dancing on the balcony as they listened to the lyrics. 'Don't be shy, satisfy me. Try and try and try.'

'You hungry? And I don't mean for the crap Casey bought,' Jarrett asked. Suddenly the aborted mission had given him a craving for a cheeseburger and French fries.

'I feel like catfish and hush puppies,' said Tracer.

'I'd settle for a burger and fries.'

'Nothing much to keep us here. I'd say Mr. Somporn ain't shown.'

Tracer lowered his binoculars and glanced at Jarrett, who lifted his head up from the scope. Jarrett still had the white feather in his hat. A broad smile crossed Tracer's face. 'Bees dying. Yeah, I dig it. We've got ourselves a situation.'

Jarrett looked down the length of the silencer fixed to the barrel of the rifle. There wasn't going to be anything but silence today, he thought. He leaned on his elbows, staring through the telescopic lens, watching the action. 'Maybe we got

166

the wrong floor or unit? Wrong date or time? Wrong something.'

Tracer smirked. 'There you have it. Wrong something. Three-nine Zapper.'

'Casey's report might've been fucked up.'

'It says the man's here every Wednesday between ten-thirty and one. Like clockwork. It says Somporn is like a German when it comes to time.'

'Then what's this punk rapper doing giving a foot of tongue to Somporn's minor wife?'

Tracer shrugged. 'Man, I'm just the paid help. But I got a feeling he don't know, you know what I mean?' A wide smile broke across his face.

'You'd better phone Waters and let him deal with Casey,' said Jarrett. 'Tell him what's happened. Let him figure out what to do.'

They decided to wait another hour, watching, making sure that the boy toy didn't slip away only to be replaced by Somporn. That would be embarrassing. Neither Tracer nor Jarrett thought that would happen. It was one of the oldest stories from the field: the men on the ground had been dished up E. coli when they thought they'd been dining on the best that money could buy. After a few minutes of cooling down, they became resigned to the fact that they'd ended up with the military's answer to a bad oyster.

'I'll let him know,' said Tracer, shaking his head. He raised the binoculars and had another good look at the couple on the balcony. The Thai man, aged about thirty, had his shirt unbuttoned and

167

his arms wrapped around Somporn's Miss Special. The way their tongues were working, some fire deep in the belly must have been heating up, making them crazy.

Tracer observed the French-kissing through his binoculars one last time. 'Whoa, boy.'

'Where's Somporn?'

'She's a beautiful creature, and from the look of things I'd say she's pretty confident Somporn's not coming around.' He stopped talking, held out the binoculars for Jarrett. 'Have a look.'

Jarrett got up from the table and used the second pair of binoculars to focus in on the lovebirds doing their ritual shifting and sliding.

He saw a couple dancing on the balcony. The young Thai was swinging her around like they were on a dance floor. She followed each step, really dancing a jitterbug, smiling and laughing. They looked to be without a care in the world. Three-nine Zapper was a disco stage, and no one was going to die that day.

After they'd packed up and locked the condo, they sat in the back of a taxi headed to the Madrid Bar in Patpong. They didn't say much during the ride, looking out the window, thinking about what hadn't happened and what it meant. They were like a team taking the bus back after losing the game.

As far as Jarrett was concerned, until they established contact with Waters and worked out the next step there was little to do, say, or think about.

Given the circumstances, he left his mind free to find some other object. It didn't take long until he'd shifted to the ying he'd left that morning. The beekeeper's daughter. Tracer had gone and talked about honey not knowing she was on his mind with memories of her face, story, and body.

'Bees are dying all over America, Europe, and Asia. No one knows why.'

'That's a hell'va thing, Jarrett.'

'I get the feeling most people have moved on. Too many other things to worry about. Bees? It's hard to get worked up over something that's going sting your ass and die anyway.'

'Human nature. If you can't figure out why something is the way it is, then block it out. No point hitting your head against the wall.'

They got out of the taxi opposite CP Tower, crossed Silom, and walked along Patpong Soi 1 until they reached the Madrid. They sat in a corner booth, an old habit, so they could watch who came in the door. The specials were chalked on a blackboard.

'Changed my mind,' said Jarrett. 'I want a pizza. One of the large specials that's got everything the cook can find in the fridge on it.'

Tracer looked up from the menu, saw the waitress standing in front of the table, and said, 'Don't suppose you'd have catfish and hush puppies?'

CHAPTER 14

McPhail swaggered like a prizefighter as he came through the door of the Lonesome Hawk Bar. A broad grin was plastered on his mug as he passed under the head of the Cape water buffalo mounted on the wall. It had been a gift from a friend of Old George, but the buffalo head had cost him a huge import duty and the years never dimmed the pain of that layout of cash for a noble head given in friendship.

'What the hell you so happy about?' asked Old George.

Before McPhail could answer, another farang pushed past him, giving him a shove without saying he was sorry. That was Casey's style.

'Who the fuck do you think you are?' asked McPhail.

'Someone you don't want to fuck with. That's who I am.'

McPhail sized him up and decided this wasn't the way he wanted to start his lunch. Pretending Casey wasn't worth the effort, he turned to the side and sat down opposite Old George. There were a couple of ways to handle a guy like Casey, and for McPhail both of them promised a kind of humiliation. Casey correctly read McPhail's gesture of boredom as a signal of surrender. Experience had taught Casey a few things about reading a man's intentions. When Casey interrogated suspects, there was a flicker of something in their eyes that would signal surrender. Interrogation techniques were designed to lead a suspect to that point, when he knows that no one is coming to rescue him, and that there's only a long drop into nothingness if he continues to resist.

McPhail had also read Casey right. He'd walked into the Lonesome Hawk like a man spoiling for a fight. Fists balled up, hanging by his sides, he walked straight back to the last booth where Calvino sat reading through paperwork on a case. Even with all the noise in the bar, compared to the chorus of crying babies in the office, the background chatter in the Lonesome Hawk was still more like what you'd hear in a library. Casey had phoned Calvino's office only to be told he wasn't in, but that he could be found in Washington Square at the Lonesome Hawk.

Casey ordered a vodka and tonic from Baby Bear. The waitress got her nickname from an Australian customer who said she reminded him of a baby koala bear. Casey slid into the booth across from Calvino.

'Casey, what's your problem?'

In the Land of Smiles, when the word 'problem' is used, the speaker isn't talking about algebra. He's referring to the kind of miscalculation that can get a man killed.

'No, you've got the problem,' he replied, clenching his jaw peppered with a three-day beard, the black flecked with little white moons.

Calvino leaned back, staring at him for a long beat. 'Maybe you ought to explain.'

Casey lowered his voice to a near whisper. 'I'll make it simple so you don't get confused. Your report said Somporn had a session with his mia noi every Wednesday. You could set your watch by his arrivals and departures. Ten-thirty to two o'clock. That's what you wrote.' He pulled out a copy of the report and slapped it down on the table.

Calvino had been called a lot of names, been the object of many curses and damnations, and had had his fair share of threats. But Casey was in a class all by himself when it came to summing up his position with a blast of pure anger. They say extreme anger turned a good man into a bad one and a bad man, once his anger was stoked up, had the capacity to inflict a load of evil that spread out far beyond his personal horizon. Here was a man accustomed to being in full control of the situation, of extracting what he wanted and discarding the source after he'd finished.

'I followed her for a month, and she established a pattern,' said Calvino.

'Why didn't you tell me about the other guy?'

Calvino frowned. 'What other guy?'

'See, you fucked up. You didn't know there was another guy. You overlooked it. This isn't some small thing. Some other guy banging Somporn's ying. Where were you? Eating donuts like a fucking traffic cop?'

'You paid me to follow his mia noi. I followed her. You gave me no instructions to follow anyone else. Now you're talking like I missed something. Casey, I didn't miss a thing.'

Casey's vodka and tonic arrived and he grabbed it from Baby Bear, who wore a tight T-shirt and low-rider jeans that exposed her belly. He drank it straight down. 'Bring me another,' he said, handing Baby Bear the empty glass. She gave him a hot lipstick smile, winking at him, as if Casey might just calm down and buy her a drink. Then she looked over at Calvino, who hadn't broken eye contact with Casey.

'And give him the bill,' Casey continued.

Calvino had been straight with Casey from day one, letting him know that he wasn't going to get involved in any revenge killing of his son. Casey had told him that he only wanted to smear Somporn's reputation, and that had been good enough to convince Calvino to take the money. His reason seemed good enough to take on the case. Though Calvino did wonder whether most people in Thailand would care about Somporn keeping another woman. In some circles it would even burnish his reputation.

Casey told Calvino about how the mia noi had another guy, a younger guy she was fooling around with during the morning she was supposed to be fooling around with Somporn. The main thing that came through from Casey's rambling half-coherent rant was that she was dancing on the balcony half-naked with a guy her own age. What a thought: a woman who might be attracted to a man her own age.

'She's screwing this guy, and I didn't know she had another guy. It should have been in your report. The one I paid for. What kind of half-assed job did you do, Calvino?'

The second vodka and tonic arrived, and Calvino waited until Casey had drunk it.

'I tailed the target you gave me, and like I told you, Somporn showed up at her condo every Wednesday. I never gave any guarantee that he wouldn't miss a Wednesday. He might be sick, or maybe he had an appointment, or he blew her off and the new guy is giving her comfort. How do I know? Three or four months is a long time in short-time affairs. People change, Casey.'

Human nature being what it is, every man thought failure and betrayal only happened to others. The belief ensured work for private investigators and lawyers. Calvino wondered when men would learn that with women the general rule did cover them; that the exception to the rule, like a lottery win, always went to someone else. It didn't take an Einstein to figure out that there were yings who knew every-trick of the game. They viewed the right man as a safe platform to stay put on so long as the money continued, but when there was the possibility of making even more money, they jumped with a predator's speed. If money could be made from two platforms, or three, why not juggle the schedules? The penalty for getting caught just meant turning one John over and finding a replacement. For such yings, romance and relationships were scheduling issues. But finding the right time to talk reason to someone like Casey, who was in the midst of an emotional firestorm, was another scheduling challenge. Yings made a good living understanding better than most that the timing of the message was just as important as the content.

'I relied on what you wrote.'

Calvino smiled. Casey had got it wrong. He'd relied on a snapshot in time as if things never changed.

'I'm not a fortune teller. I can neither predict the future nor can I stake out two people at the same time. I observed and reported a pattern of a women's behavior. I never said anything about that pattern lasting forever. You got what you paid for. That's all you could reasonably expect. Anyone who promises you any different is selling you a bridge to Brooklyn.'

Calvino watched Casey think his situation through. 'Tell me, Casey, why do you care so much if she's cheating on Somporn?'

'What's it to me? That's what you're asking?'

Calvino nodded, seeing that Casey hadn't thought this through.

'Are you afraid that she's breaking up Somporn's happy home?'

'I want you to keep tabs on her and report back on who she's seeing.'

'Starting when?'

'From now would be about right.' Casey pulled out his wallet and counted out a thousand dollars in ten Ben Franklins with watermarks so fresh they looked like they'd smudge if you rubbed them the wrong way. 'Give me a full report this time. Don't leave out anything. I want to know where she goes, who her lover is, and whether she's still seeing Somporn. And anything else you find out about her. Put it all in. This time, I don't want any loose ends.'

'It's back to tracking the mia noi, and Somporn is just one more guy in her life, is that how you want to play it?' asked Calvino.

Casey sucked in his teeth, his eyes bulged, and he swallowed hard, hands wrapped tightly around his glass. 'I'm not forgetting him. Believe me.'

Calvino believed him. What he had trouble coming to terms with was how downright certain Casey was in his belief that every loose end could be tied up. The reality was that each time someone pulled out one string, three more spun out somewhere else. No one could ever completely tie them up in a perfect ball; the best any private investigator could promise to do was to observe the patterns, to explore the knots, and to tease, tuck, and pull until a plausible scenario emerged, but never could he find every last stray strand. 'I'll do what I can.'

'Don't fuck up this time,' said Casey as he swallowed hard, leaving Calvino to bite deeply into the allegation that his work on the Somporn case hadn't been professional. A smile crossed Casey's face. 'I heard you were out of town.'

'Yeah, where'd you hear that?'

'From your secretary. Who else would I hear it from?'

'Did she tell you where I'd gone?'

'No. Was she supposed to?'

Calvino watched Baby Bear come with a drink. She rested her arm against his shoulder. 'You too serious today. Not smile. Not happy.' She pulled an exaggerated frown, put her hands on her hips. That usually made him smile, but not today.

'Later, Baby Bear.' She nodded, looked at him, and then stuck her tongue out at Casey and stormed off.

Casey pushed the notes across the table. 'That should cover baby formula for a couple of months and leave you enough to feed the bear,' he said.

A grand was enough to provide baby formula in Bangkok until the kid was six. 'I want to know if she's still Somporn's minor wife. Was it a one-off thing? Or maybe they've changed the day or the time they meet? I want that level of detail.'

'To the tattoo on her right hip,' said Calvino.

'You saw that?'

'Just checking the detail level.'

Casey turned stone-cold silent. 'Don't fuck this up.'

At the bar. McPhail was in the middle of a serious conversation with Henry, a Lonesome Hawk regular with major health problems. Henry weighed four hundred, maybe four hundred and fifty pounds. He was one of those people who didn't stop eating when he was full. Henry kept on eating until he was so tired he keeled over asleep on his plate. He had an appointment soon to have his stomach reduced to the size of an apple. At the moment, he was on his third special of the day, galloping through the food on final countdown, one last binge before submitting to a life sentence of one small spoon of this, and one little taste of that.

After the door had closed behind Casey, Old George bellowed from his perch: 'Next time I'm going to eighty-six that asshole. I don't like him.'

'You can't do business only with your friends and make any money,' said Henry from the bar.

'I'd rather go broke giving enemas to house lizards than make money from customers like him.' Old George made a fist and thrust it toward the water buffalo mounted on the wall above his head.

'I've got all the money I'll ever need. And I don't need any more friends.'

McPhail shook his head, repeating the word 'enema' as he walked over to Calvino's booth and slid onto the bench opposite. 'That guy, I've seen him before. Didn't he used to work at the embassy?'

'I don't wanna hear about embassies.' He thought about the Benz he'd clipped that morning. 'I hate diplomatic plates.'

'I get the picture,' said McPhail. 'Did you see the way he hooked his ankles?'

'You think I had my head under the table looking at his feet?'

McPhail laughed. 'I could see him from the bar.'

'You watched the way he hooked his ankles? McPhail, cut down on the alcohol before noon.'

McPhail lit a cigarette, took a long drag, let the smoke roll out of his nostrils, and leaned back. 'Some things like this matter. If you've studied long enough, you can make a profile from the way a man sits.'

'You're crazy. Casey's crazy. Ratana's kid is making me crazy. Is there anyone sane left?'

McPhail looked around the bar and shook his head. 'Not in this bar. Not in this part of Bangkok. Everyone's nuts.'

Calvino leaned forward, eyes focused on his friend. 'How did Casey hook his ankles that gave you the slightest idea about him?'

McPhail smiled. He took a drag from his cigarette and a gulp from his vodka tonic. 'I've got more than two hundred photos of the way people cross their legs, hook their ankles, and how they sit with their knees touching or wide open. There are hundreds of variations. And I can tell the personality type from the way that person deals with his legs and feet when he's sitting – or she's sitting.'

'Enough, McPhail. What did Casey's hooked ankles tell you?'

'He's a killer.'

'I want to know what's going on inside his head,' said Calvino. 'He's after something he's avoided talking about.'

'You know what I'm saying? The man's a natural-born killer. You can see it in his eyes.'

'I thought it was the way he hooked his ankles.'

'Are you fucking with me, Vinny?'

Let it ride, Calvino thought. McPhail smoked his cigarette and nodded his head to the music coming from the boom box. Casey hadn't been happy when he came in and he wasn't any happier when he left. Without a baseline to go by, it was difficult to know if this was a permanent state. Calvino pulled one of the hundred-dollar bills out of his wallet and gave it to McPhail. 'Follow Casey. I want to know where he goes and who he sees.'

McPhail rolled his eyes, 'Man, he's been gone five minutes. And do you know how hot it is outside? I'll get third-degree sunburn. Then I'm in the hospital with tubes feeding me. What good is a hundred fucking dollars gonna do me?'

Calvino smiled, peeled off another hundred and handed it to McPhail, watching him gulp down his drink. 'All you've got to do is ask.'

'I know, anyone seen a medium-height grumpy-looking farang in a baseball hat with a three-day-old beard?'

At the door, one of the waitresses pointed to the right. Casey had headed toward Sukhumvit Road. Outside the door, McPhail described Casey to a security guard. He'd seen him walk past the old cinema building with the marquee advertising the Mambo transvestite show. By the time McPhail reached Sukhumvit Road, he spotted Casey's baseball cap in the distance. He was just opposite the pond in the park on his way to the Emporium.

One of Bangkok's brown-shirted finest had stopped him for flicking ash from his cigarette onto the pavement. Casey was walking over to the police booth, arguing with the first officer and then a second one sitting in the booth. The anti-litter squad of BMA cops had caught another victim. McPhail moved in close enough to hear the charges. Flicking ashes was an offense, they told him. No question he was being told to pay a two-thousand-baht fine. And no doubt he was telling the brown shirts to go fuck themselves. He was waving his arms like a bird lifting off, and his voice could be heard over the traffic. Taking off his baseball hat, he clenched his jaw, his lips a blur, his voice a litany of curses. He looked like a coach jawing at a referee who had called his man out at first base.

In-your-face confrontation was never a good technique for negotiating a lower penalty in

Thailand; meek, playful, sorrowful – that was the path to the two-hundred-baht fine. Casey had a lot to learn about the art of expat living. McPhail decided to make a note to that effect. Standing in the heat of the day, it occurred to him that Calvino already knew this much about Casey, but he had to write something down to earn the two hundred bucks.

CHAPTER 15

Somporn had gone AWOL from Zapper three-nine on the advice of his wife's fortune-teller. His wife rarely made a decision unless she first checked with Tanat, asking for his advice on place, time, and position. Somporn's decision to run for parliament had not been made until Tanat had given his blessing. With his daughter's marriage and the election closing in, Somporn and his wife had been spending a great deal of time with the skinny, dark-skinned guru, who favored business suits, gold rings, and betel nut in the late afternoons. His roughness added a natural edge, giving him credibility as he closed his eyes, hands folded on the table, smiling, as if glimpsing some spectacle in another world.

Tanat was seated at a table on the terrace of the Oriental Hotel beside Marisa, the sister of the man who was marrying Somporn's daughter. He held her hand up, his index finger tracing the lines of her palm. He stopped, lips pursed, head nodding, and then continued until he had traced each of the lines. 'A very good hand,' he said. 'You will have three children and die at eighty-three years old.

Your husband will be foreign, and his work will take him away for many days at a time. When you are fifty years old, you will come into money.'

A large red-and-white striped umbrella provided shade from the overhead sun. Juan Carlos, the bridegroom-in-waiting, sat on the other side, leaning forward. Tanat had read his hand several times. 'Don't eat eggplant or walnuts. They are bad for your liver.' That was all Juan Carlos had remembered from the last reading.

Seated at the table were his future family, Tanat, a feng shui master, and another maw doo who specialized in reading skulls and faces, though he'd recently branched out, entering the amulet business. Marisa thought her brother's future mother-in-law had put together the equivalent of a movie star's complement of trainer, nutritionist, and hairdresser. They had come together for one last examination of the Spanish brother and sister. Marisa and Juan Carlos had grown up in Catalan culture; they could, in a way, understand the values, traditions, and love of family shown by the Thais. A vapor trail of superstition hung above the table, streaking the conversations with senti-ments from an old, traditional culture. For a moment, she almost felt at home. But that feeling passed and a more disturbing picture snapped into focus.

Several close friends of the bride's father stared into their menus as waiters hovered, ready to take their orders. They joked and laughed, stretching out the time. But despite the laughter, there was an undertone of seriousness. A lot was at stake: power, family, and influence. Marriage was a serious matter. Running for parliament was a serious and dangerous matter, too. They watched Marisa smoking as if they'd never seen a woman smoke before. It didn't bother her. She drew in another lungful and slowly exhaled.

When Marisa studied her future sister-in-law's features, she could detect what had been transplanted, softened, and made more elegant from her father's face. Somporn's face next to his daughter looked more like a first draft, a beta version of what would be realized in his children. Kalya's face had certain echoes from the father, but Marisa concluded that she had drawn more from her mother. Niran, her brother, sitting next to the mother, had her full lips and large eyes. A younger version of his father, he fiddled with a gold cigarette lighter. The whole family had been smiling since they'd arrived with their entourage of gurus, courtiers, bodyguards, advisers, and relatives.

'When I am elected, I will help my people,' said Somporn.

Somporn had no policies to sell; he felt he didn't need them. He showed up at gatherings with his funny stories and lots of good jokes, and he relied on his wit and faux upcountry charm act to ensure victory in his district. He understood Thais voted for people they liked, and to be liked, a candidate must have a good heart. And that was all that mattered. Pundits said Somporn's manner reminded them of Thaksin, the old prime minister who had been overthrown in a coup but had shown resilience in a political comeback. The campaign act left Marisa cold; she couldn't find a flicker of insincerity when he uttered such pronouncements. That was the most disturbing discovery: a politician who had convinced himself that pursuing his self-interest advanced the interest of the public.

Lawan, the mother, solid and determined. looked regal with her narrow mouth and intense eyes that constantly surveyed the people at the table. She had a clean jawline, though age had softened it. An early version of that jaw had been inherited by the bride. The resemblance was striking, as if the template of her jaw had been molded onto Kalya's face. Marisa imagined those features appearing on the faces of Juan Carlos's children. What got passed on was success; what got left behind died or disappeared into an unmarked grave.

Leaning to one side, the bride's mother nodded and stared at Juan Carlos and Marisa as she listened to a running commentary from the maw doo, who nervously fingered the amulet hanging from a gold chain around his neck.

The Chinese claimed the discovery in ancient times of the science of determining people's essential characteristics from their faces. Lawan asked the guru, who was buttering a piece of bread, about her future grandchildren's lives behind faces much like that of Juan Carlos. The next generation was a constant worry for the Chinese. She had an air of quiet resolution, a firmness of purpose. Lawan left little doubt that she was the power behind her husband's empire and had urged him to run in the election.

The bodyguards and retainers gave her special deference, as if to publicly demonstrate her status as someone who was more than just Somporn's wife. The Somporns had carefully guarded their daughter. A good marriage was everything: legacy, political advantage, and a merger. Somporn had a habit of talking up populist programs. But the family's contempt for the peasant class was only exceeded by their fear that one night they might wake up and find a horde around their beds with long knives ready to slit their throats. That fear had propelled Somporn into the political limelight. It was a fear renewed as he looked at Juan Carlos, the farang, who sat across the table smiling, unaware of what was at stake.

'Juan tells us that you work for the UN,' said Lawan, the sunlight catching the huge diamond on the finger of her right hand.

'I work on a children and women trafficking project.'

Lawan smiled and nodded; a position at the UN conferred, amongst the Thais, a high status upon the person. She seemed to like that Marisa was an official, brushing over the nature of her assignment. It was the position that mattered.

'You look like your brother,' said Somporn to Marisa.

'We're twins,' said Juan Carlos.

'Who is older?' asked Lawan. An important question for Thais, whose informal address depended on whether someone was older or younger.

'I am older,' said Marisa.

'By five minutes,' said Juan Carlos.

The table huddled as whispers shot around in Thai.

Having a twin brother who looked better than her had generated a long trail of comments since childhood. Each of them had, in their way, suffered from the comparison, and the two had been drawn closer together as a result. She was critical of herself. Marisa believed that she was two degrees short of beautiful; that shortfall dropped her into the high end of ordinary beauty. The extra two degrees had instead gone to her brother. A man should never be more beautiful than a woman; it violated a fundamental law of nature.

It wasn't the twin status that had drawn the group's collective attention, however. Juan Carlos and Kalya were holding hands beneath the table, fooling no one. What would voters think if Somporn's daughter were found to be holding hands with a farang? One of Somporn's advisers whispered in his ear. Somporn continued to smile and nodded. So long as the hand-holding occurred out of sight, under the table, like much of what took place in Thai society, there would be no problem. He was confident that his daughter knew the rules and understood the sensitivities of Thai voters as an election approached.

The wedding banquet discussion was suspended as everyone studied the banquet menu. There would be a ten-course Chinese meal with shark's fin soup. They were to be married in a country where the soup wouldn't cause a problem for a politician, and bits of dead shark would enhance his reputation. Tanat insisted that exactly 503 guests should be invited. But the number of friends and family exceeded Tanat's auspicious number by twofold. It was an election year. Somporn asked him to reconsider. They compromised on 888 guests. An independent-film-sized budget had been set aside for an acclaimed Dutch filmmaker who had been following Juan Carlos and Kalya. The couple had been filmed shopping in designer shops in Siam Paragon, walking on the beach in Hua Hin, where the family had a seaside mansion, riding horses, playing golf, and dancing at a disco. All of this footage was being edited down by the film-maker and would later be indicted on the captive audience of 888 guests before they were served any food. The wedding would be a ngan chang – an elephant event, one to display the status, wealth, and power of the family.

'Ever since we watched Dr. House on a fifty-inch flat-screen, I can't look at a regular TV without thinking I'm sneaking a look through a peephole.' Lawan laughed at her own joke.

Kalya smiled and immediately changed the subject. 'Mother, it's not the size of the screen. It's the quality of the program.'

Marisa lit another cigarette from the last burning ember of her previous one.

'I predict you will have lung problems in later life,' said Tanat.

That didn't take a fortune-teller to guess. 'I'll take my chances,' said Marisa.

Kalya's parents, at first, had been disappointed that Juan Carlos was a farang; in many ways, the love match represented a wasted opportunity for business, political, and social advancement. They had hoped to marry her into another well-connected clan, one that could deliver a block of voters from the northeast region of the country. Kalya had given them no option but to accept her choice. They were still adjusting to a middle-class farang becoming part of their family.

Kalya tried to make small talk with Marisa. 'Juan Carlos told me you've also been a journalist.'

Somporn leaned forward. 'You have done many things for someone so young,' he said.

'You might consider working for the family,' said Kalya, who was trying a two-for-one deal. She couldn't help herself.

'I'm happy in my work. I like to think I'm making a difference.'

One of the associates whispered, 'Communist.'

'Franco did his best to wipe out our culture, our way of life. He failed. In Catalonia you find proud people who never forget their heritage.' The table fell silent. A long-tail boat roared past, filling the conversational gap.

Marisa's rescue came in the form of a waiter. Young and handsome, dressed in a white shirt and black trousers, he drew attention away from her as he approached with a small whiteboard with Somporn's name written on it in blue marker. He rang a small bell as he wound his way down to the terrace level. One of Somporn's luk nongs spotted the boss's name, leaned over, and nodded toward the waiter. Somporn excused himself from the table and followed the waiter into the hotel lobby. Marisa got up at the same time. 'If you'll excuse me, I need to use the restroom.'

At the bell captain's desk, Somporn was handed the phone. His mistress was on the other end. 'Why did you turn off your phone? Where are you?'

He cupped his hand around the phone and explained that he was at the Oriental Hotel hosting a party for his daughter and her future husband. The mia noi went silent and then screamed at him. He held the phone away from his ear.

'You say I'm important, but you don't care about me.'

'It's not like that. Of course I care. But I need to do this for my daughter.'

'What about me?'

There was always the same outstanding question:

What about me? A question those in his political party asked as well. And his wife, and his daughter. It was a universal question that boomed through his dreams.

Marisa saw him in the lobby talking on the phone. He was turned away so he didn't see her as she walked toward him. She heard him whispering into the phone for understanding. It didn't take any imagination to know he was having a clandestine conversation with a woman.

When he turned around and saw her standing a foot away, he looked startled but recovered quickly. 'Tomorrow, I can make an appointment. I'll call later once I have my diary to confirm the time.' He handed the phone back to the bell captain.

The mia noi's voice screamed out through space, 'Confirm the time? Remember who you are talking to!'

'Some clients can be awkward,' he said.

'So can most women,' she replied, smiling.

Somporn thought for a moment. 'You are a clever woman. Like your brother, you will become part of our family. All families have secrets. I'm certain you'll agree that we must always keep our secrets.'

'A man with a secret leads a secret life,' she said.

Once they'd returned to the table, Somporn acted as it nothing had occurred. He launched into a politician-like speech on all of the wonderful attributes of his future son-in-law. He disclosed his post-wedding plans for Juan Carlos. He would be appointed as vice president of international marketing. With nine languages and five dialects, Juan Carlos was exactly the kind of man who could guide the company to new ventures abroad. And what was an empire without expansion plans? Either advance or retreat. And Juan Carlos had come along just as Somporn was planning the advance of his commercial interests in Europe. If his political party, the Love of Motherland, formed the next government, Somporn had been promised the foreign ministry. Juan Carlos would be an asset if that were to occur.

Having a farang son-in-law wouldn't have been Somporn's obvious first choice, but he had grown to like Juan Carlos, his charm, openness, and elegance, and sometimes he forgot he was a foreigner. He was able to see the range of possibilities that Juan Carlos represented for business and politics, and concluded that the man had the potential to be useful.

He had paid Juan Carlos his highest compliment on the ride to the hotel, when he turned to his future son-in-law and said, 'I don't think of you as a farang. You are a Thai.'

Juan Carlos had swelled up with pride. 'I am happy to hear your words.'

He had said this in perfect Thai. Those riding in the car floated high on the emotions of the moment. Somporn nodded in his likable, friendly manner. It had been settled. Juan Carlos would become part of the family.

CHAPTER 16

After work Colonel Pratt changed into his civilian clothes, picked up his tenor sax case, and headed for a gig. He was trying not to think about the scout from the Java Jazz Festival who would be in the audience to listen to him play. He focused on his driving. By the time he turned into the soi for Saxophone, he was no longer nervous. Out of the corner of his eye he saw a red Mazda RX-8, stopped his car, and rolled down his window for a closer look. It was parked in a choice spot near the entrance to Saxophone. Pratt parked his car some distance away and walked back to have another look at the Mazda. Resting the sax case on the ground, he squatted down and made a mental note of the plate number. A Thai man in jeans and a polo shirt emerged from the shadows. He positioned himself between Pratt and the car, asking, 'Is there a problem?'

He was one of the unofficial security guards who extorted twenty baht so the parked car wouldn't be damaged – an old protection scam. He cleared his throat, about to ask Pratt to move on.

'Do you know the owner of this car?' asked Pratt.

The question stopped the guard cold. 'His name?'

'Yes, his name.'

The guard said that he didn't know the name but the owner was a musician who played in a jazz band. A Ray Charles riff filtered out to the street. The keyboard player was pretty good, thought Pratt.

'What's he look like?' asked Pratt. He showed him a police badge.

The guard strained in the half-light to see the object Pratt held out. The guard's mouth narrowed as Pratt's police ID registered. He stiffened up, eyes wide, mouth going slow motion with nothing coming out. Pratt waited a few moments until the guard found his voice and described the driver: paper-thin arms and legs; long, curly black hair; and wearing a baseball cap and sunglasses.

'And he carries a cheap, ugly bag,' he added, as if that were a crime for a man driving a Mazda RX-8. The guard couldn't figure out how a new, ultra-expensive sports car went with a beat-up suitcase. But Pratt understood: the musician knew his audience. His image inside the bar was one thing, and outside the bar, something else. Each required its own branding and symbols of success.

'You need anything else, you just ask,' said the guard, walking back into the shadows. His heart was still thumping; he couldn't wait to get away from the cop who had unintentionally humiliated him.

The Skytrain screamed past overhead. Colonel Pratt waited outside a couple of minutes until he saw Calvino looking down from the walkway. Calvino waved. Pratt watched as his friend disappeared down the pedestrian walkway to the stairs. The Victory Monument gleamed in floodlights – a monument to the glory of what had gone down in some history books as a military loss but politicians had found a way to massage into a victory in what was largely a forgotten war. Colonel Pratt walked around the Mazda, considering why governments erected such structures. They built them to represent sacrifice and the warriors who had made it, all the while promising voters that under their leadership no one would ever be asked to embrace hardship. They called elections, using their victories to make money. That was the real monument they were committed to building.

When Calvino reached the street, he hurried along the broken footpath between the encroaching food stalls. A couple of vendors in their greasy aprons were packing up for the night, stacking up the plastic stools and tables. Other merchants, mostly young women, called out to Calvino as he passed their tables, stacked with neat rows of T-shirts, panties, socks, sexy skirts and blouses, and children's toys. He spotted a stuffed teddy bear and bought it for Ratana's kid. The last of the food stalls offered a special price for the last two fishheads. He gave the fish vendor a shake of the head. Calvino found Colonel Pratt standing beside the red sports car.

'What'd you buy?'

Calvino showed him the stuffed bear.

'It's from China. Be careful of the button eyes.'

Calvino looked at the stuffed bear and sighed. He'd forgotten about the reports of dangerous chemicals used in Chinese toys.

'It's like what my wife says, "It's the thought that counts."' said Colonel Pratt.

'What's the story on the Mazda?' Since Calvino had returned to Bangkok, this was the third red sports car they had tracked down.

'So far there is no story.'

'Could this be our man?' said Calvino. He was thinking that he should buy shares in the company. The other car owners had alibis; they hadn't been anywhere near Pattaya the night Nongluck had died.

Pratt shrugged his shoulders and shifted his sax case. 'I'm on soon. Afterwards, we can check out the driver. I can't stay for more than one set. I have an early-morning appointment.' 'Early morning' and 'sax player' were rarely found in the same sentence. Great sax players ate breakfast in the afternoon. A life of morning appointments was everything jazz wailed against.

But that was the political part of Colonel Pratt's job. Meetings, conferences, and seminars had become more frequent with the elections. Fear of violence and disorder had the brass worried, exchanging information and gossip about who was up and whose star was fading. The death of a ying in Pattaya hadn't registered on anyone's list of important matters. Colonel Pratt believed that she'd been murdered and Calvino had been set up for the fall. He kept his investigation low-key. Plugged into internal intelligence, he was aware how much the election had distracted his superiors. They were far more interested in controlling hired hit men on the political party payrolls than looking for the killer of a woman in Pattaya. His knowledge of how the department really worked gave him an advantage.

Colonel Pratt made himself appear busy enough on routine police matters to be largely left alone. He knew the game and it had come in handy. The two men who'd died in the motorcycle crash on Soi 33 had given him some extra work, but he had it under control. His boss had put him on an internal subcommittee to prepare rebuttals to the program of reforms promised by one party. It was a job he didn't want. The fact that he agreed with many of the reforms, especially the ones aimed at ending corruption and nepotism, was something he kept to himself. A lot of other officers agreed with him and were keeping quiet, not wanting to tip their hand; it was too early to know who would win the election.

Calvino circled the Mazda as if he owned it, the march of an owner admiring a trophy. Out of a shallow pool of neon light, a bleached-blond Thai woman in her twenties appeared, wearing tight white jeans and a pink cowboy shirt with white piping on the sleeves and collar. She smiled at Calvino, thinking that he and the car belonged together.

She stood with her hands on her hips. 'Hi. I'm Amy.'

Apple, Ann, and Rose, he'd heard. This, though, was the first Thai Amy he'd met. She had woven colored strips of tinsel into her hair, wore a loosely knotted necktie printed with yellow happy faces, and carried what looked like a legit Prada bag. It was as if Calvino had been hit by a stun gun. He stood in the road with a sappy grin on his face.

'You wanna drink, Amy?' he asked her.

'Nice car,' she said, looking at Colonel Pratt before turning her smile on to Calvino. 'Nice jacket.'

Calvino flashed a smile. The jacket is doing its thing, he thought. He winked at the Colonel. But it wasn't so much the jacket as the smile and clean clothes that signaled a willingness to spend money.

Colonel Pratt looked at the ying, then at Calvino, and having sized up the situation went inside Saxophone. 'Catch you inside,' he said.

It was just the two of them on the soi.

'Hey, would you like a teddy bear?'

He held it out, and she squinted in the half light. 'It won't bite. But to be on the safe side, don't lick the eyes.'

She grinned, taking the bear. 'He's so cute. Where you from?' she asked. She had stepped into the light leaking into the street from the half-open entrance door.

'New York.'

A closer look showed the plastic surgery jobs on her nose and chin. The breasts looked like they'd been sculpted from a giant ball of wax. She had a small diamond stud in one nostril, a starter gem looking for a man to step up the size. The overall package created the impression of a ying who was comfortable prowling for Mr Right at a jazz club. She'd thrown a line out, had Calvino hooked, and all she had to do was slowly reel him in.

'Are you on holiday?'

'I was on holiday, but things got turned around. I've been looking for a way to get back to my holiday.'

'Good goal.'

'I could use some help.'

She laughed. 'That may be the worst pickup line I've ever heard.'

Calvino looked at his fingernails, then his feet. 'It was pretty lame. So why not let me make it up to you and buy you a drink?'

She looked him over. 'You're slick. But do you like jazz?'

'I'm crazy about jazz.'

Amy rewarded him with a smile. How did men live in countries where their sex lives died when they still had another half-century to go? Calvino asked himself. How did they stop themselves from going suicidal or unbearably lonely?

'I'm crazy about cars. Red and fast,' she said, looking at the Mazda RX-8.

'I like it too,' said Calvino.

'But it's not yours,' she said.

He flashed a crooked grin. 'Any idea who owns it?'

She smiled. 'Be nice and maybe I'll tell you.'

'I'll be nice. Promise,' said Calvino, knowing this was going to cost him more than a stuffed bear.

Amy smiled as she reeled him in. He held the door for her and then walked in behind her. Sometimes a man knew when he was being played, but Calvino didn't care. What mattered was that he was also playing her. She had information he wanted.

They walked into Saxophone knowing pretty much that a deal was in progress but the fine print was still being worked out.

Calvino and the ying threaded through the crowd with a haze of blue smoke destroying visibility. They followed a waitress through the standing-room-only room, avoiding elbows and heavy trays filled with beer. She gave him a menu and pointed to two stools at a long, curved wooden counter right in front of the band. Calvino was facing the stage. The volume was cranked up loud enough that it seemed to be absorbed and rebroadcast from the throat and chest. The crowd, whacked-out on drugs and booze, moved to the music. The decibel level was a notch away from rupturing eardrums. No one seemed to mind. The music thundered, shaking the floor.

The waitress couldn't hear his order. He tried twice before mouthing the word, 'Tiger.' She knew

201

it was a brand of beer. Amy ordered Johnnie Walker Black Label – an entire bottle, with ice and mixers. He had offered a drink and she'd ordered for an entire party. After the waitress left, she pressed her cell phone to her ear and told the person on the other end that she wasn't waiting outside; she was inside and sitting at the bar directly in front of the stage. 'The best seats in the house,' she said.

'What's your name again?' shouted Calvino over the music.

She rolled her eyes, 'Amy. You don't remember?' she asked. She set the bear on the counter, facing the band.

He raised an eyebrow. He'd never had a good record with yings using farang names – or Apple, Anne, or Benz. The front end of the alphabet had usually proved a huge disappointment. He regretted having forgotten her name, but it was too late. She had already written him off as a loser, which she signaled by orphaning the stuffed bear. Spending a night with a ying named Amy had narrowed to the same range of possibilities that his night spent in Pattaya with two police officers had held.

Calvino followed Amy's eyes to the band. Assembled on a worn red-carpeted stage, the five musicians were giving it all they had. The lead guitar player attacked his electric guitar as if he and the guitar were on fire. The musicians jammed: guitars, keyboard, and drums taking a riff one direction, doubling back, and then taking off on a new high note. The guitar player with black kinky hair, gold earrings, and a deep, throaty voice, sang as the keyboard player jumped in a beat late. The packed bar watched him dance across the stage.

In the upper balcony, which wrapped around a hundred and eighty degrees, heads peered down at the stage. On a shelf above the wall behind the stage, under a layer of dust and spiderwebs, were faded album sleeves from Ray Charles and Louis Armstrong. Behind the stage a four-year-old girl dressed in a frilly dress with silver glitter in her hair danced on a table. With her mother's arms wrapped around her waist, the girl looked like part of a show-business act. Next to them was Colonel Pratt. He nodded at Calvino as he removed his saxophone from the case and pulled the leather strap around his neck. He let the instrument rest against his chest as he waited, catching the eye of the man seated beside Calvino. The smartly dressed Asian man nodded at the Colonel, saluting him by holding up a bottle of Tiger beer. He told Calvino that he was a scout sent by the Java Jazz Festival to see if a Thai police colonel playing the sax might be worked into next year's program. Pratt failed to mention that his gig was a rehearsal. Calvino smiled at the Colonel.

After he had looked the place over, Calvino's attention returned to Amy, or whatever her name was, and he reached out to touch her hand. He stopped, though, before making contact; it would have interrupted her eye-lock with the guitar player at center stage. He looked like a half-starved bird flapping its wings, jerky on its feet, head moving side to side as he worked the struts on the guitar. Amy sipped her Johnnie Walker Black and raised it to him. He returned her smile. By the end of the second set, three of Amy's friends had arrived, and Amy had written her phone number on a Tiger beer coaster and slipped it to the guitar player.

'Remember the red sports car?' Calvino whispered in her ear.

Amy turned away from her friends, who had helped themselves to the bottle of scotch. 'That's him,' she said. 'The guy who owns the Mazda.'

She nodded at the guitar player in the middle. Colonel Pratt had gone onstage and stood a couple of feet away while the band played on. Calvino tried to imagine the birdlike creature throwing Nongluck off the balcony of the hotel. He had rarely seen anyone with less muscle tone. But in the heat of an argument it wouldn't take much muscle to toss forty-three kilos off a balcony. It could have happened that way, Calvino told himself.

Colonel Pratt's eyes were closed as he played a Charlie Parker piece, his cheeks puffed out as if floating to the level where dreams are made. Onstage with the saxophone strapped around his neck, he didn't look remotely like a cop. He slowly moved the length of the stage, his head bobbing, stopping for a moment, bending his knees, arching his back as he hit a high note. Calvino had seen him play many times before but never quite in a performance like this one. Pratt's lungs and body had channeled Charlie Parker and inside that envelope of bliss, the Colonel had gone over to some place Charlie Parker was still playing. Whatever world Pratt had been transported to, he carried the audience along with him. He had the Jakarta scout tapping the palm of his hand against the edge of the counter. No one in the crowded room talked; no one took their eyes off Pratt and his saxophone; pure emotion and impulse poured from his instrument.

After the final number, Pratt and the band bowed to a standing ovation. A new band came on as they left. The Jakarta scout signaled a thumbs-up to Colonel Pratt as he walked offstage. The mother with her frilly-dressed daughter came onstage; they were part of the new act. The mother sang; the kid sang and danced. Pratt came back to the counter with the guitar player, who held the beer coaster with Amy's phone number written on it. He looked like a garuda, a mythical bird, swooping down with talons exposed. Calvino looked at the guitar player and then at Colonel Pratt. 'He owns the red sports car.' The information had set him back a bottle of scotch.

The guitar player leaned forward, bracing himself against the bar, joking with Amy and her friends. Colonel Pratt asked if he might have a word with him outside. Calvino had gone ahead and was standing by the sports car when Colonel Pratt and the Birdman, also known as Nop, came out the door.

'Nice car,' said Calvino, leaning against the side.

'Were you in Pattaya last Tuesday night?' asked Colonel Pratt.

The Birdman crunched his mouth into a pout, as if he had to think hard to recall where he was on Tuesday. 'I might have been. Why are you asking?'

Colonel Pratt showed the Birdman his badge. 'What hotel did you stay in?'

'I stayed with a friend,' he said, no longer looking cocky and strutting. Nop was becoming another kind of bird.

'That's not what I asked. What was the name of the hotel?'

'I can't keep them straight. One of the hotels on Beach Road.'

'You stayed with a woman?'

'What if I did?'

'What was her name?'

'I can't.'

'Can't what?'

'Tell you or she'd kill me,' said the Birdman.

'Have you ever killed anyone?' asked Calvino.

The Birdman winced. 'Man, are you crazy? Why would I kill someone?'

Calvino stretched his arms. 'You don't strike me as panya nim,' he said.

Being called stupid or soft in the head by a farang wasn't something the Birdman liked, but given the circumstances he had little choice in the matter.

'There's nothing wrong with my head,' he said.

'Khun Nop, we can always go to the station and check that out,' said Colonel Pratt. He was always pleased when Calvino brought a piece of Thai out like a fast right jab, a verbal flurry that propelled his Thai listener against the ropes. In this case the Colonel thought that his friend's assessment of the Birdman was right on the mark. He looked more like a Nop hanging on a thread than a Birdman ready to control an audience.

CHAPTER 17

Colonel Pratt never arrived at Calvino's office without some small gift for Ratana's baby. Manee, the Colonel's wife, bought clothes, toys, and food, making certain her husband was well-stocked. This time, the Colonel arrived with a hand puppet, a golden-velvet duck with green eyes and a red cloth tongue. Manee had picked it up at Siam Paragon. It had been gift wrapped. He handed it to Ratana before kneeling down beside the playpen and looking through the mesh at the babies. Unlike Calvino, he never had any trouble spotting John-John.

Ratana looked at the heavy silver wrapping paper until Calvino said, 'There's something inside.' She slid a letter opener into the end and carefully folded back the paper. She slipped her fingers into the pockets for the upper and lower jaw of the duck. 'John-John will love it. Tell Khun Manee I like it very much.' She pulled the puppet off her hand and handed it to the Colonel. 'You show him.'

Colonel Pratt moved the duck's head from side to side as the baby's eyes followed the movement. 'Have you eaten yet?'

Ratana smiled with delight. The baby's legs kicked and a line of slobber rolled down one corner of his mouth. 'He loves it,' she said.

Calvino sat on the edge of Ratana's desk. 'She's right,' he said.

But for Ratana, nothing could ever be as simple as pure, spontaneous enjoyment; there had to be some underlying omen expressed in the baby's reaction. 'Last life, he rose from his sleep from the quacking of a duck as the house was on fire. He would have died. But a duck saved him,' she said.

'Or he just likes cute puppets,' said Calvino.

Colonel Pratt removed the hand puppet and gave it to Ratana. 'You try it.'

She slipped on the puppet and bent over the playpen. Her son kicked his feet and waved his hands like a turtle trying to right itself. The gravity of motherhood had pulled Ratana into a world where the child was everything; each act, decision, or thought started and finished with the child. Calvino tried not to feel excluded from her new world, but he couldn't help himself. He was happy that she finally had what every Thai woman wished for: motherhood. To become the mother goddess was to have achieved a vindication, to have climbed to a sacred platform and claimed a throne.

'The Colonel's going to the Java Jazz Festival,' said Calvino.

Ratana's eyes widened.

'It's a long shot,' said Colonel Pratt, displaying no emotion.

'That scout loved you. The audience loved you.'

Ratana smiled, 'And we love you, too.'

Colonel Pratt walked ahead to Calvino's side of the office and sat down with his briefcase, unfastening the clasp.

'If Casey phones, take a message,' Calvino said to Ratana.

'He's already phoned twice this morning.'

He sighed, looking at Colonel Pratt. 'You wouldn't believe this guy.'

Colonel Pratt was prepared to believe just about anything one of Calvino's clients might say or do. The trouble with clients like Casey is that they assume their fee buys the investigator and not just his professional services. Ordering him around fell in that hard place between ego-inflated, know-it-all boss and neurotic father telling a child to finish eating his vegetables or else.

After questioning the Birdman the previous night, the Colonel had gone to his office and done some homework. Now he arranged spreadsheets, photographs, and computer printouts of emails neatly on Calvino's desk. Calvino listened as the Colonel walked him through the chronology. A red sports car had entered the hotel parking lot at 3:39 p.m. and left the following morning at 1:12 a.m., according to the receipts. Calvino placed himself in bed at the time the red Mazda must have sped out of the hotel parking lot. The attendants had a shift change at 6:00 p.m. But the descriptions of the car and driver given by the two attendants had matched. They'd both remembered seeing a red Mazda RX-8 with Bangkok plates and described the driver as a young Thai male who wore sunglasses and a hat like a movie star. No one got a good look at the driver. The police had shown the witnesses a hundred photos of possible suspects. But there had been no positive identification, and this left the investigation stranded in the zone of nowhere.

The cops, who had polished off the liter bottle of vodka, had flopped down and were fast asleep. Colonel Pratt had emailed a JPEG photo of the Birdman to his friend in the Pattaya police, who'd showed it to the underground parking attendants, who were able to ID the Birdman as the driver of the red Mazda.

'They had no doubt in their minds,' said Colonel Pratt.

'That puts him at the hotel, but not in her room.'

'We're working to find hotel staff who worked the day before you arrived and the night she died.'

'I'd start with the staff who upgraded my room.'

Colonel Pratt smiled. 'Where else would we have started?'

Calvino heard the office phone ring. Ratana picked up and told the caller that he wasn't available. He assumed from her chilled, formal tone that she had Casey on the phone.

'Was the Birdman alone in the car?' asked Calvino.

Colonel Pratt nodded. 'No one noticed a passenger

when he arrived. Or the next morning when he left.' He paused as a realization struck him. 'It's hard to miss a passenger in a small car.'

That model of Mazda had enough trunk space for a six-pack of beer, a bag of potato chips, and a few bananas.

Calvino smiled. 'There are a lot of small people in this country, in case you haven't noticed.'

'What are you saying?'

Calvino leaned forward and, fingers gliding over the keyboard, typed in a search phrase for the Birdman, and then turned his computer screen around. 'This guy gets more action than a starting pitcher for the Yankees.'

On the screen were photos of the Birdman with a dozen different women, all of them young and beautiful, with toothpaste-selling smiles and shiny hair.

'Is Nongluck in any of the photos?' asked Colonel Pratt.

Calvino shook his head. 'Doesn't look like it. But not every photo of this guy is on the Internet.'

'We questioned him for three hours, Vincent. According to his story, he wanted to get away from the big city. 'Downtime' is what he called it. A phrase he picked up from a farang. The Pattaya police confirmed that he'd checked in at the Rama Gardens a couple of miles away from your hotel. He parked at your hotel because it was close to the restaurant and the beach. Going to Pattaya alone is strange. He let something slip about a woman, but when I called him on it, he said that he meant he was likely to run into a few fans who wanted to meet him. But that he'd never met Nongluck. He said he had no idea who she was. And as far as Apichart was concerned, he knew him only from the newspapers. There were a lot of people in the hotel that day and night, coming and going. He swore that he'd been on the beach and crossed Beach Road to eat at a restaurant. The people at the restaurant remembered him. He's a celebrity. In the local jazz scene, people know him. And he has no motive.'

'You're saying he's a dead end?'

Colonel Pratt, showing fatigue, feeling a defeat pulling him in a direction he didn't want to go, nodded before he looked away. He searched for the words to explain that a search-and-rescue for a Burmese on a Thai fishing boat had been called off because of a manpower shortage. The men had been reassigned to help with the election. The reality was that law enforcement priorities gave way to political reality. How could he expect a farang, even one who'd been around as long as Calvino, to accept choices that were largely un-acceptable but necessary nonetheless? 'There's no apparent connection to Apichart or Nongluck. At least nothing we've found on the surface. I need a reason to dig beyond that. I don't see one. Do you?'

'What he's saying? He drove alone to Pattaya so he could walk on the beach alone and then eat alone? Does that sound very Thai to you? The Thais are social animals; people who do such things alone are sociopaths.'

'But that's his story, and I don't see any holes in it.'

From Ratana's side of the office partition, Calvino heard the squeak of the hand puppet, silence, and then Ratana's official office voice. The door opened and an aggressive alpha male asked to see Vincent Calvino. Calvino recognized Casey's voice.

Ratana stuck her head around the corner and announced Casey's arrival. Calvino held up two fingers, meaning two minutes. Her kid started crying at the same time. It didn't take long for the other babies to join the wailing chorus, but once she returned to the playpen, the tiny soprano voices shifted from the terror of Wagner to the giggles of Gilbert and Sullivan. Casey must have scared the babies, setting off a panic and distress. He was the quintessential figure that made dogs growl and back up. Calvino felt some sympathy with the kids; something about the enigmatic and angry Casey scared him too.

Colonel Pratt had started to put the documents back into his briefcase.

'What's the baseline? Are they putting Nongluck's death down as a suicide?' asked Calvino.

'It doesn't necessarily mean it's a suicide. It's a wrongful death under suspicious circumstances. Unless we get something more to go on, Vincent, there's not a lot anyone can do.' Nongluck's death was looking more and more like one of those unsolved cases that were swallowed into a black hole called 'open and unresolved.' There wasn't much to connect Calvino to the death. Pratt said that finding the sports car in the hotel parking lot wasn't necessarily evidence of the musician's involvement in the wrongful death. The case had splintered into many pieces, and there was no apparent way to fit them together.

'Please tell him Casey's here and it's urgent,' said Casey.

Colonel Pratt glanced at Calvino. Calvino shrugged his shoulders and shook his head.

'Is execution done on Cawdor?' said Casey in a loud voice.

'What does that mean?' asked Calvino.

'It means he knows a little Shakespeare,' said Colonel Pratt.

This hadn't been a side of Casey that Calvino had seen before.

Colonel Pratt finished putting the photographs and documents in his briefcase. He started to leave Calvino's office but found Casey blocking the narrow passage into the reception area. Casey wore his baseball hat and aviator glasses, with his hands in his pockets, chewing gum.

'"There's no way to read a man's mind by looking at his face. I trusted Cawdor completely,"' Colonel Pratt quoted Duncan's speech in *Macbeth*.

'The king in *Macbcth* said that.' A certain pride

215

was in his voice. 'I heard that you liked Shakespeare,' said Casey.

'Which makes me ask why, with such good intelligence sources, you need the services of a private investigator?'

Casey didn't like the question. His jaw pumped up and down as he chewed the gum. The Colonel had upset him in some strange way.

'Colonel, I'll phone you later this afternoon,' said Calvino. The two men continued an awkward stare down before Casey stepped aside and let Colonel Pratt walk through. Ratana hovered near the playpen like a mother hen. She had the duck hand puppet on and tried as best she could to entertain her son. Her Donald Duck aria sputtered and died. The babies continued unconsoled in a tonality colored by their boredom and listlessness until Calvino couldn't hear himself think. Calvino heard the door close behind the Colonel. He returned, brushing his fingers through his hair, wondering at what point he'd start pulling out his hair, and sat down hard at his desk. He remembered how, the night before, Pratt had fused music and poetry on the stage. But that had been yesterday's performance and he was back on the ground as a cop, in a world with a different beat where the poetry was written as tragedy.

'He's your fucking friend. Big deal,' said Casey. 'He knows a little Shakespeare like I know a little Thai. But I didn't come here to talk about your colonel. I want to know what you found out about

216

Somporn's whore,' said Casey. He spat out the gum, balled it between his forefinger and thumb, and then pulled a piece of paper from Calvino's desk. Sticking the gum inside, he crumpled the paper and tossed it at the wastebasket, missing.

This client wasn't much for pleasantries and wanted to get straight down to business. He was one of those guys who had a genius for creating an urgent, supercharged atmosphere. 'That was a senior police officer you stared down,' said Calvino. 'That's not a good thing to do in this country.'

'Colonel, general, they're all the same to me. I stopped being impressed by that shit in about 1993. So save any lectures about how important a Thai cop is for another client.' Casey rubbed his perpetual three-day-old beard and waited for Calvino. 'What have you got for me? You've done the surveillance, right?'

Calvino ignored the jab like a professional boxer bobbing to one side, instantly recovering as if no serious punch had been thrown.

'Have you come across a jazz guitar player named Nop?' Calvino remembered that this was the Birdman's real name and how his real nickname didn't quite capture the full image of the man.

Casey looked perplexed. 'I don't know what the fuck you're talking about.'

'What about a Thai woman named Nongluck? Or a businessman named Apichart? Do you know them?'

'What is this? Twenty questions? I don't know any Thai woman with luck in her name. Or anyone named Dope who plays the guitar. And who is this Thai businessman? What did you say his name was? Applecart? Never heard of him.'

Casey had a better memory for Shakespeare than for Thai names. His nasty attitude combined with impaired pronunciation made his attempts to instill fear more difficult. He stared at Calvino as if he had a growing suspicion that Calvino was trying to spin him, make him dizzy and disorientated with references to some degenerate hippie guitar player, a whore, and a businessman. He'd strung together a bunch of civilians and thrown them at him. He didn't like for anyone who hadn't worn a uniform to talk to him that way.

Calvino brushed off the bad-tempered response. Surly was about as happy as someone like Casey ever got on a good day. There was no point fighting against a mountain of anger and regret. 'Nop. I call him the Birdman. He has something going with Cat. Maybe you know something about their relationship, since you have all these sources on the street?' In most cases, it would involve a complex web with a trail leading to money. Maybe, Calvino told himself, there was a more philosophical dimension since Cat had her source of funding, and the Birdman had forged a private empire of relationships for special entertainment.

'They're fucking each other?' Casey was either a good actor, pulling down his aviator glasses to register his surprise, or he'd been caught off guard.

Calvino smiled, thinking that this was the kind of philosophy he understood. 'I can't confirm that. They could be holding meditation classes together or arranging flowers for Somporn's campaign. But probably not.'

The Birdman had been turning up in all the wrong places. He'd been at the hotel where Nongluck had gone over the balcony and at Cat's condo. Had parked his red Mazda sports car in the underground hotel parking lot in late afternoon. Calvino figured that even for a musician, Birdman got around troubled women a little too frequently to immediately write it off as coincidence.

It crossed Casey's mind that he might have underestimated this investigator. That was both a good thing and a bad thing for his plans. He started with what Calvino already knew: Cat had been going behind Somporn's back. It had fucked up the hit, but at least he could factor a jazz musician boyfriend into the equation.

'I want to know if Somporn's still seeing her,' said Casey.

'She's meeting him again on Thursday.'

'You're certain about that? That's very close to the election.' His eyes narrowed, his jaw clenched as he waited for the answer. 'I need to be certain. Not a maybe, or "she's thinking about it."' When a man spent too much of his life behind enemy lines, all he could think about was the certainty of the escape route and the men he needed to get him through that passage.

Calvino stood up, turned, and looked out his window at the soi. A van was delivering office paper to the translation service on the ground floor. It looked like business was good.

He turned back to Casey. 'It's not like he's made an appointment for open-heart surgery. She's a mistress. He might have a conflict and cancel. Maybe she got her period. You know that happens every month, right? Or he might have a press conference or a speech to make. Any number of things can happen. From what I know, they plan to see each other late morning on Thursday.'

'You got a tap on her phone?' Like an animal licking an old wound that would never heal, Casey never let up the pressure.

'I'm listening to her every word.'

Casey seemed tone-deaf to irony. In a way. Calvino envied him the simplicity of his literal world. 'You hear anything different concerning their next love fest, you phone me. How much do I owe you?' Casey pulled out a wad of cash. It was his way of dealing with civilians; they were a cash-and-carry crowd who'd howl at the moon if they thought it would cause money to rain from the sky. The men he'd served with lived by a code other than money. It was called honor. Calvino wrote down 'forty thousand baht' on a sheet of paper and showed it to him.

'Give me an extra fifty baht for the paper you threw away. I have to print it out again.'

Casey handed him forty thousand in thousand-baht notes plus a one-hundred-baht note. 'Keep the change.'

Calvino heard Ratana sigh with relief once Casey had left. He walked to her side of the office. She had Colonel Pratt's duck puppet on her hand. She pointed it at the door. 'Jai dam,' she said in a Donald Duck voice. 'That is a very jai dam man.'

He thought about Colonel Pratt's immediate reaction to Casey standing in front of him, chewing gum, looking hostile. He liked that the Colonel had nailed him to the floor – 'There's no way to read a man's mind by looking at his face.' It was one of Pratt's talents, matching Shakespeare to the real-world petty thugs and big-time villains.

Ratana had nailed Casey in her own very Thai way. A black heart was a condition Thais wished to avoid in others. It meant a person who had a capacity for evil, and anyone who got in the path of such a person paid a price. The people around me are good judges of character, Calvino thought. They also warned me against sending a coffin to Apichart. He promised himself to listen better.

The babies had been brought under control, the silence ruptured now only by an occasional cough or fart. Whatever instinctive threat Casey had brought into the room had vanished. Ratana held John-John, hugged him, kissed his cheeks, and sniffed his neck.

There were clients Ratana didn't like. There were others who made her skin crawl. Even one or two she thought had been overshadowed with coldness and embroiled in a world of deception from which they desperately sought escape. Casey, she thought, was in the unique category of men who showed no sign of wishing to escape from their secret universe.

As he sat back at his desk, Calvino put on his leather shoulder harness with the .38 police special snug inside. There was something about Casey that he'd left behind him: a man with self-inflicted wounds, a casualty of beliefs and action that were on a course to destroy him. Most of Calvino's expat clients had something shameful they tried to hide. Calvino understood such feelings as being normal; a tainted reputation was hard to shake off, and when the damaged reputation got out into the expat community, the person was finished. But Casey's wound was deep and jagged. What festered inside was the memory of a murdered son, and Casey's personal redemption – and reputation – depended on his ability to right that injustice, and until that happened, his outrage would eclipse civility, decency, and tolerance.

CHAPTER 18

The beekeeper's daughter, Wan, sat on a plastic stool brushing her hair in front of the mirror, one elbow resting against the edge of the sink. Standing behind her, two other dancers checked their makeup in the mirror. Wan's orange and black striped backpack rested at her feet. Everything she owned was inside it. Like the other yings in the back of the bar, Wan was naked. The natural aversion to nakedness in front of strangers had worn away, and she was no longer self-conscious of a public display of her body. The bar had overcome the native shyness of the country ying and killed it stone dead.

Another ying pushed back the beaded curtain and shouted, 'Farang ma laew!' That was short-hand for Jarrett's having just walked into the bar. Wan's eyes grew large. She glanced at herself in the mirror. It was the moment she had been waiting for. Sitting on the stool, she wondered whether to put on her street clothes and leave, go onstage and dance, or stay and brush her hair and wait for some sign of good fortune.

She decided to let Jarrett decide her fate. He is

a good man, she thought, smiling, putting down her brush. She'd had a feeling he'd be back.

It had been Jarrett's idea to take a break and go out for a drink. Tracer had the feeling that Jarrett had been thinking about her; she was in his system, and it only made sense to go out with him and make certain he didn't get into any trouble. Maybe get himself mistaken for someone else; his history included identity mistakes, and Jarrett and Tracer only rarely brought it up, but that didn't much matter as there were constantly the background reminders, like the *Hua Hin Today* newspaper that Casey had left behind in the condo. The lead story was about an unsolved bombing in Narathiwat, which ran along with a photograph of a smoldering wreckage of a pickup truck.

Reno, the bar owner, ushered them to seats and told the waitress to bring two cold Belgian dark beers for his friends. Jarrett and Tracer eased onto the bench at the far end. This position allowed them to see who came in the door, and their backs were to the wall. Someone would have to look twice to spot them.

Jarrett looked at the yings dancing onstage and didn't see the beekeeper's daughter. 'Don't worry,' said Reno. 'Wan's in the back making herself pretty and waiting for you.'

Two bottles of dark Belgian beer arrived on a tray, and a waitress filled their glasses. Jarrett glanced at the beaded curtain in the back.

'She ain't going anywhere,' said Reno. 'How was she? Another customer swears by her.'

That wasn't something Jarrett wanted to hear. Tracer raised his glass to one of the dancers who stood motionless with one hand grasping the chrome pole, as if she were a performance artist in a state of total stillness. Only she wasn't an artist; she was tired of dancing, and not that many black men came into the bar. She stared as if Tracer were the first one she'd ever seen.

'Wan says you put some crazy idea into her head about going upcountry and raising bees. Apiculture? You gotta be joking.' He said 'apiculture' like it was a dirty word. 'But I told her that didn't sound right; all the bees are dying. And all the honey is in Bangkok. But she said you'd told her to go home. That can't be right. I told her I'd discuss it with her later.'

'There's nothing to discuss. I gave her money and said she should go home.'

The bar owner bit his lip, stroking his moustache, deciding whether Jarrett was being serious. 'You're not one of those guys who falls in love with a bar girl and gets a mission to reform her? After she's worked in the bar, you think she can go back and sleep on a dirt floor, take bucket baths, go to sleep under a bamboo roof, and not go a little nuts?'

'If that's what she wants.'

The bar owner rolled his eyes. 'Man, what she wants is fucking money. And unless she works in the bar, then she ain't gonna have squat. You guys are tourists, so you don't understand anything about these girls. They ain't got anything that you would call an education, but they understand better than most what they need to do to get ahead. Some of these girls make more money in a month than you do. That's the reality. And you want to take away her prime earning years so she can look after bees? How fucking crazy is that?'

Tracer leaned forward. 'I've known Jarrett a lot of years. And nothing about him is crazy. He's careful about what he does. He plans and thinks things out before he acts. If he says the girl wants to go home, then she wants to go home. Cash isn't always the line drive that wins the game.'

'For you, money is the only game,' said Jarrett.

'Yeah, yeah, and that makes me shallow and materialistic,' said Reno. 'Don't believe me? Wait a couple of weeks. She'll be back with bee stings on her ass, asking for her old job back.'

'You wouldn't want to put some money on that?' asked Jarrett.

'How about a hundred dollars?' asked Reno, raising an eyebrow, balancing against the countertop, his weight placed on one elbow. It was a good position for observing the customers and the stage.

'Why not make it interesting? Let's call it a grand. If she's not back in a month, you pay me; if she's back, I'll bring in the money and lay it on the table.'

Reno's eyes bulged, his lower lip disappearing beneath his moustache. 'I like interesting but I don't like extremely interesting. Keep it at a hundred dollars. Maybe you're right. She might become the honey queen of Isan, export the shit to America, and make the Forbes list next year.'

A young woman's head poked out from the beaded curtain and then disappeared. Like a forward scout, one of the yings had been detailed to check on Jarrett and Tracer. But in the ying army the loyalties were never certain. As she stared into the bar, she looked for a soft opening, wondering if she could add Jarrett to her dance card, or whether he was fully committed to Wan. That could only be established after the beekeeper's daughter walked back into the bar with the backpack strapped to her back and Jarrett acknowledged her. Until that moment, technically, under the rules of engagement Jarrett was hers to lose.

As Jarrett leaned forward to get up, the bar owner pressed his hand on Jarrett's shoulder. 'Before you go, I have to ask you something.'

Jarrett stared hard at the bar owner. 'And what would that be?'

'When you get tired of each other, send her back. She's a good kid. Works well with the other girls. I hate to see her go.'

Jarrett stared at him in the half darkness. 'You'll find someone else.'

Reno laughed. 'And so will you.'

★ ★ ★

Jarrett slid out of his seat, crossed the bar, and pushed back the beaded curtains. Inside the backroom, half-naked girls smoked, chatted, put on makeup, read comic books.

Framed in the doorway, Jarrett thought he'd seen this scene before – in a counting room in Cali, Colombia. His skin let him pass as a Latino. His Spanish was good enough to carry on a conversation. He froze; for an instant, it was really as if he were in the Cali counting room. Same people, smells, nakedness; it was happening all over again.

In an old warehouse on a side street was a room lined with gym lockers. Wooden benches with initials carved into the side were stacked with shoes, socks, and ashtrays spilling over. Showers were located behind the lockers, and a solid metal door stood on the opposite side. On the other side of that door had been fifteen naked men and women. The scene had shocked him – so much flesh, like a slaughterhouse. They worked at tables. Some sat on chairs in front of tables; others worked standing up, lifting and stacking. But what at first blush seemed like an orgy had nothing to do with sex.

The naked workers were assigned various tasks in the counting of hundred-dollar bills. They counted one hundred at a time, slipped a band around the stack, put it on a pile, and then counted another hundred notes. When they had a hundred stacks, they loaded them into a box. That was a million dollars. The workroom was piled with boxes. They worked eight-hour shifts, and there were three shifts, twenty-four hours a day. Working naked, they had nowhere to hide a stolen stack of notes. A woman employee had once tried to hide a bundle of hundreds inside her vagina. She'd been caught. They'd marched her into the shower and shot her in the head. No one ever tried to do that again.

The counting room had been on the second floor of a four-story building sheltered behind a fence and trees. Guards watched the entrance, and anyone who didn't belong there was ordered to turn back. Jarrett had ridden in with an operative. The guard looked in, saw his companion, and waved them through. They entered the building from the side and walked up the stairs to the second floor. To the left was a long corridor where security guards in jeans and T-shirts frisked them, took away belts, shoes, trousers, and shirts, and gave them each a paper surgical gown. They dressed in silence.

When they finished each shift, the workers returned to these lockers. That made sense. They'd worked naked together for eight hours; it would be crazy to go all shy about showering and dressing in the same room. The ceiling was one solid mirror, and upstairs, people worked on the other side of the mirror watching, recording on video. The obviousness of the surveillance was likely the point; they wanted people below to know they were being clocked.

The local operative, a thin man not quite thirty, with a goatee and gray eyes, said nothing and walked ahead, opening a door and holding it for Jarrett. He waited until Jarrett was inside and then closed it hard, sealing him inside as if he were in a vault. Fifteen naked men and women kept their heads down. They worked like drones or robots. The workers had mastered a mechanical, precise system, one that could be done in a twilight state of consciousness. All of them were busy working at two long tables. What they were counting had everything to do with sex, but sex had nothing to do with their jobs.

When the big boss came in the door, everyone stopped counting and looked up.

'Mr Lopez, welcome to our house. This is the money that you will be investing for us. I think gold is good. American currency is not worth keeping, you agree? And oil is good. Oil is the new gold. The rest should be put in Euro bonds. We must keep up with inflation. Of course, you have your plan. You work for us, and we only want the best and brightest bean counters – that's a good name – on the payroll. Each and every dollar is precious. No leakage is permitted. Not a single bill goes uncounted, unrecorded.'

That had been his cover. In reality, his intensive one-week training in banking and accounting had summarized key phrases. He'd tried to remember information from a week of tutorials. There'd been material and lectures about cost principle, revenue principle, audits, and GAAP. They'd given him sufficient background so long as the conversation didn't turn too technical. If that happened, he was told to repeat the necessity for following the consistency principle; this principle appealed to the conservative interests of drug dealers who actually knew a great deal about the subject.

The workers had returned to their methodical counting of notes, straightening them, unfolding the corners, smoothing them out the way a mother touches the cheek of a baby. He'd been briefed on Ruis, a low-key, under-the-radar drug lord with a reputation for brutality. The first time he met Jarrett, he asked, 'Remind me, is an Accounting Principles Board Opinion Category A or Category B?'

Jarrett drew in a deep breath and recalled a chart from his lectures.

'APB's opinions are Category A,' he said.

Ruis smiled with welcome to the backroom and slapped him on the back. He squeezed his shoulder. 'Let's get started.'

Ruis's smile faded and Jarrett felt Wan's hand on his shoulder, standing on her toes, sniffing his neck. The Cali counting room had vanished. He found himself where the counting was being done on fingers and toes in the back of a Bangkok bar.

Jarrett emerged from the backroom with Wan dressed in jeans, sneakers, and a T-shirt, her backpack strapped on her back. The yings on the stage, who had been barely moving, squatted down and called for her to come back soon. They didn't want her to forget them. Wan stopped along the way, saying her goodbyes as the bar owner lit a cigar and blew smoke, shaking his head, eyebrows raised. Tracer sat on the opposite side of the stage, watching Jarrett's reaction. It was as if he had locked onto a target and was about to squeeze the trigger. His whole being was focused on the girl and on getting her out of the bar.

'Come on, Wan, you sweet girl, let me buy you one more before you leave,' said Reno.

The beekeeper's daughter put her fingers together as if in prayer and waied him, her head slightly bowed in an act of respect. He had selected a blues song and the singer's voice wailed through the speakers, 'I'm going home.' In the blues someone was always about to go home. But something or someone stood in the way. And everyone in a Bangkok bar, customer and ying alike, listening to the blues had a familiarity with being homesick and accepted that what life delivered up was the promise of hard times.

As she ended her wai, she went around to the side of the bar where Jarrett and Tracer always sat. She turned and smiled at Tracer. The wai to the bar owner was still stuck in Jarrett's throat, fishbone-like. He couldn't swallow it, couldn't cough it up. Her wai had been the kind of deference that Jarrett hated. The same kind that had led her to the bar in the first place, and the last act before she could leave. If she wants to square that circle, let her try, he thought.

Just as there is no easy shot in the field, there is no easy way to get a ying out of her bar. All the conditions had to be right, or the attempt would fail. Failure had consequences that were almost never good. There was rarely a second chance once the first shot had missed the target. Jarrett listened to the music, holding Wan's hand. She squeezed his fingers, looked him in the eye, waiting with eternal patience for him to lead her out of the world of misery, loss, and cruelty. She looked at him as if he were her hero. But he was, he told himself, just another customer listening to a tenor sax hitting a high note.

Tomorrow Jarrett and Tracer would return to the rented condo unit. Their intelligence source had promised Somporn would be visiting his mia noi. Same-place-same-time kind of guy, thought Jarrett. Waters had run every special operation they'd been sent on. Harry Jarrett, Jarrett's father, liked him, and said Waters had something that reminded him of Jack Malone.

While Jarrett had been in his fuguelike state at the back of the bar, Tracer had gone outside and called Mooney, who was bitching like an angry husband about not having Kate back. Tracer promised that the rifle was safe and sound. There had been an unscheduled delay, nothing serious. A blip on the screen, Tracer had told him. He'd seen Jarrett go into one of his haunted states, but he'd always come out and got the job done. Tracer had drunk his beer and wondered whether his partner might open up a little and talk about what was bothering him, but it was easier to get a brass drum out of a metal bucket than to get a closed man to open himself up. Tracer glanced at his watch, getting enough light from the strobes over the dance stage to read the time. He wanted to get back to the condo and turn in for a good night's rest.

Colonel Waters had said they could count on Somporn being at the condo in the morning. 'Be there. Take the target as you find the target. If someone is in the way, take it. Under all circumstances, take the target down.' That was good enough for Jarrett.

In straight talk, if the mistress is in the line of fire and there is no other shot, take the shot.

'Am I clear?' asked Waters.

'Roger that,' said Jarrett.

Paying back Jack sometimes meant going through Jill.

CHAPTER 19

C alvino emerged from the subway and rode the escalator up to the Skytrain station. Ratana had touched up his new sports jacket so he'd been saved the expense of the dry cleaner. It was a night out and anyway, dressing up was on his New Year's resolution list, along with doing some meditation exercises passed along by General Yosaporn. His new look and new mental state were supposed to bring about an overall improvement in his life. Just in case self-improvement didn't work out, the self-help alternative underneath the sports jacket in the form of a .38 police service revolver might prove useful.

Apichart had denied any connection with Birdman or Nongluck, but that was to be expected. He'd also denied any knowledge of the hit team he'd sent to kill the General. Pictures of the two fried assassins, the jazz musician, and the dead ying hadn't improved Apichart's memory. 'Never seen them before,' said Apichart with his lawyer at his side. 'Don't know them.' He was in advertising and told lies for a living; his training had come in handy during the police investigation.

At the top of the escalator, stairs led to the platform. It was jammed with passengers who had been disgorged from the train in a single knot of humanity a moment before. Office workers, the Bangkok middle-class, swarmed as if someone had knocked over their hive. Bodies briefly stalled and clotted into a large immovable mass as each passenger waited his turn to pass through the exit stalls, using an electronic plastic card or a small, black, poker-like chip – one at a time, slipping through as the barrier flipped back for a couple of seconds. The passengers, like the Skytrain tokens, looked used and recycled after a long day at work. The women had touched up their makeup, applied fresh lipstick, and sprayed on a whiff of perfume to create an appearance of freshness. There was one woman who hadn't bothered. She was a mem-farang who was almost beautiful.

Calvino bumped into her, a glancing touch, brushing against her shoulder. 'Sorry, I wasn't watching where I was going.'

'That's okay. It's very crowded,' she said, looking directly at him.

She's got an accent from somewhere in Europe, he told himself. And she had an exotic look that caught his eye. He told himself it was her dress, but then decided it was nothing special. Then he thought it was her hair, until he saw a hairclip that vendors sell on the street. Then he wondered if it was her seriousness of look, a quiet, forceful determination to be somewhere, an attitude that reminded him of someone from New York.

Casey's last visit to the office had got Calvino thinking about the world he'd left behind. When he was young, life had held promise. He'd been happy and free, and everyone around him assumed life moved forward, opening up unlimited possibilities.

What this woman in Bangkok brought back was the moment he'd met his future wife. It had been an accidental meeting on the subway. He'd picked her up and one thing had led to another – they'd moved in together, got married, had a kid, and inevitably divorced. He wondered if his ex-wife still rode the subway. Even after she'd found his replacement, she was the type who loved the attention of a stranger tossing her a look.

He had told himself it was a mistake to underestimate the role of some random event upending the course of one's life, one accident that destroyed a warehouse of carefully drawn-up plans. Chance could be good, bad, or neutral; a man never knew until it had overtaken him, bucked him up, pulled him down, and passed him by. Calvino's law said chance alone was an insufficient guide through life; another lesson kicked in, most of the time; chance, like a bus you waited for, sooner or later arrived a second time, and then a man had better be prepared to climb onboard and hold on for the ride. A small robotic voice, like the ones used in high-rise elevators, told him to move away from the mem-farang, walk to the nearest exit, and leave the scene before there was an accident. Everything he'd learned told him to turn and walk away. But he ignored the alarm bells, the flashing warning lights, and the voice of past experience.

He felt himself drawn to her presence – something that made it difficult to turn and walk away. There should always be an escape hatch, but that wasn't really the case. The hatch was sometimes locked down. The Thais called it saneh – a black magic spell that people along the Cambodian border swore could capture the heart of any man. He stared at her like he was a stupid teenager.

One face, one person, had knocked out the scaffolding that held up his Bangkok. For a moment it was as if the city had vanished. He felt himself falling back to somewhere he hadn't visited in years.

'Can I buy you a drink? You know, make it up to you?'

She smiled. 'That's not necessary. But thank you.'

She started to walk away, but he followed her, pushing through the crowd. 'Hey, what's your name? Mine's Vinny. Vinny Calvino.'

'Another time, Vinny.'

'Tomorrow for lunch.'

'I really have to go. But thanks.'

Then she turned and rushed down the stairs from the Skytrain to the Asoke and Sukhumvit intersection. He wanted to tell her about taking the underground passage beneath Sukhumvit Road. But she'd vanished before he could make his next move.

McPhail, who had been walking alongside Calvino and carrying on a conversation with him, had sailed ahead until he'd realized he was talking to himself. He turned around and saw Calvino scanning the crowd for the vanishing mem-farang.

He walked back and pulled Calvino's arm. 'What's with you?'

Calvino shrugged, looking hard at McPhail, who was supposed to be his wingman. And a wingman didn't just go dancing off into the night talking to himself. He was supposed to be engaged enough to see what was happening when he stopped and talked with someone.

'Nothing's wrong. I just had a flashback.'

'I've had more flashbacks and flash-forwards than Timothy Leary. Wasn't that a mem-farang that had you stepping on your tongue?'

Calvino didn't deny it. 'She was something.'

'She brushed you off.'

'She had an appointment.'

McPhail sighed. 'Are you nuts? She didn't have an appointment. She blew you off. You'll get over it.'

They walked to Suda's outdoor restaurant and sat at one of the long tables under a ceiling fan. The tables were packed with tourists in shorts and T-shirts, backpacks stacked beside them. The restaurant was noted in many guidebooks for its cheap Thai food and good service. It was the kind of place with a roll of toilet paper on each table instead of napkins. McPhail had his eye on one of the waitresses. She would never go out with him, but that only made him go back. That and the fact she knew he always drank Singha.

McPhail ordered fried chicken with a side of roasted nuts, and Calvino ordered a beef curry and rice. The waitress smiled at McPhail. He tried a move but she only looked down at her notepad and repeated the order before walking back to the kitchen where she could stay out of sight as she always did when McPhail came to the restaurant.

McPhail lit a cigarette, turned his head, and blew out a lungful of smoke. The hit calmed his nerves. The Singha beer came before the food, and McPhail downed half his glass in one long elbow-levered tip-back. He wiped his mouth with the back of his hand and picked up his cigarette.

'That woman wants to go out with me,' McPhail said.

'Like she wants to get run over by a bus,' Calvino said.

'And look at you. What were you doing chasing after the mem? She couldn't get away from you fast enough. Anyone would have thought she had rockets attached to her shoes.'

'Okay, we're both losers. You feel better?'

McPhail sucked his breath in. He was annoyed. The waitress had snubbed him, and Calvino had rubbed salt into the wound. 'Do you want to hear about Casey? Or do you want to sit and day-dream about some mem-farang who looked at you

240

like you were a telephone box covered in a sports jacket?'

Calvino drank his beer straight from the bottle. As he lowered it, he saw McPhail grinning at him.

'What are you looking at?'

'Hey, bud, you're drinking from the bottle.'

'So what?'

'It's a habit you're gonna have to lose if you want to go over to the other side.' McPhail called the Western world the other side. Life in America had become like a Norse legend, where warriors coexisted with the undead who continued to breathe, eat, sleep, and forgo lovemaking. And no one in their right mind with any choice in the matter would even think of visiting there.

'You're changing the subject because you're going to tell me you came up empty-handed with Casey. Nothing. Nada. And all this talk about mems is your way of distracting me. But it ain't working.'

McPhail glanced back toward the kitchen. His waitress was nowhere in sight. He shuddered, drank from his glass of beer, and belched. 'About Casey. He's ex-special forces. A tough, mean motherfucker who did three tours in Vietnam. He couldn't get enough. He ended up in Florida at MacDill, and was stationed on base. Special-ops missions on one of those special tactics teams. Somalia, Bosnia, Colombia. Then he got a job with one of those private contractors out of Kuwait. They send him to jungles, cities – wherever Casey goes, he leaves bodies behind. But

Casey always manages to walk away. His nickname is "the Ghost." His medals have medals.'

'How'd you find this out?'

'The Pentagon hotline. The operator told me everything.'

'JUSMAG,' said Calvino. JUSMAG stood for 'Joint US Military Advisory Group.' There was a JUSMAG in the Philippines, one in South Korea, and another in Thailand. It acted as a joint American and Thai military operation, with Thai military providing the security. The buildings had been erected in the 1960s at the height of the Cold War and had the feeling of something off the set of M★A★S★H. Except that all the modern electronic gear dotting the roofs indicated that the Americans had tuned their satellite dishes to the local chatter.

'Bingo,' said McPhail.

He meant the game. McPhail had hung around the JUSMAG restaurant on bingo night and found a couple of old Vietnam veterans who had known Casey from the war. Talking about Casey came naturally to them, as they'd grown tired of losing at bingo.

'And I won twenty-eight dollars that night,' said McPhail. 'They hate it when an outsider wins the money.'

'You're the winner, my man.'

'After a dozen beers, this vet named Larry said, "This is borderline classified. I shouldn't be telling you this. But . . ."'

'But what?'

McPhail had fired up his vintage Zippo lighter for his bingo pals, leaning his new cigarette into the flame and snapping back the lid. That always worked as a conversation stimulus at a bingo night. There were people whose eyes came alive when that lick of flame shot torch-like out of the silver wafer. This lighter had a map of Vietnam on one side and '81st Cal.' on the other side, with the insignia. McPhail pushed aside his glass and tipped back the rest of the Singha straight from the bottle, his mouth coming up red and wet. He didn't bother to wipe it this time as he stuck the cigarette in the corner of his mouth.

'Casey worked in a prison in Baghdad.'

'Doing what?'

'Helping prisoners remember shit.'

'Thumbscrews, waterboarding, wiring to the balls – that kind of memory aid?'

McPhail shrugged. 'Who knows? But Casey's private contractor liked his work well enough. He got results that let them charge zillions for their contracts. He got reassigned by his people to do the same kind of shit here.'

'Are you sure?'

'That's one theory,' said McPhail. 'The other was some journalist was on his tail in Baghdad and he volunteered for the Bangkok assignment.'

'What do you think?'

McPhail rolled his head back and forth. 'I think Casey likes his work, and he doesn't much care where it takes him.'

'He's working at a prison here? Which prison?'

McPhail shrugged his shoulders. 'I couldn't get anyone to give the location. I don't think they knew. But it's some kind of interrogation facility buried in the outskirts of the city. No one wanted to talk about it. All I got was that his job is to question bad guys.' McPhail lit a cigarette and leaned forward, whispering over the table. 'They didn't say who the bad guys were, and there weren't any other details.'

McPhail's sources had another beery theory or two. They said Casey had found his way to Thailand and settled down – or what approximated settling down for someone like Casey, who changed apartments every six months. He was calm under fire, a man who could wait for days with little water or rations. Once on a mission Casey didn't return to base until he had what he'd been sent for. A scalp, a map, troop or motorized-vehicle-movement intel, supply road activity, security around a camp or bridge – he'd done all of them.

No second best, nothing less than what the commanding officer had said was essential. Casey knew the difference between essential and nice-to-have. That had given him a huge head start in life, but the advantage largely had been erased by his easy anger as he tried living among civilians who changed their minds about what they wanted, when they wanted it, and what it meant once they got it.

'Casey got to the point on the airforce base at

MacDill that his CO couldn't control him. He didn't listen. When he went to work for Logistic Risk Assessment Services, his bosses didn't bother to try to control him. The corporate deal is you can be a cowboy so long as it makes money and you don't fuck up. But it's just a matter of time before that happens. There's only so much luck. Each time you go into the field and come back alive, you use up some of that luck. That's what Larry said happened to Casey. He used up the last of his luck. One of his prisoners died during an interrogation. Ruptured spleen, his face bruised and bloated. Someone turned him in and threatened to take it further. Next thing, LRAS sends Casey to Bangkok. This kind of guy makes a good interrogator. He's an asset for them. But he's also a little too angry, he's a patriot who has no trouble inflicting pain. And his second career had always been his son. Casey's one of those guys who lived for his kid. You remember a few years back, the young American guy who got whacked upcountry?'

Calvino nodded. 'Casey told me.'

'He went to audit the company books at some factories along the Burmese border. He couldn't help but sniff around. He found kids hiding under beds in bamboo huts. Casey's son was going to blow the whistle. You know how these big brand guys operate. They take out ads for millions of dollars during the Super Bowl. During the halftime show, right on TV, they promise the world that their shit isn't made by slaves or kids. Not that they really wanted to know. But he didn't play their game. That's where he fucked up.'

'Joel was his name,' said Calvino.

McPhail nodded. 'That's it. Joel. He'd got a couple of warnings. You know how tolerant the Thais are. The kid didn't understand chon taw. Every Thai knows that when the big guy smiles and tells you politely to go away, you go away. He offers you cash, women, whiskey, wine – you back off. They're always smiling, which is what makes it so dangerous, because you see only the smile. Joel kept snooping around and scribbling notes, taking photographs. The same guys came back. "You're still here," they said. "Good idea you go to the airport. This is Thailand, you know." Smiles all around. Next time Joel doesn't see the smile. Joel don't see nothing, because he's dead. That's what happened to Casey's kid. The fucked-up thing was the way they killed him. Not the bullet or two in the head. Looks like they killed him real slow. Like they were making some kind of a statement. The body was in pretty bad shape by the time Casey got to his son. The police had a lot of pressure from the press, the embassy, all down the line. A Thai big-shot named Somporn was questioned a couple of times. They were his factories that Joel had been auditing. He said he'd never met Joel Casey, that he didn't know anything about Casey's visits up-country. He shrugged it off. I could tell what he was thinking: "I'm way too fucking important to deal with an ant like Joel Casey."'

'The same guy who's running for parliament,' said Calvino.

'Hey, murderers are entitled to representation,' said McPhail.

'It happens,' said Calvino.

'What's that mean?'

Calvino smiled. 'A man silences someone who has the capacity to betray him.'

'In that case, it's no wonder there's blood in the streets.' Calvino had finished his beef curry and rice and had his wallet out. 'Why are you wolfing down your chow at the speed of light?'

'I want to head over to Soi Cowboy,' said Calvino, getting up with his mouth still full. He paid the bill.

'Hold on.' McPhail rose from the table.

'You coming along?'

'Wouldn't miss it. I can see you're still thinking about that mem.' He shook his head, following Calvino to the street. 'What is it with guys like Casey and you? I want to spend my time getting unfocused, and you get all tense and twisted up with all of that concentration. You sure you weren't in the army?'

'I'll buy you a drink and tell you how I once won fifty dollars off of a marine recruitment sergeant in Brooklyn.'

McPhail hadn't heard that story. 'You were gonna join the marines?'

'I was running a backroom poker game for my uncle.' Calvino grinned. 'And it was payday and the sergeant was flush, feeling lucky, and thinking, "This dumb-ass fucking kid, what does he know about poker?"'

They'd already crossed the sky bridge to the other side of Sukhumvit. McPhail, following at a half-trot, cupped his cigarette and coughed. The light changed on Sukhumvit and they crossed, McPhail hacking out his guts and bending on the opposite side to catch his breath. 'I hate this fucking street.'

'I didn't tell you what happened to the sergeant?'

'You still exchange Christmas cards, and he thanks you for rescuing him from a life of gambling.'

'He got killed in Vietnam the next year. They'd offered him a big bonus to go back. He'd taken it. He struck me as someone who overestimated his luck. You know what I mean?'

McPhail shrugged, lowered his chin to touch his neck. 'Joel Casey's luck ran out. He made a fatal mistake. And he should've known better. His old man could have told him to keep his head down. Or maybe he did but he didn't listen to his old man. I never listened to mine.'

'Joel's father may be making some mistakes himself.' They were the kind of mistakes a man made when everything in his life was turning south on him.

McPhail looked surprised, smiled, and finished his beer. 'Like what?'

'Like hiring me to follow Somporn's mia noi. Unless he thinks I'm stupid, he's gotta know what's going through my head as to why he wants that information.'

Calvino had tagged Casey as the careful-planning type, the guy looking to anticipate everything that could go wrong, the kind of man who knows his exit before he goes into a situation. He'd hired Calvino to find out when the ying was scheduled to see Somporn. And if the police started asking around, they'd find only one person who'd been snooping around the mia noi: the guy who'd been held in Pattaya when a woman – some eyewitnesses said – had been pushed from his balcony. It had the classic feeling of a breakaway by the Knicks' power forward, racing downcourt for the layup, a twist, a fake, slamming the ball into the net. Calvino understood that move; he'd used it to take down the recruitment sergeant in poker.

CHAPTER 20

A feeling of nausea swept over Marisa as she worked her way through the middle-aged farangs drifting between bars on Soi Cowboy. The heat of the day remained in the early evening like a blowtorch on her skin. The air was heavy, suffocating. Lining both sides of the narrow soi were rows of neon-lit go-go bars. Overhead, a sliver of moon looked like another neon sign. But it wasn't the heat or that a man hot with desire had tried to pick her up; she'd had one, then two false starts. Little girls who looked like Fon but turned out not to be her. Each of them had nodded with sad eyes, offering to sell her flowers or gum. She moved on. Standing in front of the bars, yings in short skirts and bare midriffs pulled, tugged, pleaded with farangs, grabbing them by the arms. 'You handsome man, welcome inside please. Many girl inside. Look, look!'

In the muggy night air, the old hands among the crowd wormed their way out of the sweaty stranglehold; the newcomers allowed themselves to be reeled inside where the chilled air brought relief. Marisa repressed the urge to scream from the helplessness she felt. She stopped herself from throwing one of those out-of-desperation punches that made a person look like a complete fool. Though she thought of herself as a tough, experienced woman, Cowboy inevitably turned her stomach. It was degrading, base, the worst of animal instinct unhinged from reason. She was no prude, but the obvious loss of dignity among the women sickened her. It gave her all the more resolve to continue her search.

As she walked along, looking for the child, the same routine played out at bar after bar. The competition for customers was intense, and Marisa watched as one by one the farangs – including the old-timers – were picked off and disappeared into the bars.

Marisa had been at her condo when she'd received a phone call from Gung, a woman from a Thai NGO whom she thought of as a colleague. Gung understood the problem of dealing with a corrupt, self-serving, and compromised political and policing system; a system that consumed weeks and months before making a decision, only committees and memos, and then an attempt at consensus. In the vacuum, gangs that knew whose hands to grease distributed children to the red-light district along with a steady supply of trinkets, flowers, laser pens, and chewing gum for the tourists. Hundreds of children in dozens and dozens of red-light areas scattered around the city.

Gung guessed the gang rotated about twenty kids in and out of Cowboy. Meetings had been held and reports filed, but on the ground nothing had changed other than that the kids would be off the streets for two weeks before they slowly filtered back.

Digital photos of kids as young as eight or nine had been attached to one of the reports. In one photo, a girl who sold flowers and chewing gum on Soi Cowboy haunted Marisa. The girl wasn't more than eleven years old. Gung had said she'd heard from the bamboo telegraph that the girl had been trafficked and was being watched as she made her rounds. Marisa had said she'd get the girl out. In a meeting with officials, Marisa had laid out the facts. Everyone had sympathized, but emotion hadn't carried the day. Too much money was involved; too many people upstream and down-stream were feeding from the action. By the end of the meeting, Marisa had been told to back off. Her superior took her into the the corridor and told her not to get personally involved. She reminded Marisa about the policy of non-interference in local affairs; going around the authorities would be counterproductive in the end.

When Marisa protested, she got the full Thai treatment: she was told point-blank that she was being selfish and stupid. Tackling the larger problem meant playing the local game. Sometimes sacrifices were unavoidable, but so long as the war was being won, casualties along the way had to be accepted. That was the nature of war: not everyone got out alive. Bakhita, who was her supervisor at the UN, reminded Marisa that hundreds of new refugees were crossing the border from Burma every day. The organization needed local officials on their side to help with the refugees. These were compelling intellectual arguments – like those of field commanders who threw men into battle, knowing the mission was hopeless, because it distracted the enemy from the main front elsewhere.

War had a cruel and terrible face.

Marisa was being asked to accept the price of saving children and women swept across frontiers. She had to let go of her personal desire to save the kid on Cowboy. That was the deal.

She had done what she had been asked to do. She'd let go of the idea of any individual intervention. The police had been contacted, and they'd said they would handle the matter.

But Gung hadn't surrendered. She resolved to step up the pressure on the farang to do the job and take the heat. When she phoned Marisa, Gung had said, 'Fon has only a couple of days. They have found a Chinese man who has paid for her virginity. He's coming in on a flight from Taiwan in two days. After that, everything will change for her.'

Then a child's voice was on the phone: 'My name is Fon. Can you help me? I think Auntie sell me soon.'

Gung came back on the phone. 'It's up to you.' Gung broke the connection.

The child's presence night after night on Soi Cowboy told Marisa that the girl was probably Tai Yai or, as it turned out, Shan, an ethnic minority from Burma. If she had been a Thai child, the police or social welfare might have taken her off the soi and put her in a shelter. That wasn't standard procedure for kids like Fon. She'd been better being a Karen, another ethnic minority from Burma that had been displaced by fifty years of civil war. Why a Karen? Because even after their villages were overrun and they ran out of food, the Karen rarely sold their daughters. But the fate of Shan and Tai girls wasn't the same; their villages had a long history of exchanging daughters for money or its equivalent.

Fon translated as 'Rain.' Marisa thought it was a suitable name for a kid who never saw much daylight and whose future was clouded. Unless Fon at the end of the night had earned at least three hundred baht, her handlers would beat her and send her off to bed without a plate of rice and fish sauce. She had fallen between the cracks; she was another kid who had been purged from a normal life of school and play.

Marisa reminded Gung that her job prevented her from going out on rescue missions.

'I could be fired and kicked out of the country,' Marisa said.

'You have big puuyai to protect you. No one can touch Marisa.'

'You don't understand,' said Marisa. 'It doesn't work that way.'

Gung paused for a moment, trying to figure out why Marisa, being a farang, didn't get the seriousness of the situation. Or was she just playing a mind game? She tested the waters with one name. 'Khun Somporn.'

Marisa's brother wasn't even married into the family yet, but the word had already fanned out through the NGO community. At first she laughed when a Thai colleague said she was untouchable. Then she stopped laughing and felt disgust. Gung had made it clear that Marisa had entered the magic circle where people are protected, and that the locals would no longer view her as just another farang. She was now someone whose power and influence could prove useful at the street level. Gung had told her that this was the only way to deal with the police. They'd bend as soon as Somporn's name came up. Her first reaction had been that she'd never go to Somporn for any favors, knowing that the moment she crossed that line, he would own her. She thought of him on the phone with his mia noi in the lobby of the Oriental Hotel. He was a man who owned women.

'Helping this child has nothing to do with Somporn,' she said. 'I would never ask him for anything.'

That was about as un-Thai a statement as anyone

could have uttered to a Thai. Not using your power and influence to give help to someone who asked for it was a gross affront. And Gung took Marisa's words as a personal rebuff.

'It doesn't matter whether you ask him or not. You don't seem to understand. You aren't like us. Nothing can ever happen to you. You want another job? No problem. You want anything, no problem. Someone makes a problem for you, they have a big problem. So why don't you think about Fon? Who does she have? What other life will she have? Maybe you don't care. I thought you were different,' said Gung. 'Sorry.'

The line had gone dead. Marisa stared at her phone and thought of calling Gung back. She was about to say that Bakhita had ordered her not to get personally involved in any individual case. It was an argument that would have sounded hollow. Marisa was upset not because the call had been terminated before she could explain the policy – being cut off had saved her from that embarrassment – but because she realized that her brother's marriage was about to turn her own world upside down.

Marisa had paced the living room of the condo where Juan Carlos was working at the table, going over a thick file delivered by one of Lawman's assistants.

'What's wrong?' he asked, looking up.

'Nothing. But I need to get some fresh air,' she said.

'Good idea, why don't I come along? I could use a walk.'

That was the thing about Juan Carlos: he was joyful, trusting, upbeat, and in love with the world and life. She wished so much that she had inherited these qualities in equal share, but Juan Carlos got the full payload. He looked at her so openly, and she was not telling him the truth. She wasn't just going for a walk. But what point was there in getting her brother involved?

'I need some time to think, Juan.'

He tapped the end of his pen on a stack of documents and stretched. 'Phone me after you've done your thinking, and I'll join you later.'

She nodded, grabbed her handbag, and went to the door.

'You seem upset. Are you sure you don't want company?'

'I'll be okay,' she said. 'Really, I'm distracted, that's all.'

'It's your work. You shouldn't bring it home.'

She smiled and gave him a hug. 'Of course, you're right.' She hated lying to her brother, but telling him the truth increased the risk that he'd want to help her. That was exactly what she didn't want to happen. She had to do this on her own terms.

As she rode the Skytrain, she'd thought about what she should do, what she could do – thought about the likely outcome, and how she had truly wanted to follow Bakhita's advice. But on the ground, things looked different; it was no place for policy wonks who focused on the abstraction of children but rarely got down in the dirt to save an individual child. She didn't want to be like them. Gung hadn't fully understood what was at stake. She could lose her job and be thrown out of the country for breaking this rule. It hadn't carried any weight with Bakhita when she'd argued that the rule that barred intervention was wrong. She was simply told that, wrong or not, it was the rule and she was bound to follow it. If puuyais don't have to follow the rules, why do I? she'd asked herself. The meeting had ended in a stalemate, much like the call with Gung. Everyone had her own position to uphold, and squeezed in between was a little girl named Fon, who was about to be sold to a sex tourist.

As Marisa had walked along the platform at Asoke Station, she'd almost decided to turn back when a farang had bumped into her. He'd tried to pick her up. At least she was still attractive enough for a man to make a play. She'd drawn in a deep breath. That's it, she thought. Give Fon a chance to grow up. Bakhita had said the world had millions of Fons. As she walked down the street, every ten meters there had been a woman, sometimes old, sometimes young, clutching a baby in one hand and begging for change with the other, reminding her of Bakhita's view of the larger dimensions of the trafficked children network.

At the top of Soi Cowboy, Marisa stopped and

thought again about turning back. Then she convinced herself that since she'd come this far, she owed Gung the courtesy of at least talking with Fon. Bakhita's warning played in her head: 'Thais have a thin skin when it comes to foreigners exposing anything to do with child exploitation, the sex trade, or the informal networks, official and unofficial, that feed off each other, making it all possible.' Thai sensibilities can go stuff themselves, Marisa had told herself. It was always the sensibilities of the wealthy, the bullies, and the influential criminal class that had to be weighed. Somporn and his kind of people created the environment. She had already worked herself up by the time she turned onto Soi Cowboy. If she lost her job and got kicked out of Thailand, she could go back to Spain. She would never ask him for a thing.

'You can't make a difference with a group unless you start with an individual,' she'd said at the meeting at UN headquarters. She'd regretted the declaration the moment it had come out of her mouth, but she'd said nothing to express her regret. She'd let it stand. Bakhita had chosen not to respond. Everyone had known exactly where they stood.

Marisa walked the full stretch of Soi Cowboy from Soi 23 to Asoke and back twice before spotting a flower girl coming out of a bar, moving her way through the door girls and touts. The girl sidestepped a food vendor who dumped a large plastic basin of dirty water into the gutter. Marisa looked at the photo of Fon and then up at the flower girl. It was the same child. Then she saw Gung.

'I knew you'd come,' she said. 'That's her.' She turned and started to walk away.

'Where are you going?'

'I've got two more kids at Lumpini Park to find. Good luck.'

Marisa watched Gung disappear down the soi, lost in the crowd. Marisa glanced back at the kid, who had her eye on a couple of farangs who were getting the treatment from three of the door girls. 'Handsome man, welcome inside,' one quoted from the familiar script. It suggested a level of English vastly superior to the actual language skill of the girl.

Marisa knelt down and looked the girl in the eye. 'Gung's gone. I want to help.' The response was restless, bored, no eye contact. With Gung out of the way, she'd reverted to flower-girl mode.

'Are you Fon?'

The little girl looked scared. She held out a packet of chewing gum. 'Twenty baht. You want?'

Marisa handed her a hundred-baht note. Fon smiled, her hand offering five packets of gum.

'How would you like some noodles?' Marisa asked, ignoring the gum.

'You don't want gum? You buy laser pen? Very good quality, too. From Taiwan. Not expensive.'

'You spoke with me on the phone, remember?'

'Laser very good,' she said.

'Why are you doing this?'

With Gung gone, it was as if Fon wanted nothing to do with her.

Fon spoke standard street-kid English, good enough to flog flowers and gum. Worthless stuff she had to push. If people bought, they did so out of sympathy rather than genuine need. She backed off as Marisa reached out to touch her hand.

'Aren't you hungry?' She could see from Fon's face that she was scared. Her small black eyes darted, looking in either direction. Although it looked like she was wandering around on her own, the kid instinctively knew she was being watched all the time. Auntie had told her so. The woman she called Auntie had given her a new dress and makeup and showed her how to put on lipstick.

For the past few days Auntie had been nice to her and told her she'd soon have a surprise. It had given her the feeling that she was special, not like the other kids. Fon had decided it was probably okay to hustle a meal from the mem-farang. At the same time, Auntie had said, mem-farangs might cause a problem. She should never, never trust one or believe anything a mem-farang said. All the kids in the house where she slept were told the same thing.

Marisa took Fon's hand. They walked to a food stall in front of one of the bars and sat on plastic stools. Marisa ordered two plates of chicken and sticky rice. A waitress set the plates down along with spoons and forks. Fon greedily ate with her fingers, stuffing her mouth with chicken.

'Gung says you're from the Shan State in Burma. Is that true?' asked Marisa.

Fon nodded, her mouth full, looking around to see who on the soi might be watching.

'Shan?'

The girl nodded, eyes lined with heavy, gleaming mascara.

'Where's your mother and father?'

'Mother's dead. Father works by the river.'

'What river?'

Fon shrugged. 'On the Thai side of the river. He has a card to stay. I will go visit him soon.'

'Who said?'

She blinked. 'Auntie.'

'Do you think I could talk with your Auntie?' asked Marisa. As soon as she'd asked the question, Marisa knew she'd made a mistake.

Fon pulled a face, scooping up the last of the sticky rice. 'Finished. I go work now.'

Marisa put her hand on Fon's wrist. 'On the phone you said that you wanted help. Have you changed your mind?'

The child sighed, stared at the table. She hadn't connected the mem-farang with the woman who had been on the phone. Besides, that had happened what seemed like a long time ago, and she had so much wanted to please Gung. Now she wasn't so sure what she wanted.

'I'll get in trouble.'

'From Auntie?

Fon looked unhappy, frightened. She had retreated to her nonresponsive space. She twisted and turned on the stool, scanning the crowd. Marisa wasn't certain how to get through to her – a kid who'd been programmed to distrust a strange foreign woman, her mother dead, separated from her father. At eleven years of age she was still cocooned in the last part of childhood, but her handlers had done her up to showcase her first hint of womanhood. Fingernails painted red; her hair, grown long, had been carefully brushed; and lip gloss and makeup signaled she was selling more than chewing gum.

'Has Auntie told you that in two days she will give you to a man, and that man will want sex?'

Fon rocked back and forth on the stool, her lower lip in a pout. 'Auntie wouldn't do that, I know. She takes care of me.'

'Auntie sometimes forces a girl to have sex with a man. You know that.'

Fon sighed. 'I have to work now.'

Marisa handed her another two-hundred baht. 'You've got your money for tonight. You don't have to worry.'

The worry lines on her forehead suggested otherwise. 'Auntie send me to my papa.'

'She's lying to you, Fon. Gung told you not to trust Auntie's promises. I know she said that. And you told Gung that Auntie plans to make you sleep with a stranger. That's why you asked me to help you. If you don't want to sleep with a man, just tell me. And I'll take you out of here. You can go to school, go see your father, have friends, a life.'

'Auntie say mem-farangs say these things but they are not true.'

It was Marisa's turn to smile. 'Auntie would say that. Has she ever beaten you? Threatened you? Or hit the other kids?'

They both knew the answers to those questions. 'You do know that Gung wants to help?'

She nodded, a flicker of softening in her eyes.

'I can't help you, Fon, unless you leave here with me. Auntie can't punish or hurt you. No one will hurt you. I promise.'

Fon searched Marisa's face for a long moment. 'You don't know things.'

'I know one thing.'

Fon waited, staying very still as if holding her breath. She had only experienced a world of broken promises.

'Let's get out of here.' Marisa held out her hand.

CHAPTER 21

Beneath the neon lights of the Sheba Bar and the huge King Tut head with a striped headdress advertising it, three short, skinny Thai men in flip-flops and worn, patched clothing slowly maneuvered a baby elephant they'd brought all the way from Surin province. The men fanned out, selling bags of bamboo to tourists for twenty baht. No one used elephants on construction projects anymore; the forests were gone, so the elephants no longer had any logs to lift. Beasts with proud working pasts had become carnival sideshows in Bangkok's red-light district.

Two of the men offered small bags of bamboo to a couple of bulky tourists who stopped to sort through their Thai baht. Turning them over, they squinted at the strange banknotes and tried to figure out in the neon light which one was a twenty. Hundreds of yings outfitted in hot pants and bikini tops with nylon robes slung around their shoulders paraded in front of their bars, holding signs advertising the cost of a beer.

'The cops said no elephants in Bangkok. What the fuck is this?' asked McPhail. He waved off one of the men who shoved a bag of bamboo into his face.

'That was last year,' said Calvino. He wasn't looking at the elephant. 'That's her,' he said.

McPhail approached the elephant and touched its trunk with the back of his hand. 'What do you mean that's her?'

It was the woman from the train station who'd told him in so many words to get lost. She sat at a roadside table with a kid dressed like a whore. The vendor stood behind his counter, hacking up chicken and folding the meat over a perfectly formed scoop of rice. A couple of dancers sat at the table wolfing down bowls of noodle soup. Marisa watched Calvino as he approached. She stood up and smiled. With the young girl in tow. Marisa walked into the soi and threw her arms around Calvino, kissing him first on both cheeks and then with a long kiss on the lips. Pressing against him, she felt the hard steel of a .38 caliber police special inside his shoulder holster. Marisa knew the feel of a concealed gun on a man. Her father had been a police officer.

'Vinny, I'm so happy to see you.' Her voice was a little too loud, as if the volume was raised to make a point.

He grinned, glanced over at McPhail, who had a smirk that looked like it risked becoming a permanent feature.

'Never think it's about you,' said McPhail, but his words were too soft to carry over the roar of the elephant that belched a huge cloud of gas from half-digested raw bamboo.

Only then did Calvino notice the flower girl holding packets of chewing gum in one hand and laser pens in the other. Marisa's arm circled Fon's shoulder in a motherly fashion, holding her in the tight possession of a mother or close relative.

'Please help me,' she whispered. 'Those men behind you want to take this girl. I can't let that happen.'

Calvino's grin disappeared and he took one step back. 'What are you talking about? What men want to take her away?' He looked around and only saw the usual milling crowd of touts, yings, farangs, vendors, and motorcycle drivers.

'Her name is Fon. She's in danger. Please help me.' Her lower lip quivered. Her eyes were wild, darting from the kid to him and back. The woman who had looked in complete control at the train station had unraveled, and what was left was a terrified human being.

He was trying to understand what she and the kid were doing. Marisa had said the words 'help me,' but help do what? Less than two hours ago she had brushed him off like a piece of lint. 'Phone the police,' he finally said.

That wasn't the response she wanted. She pursed her lips, shaking her head, afraid to let go of Fon.

'It won't work. I need to get her out of here. Believe me, the police won't help.'

'I liked the kiss,' he said. 'I made a mistake. I took it for something more than a cry for help.'

It wasn't what she expected. He was a man, and men had to be handled in a delicate way. 'All kisses are a cry for help,' she said, trying to smile. If guile was what was required, then she could play that game, too.

McPhail was the first to spot two Thai men closing in from behind Calvino and blocking their path. 'If you're going to help, now would be a good time.'

Calvino took Marisa's hand and walked her and the child across the soi to the entrance of a bar where he knew the owner. A thick curtain covered the entrance. Calvino slipped his fingers into the fold and parted the curtain wide enough for Marisa and the kid to slip inside.

Without looking over his shoulder, he followed them. McPhail spoke to the Surin men who owned the baby elephant and gave them a hundred baht to stay put outside the bar. A small crowd of yings and tourists gathered, and the two Thai men who had been on Calvino's tail backed away, taking up a position behind the crowd. The Thais looked patient, arms folded over their T-shirts; one broke out a pack of cigarettes and passed it to the other.

Several more Thai men joined the first two, filtering in from the Asoke side of Cowboy. No one could enter or leave the bar without going through them. As a line of defense, McPhail admitted they looked impressive. A woman and a child would offer them little challenge. Calvino was packing, but pulling a gun on Cowboy was something that would make things even worse. McPhail curled his lips and spat on the ground before he slipped inside through the curtains.

'Man, there are at least four or five of them waiting outside. They ain't going anywhere soon.'

'They want Fon,' said Marisa, squeezing the kid's hand.

'Of course they want her,' said McPhail. 'She probably works for them, don't you sweetheart?'

'Is this your friend?' Marisa asked.

Calvino nodded. 'He sometimes gets carried away.'

McPhail rocked back on his heels. The blues blared from speakers positioned like ceremonial Chinese urns hung in the family cellar. The lyrics got to him, giving him the crazy sensation that the song had been written just for him. 'I was in trouble around midnight, and you were on my mind. Yeah, I love you baby, and if I get out of here alive, I'll tell the whole wide world that you're mine.'

A half-dozen dancers dressed only in cheap high heels huddled onstage, watching a kickboxing match on the TV suspended from the ceiling. They weren't listening to the blues. The kickboxers, a Thai and a farang, circled each other in the ring. Every time the Thai landed a kick, the yings cheered.

Calvino pulled Marisa to the back of the bar,

where the owner, Reno, sat in the DJ booth singing out of tune into his microphone: 'I love you, and if I get out of here alive, I'll tell the whole world that you're mine.' Reno grinned, keeping time with one foot as he stuck his head out from the booth and waved his cigar at Calvino. He crossed the floor and gave Calvino a bear hug.

'Vincent Calvino, where the fuck have you been?' He looked behind Calvino and saw that he hadn't drifted into the bar alone. It was never a good thing when Calvino showed his face with a group that included McPhail. Glasses got broken, tables got overturned, yings cried and moaned. Then he registered the presence of a mem-farang, and Calvino holding her hand. Reno pulled the cigar out of his mouth and put a hand over it.

'Sorry, I didn't know it was a BYOY night.' A bring-your-own-ying night. In Reno's business, some guys showed up with beer they'd bought at the 7-Eleven so they didn't have to pay the bar price, and then there were guys who showed up with a woman for much the same reason. Cheap Charlies, like rats, came for the fun, the slap and tickle, and sometimes raced away with the best meat before anyone could catch them.

'There's a problem.'

'Brother, the world shuttles from one problem to another,' said Reno. 'The trouble is if you don't learn to jump out of the way, you can get run over.'

'The situation's fluid,' said Calvino.

'Like fucked-up,' said Reno, expecting the worst. He looked at Calvino's expression. 'Okay, seriously fucked-up then. What do you need?'

'Help me get these two out the back way,' said Calvino. He walked over to the main bar and rang the bell. The yings watching the TV cheered. The customers applauded. The sound of the bell meant drinks for the bar, and the yings were parched from screaming in support of their man in the kickboxing match. Calvino peeled off three thousand baht and handed it to Reno. It was just under a hundred dollars but it would cover the round of drinks he'd bought. Reno played a new blues song: 'My happiness depends on my baby coming back home. It makes me so sad sittin' here, thinkin' you're being bad. Tell me how I can bring you home tonight, baby. I'm missing you.'

Marisa had moved halfway down the main stage away from the door. McPhail stood at the curtains, holding them tight, peering out, shaking his head, then squeezing the curtains into his fist. 'Mean-looking motherfuckers,' he said. 'And it don't look like they're going anywhere soon, Vinny.'

'The police catch this kid in my bar, it's gonna cost me.'

'Not if we get her out over the roof.'

'I don't know if that's such a good idea.'

'Reno, I just paid the bar.'

Reno rolled his eyes, fanned the three notes out and touched the body of the nearest dancer.

271

He sniffed the money, then looked at the three-thousand-baht notes and signaled for Wan to join him. She looked at her boss, then tried to let go of Jarrett's hand. He held firm.

'You don't have to go,' he said.

'It's okay. He's my boss.'

'Not anymore.'

He saw that she didn't agree with him, and he let go of her hand.

'I want you to show my friend the old Indian rope trick,' said Reno, an unlit cigar hanging from the corner of his mouth.

'We won't need a rope.'

Reno pulled out a lighter with a blue flame that rose a meter high. He pushed the button to shoot out the flame and sucked on the cigar. 'Yeah, as if that's going to make my life any easier.'

Calvino caught a glimpse of the customers sitting on the other side of the stage. Through the bare thin legs shuffling in high-heeled shoes, he thought he'd recognized her but decided she'd fit a general pattern he'd seen thousands of times, fooling his mind into believing that the ying's face was familiar. The strobe lights on the stage reached to the end of the platform, and then the benches beyond were shrouded in muddy shadows. Reno cracked up the blues a notch, and the red and yellow lights flashed above the dance platform. Moving down the bar, he got a better look. A white guy and a black guy were on the opposite side. It was the same two early birds with the parked Benz in Washington Square.

They pretended not to see Calvino and he looked away. It didn't matter, he told himself.

Calvino listened as Reno instructed Wan on what she had to do to get the mem-farang and the kid out of the bar the back way. Wan said she understood the situation, even though she had no idea what she'd gotten herself involved in.

Calvino looked around in time to notice that Jarrett was staring at Marisa, looking at her like he knew her from somewhere. He didn't have time to think about it. Distracted by the kid, she wasn't aware of his attention. Calvino stayed close to her side, his arm brushing against her shoulder. 'It's fixed up. Let's go.'

McPhail was at the entrance when one of the street enforcers used a knife to cut through the curtain, nicking the edge of his hand. He yelped, instinctively shaking his hand, blood going over his shirt, the ripped curtain, and the walls. Calvino ran back to the door, drawing his .38 out of its holster, and brought the butt of the gun down hard against the intruder's head. He dropped heavy, like a stone from a third-story window. His knife clattered along the floor. The lead ying on the stage screamed, her hands grasping her throat. She saw McPhail's blood and fainted.

'Get the fuck out of here,' said Reno. He cupped his hands and yelled into his DJ microphone. Wan turned and looked at Jarrett. He nodded to let her go. He was the man who never took the same ying twice. Sending them off was the price of staying out of the zone of recurring obligation. There was no goodbye, because there was nothing between them that hadn't been settled.

As Calvino, Fon, and Marisa ran up the back stairs, Reno wrapped a towel around McPhail's hand and poured him a double Jameson. The men outside had no idea what or who might be waiting on the other side of the curtain. Trouble, they knew. But how much was yet to be determined. They hesitated the way hired thugs often did in the street. They had to make a hard decision without the adrenaline surge that high personal emotions pumped into the system, making a man act without any thought of getting hurt. By the time they got the courage to enter the bar, McPhail had gone, and so had Jarrett and Tracer. Most of the bar had paid up their bills and vanished into the night, leaving the marnasan to tell the Thai men that she hadn't seen anything, and no, she had no knowledge of a kid and a mem-farang. One lie after another said in calm, caring tones. They saw right through her, but searching the bar they found nobody except a covey of yings frightened out of their minds.

CHAPTER 22

Marisa clutched Fon's hand, guiding her as she stepped first onto the roof. Fon froze. 'Don't look down,' said Marisa.

Four floors above the soi, Marisa glanced down at the crowd. Wan knelt beside the flower girl that she'd seen before around the soi.

'You follow me. No problem,' Wan said, putting her hand on Fon's shoulder.

Fon drew in a deep breath and tried to smile. 'Let's go,' said Marisa.

Calvino circled back and knelt beside Fon. 'You'll be okay, kid. We'll be out of here soon.'

Fon searched Calvino's face as a child does, trying to decide if he was lying to her.

'It's no problem for you,' said Wan.

A flicker of a smile crossed the child's face.

'Now,' said Calvino, 'we need to get a move on.'

Most of the yings knew about the escape route on the roof. When the outside tout signaled the police were coming, the younger yings, like in a school fire drill, ran up the stairs, out on the roof, where they waited for the all-clear. Wan, who was more curious than most, had checked out the roof her first day on the job. She turned, waved for the others to follow, and ran ahead.

The community of working yings on the soi was small. After a week, most of the yings knew who worked at which bars, which yings walking the soi were freelance, and which gangs owned which kids. It was like an international air terminal in a bad storm. The yings looked at each farang as a potential boarding pass for an onward flight. That didn't much matter. Even if they did get out, others arrived to take their place. Cowboy was a rough mirror of their own family lives – unstable, uncertain, and with everyone waiting to take advantage of someone else. Before Wan's father had abandoned the family, he had carefully planned his escape. It had been the one valuable lesson Wan had learned from him. Two days after she'd gone to work at the bar, one of the old-hand yings confided in her that, in the event of an emergency, the best escape route was over the roof to the underground station.

An outline of a man running toward them emerged. Calvino dropped to one knee and waited, looking to see if the man was armed. The roof wasn't such an empty place. A moment later a ying, barefoot, cursing and out of breath, was visible. Calvino leaned behind the shadows cast by the drying clothes, waited, stuck out his foot and tripped the running figure, who tumbled headfirst, hitting a clothesline, ripping it down and falling hard into damp sheets. It was as if his engines had cut out and he crash-landed. He was a Thai male in his early twenties; blood dripped from the corner of his mouth. 'Keep running,' Calvino shouted at Marisa and the others.

Calvino touched his gun but didn't pull it out of the holster. 'What the fuck do you want?'

The young Thai male, his shirt unbuttoned, looked meek as he pressed his hands into a wai.

Calvino looked up and saw the women had stopped. He shouted and pointed to the end of the roof. 'Don't stop. I'll be right with you.'

A ying, huffing and puffing, holding a cigarette in her hand, finally caught up. The run had worn her out; her knees wobbled as she plunked herself down beside the fallen man. 'He cheat on me. Butterfly man. I kill him.' She assumed the Asian squat, feet splayed, sucking on her cigarette. She blew smoke at her boyfriend and shook her cell phone at him. Whether that was her way of killing him or a lull before she worked up the courage to finish him off, Calvino couldn't be sure.

Calvino continued to squat on the man's chest, watching as Marisa and Fon ran toward Penny Lane, ducking under lines of towels, bikinis, panties, and bras drying in the hot night. Then he turned his attention to the couple. While she'd been ready to rip his heart out, her anger shifted once a farang sat on her boyfriend.

The man groaned under Calvino's weight. 'You hurt him, I kill you,' she said, rising to a crouching position, her fist ready to strike Calvino. He grabbed it and pulled her down until she was eye-level with her boyfriend.

Ahead, Calvino saw them weave through air-conditioning compressors, water tanks, and piles of garbage. Fon no longer thought of it as a game as she knocked down a towel.

'Kiss and make up,' he said.

'He bullshit man. You bullshit man. All men bullshit,' she shouted. Suddenly she was no longer certain of whom she wanted to kill more.

While the ying didn't have much of an English vocabulary, she got her point across. Calvino eased himself off the Thai, holstered his gun, and waited half a second for the ying to hit the young man with an impressive right hook, sending him back to the mat. He barely caught the whisper coming out of her throat. 'I hate you,' she said.

Calvino slipped away, joining the others as they reached the end of Penny Lane. As he looked back, he saw that the Thai male was on his feet and the ying was on her cell phone. She definitely wasn't phoning for a pizza delivery.

'What happened back there?' asked Marisa.

'Lover's quarrel. They're making up in their own way.'

Marisa looked at the couple embracing against the backdrop of neon and white sheets, and then she looked over the roof edge. It was a long drop. Wan also looked down at a metal ladder leading to the street. Fon had stumbled and fallen in the darkness, scraping her knee. She was rattled and scared.

Calvino picked her up and carried her. 'It's okay,' he said. 'We're here.' He gestured toward the ladder. 'But we don't have that much time. Once those two return to the street, the word will be out.'

Marisa's face had gone ashen. 'Look at how afraid she is.' The threat of more violence on the roof had them all squirming. Wan, her body shaking, held on to her hand. Neon signs stretching the length of the soi threw off enough light to make out the ladder. Wan wasn't winded, despite having doubled back a couple of times to check on Fon. Calvino kept an eye out so no one got separated.

When Calvino looked back, the couple had vanished. They had no more than a couple of minutes before the thugs would hear that the kid had gone onto the roof. Marisa and the two Thais fumbled around in the dark. 'What do we do?' asked Marisa.

'Take the ladder,' he said, looking over the edge. 'Wan, you lead the way.'

From the moment they'd climbed the stairs to the fourth floor, it had been clear that she knew where she was going. Calvino looked back and saw movement in the distance. The young couple hadn't just made up, they'd spread word of a farang with a gun on the roof. He said nothing to Marisa. With the neon sign for Penny Lane blinking a couple of feet away, Wan stared at the fire-escape ladder.

'You go first,' Wan said, looking at Calvino.

'Any reason for that?' he asked, with a dose of old-fashioned suspicion.

Wan clicked her tongue, cocked her head. 'There's a long drop. You need to put Fon on your back and carry her down.'

He picked Fon up and swung her over his shoulders. 'Hold on tight.' He twisted back and saw the terror in her eyes. She said nothing, but the way her small hands clawed around his neck, she didn't need to. As he climbed onto the ladder, he told the others, 'Keep down and quiet. Then come after me. Wan next and Marisa, you come down last.' He went over the edge, feeling the full weight of the kid on his back.

He didn't see he had much choice. Putting his life in the hands of a bar ying violated several of Calvino's laws, among them, 'If a ying asked for something, she was asking for money.' He slowly climbed down the stairs with his toes pointed to the brick wall. He had underestimated Wan, he thought.

When he reached the last rung of the fire escape he measured the length of the drop. Below in the near distance he saw the Asoke underground station. But the pavement was a four-foot drop from the last rung of the fire escape. He reached back and tapped Fon on the shoulder. 'Almost there, kid.' Once they were on the ground, it would be a couple of seconds until they passed the security guard and entered the subway station.

'Climb off my back. And stay on the fire escape.'

She froze again, clutching him with all of her might.

'You've got to trust me, Fon. I'm not going to leave you.'

But the kid hung on tight. She didn't want to climb anywhere. The drop was high enough to break a leg if you landed the wrong way. Having a kid on his back was increasing the risk of getting hurt. He could hear, in the distance, angry Thai voices shouting Fon's name.

Wan whispered to the kid in Thai, 'Climb up two rungs and wait or everyone will have a problem. You don't want to make a big problem, do you, Fon?'

Calvino felt the kid's hands release from his neck. Her hands grasped the rungs as she lifted herself off Calvino's back. He looked up and smiled. 'After I'm on the ground, I'll catch you. You understand?'

The beekeeper's daughter, just above them on the ladder, translated for Fon. The kid glanced at Wan and nodded. Calvino saw the exchange as he looked over his shoulder. He tried to judge the distance to the ground. He climbed down until he could lower himself from the last rung, holding on till the last moment. His body extended a couple of feet from the surface and then he let go. He dropped to the pavement and landed on his feet. Fon had watched him, and she climbed to the last rung, hung on with two hands, her tiny dress fluttering, and dropped. Calvino caught her. Wan and Marisa followed one after another.

Calvino grabbed each woman as she dropped to the ground. At the entrance to the subway, a uniformed security guard checked Wan's backpack. From the roof, Calvino glanced back to discover two men bent forward from the shadows and staring back at him. They quickly moved, disappearing like a bad hallucination. But Calvino knew that they would have phoned their friends on the street to intercept them in the station.

'We're about to have company,' said Calvino, as he slapped a hundred baht down on the ticket counter.

'Where to, sir?' asked the woman seated on the opposite side of the glass.

Calvino turned to Marisa, 'Where do you want to take her?'

Marisa looked pale as she stammered. 'To my condo on Silom.'

'Sala Daeng Station. Four people.'

They ran down the escalator to the platform as they saw the light from the train moving down the tunnel. No one talked as they waited for the train to arrive. Calvino paced beside the down escalator, watching for men from the soi. Wan, Marisa, and Fon waited on the platform, palms sweaty, eyeing the other two or three people at the opposite end of the platform. No one said anything. A commercial for shampoo blared from large LCD screens on the platform. So far no one had followed them from Soi Cowboy. It seemed forever until a train arrived. When it did, they rushed inside, found seats, and flopped down, exhausted. Calvino caught a final look at the stairs and saw two Thai men running alongside the train, shouting and gesturing. The train soon picked up speed and the men disappeared. Calvino sat close to Marisa and she leaned her head against his shoulder.

'That was close,' said Calvino. He closed his eyes and exhaled, trying to clear his mind from the mistakes of the evening.

'You might have killed that man in the bar,' she said. 'And the man on the roof. You hit him hard.'

He glanced at her and saw that she looked scared. There was only one source of fear remaining: she was staring at it. Her body tensed as he touched her hand.

'They'll have a headache. But no lasting damage.'

She'd seen him use his gun to knock out the man who'd drawn first blood, and again he'd used violence on the roof. She had seen violence before, but it had been propelled by anger. What she had witnessed was cold-blooded, methodical violence carried out as a matter of efficient routine. At first Calvino's actions repelled her, making her feel vulnerable, then they excited her, making her feel confused. 'It doesn't bother you? To beat someone up and then . . .' she paused, looking for the right words. 'Then acting as if what you did was just another part of the day. It's what I imagine a hit man's emotions to be.'

'What do you know about hit men?'

She looked away, shrugged; whatever fear bubbled

below the surface, what she showed on her face was part revulsion, part terror as she struggled to reply. No words came out of her mouth. Ice water for blood is what she had wanted to say, but couldn't get the phrase out.

'I've got some news for you. Violence always has and will have a place and purpose. It is part of life. You do move on and be glad that you can,' he said. 'You don't swing open a switchblade at a wedding and expect to get a piece of cake.'

'This happened in a bar,' she said.

Calvino smiled, hands behind his head, 'No argument there. No cake either.' Violence was a secret companion haunting any bar. Most of the time it was inside the box with the lid on; other times, with enough liquor, a sideways glance, the wrong word, it flew out of the box at the speed of light, surprising everyone with how fast a room could fill with the smell of blood.

'Afterwards, you feel nothing, do you?' she asked. 'It entered you and left without leaving a mark. No damage. No nothing. Doesn't that scare you?'

He saw that it scared her. 'I don't take my work home with me.'

She nodded, biting her lip, as if she understood.

Flashing red and yellow lights shone on an empty stage. A dozen naked yings huddled in the back, smoking cigarettes and drinking rum. When the police showed up at the bar, the mamasan and two of the waitresses had finished cleaning up the blood

284

left behind by McPhail. She hadn't bothered to ask where Reno had gone. She didn't want to know; lying was much easier that way. No one had seen him slip away on the soi. 'Reno, he go home,' she told them. They looked around the bar, their walkie-talkies springing to life with grainy, deep-throated voices before going silent again.

'You tell Reno, we catch him with an underage girl, we close him for sixty days,' said one of the cops.

'I'll tell him, sir,' said the mamasan.

'Tell him we have a strict rule. Cannot break it.'

She nodded, agreeing with the seriousness of the allegation.

'We have four witnesses who saw a small girl come inside the bar. Where is she? Tell me and nothing will happen to you.'

'I saw no small girl, sir.'

They tried a few more times, but it took a sledge-hammer to crack a mamasan, and what was inside was mostly rotten anyway. The lead officer made the calculation that Reno had gotten away this time, but they'd be watching the bar. 'Tell Reno he's on our blacklist.'

'I'll tell him, sir,' she said, giving him a wai, which wasn't returned.

The cops left after a few minutes, and she saw them talking to the thugs who'd been waiting outside. The mamasan smiled, leaning on the mop as she peered through the torn curtain.

CHAPTER 23

They stood in the door to Marisa's three-thousand-square-foot condo – four bedrooms, three baths. Polished teak floors, Burmese artwork, Chinese vases, African ceremonial masks, and a Japanese samurai sword studded the vast living area along with tables and three sofas. The others behind Marisa stopped dead in their tracks, staring. Wan, the beekeeper's daughter, slowly pulled off her backpack, mouth open, looking around the largest private living area she had ever seen, and Fon walked straight to the African ceremonial masks to peer through the empty eyeholes. Calvino removed his shoes, staying close to the door. It wasn't clear whether he'd been invited inside or whether his duties were finished by delivering the others to the door.

'How many families live here?' asked Wan.

'My brother and me,' she said.

'You must be very rich,' Wan said.

Fon had taken one of the masks off the wall, walked over, and sat on one of the sofas, resting the fierce-looking witch doctor's wooden face on her lap. Her feet didn't touch the floor. 'Can I have it?' she asked.

'Keep it as long as you want,' said Marisa. The mask belonged to Juan Carlos.

Marisa had recovered some of her color, but still looked like she'd seen a ghost. 'Vinny, would you like a drink?'

'A drink would be a good thing,' he said, looking around the room. 'Where do you work?'

'The UN.'

He paused, looking around the apartment. 'You people at the UN are paid like bankers.'

Her hands continued to shake as she walked over to a cabinet and fiddled to open the door. Dozens of bottles were inside. She pulled out two glasses, bent her head forward as if she were bowing. Her forehead touched the cool glass, and a long sigh passed through her lips. Recovering herself, she turned back to her guest.

'I can't believe we did it. I don't want to think what would have happened if they'd caught us.'

'It's not over,' Calvino said, as she pulled a bottle from the liquor cabinet.

'Scotch?'

'You look a little shaky.'

'I'm okay. Really. Just out of breath.'

He nodded, watching as she screwed off the cap of a single-malt scotch, the same brand the General had given him. It made him smile. Maybe his luck was changing.

'You're smiling.'

'It's just that you're pouring my favorite scotch.'

Raising one eyebrow, she poured three fingers

into a whiskey glass and handed it to him. 'I'm guessing ice isn't something you like in your whiskey.'

'Straight is fine,' he said, taking the glass from her.

He sipped the scotch. It was the first time he'd actually tasted the General's choice. Edging away from the door, he walked to the middle of the room, looking around at the kind of luxury that he'd read a few expats at the top of the food chain enjoyed in Bangkok.

'Let's toast to happy endings,' she said.

He choked on the scotch. 'Excuse me? This is just the beginning. I don't see how happy is gonna figure into anything at the moment.'

'I thought Americans were more positive,' she said.

He ignored the play on nationality; it was a mug's game, one he refused to play. 'Here's how I see this situation playing out. The kid has value to the people you snatched her from. They won't let her go. They'll go to the police and file a report that she's been kidnapped. That's the way they work. In their mind, they own her. It's like you've stolen their SUV. It's not likely they'll throw up their hands and walk away.'

'They were planning to prostitute Fon.'

Fon sat across the room beside Wan, who was telling her stories about the faces on temples at Angkor Wat and about the Khmer people who'd built the temple. How these people also had ceremonial masks with the same hooded eyes, large lips, and flat nose. Wan's father had taken her to Angkor Wat when she'd been about the same age as Fon, and she remembered the faces of slaves, soldiers, kings, and courtiers carved in sandstone. Wan lifted the African mask from Fon's lap and raised it to cover her own face. Fon giggled as Wan lowered the mask.

Calvino watched the two Cowboy yings bonding, one a child and the other just beyond childhood. How was he going to say this so that he wouldn't come across like an asshole? Of course the kid's handlers had planned to pimp her. To them, she wasn't their kid. She was some poor peasant's kid.

'That's how they make money on their investment,' Calvino said. 'It's all about business. Profit and revenue and, of course, expenses. Keeping expenses down is something they're good at. Tomorrow, some relative, or someone pretending to be a relative, will sign a paper at the police station saying they never authorized you to take their kid. And the police have to make a decision. A Thai kid has been taken from her Thai family by a mem-farang. Whose side do you think they're going to take?'

He thought about the bar ying on the roof who'd chased her boyfriend down to kill him until she decided the farang on his chest was a greater affront to her honor than the boyfriend's infidelity. The clan always closed in behind each other in the face of a challenge from an outsider. Marisa wasn't their clan.

'She's not Thai. She's Shan, Burmese.'

Calvino shrugged, knowing that clan suddenly expanded to include neighboring ethnic minorities when a farang became involved in a conflict. Or they could play another card. 'An illegal immigrant has no rights. She's not a free agent. You can't just grab her off the street because you think it's the right thing.'

The traditional system had been tailored to operate on a highly personal basis. It wasn't modeled on law or rules, but survived on the basis that each level was connected, and breaking one of those connections threatened to collapse the entire structure. Marisa had pulled out one of the wires. That wire had to be put back. And the question was whether Marisa understood that her diplomatic passport, her UN position, and her ideals and values would not shield her.

'I have Thai colleagues who will help,' said Marisa. She so wanted to drop Somporn's name.

More people to draw into the line of fire, thought Calvino. 'Is carrying out rescue missions part of your job?' he asked. 'If it is, next time you ought to ask for backup.'

'My supervisor won't be happy about it. But it's done.'

'I don't know how to say this well. But I'd ask you to believe me. Nothing in Thailand is ever done in such a way that it can't be undone in the blink of an eye. You think you've crossed a finish line. But the line you just crossed is the starting line, and the people who were after the kid tonight are long-distance runners. They have endurance. Do you?'

Marisa poured herself a drink, steadying herself against the liquor cabinet. The last thing she wanted was to appear the stereotypical scared, weak female who couldn't stand on her own feet, make her own decisions, and fight her own battles. The moment she asked Somporn for help, she would be lost inside a world she would never escape. 'Thank you for your advice and for your help. What you did tonight, I can't begin to say how grateful I am for.'

He shrugged and finished the whiskey, setting the glass down on the long coffee table. 'I should go.' The three words every man utters when he understands that sex isn't going to happen and another day is waiting around the corner.

'Please. Not yet. I'd like you to meet my brother. He'll be home any time now.'

Meeting a brother, what an attractive alternative, he thought. 'Where are you from?'

'Catalonia.'

'Isn't that Spain?'

'Like Scotland is England,' she said. 'Or New York is America.'

He was starting to like the woman – her humor, her choice of whiskey, her fierce sense of right. 'It's just that I couldn't place your accent. I thought maybe Italy,' he said. Italy was Calvino's default; being half-Italian, he assumed a mem-farang had to be either Italian or Jewish.

Calvino walked over and squatted down beside Fon, her child's face painted like a whore's, her dress seductive and sensual, advertising her arrival to the marketplace.

'You did well tonight,' he said.

She pulled a face, stuck out her tongue, and raised the African mask. She had been someone's investment, but perched on the expensive sofa and wearing an African mask, she was still just a kid playing a game. Beside her was her stash of chewing-gum packets, a few wilted flowers, and half-a-dozen laser pens. She lowered the mask, laughing. She reached over and threaded her arm through Wan's as if letting go would mean that she'd tumble into a freefall. Wan had also made murmurings about leaving. She had a bus to catch to Surin. Her backpack had been left beside the door, next to her shoes.

'Stay the night. It's late. Tomorrow you can catch the bus,' said Marisa. Wan started to say something but stopped. 'I have a spare guestroom,' Marisa said. 'Please stay.'

Wan felt the kid's grip tighten, and she couldn't think of any good reason not to trade a hard seat on a bus upcountry for a soft bed in this palace. Calvino held his breath, hoping his own invitation would follow.

★ ★ ★

292

Fon and Wan padded off to a large bedroom of their own. At last the two adults were alone. Calvino sat on the sofa with Marisa, waiting for her brother. 'You're close to your brother, aren't you?' asked Calvino. He was killing time. Was he going to spend the night, or was he out the door? He'd delivered the kid. What else did she want? He moved closer, stretching his arm across the back of the sofa, just behind her head. She didn't seem to mind.

Marisa explained that she'd been born five minutes before Juan Carlos. She had slipped out of the womb as the advance detail. From the beginning Marisa had had one mission in her life: looking after her brother. It had been the twenty-first of June, and Juan Carlos had been born after midnight, making his birthday fall within the sign of Cancer. He'd left his sister on the other side as a Gemini. Different zodiac signs, different missions, same mother. Juan Carlos spoke nine languages. Calvino was impressed. In America he'd never met anyone who spoke more than two or three.

Marisa said, 'When I say, 'speaks nine languages,' you have to understand what I mean. He doesn't just speak these languages; he recreates them, acts them as if onstage, becoming a native speaker as he says the words. He becomes an Italian, a German, a Frenchman, or an Englishman. It's quite remarkable. I'm not saying that just because he's my brother. Others have said the same thing.'

'He speaks Thai?' asked Calvino, slowly removing

293

his arm from above Marisa's head. The brother was becoming a more intimidating force by the moment.

'Do you speak Thai?' she asked.

This was a dreaded question. There was speaking Thai and then there was speaking real Thai. Calvino spoke Thai like an Italian working-class immigrant spoke English. 'I get the message when someone threatens to kill me,' he said.

Marisa explained how there was something unearthly about watching Juan soak up Thai. He was a language sponge. He nailed the mannerisms, the gestures, and the facial expressions of a Thai, cool and friendly. Juan Carlos had an actor's talent to transform himself through language. 'It's like having eight brothers in one,' she said. Marisa spoke five languages. 'We have our language games. And we use our private codes and secrets in each language. Some people find that strange or annoying. For us, it's quite natural.'

Calvino resisted the urge to lean over and kiss her but for how long he could, he wasn't sure. He had a secret code of his own he wanted to share. But she got up and poured him a fresh drink, talking as she poured. 'Everyone has a favorite story. Would you like to hear mine?'

He glanced at his watch. Why not? he thought. What else did he have to do but pay McPhail's hospital bill, face a bitter bar owner named Reno, and proof-read a fifteen-page article that General Yosaporn had written about the history of holy water in Thai culture, how it had been taken from

India, and how it was different from Western holy water.

'I'd like to hear it,' Calvino said. He used every known facial muscle to not roll his eyes.

Marisa began her story. There was a Spanish naval officer who sailed with Vasco Núñez de Balboa. They set out on the same ship from Spain in 1500. Their journey had one goal: to return to Spain with two tons of pearls from the wilds of the New World. Travel at that time was very dangerous, and the outcome of any mission like this one was uncertain. They journeyed to many exotic places, crossing rivers, hacking through jungles, being attacked by Indians. They walked long expanses of virgin beach. Their divers submerged themselves in the offshore coves but found nothing much in the way of pearls. They discovered that the reports of pearls were nothing but a bar-room boast. But they pushed on, refusing to give up.

Along with other members of Balboa's crew, the Spanish naval officer crossed the Isthmus of Panama. They were fighting off mosquitoes in a dense rain forest when they were ambushed by local Indians, one of those tribes that specialized in shooting poison darts from a blow tube.

Despite the difficulty of the journey up to this point through dangerous and hostile country, this naval officer had insisted on one thing: that he must always travel with a wooden coffin.

'Why a coffin?' asked Calvino. She had hooked

him. After his experience with Apichart, he was a sucker for a coffin story.

'Exactly,' she said. 'He was afraid of dying in a strange place: He didn't want his body abandoned on a jungle path where it would be eaten by wild dogs. In death, he wanted dignity and honor as much as he had wanted it in life. And when he was killed, they buried him in that coffin. They placed a simple white cross above his grave and said prayers. He got the one thing that he'd wished for: not pearls, but a decent burial done with dignity.'

His arm had inched back around her neck. 'I have a coffin story. Do you want to hear it?'

'Love to,' she said. The man continued to surprise her.

He told her about General Yosaporn's deadbeat Chinese-Thai tenant and his coffin trick. He wanted to tell her what had happened with the hit team on the motorcycle, but he thought better of ending the night on a story of violence. He couldn't imagine that this woman had ever witnessed such a death.

'Do you carry a wooden coffin around?' he asked.

She started to laugh. His story, his question had connected. The ultimate seduction drug was laughter. She laughed until tears came into her eyes. Before she could stop laughing, his arm had moved down with the speed of an anaconda dropping from a tropical tree onto a small deer. Calvino started unbuttoning her blouse. Before he got to the second button, they were both stripping off each other's clothes. He slipped his arms around her, finding that she returned his embrace. He pushed his tongue against her lips. Marisa returned his kiss. She pulled back and took his hand to lead him into her bedroom. The single-malt whiskey and the bonding of the escape were making her do something she would normally never dream of on a first meeting.

He uncoupled the leather gun holster and laid it on a side table. Her eyes widened as she stared at the gun.

'I have a license.'

'Have you used it?'

'Never in the bedroom.'

'Should I be encouraged?' she asked, switching off the lights.

Calvino slipped out of his trousers and pulled her onto the bed. 'To carry around your own coffin.'

Her smile returned. The threat of the weapon had passed.

They fell into silence, touching each other in the dark. The first touch of a stranger's body, the smell of the city on skin, the smoke from the bar, perfume, scotch with a residue of chicken and sticky rice.

She reached over to a side table, opened a drawer, and took out a lighter. She lit two candles and three sticks of incense. The smell of sandalwood overpowered the other smells, and the flicker of the candle did wonders to hide the wrinkles around the eyes. She brushed her hand against his cheek.

'You're a nice man,' she said, finding his eyes in the candlelight.

'I was clumsy on the platform earlier. I'm out of practice.'

'What do you mean?'

'The things guys say to women they find attractive. The things that make them feel good about themselves, that make the women feel at ease.'

He didn't have to explain that with yings for hire no smooth-talking was required. The coffin story hadn't been his idea of foreplay. But it proved that foreplay can never be planned; it has to be improvised – matching his coffin with her coffin and above all making her laugh in the process.

Afterwards, his body lay braced against hers. 'No boyfriend?'

She shook her head, which lay on his chest.

Raising her head, she found his eyes in the candlelight. 'And you, do you have a wife?'

'No wife.'

'Foreigners usually have a Thai wife.'

'Usually doesn't mean always.'

She looked over his chest at the holstered gun. 'I don't like guns,' she said.

'Most people don't.' He thought she looked offended as she turned away. 'Did I say something wrong?'

'You don't understand. I'm not like most people. Not about guns. I know what they can do.'

She was getting more than interesting, a woman with knowledge of what a gunshot inflicts on another human being. There weren't many women in that category.

'I'd like to hear the gun story,' he said.

Her mother had told her that like her father, Marisa had a stubborn, independent streak. She dyed her hair and kept it short, tying it with red and yellow ribbons. She wore earrings bought from a gypsy in Mexico City who had told her they would always keep her safe. She'd worn them on the beach in Gijón the day a drug warlord from Colombia had been shot no more than three meters from where she stood.

Gijón, Spain – 2003

Marisa looked at the open blue sky stretched across the water, their meeting point blurred in a seamless aqua apron. She glanced at her wristwatch as she walked along the quay. It was 5:05 p.m., giving her another five hours of sunshine until the last rays disappeared into the sea. Marisa was in her mid-twenties, carefree and happy – more than happy: radiant, as if the sun had transferred some of its energy to her body. Her head felt light as she moved through the crowd. It was as if she were many years younger. Time had reversed itself and she felt like a teenager, free and wild, as if anything were possible.

She had been reading Flaubert's *Madame Bovary*. She hadn't read it since university and was just beginning to re-enter its remote world. She nibbled on a piece of apple and turned the page. Feeling hot, she put on sunscreen and drank from her water bottle. She laid the book on her blanket and set out to dip her feet in the water. She hadn't registered the men who were walking toward her. When she did look up, she saw a man's head explode. Bone, brains, tissue, and blood shot outward. She felt the warmth of blood on her face. When she touched her cheek and looked at her fingers they were sticky red. The headless man crumpled beside the edge of the sea.

The other men – she assumed that they were the dead man's friends but later learned they were his bodyguards – stood beside him with guns drawn. They knelt beside their fallen comrade, scanning the beach, the quay, the buildings along the beach road. There was no second shot. Most people were unaware of what had happened. Twenty meters away children played. Bathers slept on their blankets, the sun hot on their faces. Only a couple of other people had seen the man die. Her hands outstretched, Marisa dropped to her knees and washed her face in the sea. She splashed the water over and over again as if the stain, the smell, the feel of death wouldn't leave her.

In the following days, she went back to the location again and again. She isolated the possible locations of the shooter to a half-dozen and gradually reduced those down to one: the corner unit of a building's seventh floor. The balcony had an unobstructed view of the beach.

Everyone, including Juan Carlos, her father, the police, and even her mother said she had to be mistaken. From that balcony, a shot would have had to carry a distance of over one-thousand meters. She had measured the distance herself. From the balcony to where the man was killed was exactly one thousand, one hundred, and four meters. Blinds covered the windows of the corner unit. No one would have seen the scope, or the spotter next to the sniper watching through high-power binoculars, the two of them scanning the beach until they'd found their man.

She stood before the building of sandstone, the same as the church at marker number two. In front of the building was a bar, Zafiro and Juber Motor. Behind the building was a towering construction crane. Some said the shot might have been fired from the crane. But no one knew. The police learned the dead man was from Colombia and had been linked to the drug business. The Americans had indicted him for cocaine trafficking. But he had never been extradited. The dead man's mother lived in Gijón, and the son had come home to pay respect to his mother. He died on her sixtieth birthday.

Was what had happened that day like a black swan? No one could say. But, again, in Gijón, everyone agreed that black swans were common.

★ ★ ★

As she finished her story, Calvino took her hand and squeezed it. 'I'm sorry for what happened,' he said.

'In Gijón I was in the wrong place,' she said. 'Maybe Bangkok is another wrong place. I don't know after tonight if there is a right place for me.'

'You don't forget seeing someone killed.'

'You've seen this?'

Calvino sighed, nodding, and kissed her forehead. Then he told her about the ying at the Pattaya hotel and how he'd seen her fall, and about the two motorcycle gunmen who'd died in the soi. 'I know how you feel,' he said after he'd finished describing the police investigations into the deaths.

'Our lives are complicated in similar ways,' she said. 'I don't know if that's good or bad.' She was looking for reassurance.

'It's neither good nor bad,' said Calvino. 'Some people are connected by friends, neighborhood, and family. Others by the violent acts of strangers.'

'I'm glad I'm not the only one these things happen to.'

She was about to kiss him again when she heard Juan Carlos open the door to the condo and walk in.

'Marisa? Are you back?'

He stood in the entrance looking at three pairs of strange shoes, one of them belonging to a man with rather large feet.

Calvino sat up in bed, instinctively reaching for his gun.

'It's time you met my brother, Juan Carlos.'

'I'd like to get dressed first,' he said.

She started to laugh again, burying her head in the pillow to muffle the sound. From the huge living room, Juan Carlos called to her again, 'Marisa!' When he stopped, Marisa knew that Fon and Wan had already crept into the living room. 'I am Juan Carlos,' she heard him say with his usual charm. Nothing ever disturbed her brother. He rolled through the waves of life as if he had a gyro system that always kept him even-keeled.

Calvino's cell phone rang and he pulled it out of his pocket. He saw that it was McPhail's number. 'Excuse me, but I have to take this call.'

He disappeared back into the bedroom and closed the door. McPhail waited on the line. 'Hey, buddy, I just got nineteen stitches. And it takes you five rings to pick up. Nineteen. I counted each one. I guess I'll play that number on the lotto tomorrow.'

'You did well. I'll cover the hospital bill.' He could hear the sound of drunks in the background, the slurred voices, hacking coughs, laughter and squeals from a ying.

'I know that. Here's Reno. He wants to talk to you.'

'Jesus, Calvino, thanks for fucking up my business. The cops want money. McPhail wants an advance to pay the hospital. My lead dancers want a raise after the bloodletting. My mamasan is making a power play to take over the business.

And that isn't even the bad news.' Calvino waited while Reno sucked air. 'And I probably lost two of my best customers tonight.'

'What are you talking about?'

'The black guy and his friend. They were becoming regulars. I doubt I'll see them again after what happened.'

'They didn't look like men who scare easily,' said Calvino.

Reno ignored the reassurance. In his mind they were history. 'I don't mind helping a friend, Calvino. But you gotta understand I'm running a business, not some half-assed rescue operation.'

Everyone licked their wounds, counted the cost, glanced at the map of power to see what had changed, and trudged back to the bar, waiting for more bad news to find their address.

CHAPTER 24

Folded inside the tight coil of greater Bangkok, like hidden dimensions of the universe, were other, stranger Bangkoks. Places that farangs never passed. Or if they did, they wouldn't understand what was in front of their long noses. There were many such places inside Bangkok, places locked in other times, places where even most Thais never ventured?

Calvino found himself in such a place as he was trailing Somporn's mia noi. She had led him to a hole-in-the-wall in the middle of a self-contained neighborhood of hypnotic ugliness. What the Thais called a moo baan, recreating a small village atmosphere of narrow lanes with big-city three- and four-story row houses, shacks, howling dogs, runny-nosed kids, dust, poverty, and gossip. This moo baan ran along the rim of old Don Muang Airport. Election posters had been plastered on the front of the squalid shop-houses selling rice. Through his car window he stared at the three grinning Thai men in the posters with medals pinned to their suits. It took him a minute to spot that the candidate in the middle was Somporn,

305

who wore a chest full of medals on a white uniform. Thais rotated between top-down coups and bottom-up elected governments. Somporn was hoping to gain leverage once his small political party would be needed to form a coalition government.

Calvino drove ahead, keeping an eye on the gray Camry. As he passed several more of the posters, it seemed like Somporn was following him. He had another look at the photograph. The candidates on the posters followed anyone passing as if tracking them, whispering, 'Vote for me.'

Bangkok had the nickname of City of Angels, but few people believed that any angels lived inside the perimeter anymore. No one knew where the angels had gone, but they knew that those who had taken their places were not heavenly creatures. In the old days, the travelers called Bangkok the city of canals, the Venice of the East, but since then most of the canals had been entombed in concrete. More recently, public relations spin masters had come up with the phrase 'Land of Smiles,' but like the angels and the canals, smiles had vanished.

After the last coup, a client had told Calvino to wind up his clock to see if it still kept time; if it failed to do so, who was the timekeeper? The military junta that had been running the latest show had withdrawn into the shadows – setting up camp, waiting to see if they could live with the next round of elected civilians. People closed in around family, friends, and colleagues. With an election coming up, the military was doing whatever it could to retain its influence in the post-election era, and that meant backing the right-thinking people. Somporn thought of himself as being among those who thought and acted right. The difference between victory and defeat, all the players understood, wouldn't emerge only through an election; it would arise once the ever-shifting power connections had made a new deal everyone could live with.

In small, isolated pockets of Bangkok like this one, it didn't much matter who pulled the strings. Casey hadn't mentioned that Somporn was running for public office. But why would he? Calvino couldn't vote for him. An old woman rode past on a bicycle, giving him a betel-nut grin. You didn't see many faces like that on election posters. It was reassuring, he thought, that there was still one part of Bangkok where people rode bicycles as their main means of transportation – people who frequented mom-and-pop shops and massage parlors with rusty grills and green splashes of algae colonizing the outer walls. How much money is Somporn paying voters? he asked himself. From the look of the neighborhood, he could bag a lot of votes with a five-hundred-baht note.

With the sun overhead, Calvino kept his eyes on Cat's Camry. He stayed far enough behind to avoid her attention, but he was still close enough to see the back of her head. He would have thought Somporn's mia noi would at least glance at the campaign posters. But as far as he could see, she never gave them any notice. If anyone could know the bullshit of a politician inside and out, it would be his minor wife.

He watched her park and wrote a note in his logbook. She popped the trunk from the inside and then got out of the car. Lifting the trunk lid, she pulled out a black carry-on case, the kind flight staff wheel through airports. She crossed the street, pulling the case behind her. A couple of motorcycles shot past in a blur. The humidity and heat had bred two competing organisms: a black fungus and a green algae that fought over the right to the half-melted caulking in the window. The street could have passed as a petri-dish experiment in a nineteenth-century science lab. An ice cream vendor slumped over his cart in the shade, quietly enough that bacteria could have been culturing on the side of his sleeping face.

She turned into a beauty salon with faded posters of Thai movie stars on the walls. A couple of old ladies with their poodles and baskets of snacks talked over moaning hair dryers while getting a wash and set. Two Thai women in their late twenties dressed in blue jeans and T-shirts were snipping, cutting, separating strands of wet hair.

Calvino parked a short distance away. He walked over and looked through the window long enough to confirm his target was inside. Then he turned and spotted an open-air restaurant across the street. He pulled up a metal folding chair, sat down, and ordered a coffee. Opening the *Bangkok Post*, Calvino pretended to read. Then he actually started to read one of the news stories about the election. He scanned the article about the major players in the upcoming election, but there was nothing about Somporn. He folded the newspaper and looked across the street, then at his watch.

Cat had led him to a place in Bangkok from which no news ever filtered out to the English language press. He tried to remember if he'd ever read something about Somporn's election campaign in the newspaper. He drew a blank. He sipped his coffee before adding another spoon of Coffee-mate. Behind cover of the newspaper, he took out his digital camera and snapped several shots of the beauty salon and the gray Camry, making certain to zoom in on the registration plate.

Finishing his second cup of coffee, he looked over at the row of buildings across the street. There were hundreds of beauty salons closer to where Cat lived. Yet she had driven her new Camry all the way to the boondocks to sit in a rundown place that looked like its business plan had imploded long ago. But the hair-cutting yings who worked inside and their customers had kept the business alive. The shops and the people inside existed in an archway, figuratively speaking, with the old ways on one side and, on the other, the modern world that was looking to displace them.

It was a transition zone between two ways of life. If they wanted to see the future, they could go on the rooftops of their shop-houses for a glimpse of the big city sliding like an avalanche toward them.

Cat was inside for nearly an hour before the beauty-salon door opened and one of the beauticians followed her to the Camry. Cat was no longer pulling the small suitcase she had taken inside the salon. The two talked for a few minutes, Cat seated in the driver's seat, the air-conditioning turned on, and the beautician standing in the sun. Calvino couldn't hear what they were saying, but that didn't much matter. He waited until Cat had pulled away before he folded his newspaper and paid his bill.

Calvino flashed a smile at his waitress. 'What's your name?' he asked.

'Dam,' she said. That was the Thai nickname that meant black. It was a traditional out-of-fashion nickname, light-years away from the trendy Bangkok nicknames of Seven, Benz, or Starbuck. The waitress's skin didn't look black or even coffee-colored, but that wasn't important. Her father must have thought her black enough at birth to pull the name out of the air. But then there were also color nicknames that depended only on the days of the week: Yellow for Monday, Orange for Thursday. Or if you were born on Sunday, you might get stuck being called Red for the rest of your life.

'Dam, do you see that beauty salon across the street?'

Always start with a simple, easy question. Assuming she wasn't blind, of course, she could see the salon. Dam nodded.

'Do you know the name of the woman who came out with the customer a moment ago?'

Then give them a simple test. Names are easy for most people. The salon was across the street. Dam would know the names of every person inside. But it was better to go slow and easy, keeping the questions light and friendly.

'That was Fah,' Dam said.

'She must have been born on a Friday,' said Calvino, leaving a hundred-baht tip. That was big enough, he thought, to make him a big spender in this version of Bangkok. Then he remembered there was an election and everyone was laying down money on the table, looking to buy votes. She picked up the hundred-baht note and slipped it into the back pocket of her jeans.

Dam smiled, 'You are very good.'

'Is Fah good? Can I get a good haircut?'

'She cuts my hair.'

'You think she'd cut mine?'

'I think no problem,' she said with a large grin. 'Tell her Dam sent you.'

'I'll do that. Thanks. Oh, by the way, all these election posters on the street. Who are you going to vote for?'

A pensive look replaced the smile. 'Person who will help the ordinary people.'

'That should be a challenge,' said Calvino. 'What

about Khun Somporn? I see his posters up and down the street. Does he help the ordinary people?'

'He helps Meow,' she said with a sigh.

'Meow doesn't look all that ordinary to me.'

As he walked into the beauty salon, all eyes turned his way and stared. The two yings working to shape the hair on ancient heads stopped, their scissors frozen in midair. Four old women sat around a polished teak table playing mah-jongg, slapping the tiles. But the game had stopped too. The players looked up, a pile of bank notes on the table beside each one. There is an element of violence and spite inherent in that old Chinese game that seemed to perfectly fit the atmosphere of the place.

'Can I help you?' asked one of the yings.

'I'd like a haircut. And I'd like Khun Fah to cut my hair. That is, if she's available.' He sat down in the barber's chair and smiled.

'I am Fah,' said the ying with a T-shirt that read on the front SAME SAME and on the back BUT DIFFERENT. 'How you know my shop? How you know my name?'

The ladies waited for Calvino to answer. The women's interrogation was more like a job interview than a haircut.

'Khun Dam across the road said you cut her hair. And there was another person who said you did good work.' He closed his eyes as if concentrating and then slowly reopened them. 'Cat. I mean, Khun

Meow, tells me that you cut her hair too. With those recommendations, I'd say you're good.' He finished with a broad smile.

'How do you know Meow?' asked Fah. The other yings in the back strained to hear his answer.

Calvino raised an eyebrow. 'We go way back in time. We both like the music scene.'

'She was just here,' said Fah.

Calvino raised an eyebrow. 'Sorry I missed her.'

'You'll have to wait,' Fah said. 'And I don't have air-conditioning.'

For someone without a lot of customers, you should try to be a bit more positive, he thought. Normally the Thais were friendly, happy, and playful. This group looked at him as if he had some intention of robbing the place. He hadn't worn his leather shoulder holster, so it wasn't because of any mysterious bulge under his jacket.

The beautician came back with a glass of water for Calvino. Twenty minutes later, after he'd flipped through several women's magazines – all in Thai, so he had just looked at the pictures like a three-year-old – Fah tied the apron around Calvino's neck. He'd settled in long enough that the ladies had gotten used to his presence and stopped staring at him. Slowly they resumed their gossip about neighbors, the price of chicken, the local Mafia, and the daughter of a friend who had married a rich farang who had delivered ten grand worth of gold for his mother-in-law's birthday. One of the old women threw a glance at Calvino after the story about the gold, wondering about him in the way Thais wondered about farangs. Was he married? Was he rich? She licked her old, parched lips before thinking of the possibilities represented by so much gold. It was tied in with some demand made by the Mafia and a three-year-old gambling debt.

'How would you like it?' Fah asked him, looking at Calvino in the mirror.

Through the mirror he looked at her, standing behind him with the scissors. 'A light trim. Very light.'

She pulled the comb through his hair and, after reaching over to a side table for a plastic sprayer bottle, wet his hair down. The salon had a closed-in musty smell cut with cheap perfume and cat mange.

'Meow could go to any salon. But she comes here,' he said, watching her face in the mirror.

'She's very loyal to her friends,' said Fah.

Calvino thought about Cat going around Somporn's back with the Birdman. There was loyalty to men and then there was loyalty to the salon. The two would never be confused in the mind of a ying, he thought. The mah-jongg players pretended not to listen. He noted that Cat's suitcase rested beside one of the women at the table. On one corner of the mah-jongg table were several stacks of small campaign cards with the faces of Somporn and two other candidates. Next to the cards were a stapler and a box of staples.

'She's been coming here a long time,' said Calvino.

One of the old ladies whispered loud enough for everyone to hear that she was increasing her wager on the game. She then discarded a tile.

'Even after her sister died, she didn't forget us.'

Calvino raised an eyebrow. 'When did that happen?'

'Two, three years ago,' said Fah.

One of the old ladies piped up, 'She died three years ago last month. I remember the funeral. Her two young boys cried their eyes out. They had no father around to hold them.' The gambling hadn't kept any of them from absorbing the gossip flying around the salon like mah-jongg tiles.

'How old was the sister?'

'Jeab was twenty-four,' said another old lady.

'No, she wasn't. She was at least twenty-five,' said the first one.

'She wasn't quite twenty-five,' said Fah. That seemed to satisfy the two old women, as there was no clear winner in the age sweepstakes.

The subject had opened up the collective wisdom of the salon, and Calvino pushed ahead with his questions. 'That's young to die.' He considered the possibility that the husband had passed along a dose of AIDS before he turned into a coil of smoke going up the temple chimney.

'Jeab worked here for two years before she died.'

'She was the best,' said one of the old ladies. 'I still miss the way she cut my hair.'

Watching her face in the mirror, Calvino saw

the remark had annoyed Fah. 'What happened to the kids?'

'With no father, Meow supported them.'

Resting against the elbow of one of the ladies was a stack of thousand-baht notes with campaign cards stapled to each one.

'Saved their lives is more like it,' said the other hairstylist.

'Gave them hope,' said one old lady. She slipped the stack of banknotes off the table and out of sight.

'She put them in an international school, a school that is only for the very rich. But she pays for it.'

It turned out to be the old story of the husband running off with a younger woman. Jeab had it in her head that she'd been thrown overboard because she had a number-three nose, the kind of nose outside of Asia that takes a lot of punching before it gets that flat. And if she had a more beautiful nose, she thought, then she could reel her husband back in, or if that failed, she'd find another man who would appreciate her new beauty. A friend had recommended a clinic. The price was cheap and the doctor was, well, a doctor, and he had done a lot of nose jobs. Jeab had gone into the clinic at ten in the morning and lain back on the cot where the doctor administered the anesthesia. But he somehow used too much, or she just had a reaction. No one ever knew the reason for sure, but Jeab's heart stopped, and by the time they got her to the hospital, her brain had swelled up, and the emergency room doctors had to punch holes in her skull to relieve the pressure.

She'd lingered a while in ICU, hooked up to machines to keep her breathing. When her heart stopped again, no one attempted to revive her. Cat took in her nephews, something that had made it easier to accept Somporn's offer at the car show. Old-fashioned capitalism, supply and demand, had worked for both of them. In three years the two boys had prospered at the international school. Cat kept a rented house near the school with a full-time live-in maid. Twice a week she visited her nephews, and they adored her as if she were their mother.

'She goes to all the boys' school functions,' said one of the old ladies. 'That's a fact.'

Cat the saint, thought Calvino. He also thought of Marisa and wondered what it was about women that made them rescue children while the men walked on past.

'Meow must be rich,' said Calvino.

Fah held the scissors an inch away from his cheek, finding his eyes in the mirror. 'She has a rich husband.'

'Yeah? She married?'

'I thought you said she was your friend?'

'I've never met her husband.'

'She's a mia noi,' said one of the mah-jongg ladies. 'But what is the harm in that? A man with that much money should spread it around with more than one wife. I've always said that.'

Another old woman shook her head. 'Not always. Only since your husband died have you said that.'

'People change,' said the old woman, who had the kind of permanent smile that plastic surgery leaves. 'And Meow has got herself a good man. He takes care of her.'

'And she takes care of him,' said her friend, winking. 'If he's elected, it's because of her. But elections cost a lot of money. That is, if a candidate wants to get elected.'

They saw him looking at the money. 'Friends help friends,' said one of the women at the table.

Calvino nodded, turned back, and looked in the mirror. He gave Cat full credit and an extra star to Somporn, who had found a way to get his money into the hands of the voters while staying far away from the money trail himself. Using the game of mah-jongg as a cover was a particularly nice touch.

Calvino scratched his head, sitting in the barber's chair and looking at the cash and the women at the table. 'I thought Meow was single,' he said. 'I saw her hanging out with a jazz musician. He plays with a band at Saxophone.'

'That's Nop,' said Fah. 'That's not her husband. Ball teaches the boys guitar once a week. He works for Meow.'

'Everyone calls him Ball. He's a celebrity, you know. A lot of people work for Meow. Some of them are quite famous,' said one of the women at the table.

Not everyone, thought Calvino, who had grown accustomed to thinking of him as Birdman.

Fah held a mirror behind Calvino's head. He had a look at her work and nodded. 'Ball's good on the guitar,' said Calvino as he started to rise.

'But I'm not finished,' said the beautician, clicking the scissors as if she had a nervous habit. Calvino removed the apron around his neck and handed it to her.

'Just a trim was all I wanted,' he said.

'I only did the back.'

'That's where it grows the fastest.' He pulled out his wallet and gave her a five-hundred-baht note.

'It's one hundred baht. Do you have anything smaller?' asked Fah.

'Keep it,' he said. 'Make certain you vote for Somporn.'

'Oh, we will,' said one of the mah-jongg players, slapping down a tile.

As he walked to the door, Calvino stopped and looked back at the women.

'I forgot something,' he said.

The women looked at him and then at each other, waiting to find out what he'd left behind. Only he hadn't left anything like keys, glasses, a wallet, or the other things geezers forget.

'Meow had a friend. Her name was Nongluck. Did Meow ever talk about her?'

The women at the table looked down at the tiles. It was the first time they'd had to prepare for the passage of a freight-train-sized lie. 'No, I don't think Meow said anything about a Nongluck,' said one of the women. The others agreed.

The thing about lies is that the truth is lying just out of reach, waiting. In most cases, it's waiting for money. He wondered how much the ladies might be siphoning off. Something, of course, but not enough to defeat the larger purpose. The Thais understood that crossing a line over into greed was a money handler's death warrant. None of these ladies looked like they wanted to get themselves killed. Calvino removed his wallet and took out a thousand-baht note – later he kicked himself for not taking out the five-hundred-baht note next to it – and walked back to the chair where he had got the haircut. He laid the note on the seat of the chair. 'Tell you what, the first lady who can remember something, anything Meow might have mentioned about Khun Nongluck, gets the thousand-baht note.'

A group of women neck-deep into rigging an election could definitely be bought. It was just a matter of time. He waited a minute and then paced between the chair and the door, staring down at the banknote. Making them believe that at any moment he was going to stick it back in his wallet.

Cat was a good customer, and she'd left behind a load of cash, but she was gone. That was the reality. Absence was a problem. There was no shield other than a physical one, and the temptation of a quick cash transaction was what determined elections, paid school fees, and smoothed the transmission of information. The ying who had cut Calvino's hair grabbed the thousand-baht note just a fraction of a second before the other stylist, who was at a distance disadvantage. 'She didn't like Nongluck. She said Nongluck was no good, a cheap woman. And what did men see in a cheap woman?'

'Any reason for Meow to say Nongluck was a cheap woman?'

'A woman's thing,' said the winning stylist, having pocketed the money.

'Meaning the bad blood was over a man,' said Calvino.

Behind their faces, upon the recognition of truth being spoken and before a switch could be flipped, he saw a gnat-sized object of truth whip past at the speed of light.

Walking out of the beauty salon, Calvino felt he'd gotten far more than he'd bargained for when he'd followed the gray Camry to the moo baan. He'd walked into an old Bangkok sealed away in the past. It was in such places that some men found a way to secure their future. Casey, the private contractor with interrogation expertise, good street contacts, and a payload of anger over a dead son, was locked in a version of the past fueled by hatred. Then there was Somporn, the businessman and politician, with a ying salting cash around his election district.

But there were a couple of troubling things about

Casey. He'd hired Calvino to follow Cat. But he claimed not to know about the dead ying in Pattaya. Maybe he was telling the truth, unless he had a reason to lie. That left open the possibility of Apichart, still the man who had a motive to frame him with a murder rap. It occurred to him that Casey might have a use for the information about Cat's movements and associations beyond the one he had disclosed. Was he going to use the information only to ruin Somporn's election chances? That seemed too subtle and indirect for Casey. Besides, the disclosure of a mia noi might help Somporn get votes. Eliot Spitzer, the ex-New York governor, had been born in the wrong country, he thought. Calvino decided he'd leave out of his report the detail about Cat's role in acting as Somporn's bagman to the constituency. It was always good to hold something back from a client who was holding back his motives for hiring you in the first place.

CHAPTER 25

Jarrett leaned forward, the Sorbothane recoil pad firm against his right shoulder. His eye touched the outer rim of the telescopic lens. For a couple of minutes he didn't move; it didn't even look like he was breathing. A soft quiet filled the room as Tracer changed the music. During that moment, as his finger rested firm against the trigger, Jarrett felt like a god, the Old Testament god perhaps, with the absolute power of death. He knew that feeling of power from his work in Bosnia, Somalia, Cali, Gijón, Baghdad, and Kabul. To take a life is the ultimate act. Snipers are gods.

The inner city core was a common factor in most of these jobs, with its concrete and steel and glass on all sides, and canyons filled with people and cars. And at night, the lights came on and the target appeared like a white ghost through the infrared scope. He leaned back from the rifle, his back pressed against the chair, arms folded over his chest.

Tracer stretched out over the pool table, looking at the cue ball and the yellow number-one ball for a long shot into the far-corner pocket. He executed the shot, dropping the red-striped eleven ball into the corner pocket, the cue ball rolling back with lots of backspin. Smiling, he chalked up the cue stick, looking at the lay of the table, contemplating his next shot as he walked the side of the table.

'I've been thinking about Casey. You ever wonder how he came up with forty-grand cash? He's working an interrogation assignment. That means he's on a monthly salary. How do you save that kind of money and live?'

'Waters said Casey used his life savings,' said Jarrett. 'Besides, that's the deal. Always has been. No more, no less.' Forty grand had been the amount Ian MacDonald had left behind with a note on the table of the beach house. When they'd returned with the boat, they went back into the house. Jarrett's father had found the note and money. The note had said, 'For Jack.' MacDonald was gone.

'I am aware of that. But Casey doesn't strike me as a man with that kind of money.' Tracer sank the blue-striped ten in the side pocket.

'Then I don't get what you are saying.'

Tracer shrugged and rested his head on the back of the sofa. 'I thought that was a pretty good shot.'

'You got a problem with Casey?'

'Just wondering. In my experience, guys like Casey no more have forty grand than pigs got wings.' Tracer missed a bank shot on the green-striped fourteen.

Jarrett walked around the table, leaning down, lining up for a straight side shot at the red three ball. 'If he didn't save it, where'd he get the money?' The cue slid smoothly over the blue felt. He made the shot, missing the pocket.

'Fuck if I know. But at the same time I don't wanna be fucked around for not knowing. I mean, it's something to think about. That's a bunch of money.'

Jarrett couldn't concentrate on his game. He glanced up at the whiteboard. On one side, they kept score of their pool games. But the other side was strictly reserved for business. He sighed and shook his head. Seeing that he was behind, he lay down his cue and walked back to the rifle. He sat down and peered through the telescope sight, looking at the activity inside Ripper before moving next door to the chrome and glass of Papa Bear, then over to the office tower Grizzly. He fit his eye on the scope, scanning windows from Scorpion, Firebird, Rooks, and Black Sheep before stopping back at Zapper three-nine. 'Clear,' said Jarrett.

'You give up?' asked Tracer, standing at the pool table.

'I never give up.'

Tracer knew that was true. Jarrett was dogged; the man never got tired, never flinched, never broke his concentration with his job. But pool was another matter. That was understandable, as shooting had some history attached to it. 'Another thing,' Tracer said after a pause. He had picked up his binoculars and focused on a young woman doing yoga on a mat inside her condo sitting room. Sitting like a Buddha in the lotus position, eyes closed. He wondered if Jarrett ever relaxed. He looked at the woman's face; it was serene and radiant like she was witnessing eternity at the end of a long tunnel.

'What other thing?'

'It's about your beekeeper's daughter taking off with that guy, the kid, and the white woman. He's the same guy who ran into our car. Early in the morning he's snooping on some poor married guy in Washington Square. Then he shows up in your bar with a white woman and a street kid. What's with this guy? You looked at that white woman like you knew her from somewhere.'

Jarrett stretched back, arms over his head, yawned. 'Just wondering what she was doing in the bar with the kid.'

'I'm not worried about her. It's your Thai squeeze I'm talking about. What's she doing with that investigator? Because that's exactly the kind of guy who could cause a problem.'

'Wan doesn't know anything. I slept with her. There wasn't a lot of conversation. It was a crazy idea, I know, but I wanted to give her money to quit the bar and go home.'

So much for free will, thought Tracer. Like the blues song said, a man with a woman is gonna leave his mind in the ditch. He's only going to talk from his heart, and that's going to throw him into a bigger ditch down the road.

Jarrett rocked the pad against his shoulder, feeling the weight of the rifle. 'You worry too much about stuff. Reading things into something that's not there.'

'Like the forty grand,' said Tracer.

'That's a good example. You know the history. That's the number.'

'You ever go to a bank and ask for forty grand?'

Jarrett smiled and shook his head. 'What are you saying?'

'I got a close look at a couple of the bundles of cash. It didn't look like those hundred-dollar bills came from any bank vault. That money had the smell of street money. Those bills came from under the floor in a basement.'

'What if they did? I don't see your point. Do we care where Casey got the money? It doesn't concern us.'

It wasn't the first time they'd freelanced a special-ops mission that Waters's boss hadn't signed off on, but it was unusual. The company's rules for such an engagement were strict. Employees worked for the company and followed company policy, and that policy was to make money from government contracts. Any assignment that threatened the company's government revenues would never make it through the approval process. There had to be a good reason to go outside the company's structure for a mission. Paying back Jack was a fail-safe reason for bypassing the system. If no one else was willing to do the job, then Jarrett and Tracer got the call.

Tracer lowered the binoculars and walked back to the pool table. He retrieved his cue and started chalking up, the blue powder getting under his nails. 'You gonna finish this game or forfeit?'

'We ain't finished talkin' about the money.' Jarrett left his position and picked up his cue, shifting it from hand to hand.

'We can talk about the money and play.'

Jarrett looked over the sea of solids on the table, knowing he was in trouble unless he started dropping some balls.

'In Casey's case, the locals didn't give him any justice,' said Jarrett. He nailed the solid-green six in the corner pocket.

Tracer raised an eyebrow. 'Good shot.'

Jarrett followed up with the solid-red three in the side pocket. He felt that he'd found his groove and relaxed, chalking up his stick.

'That leaves a man with one alternative: revenge,' said Jarrett. 'It's a word we both understand. You kill the man who killed your son. It don't get any more basic than that. If that happened to you, Tracer, you'd find a way to get forty grand. You'd make it happen.' He banked the solid orange in the side pocket. Jarrett looked up, letting the pool cue slide down his hand until the bottom touched the floor. 'I'd make it happen. What man wouldn't? This is payback, Tracer, pure and simple. Casey's a patriot. You know that. The man did three tours in 'Nam. A special-ops guy like Casey could pull forty grand out of a hat. He probably had it buried in some Vietnamese village, figuring that one day he'd need that stash.'

'The bills he used were from the early 1990s,' said Tracer.

Jarrett slowly moved around the pool table, stopping behind the solid-blue two. He sent it into a corner pocket and looked up. 'Does it matter, Tracer? He got the money. He had every reason to come up with the cash.' Jarrett ran oil along the barrel of the rifle. Tracer could see he was still thinking about the money.

'How'd you know about the bills?' Jarrett asked, eyeing the solid-yellow one ball.

'Colonel Waters. I asked him.'

It made Jarrett smile as he sent the cue ball and dispatched the number one into a side pocket. The fact that Tracer continued to use Waters's old rank when he talked about him amused Jarrett. He was a company man now, a vice president at Logistic Risk Assessment Services. 'Colonel' was a relic from his past.

'Why'd you do that?'

'Where a man gets his money tells you what kind of man you're dealing with.'

'What did Colonel Waters say?'

Tracer's eyes grew larger as Jarrett sunk the purple and orange balls, leaving only the wine-colored seven and the eight ball to finish the game.

'Pretty much what you said. Casey had all the

reason in the world to nail the motherfucker who put a hit out on his son. But he's on special assignment in Bangkok. He'd compromise what he's doing if he did it himself, and he's not gonna risk the mission. Not even Casey. Waters said forget about where it came from.' He paused. 'You gonna let me have another shot or not?'

'But you aren't forgetting.' He turned his attention to the seven ball, just missing the side pocket. Looking up, he was rewarded with a big smile on Tracer's face.

Tracer hummed along with the background music like he'd gotten a fresh start. 'You forget something important, you lose. Pool or your life, it's all the same thing when you stop paying attention.' He lined up on the striped purple and sent it sailing to the side pocket. The successful shot made him feel better until he saw that his follow-up shot on the striped green was snookered by Jarrett's solid seven ball.

'We've got the perfect cover for the assignment,' said Jarrett. 'With this election in a couple of days, everyone will assume it was a political job. They won't be looking for us. They'll be looking for Thais with military connections, a business conflict, even his wife. He's got a list around the block of people who'd like to see him dead.'

'I've got no complaints about the timing,' said Tracer. He tried a bank shot that set up an easy corner-pocket shot on the solid seven for Jarrett.

Jarrett took his time chalking his cue. The silence

between them lasted until the seven dropped into the pocket. Only the eight ball remained between Jarrett and winning the game. 'I asked Wan why the bees were dying, and you know what she said?'

Tracer liked the idea that somehow Wan, with a ninth-grade education, had figured out the scientific mystery. 'What'd she say caused it?'

'Someone had dishonored the spirits and they were taking revenge.' Jarrett leaned against the pool table, taking his time.

Tracer scratched his throat and sighed, waiting for the inevitable loss of the game. 'In New Orleans, we knew that disturbed spirits could never cause anything good.' He stroked his mojo bag and smiled, thinking that maybe this beekeeper's daughter knew something about life outside book learning.

But that mojo didn't stop Jarrett from rolling the eight ball in the right-corner pocket. When Jarrett looked up, he watched Tracer fingering his mojo bag, hoping against hope for a win. He was a practical man, and that meant relying on tangible things – wind, water, and fire – not as signs, but as real elements that could be used to heal or to destroy. There were no spirits, demons, or ghouls, only distance, wind, velocity, load, and opportunity. Sniping was taking that opportunity to the next level.

Tracer racked up the balls for another game. 'I let you win the first one.'

A crooked grin crossed Jarrett's face. 'Harry always said, "Son, never insist on too much reality.

331

People just don't have the capacity for knowing too much."' That came from a man who had made a career of tracking high-value targets who'd taken refuge in failed states. His son had followed in his father's footsteps, keeping up the family tradition.

'Your father was a wise man,' said Tracer. 'My daddy believed in voodoo, and I'd say he was a wise man, too.'

'Yes, he was,' said Jarrett. He'd once met Tracer's father when they were on leave from the marines. Watched him kill a chicken and mix the blood with rum and pass the cup for Tracer to drink, and then over to Jarrett. All eyes were on him as his lips touched the rim of the cup and he drank. The old man said that this had made them brothers. Tracer's father had enough voodoo to get a French woman wild enough to leave her family in France to come live with him, as he ritualistically killed chickens, cast spells, and expelled demons. Wild enough to produce a man like Tracer.

Jarrett's father, Harry, had served three tours of duty at JUSMAG and performed his own kind of voodoo in marrying a woman from Istanbul. He was a senior adviser at USSOCOM at MacDill Air Force Base, a jumping-off point for assignments that took him from Berlin to Jakarta to Beijing and finally back to JUSMAG in Bangkok. He'd retired a year and a half ago. Harry and Lee had produced three children: Sam, the doctor; Janet, the Ph.D. in biotechnology; and then came their youngest son, the ex-marine sniper with a degree in criminology from John Jay College, who worked for a private contractor in Kabul with special-op assignments that took him in and out of Baghdad. His brother was pulling in five hundred grand a year, and his sister was working toward a Nobel Prize at Stanford.

But which one did the old man love the most? Jarrett had been the child invited to Hua Hin to celebrate the twenty-five-year reunion with Jack Malone. After Jack had gone missing, they'd gone to Ian MacDonald's beach house, snuck in through the backdoor. Harry witnessed his son shoot a man whose assignment had been to kill MacDonald. Alan's brother or sister could never compete with the bond created that night. Harry had himself one child who was practical. Who hadn't been afraid and acted out of instinct; in a split second, as Varley swung his gun and fired on his father, Jarrett shot him in the head.

'Harry's most important lesson was to take life ten meters at a time.'

When Jack Malone didn't show, Harry returned to the hotel to wait for his call. After the third game of pool with Ian MacDonald, he'd pretty much told Jarrett the outline of his story. A Perth businessman named Cleary, who made his money in shady real estate, gold mines, pearls, and shipping, had made a death threat. But MacDonald said he wasn't too worried. He called Jarrett around to the side of the pool table, patted his ankle with the cue stick, and then used the end to raise his pant cuff to reveal a handgun in a holster. Cleary bragged about the number of people he'd had killed before. It was part of doing business. Once in New York, the Perth businessman called in a favor with a drug-dealer connection to arrange for the murder of a banker who'd repossessed a couple of antique cars to settle a debt.

Afterwards, Cleary had gone into his office, closed the door, and showed him a clipping from a New York newspaper, an obituary, describing how the guy had been murdered. He wanted the two million that MacDonald received from cashing in shares in Cleary's company. And Cleary wanted his money back. It was his money, he said, with no shade of doubt. And like the banker, MacDonald could run off to some remote place, but Cleary would find him and that wasn't something that MacDonald should ever want to happen.

Jarrett was still waiting for Jack to appear when Daws and Varley, the two men sent by Cleary, walked into the pool hall. It didn't take MacDonald more than thirty seconds to figure out that Cleary had sent them. They said they wanted to talk to him, alone, in private. Jarrett looked on as MacDonald said he didn't want to talk to them in private or anywhere else.

'That's not an option,' the hood called Daws told him. His partner, the Aussie named Varley, told Jarrett to get lost, as he was getting in the way of some personal business.

Jarrett's hands gripped the pool cue as one hip leaned against the pool table. 'Either of you guys see a redheaded guy coming into this place a few hours ago?'

Daws, the taller one with a military brush haircut and a Hawaiian shirt worn loose outside of his pants, said, 'This is the redhead we want.'

'What he's saying, in case you aren't listening, is piss off.'

Jarrett noticed that the skin had been scraped off the knuckles of Varley's right hand. What looked like a streak of blood had dried above one pocket as if he'd put a bloodied hand into it for something. There was a fresh bruise under Daws' right eye where someone had landed a solid punch. Daws showed no signs of a crashing headache or double-vision, but that newly born mouse cried out for a piece of raw steak.

Just as Jarrett was ready to make his move with the cue stick, Ian raised his hand and smiled, 'It's okay. We'll catch up a little later on the beach. Hope that you find your friend.'

'Yeah, me too,' said Jarrett, holding the pool cue; he'd understood what was going down and what MacDonald wanted. They'd shot a number of games, and fell into a pool-room bullshitting session. MacDonald had written down the location of his beach house and stuffed it in Jarrett's shirt pocket. He must've figured that maybe these guys would have turned up. 'Bring your dad and Jack. It's a big place. I've got a boat.'

Tracer saw that Jarrett had that faraway look. 'Why don't I break this time?'

'Winner breaks,' said Jarrett. 'But why don't I make an exception?' He gestured at the table.

Tracer obligated with a solid break, scattering the balls with the orange thirteen ball dropping in the corner pocket. 'Looks like I got stripes again. I got no luck with stripes. And when you get that faraway look, I wonder what is going on in your head.'

He waited until Tracer lined up over his next shot. 'Thinking about the smell of the sea.'

Tracer pulled a face. 'When I think of the sea, I smile. You weren't smiling.'

'It's not just me. Something's bothering you. Maybe you were thinking about something but keeping it to yourself,' Jarrett said.

Tracer studied the lay of the balls on the table. 'I can't say one way or another. Somporn being a no-show was a sign. But then that kind of shit happens. The man's running for public office. His time isn't his own. Then I think, what about tonight in the bar? That guy who hit our car in Washington Square walks in and all hell breaks loose. Maybe it's got nothing to do with our job, or maybe it's a sign we ought to think about.'

'There's no connection I can see,' said Jarrett.

Tracer seemed rattled, missing an easy shot on the striped-red eleven in the side pocket. 'Fuck, how did I miss that?' He shook his head and picked up the chalk.

Jarrett put down his cue. 'Why don't we turn in? We could use a good night's sleep,' said Jarrett, 'and then tomorrow we take another look at this thing that's bothering you.'

'Tomorrow we finish the job and fly back to Kabul,' said Tracer. He grinned, running a hand over the silencer fitted to the barrel of the rifle. This would muffle the shot. 'That's what I like about you. You are always looking at the next ten meters ahead and ready to roll out.'

'I've been thinking about that woman who came in with the detective,' said Jarrett. 'Did you see how scared she looked?'

'I saw the fear.'

He sat on the edge of the pool table, ran his fingertips down the nap of the felt. 'There was something familiar about her.'

'Déjà vu,' said Tracer.

'She was that woman in Gijón.'

Tracer had remembered her, and he'd been hoping that in the dim light of the bar, Jarrett wouldn't have drawn the connection. The last time either one had seen her was through a telescope. Jarrett had hit a target smack in the head one thousand meters away, and a girl reading on the beach next to the guy had got herself splattered head to toe. He had seen her wild-eyed face through his spotter binoculars, and Jarrett had seen her frozen in the crosshairs of his scope. It was as if time had stopped. No one moved, said a thing, or breathed. Then the clock started again. The blood dripped down her chin, but they were too far away to hear the scream. The hit had been a job. He hadn't felt anything for the target. But in his mind he'd seen that girl on the beach for months afterwards. Whatever else had happened in that girl's life, he'd chopped off a huge shank of innocence. Tracer thought about what to say, scratched his head, and looked to a blues song for a little inspiration.

'What was she doing in the bar tonight?' Tracer said, rolling one ball after another on the pool table. 'Man this is seriously fucked up.'

'I don't know. I don't think it means anything. She's never seen me. We were too far away. There's no way she could know,' said Jarrett.

'But she was looking at you.'

'I reminded her of someone. Mistaken identity. It happens. It happened to Jack Malone.'

Tracer paced up and down alongside of the pool table. 'You're right. So what if it was her? It don't make any difference. She don't know you. She don't know me. And besides what happened in Gijón was a long time ago.'

Tracer had been right. Jarrett had been thinking about Gijón and the girl on the beach, and then thinking about the girl on the balcony. And thinking about Jack Malone. He remembered what his father had said about there being a borderline between regret and remorse. The line was different for every man. If a man failed to act, he was going to find himself with a load of regret sitting on his heart and scratching his head. What made the choice hard was when a man did something that seemed right but some emotion had colored his action. Sometimes later, when he recovered his senses, he'd look at the situation rationally and feel remorse for the pain his actions caused the other person.

'So when you're paying back Jack,' Harry had said, 'remember that no one can tell you what is heavier to carry: regret or remorse.' It wasn't anything his father ever had to tell him twice; he'd been there, he saw it unfold, he'd acted when it mattered.

CHAPTER 26

Juan Carlos, after an hour, had warmed to Calvino, taking into account that the stranger had come out of his sister's bedroom with the easy kind of smile of satisfaction. His initial suspiciousness gave way to his characteristic openness and friendliness. Calvino sat close to Marisa on the sofa. The proximity along with the rumpled state of Calvino's trousers and black T-shirt hadn't gone unnoticed. He'd left his sports jacket and holster in Marisa's bedroom. Marisa wore a yellow short-sleeved blouse and black slacks, a different outfit from what Juan Carlos remembered her wearing when she'd left the condo earlier that evening.

'Vinny, thank you for helping my sister,' said Juan Carlos.

'I walked her home,' said Calvino.

'I remember running,' said Marisa.

Calvino shrugged, looking at Juan Carlos and then at Marisa. People often thought someone had saved their life when most of the time their life had not been at risk of ending. Inconvenience, a slap-down, a kick, or pulling of hair, but rarely did death enter into the mix. The men at Reno's bar had no intention of killing Marisa; that would have been bad business. They just wanted the kid back, and a bit of shoving, grabbing, and a hint of violence would have been enough to do the job.

Juan Carlos sat forward on the edge of his chair. Marisa's account of the evening had pumped him up with a range of emotions – anger, fear, hatred, and finally gratitude. 'I'm grateful for what you've done.'

A twin quality connected them. 'My sister insisted that she go out for a walk on her own. I urged her to let me join her.' His tone dropped off with a long sigh as if his failure of persuasion was to be blamed for the encounter that evening. 'Do we know who attacked Marisa?'

'No idea,' said Calvino, keeping it sweet and simple.

'Traffickers,' said Marisa.

Juan Carlos leaned forward and hugged his sister. 'I should have been there,' he said. Calvino liked the brother but knew that if he'd been in the bar, challenging the Thai thugs to defend the honor of his sister, the result would have been worse for everyone.

'No one was hurt,' said Marisa from the sofa. She sat with her legs crossed, her arms stretched out.

'Except for a good friend whose arm got cut up,' said Calvino. McPhail had gone to the hospital.

'I hope that he will be alright,' said Marisa, squeezing his hand.

'Let me get you a drink.' Juan Carlos moved to the liquor cabinet.

'Scotch,' said Calvino.

'The single-malt,' said Marisa, smiling at Calvino.

Juan Carlos pulled out the bottle of eighteen-year-old single-malt and filled the glass half-full. A man who had saved his sister's life deserved nothing but the best.

Earlier that evening, after Marisa had left, Juan Carlos had gone out with a friend who was passing through Bangkok, a journalist from Madrid. Arnaldo had phoned from the Dusit Thani Hotel, which was near the condo.

'Arnaldo was in such good form earlier tonight,' Juan Carlos said. He was fully relaxed, speaking as if he'd known Calvino his entire life. 'He said to me, "Juan Carlos, there are only three important things for a man." And I asked Arnaldo, "Only three?" And he nodded and said, "Yes, three things matter to a man – meat, soccer, and women."'

'I told Vincent what happened that day on the beach in Gijón,' said Marisa. Juan Carlos handed Calvino the glass of scotch.

The smile had disappeared from his face as he looked at his sister. 'Why don't I get you a drink, too?'

'Juan Carlos thinks I should have forgotten about that day.'

'That's not true, Marisa,' he said from the liquor cabinet halfway across the enormous living room. 'Forgetting is not possible. But returning to the place with a stranger doesn't help your mental health.'

'Vinny isn't just a stranger,' she said.

He was about to switch into Catalan and ask her how someone she just met on the street – even if he had saved her life – wasn't a stranger. Catalan was their private, tribal language, the one spoken at home with their mother and father, which they could safely assume almost no one from outside the region could understand. A nice, good, and decent stranger, yes, but the man in their sitting room was still a stranger nevertheless.

'Meat, soccer, and women?' asked Calvino.

The smile returned to Juan Carlos's face. 'That's the holy three for Arnaldo. But he says it's true for all men. What do you think, Vinny?'

Calvino squirmed on the sofa, his knee brushing against Marisa's leg.

'I'd say the first two were optional. But I'm not Spanish. I'm Italian and Jewish.'

Juan Carlos laughed. 'I like you.' He raised his glass of red wine to his sister. 'I like Vinny's sense of humor.' He sat a couple of feet away – in the excluded zone – from his sister and Calvino on the sofa. He had given Marisa a fresh glass of red wine. Calvino held his glass of scotch in both hands, wondering how he was going to get his holster and jacket and gracefully leave the condo.

'The authorities reported that the man who was shot in Gijón was a big-time drug baron,' said Marisa, sipping from the wine. 'The authorities thought it was a professional job. Maybe the Americans assassinated him. Or it could've been another Colombian wanting to take over his drug cartel.' She stared at Juan Carlos, who remained silent for a full minute. On paper that isn't much time, but right then the minute stretched on for an embarrassing period.

'I need to get back,' said Calvino, catching Marisa's eye. He brushed the top of her hand and she nearly spilled her wine. 'Sorry, that was clumsy of me.'

'Give me your card,' said Juan Carlos. 'I want to invite you to the wedding.'

Calvino's half-grin betrayed his anxiety. 'Wedding?'

'Marisa, you didn't tell our friend about the wedding?'

She tipped the wine glass back, finishing the wine. 'Juan Carlos is marrying next month.'

'Congratulations,' said Calvino, extending his hand. He thought for a moment that Juan Carlos was going to kiss his cheeks.

'My sister is trying very hard to accept that her little brother will have a wife,' he said, shaking Calvino's hand again.

'That's not true,' said Marisa.

Calvino sat in the middle. He wanted his sports jacket. He wanted his gun and his socks and a taxi back to Sukhumvit Road. Marisa reached over and squeezed his hand.

'The father of the bride is running for parliament. I'd never heard of his political party. But I

344

understand he stands a very good chance of getting elected. He has big plans for Juan Carlos; he'll work in the family corporate empire and play an advisory role in the political empire. What I'm finding hard to accept isn't that Juan Carlos is getting married but that he's being absorbed into an enterprise that will own him. Somporn's his name.'

'Somporn?' asked Calvino, his head resting back on the sofa.

'You've heard of him?' asked Marisa. 'I'd never even seen his name. You're the first foreigner I've ever met who knows him.'

'That's not fair,' said Juan Carlos, the smile reappearing on his face.

'Why isn't it fair?' she asked.

Calvino experienced the back and forth of a verbal tennis match.

'Because foreigners don't vote. He doesn't care if foreigners don't know his name. It makes no difference.'

'But he wants to be foreign minister. Shouldn't some foreigners know him?' asked Marisa.

'What do you think, Vinny?' asked Juan Carlos

Calvino saw the situation was heating up between brother and sister, but couldn't figure out the context of what was fueling it. He'd been in a beauty salon where a game of mah-jongg was used as cover for a voter bribing operation. He'd been trailing Somporn's mistress, who happened to be involved with a guitar player some called Nop, others called Ball, and whom he called Birdman. Birdman had been in the hotel where a ying named Nongluck had tumbled off a balcony. He'd already heard more than he'd ever wanted to hear about Somporn.

'Politics gives me heartburn.' He looked at Marisa and nodded at the bedroom. 'I find politicians boring. Don't you?'

Calvino saw a red dot appear on Juan Carlos's forehead. Instinctively, he pushed him off his chair. He crashed hard onto the floor. In the confusion, Fon appeared at the far end of the room. In her hand was one of her laser pens. 'What's going on?' asked Marisa.

Calvino looked back at the child. 'Nothing, I saw a red dot of light on your brother's forehead, but it's just from a child's toy,' said Calvino. He motioned for Fon to come closer. She quietly walked from the bedroom door and stood a foot away. 'Show me what's in your hand,' he said.

Fon opened her hand and a laser pen rested on her palm. 'It's for you,' she said. It was all that she had to give. She stretched out her hand toward Calvino. He looked at the laser pen and smiled as he took it. He pointed it toward the wall and turned it on. A single red dot appeared. He moved across the wall until the red dot settled on the bottle of single-malt whiskey on the dry bar.

'Good for ordering drinks,' he said.

'It keep me safe,' said Fon.

Calvino tilted his head to the side. 'How does it keep you safe?'

'If I have problem, I flash and someone come to protect me.'

'You don't need it now.'

She hesitated, looking at Marisa and then back at Calvino. 'Maybe not.'

Marisa leaned forward, hugged her, kissed her on the forehead, and led her back to the bedroom. Calvino looked at the laser pen. He shone the red laser dot on the bottle again. 'I could use another scotch. But I'll pass. You okay, Juan?'

Juan Carlos nodded, smiled. 'Okay.'

As Marisa came back into the room, Calvino rose from the sofa, knocked back the rest of the scotch, and walked into Marisa's bedroom. After strapping on his holster and putting on his jacket, he walked back out. Brother and sister remained seated, caught off-guard by his abrupt departure.

It was the line that Calvino knew from experience would get him out the door: 'I have some work I need to finish, so I'll be on my way.'

He was showered with goodbyes in languages he didn't understand. Calvino assumed the message was goodbye, but given the evening, it could have been 'Watch your step. It's a long way to the bottom.'

CHAPTER 27

C asey folded up the subpoena and slipped it back into his pocket. It had been on his desk when he arrived for work. Each time he read his name on the subpoena, he balled up his fists in a flare of anger and paced his office. He phoned the company headquarters. He was told not to worry. It was a formality. Showing up in a suit and tie at the Russell Senate Office Building in Washington, D.C., before a subcommittee of the military intelligence committee, seemed no formality. The committee was holding hearings on the role of private contractors in the secret-prison system, and they were out for blood. His boss told Casey that at the company level, Casey had their full support. They promised him that he'd have at his side one of the best lawyers around.

Casey knew the game. They were telling him what he wanted to hear because they wanted his cooperation. What burned him was the company's using classic interrogation techniques, the same ones he'd used on insurgents before taking them down, inflicting pain, getting to the truth of what they knew. What Casey had wanted to hear was he didn't have to testify, just keep doing your job.

Instead, he had less than a week until he boarded the plane for Washington and the committee room. LRAS was preparing to cut him loose. He felt it like a man who sensed a subtle change in his wife's attitude as she put in place her plan to leave him.

Logistic Risk Assessment Services had been as cold-blooded as any private interrogator; what they were doing was nothing personal, but someone at the operational level had to be isolated and set up to take blowback. The handwriting was on the wall when the CFO at LRAS gave him the details of his legal representation: a twenty-six-year-old lawyer two years out of law school whose only job had been as a White House intern. His political connections would help them offer up Casey in a deal. Waters had told him that this was in the pipeline. 'Be prepared, act first,' Waters had said. Waters had tipped him several months earlier that an investigation was likely and warned him to cover his ass. That was something Casey had a lot of experience with doing. He had zero intention of showing up in a committee room in Washington and testifying about activities in Baghdad and Bangkok. He'd tie up some loose ends and then disappear, something he knew how to do. He'd been trained to make independent decisions in the field – whatever was needed to accomplish the mission.

Casey never forgot his training. He had already

bought his outbound ticket. But it wasn't to Washington, D.C.

Casey walked into Calvino's office wearing his interrogator's smile and a floppy-eared dog hand puppet. He stood erect before Ratana's desk and barked, the puppet hidden behind his back slowly emerging. Ratana brushed back her hair to one side, ignoring his intrusion but keeping an eye on him to see what he would do next. 'Say hello to Ross,' he said, bringing the puppet within a couple of inches of her face.

'Ross?'

'The name of someone who works in my company,' he said. Ross was the company's CEO. 'Ross and Mr Casey would like to see Mr. Calvino.'

He stripped the puppet off his hand and laid it on her desk. 'Or I could just surprise him. I think that would be better,' he said with a broad grin.

Casey breezed past her like she didn't exist and walked straight into Calvino's office. Calvino had told Casey on the phone that he had a report on Cat and he wanted to deliver it personally. Calvino had expected to find Casey hardwired with his usual default settings: belligerent, self-confident, with a talent for discovering the weakness in the defense and destroying it. It had troubled Calvino that Casey had been gathering information about Colonel Pratt. He wanted to hand over the file and get Casey out of his life.

The blinds on the window were open far enough

for them to watch the neon One Hand Clapping sign. It looked like a dead hand in the daytime. Casey glanced in that direction but quickly looked away. What was outside didn't interest him.

'You know personal details about Colonel Pratt. It's not too much of a jump to say you know a great deal about Cat,' said Calvino. 'But you do a good job of pretending you don't. A good job pretending that you need me to get information that you already have. Maybe you can explain why you've gone to all of this trouble?'

Casey raised his hand as if to interrupt what was coming next. Calvino waited as his client paced up and down the wall, looking at the paintings. His training as a professional interrogator meant he looked for the breaking point, and when he found it, Casey had no trouble doing what was required at that point. Throw him off-balance, humiliate him, make his head spin.

'In the intelligence business all information needs to be cross-checked, Calvino. Sure, I know about her. What does that matter?' He moved along the wall, turned around, narrowing his eyes and talking through his teeth. 'What does matter is you. Who is Vincent Calvino? That's a good question. I look at the wall. But I don't see any degree in criminal justice. A real PI has it framed because it shows he's had the training for the job. Also no license. Do you have something to show that you've met some minimal requirement or passed some test? Not likely. I don't even see a

351

framed certificate from some tin-pot association saying you've paid your dues. From the look of it, I'd say you fly by the seat of your pants. You take the money and do your best. But I heard about your police connections. In this place, forget about a degree or a license; it's the guy who's connected at the street level who delivers. That's why I hired you. Beyond that, I don't give a shit who you are.'

Calvino leaned forward on his desk, his .38 police service revolver inside his shoulder holster. His jacket hung loosely from a coat rack to the side of his desk. He stared across his desk at Casey, trying to imagine him in an interrogation room with someone tied up, bloodied, yapping out of control, admitting anything to stop the pain.

'I've heard that you're in the pain business. I don't like doing work for that kind of man.'

Casey rolled his neck and a small cracking noise echoed from the bones inside. 'If you worked only for people you liked, you wouldn't cover your rent.' He smiled as if the exercise had eased up some stiffness. 'That's why I've thrown some business your way. I was never much into judging a man by what he has on paper. It's what he can do in the field that matters. And if you play this right, I can throw you a lot more, if you're interested.'

Calvino had come across his fair share of con men, grifters, and boiler-room operators in Bangkok, men who were always just around the corner from starring in the biggest role of their life, and inviting you into their movie as the second lead. Suckers fell for the performance more times than Calvino cared to count. Behind Casey's mask, beneath all the bluster, something about the man told Calvino that he had known Somporn wouldn't show up for his usual appointment with Cat. Otherwise, Casey would have thrown him off the case. Why would he have bothered to shell out more to an investigator if he believed he was no good at his job?

'What did you find out about Cat that you can't tell me over the phone?'

'She's looking after a couple of her sister's boys, putting them through international school.'

'Her sister's out of the picture, right?'

Calvino wanted to reach across the desk and grab Casey by the neck and shake him until he was blue in the face. 'Her sister's dead.'

'Sisters, brothers, dead or alive. I don't care. All I want to know is her connection with Somporn and whether she's showing up on a regular basis.'

What was it that had wormed into Casey's heart at an early age and turned it to stone? thought Calvino. An abusive father, an indifferent mother, an uncle or neighbor who beat him and made him eat dirt for some minor infraction of a silly rule? With a guy like Casey, it could have been anything, including the possibility that he'd been born without a heart. Or was that just another part of his act?

He'd been thinking about the women in the beauty parlor, gabbing over their mah-jongg tiles and stacks of money, letting him know Cat knew about Nongluck. He looked hard at Casey, and he wondered if Casey knew about the love triangle as well. 'Cat knew Nongluck was seeing Somporn. Convenient for her that Nongluck died in Pattaya. Someone pushed her off a hotel balcony. It makes you think, what if?'

A slight twitch of Casey's upper lip threatened to turn into a sneer for only a flash and then he regained his control. 'What if what? I don't see the connection.'

'Somporn is an active man. There's Cat, and then there was Nongluck. Women are natural-born monopolists. They hate competition.'

'You're moving away from the assignment, what I paid you to do. I'm interested in Cat and when she meets up with Somporn.'

'I'd have thought Nongluck's death would have interested you. If your endgame is to get Somporn, why not link him to a murder? It would make life messy for him.'

Casey smiled. 'I like that possibility. It's good, Calvino. Real good.'

Calvino got the impression that the compliment was false and that Casey was toying with him. Calvino rose from his chair and walked across the room. He opened a filing cabinet and removed a folder. He walked back to his desk and opened it. Inside were newspaper clippings about Nongluck's death and more clippings about the murder of Casey's son, Joel. One of the photographs was of Joel. He pulled out the clipping of the fresh-faced man, half as handsome as his father, and laid it on his desk.

'Personally, I don't think you have any intention of framing Somporn. You plan to kill him.'

Casey laughed but was clutching his fists into balls at the same time.

'Something happens to Somporn,' Casey said, 'and I'm one of the first people they'd pull in to question. And they know where I live.'

'He killed your son. A man might take some risk to put that right.'

Casey didn't blink. In the years that had passed since his son's death, Casey would have had other opportunities to kill Somporn. He hadn't done so. Why not? Calvino had to look him in the eye as he answered. There was an old Chinese saying about how the wise man waits until the dust settles and the emotions cool, and then takes revenge.

'There's more than one way to destroy a man,' Casey replied. 'Ruin him in ways far more painful than killing. Somporn's running for election. Your idea of pinning the Pattaya murder on him is good. I want you to run with that.' Casey smiled and looked away from the photo of his dead son. He'd seen a lot of photographs with the faces of anguished men who'd been tortured. He'd taken some himself. But when the man photographed was his son, all the professional detachment vanished. He'd stared at his dead son's body in the photograph many times; it was an image he carried around in his head day and night.

'I don't want to work for you after today,' said Calvino.

'Now you're starting to fuck with me. I strongly suggest you don't.'

'Here's the report on Cat.' He handed Casey an envelope.

'You'll regret this,' said Casey.

'My only regret is not doing it before.'

'You'd be wise, and your colonel friend would be wise too, to not get too close to things that don't concern you.' Casey had an eerie way of flaring up into a white heat then pulling back a second before he exploded. Signaling his return to self-control with a knowing smile, Casey shook his head, slipped on his aviator glasses, smacking his lips before breathing out in a long sigh. 'We all need to pull back a couple of steps. Give each other space. You and your colonel go back to your corner because my fight's got nothing to do with you. Don't ever get into a fight unless you have to. That's my advice.'

Before Calvino had arrived at his office, Colonel Pratt had stopped in and shown Ratana a set of cards like the ones they had found in Nongluck's hotel room in Pattaya. He asked her if she had any opinion about them. Pratt bounced her baby on his knee, keeping him happy with another hand puppet – a penguin with large black button eyes – that he'd found in the kids' department at the Emporium. Gifts for the baby, question for

356

the mother. It was the Thai way of doing things: sweet, informal, and polite.

Ratana thought about the cards. 'Was she a gambler?' she asked. Women who gambled sometimes ran up large debts with the wrong people, the kind of people who might finally push the indebted gambler off a high place.

'They were held together with a rubber band.'

He laid the cards down in the order in which they'd been found. 'That's how the Pattaya police found the cards,' he said.

'These are Nongluck's cards?'

The Colonel shook his head. 'I bought these cards, but they're identical to the ones found in her handbag. I've been wondering why she only had eight cards. Unless it was a poker game and that was the last losing hand she'd been dealt.'

Ratana slipped off the rubber band and turned over the first card: the ace of hearts. The next card was the eight of diamonds, followed by the six of clubs and the six of spades. The last four cards were the seven of hearts, the six of hearts, the five of hearts, and the nine of spades.

'Doesn't look like she won anything with this hand,' she said. 'But I can't think of a poker game played with eight cards.'

The Colonel nodded, slowly moving the penguin up and down in front of the baby. 'It must have been some other card game.'

'You didn't find the rest of the deck?' Ratana asked.

'It hasn't turned up.' Colonel Pratt lifted the baby back into the playpen and put the penguin beside him. The baby started to cry for his mother. 'Tell Vincent I stopped by. Nothing urgent. I just wanted to drop in and see if everything was okay.'

'I'll tell him about the cards. Maybe he can figure it out. Farangs know a lot about cards,' she said. Her baby was half-farang, but it didn't stop her from thinking there were things that farangs knew that Thais didn't know, and that it worked the other way around too.

Colonel Pratt had restrained himself from saying that inside the skull the basic raw material was pretty much the same; there was no farang brain or Thai brain, just brains that absorbed what they found in the environment. Like a penguin puppet. 'Keep the cards. I've memorized them. You might want to show them to Vincent.'

By the time Calvino had arrived back from the beauty shop, Ratana had stared at the cards for some time, as if they might speak to her. Ratana thought that a man who finds eight playing cards in a woman's handbag would assume that she wasn't playing with a full deck. A man would get sidetracked wondering about the rest of the cards. But a woman would understand that a deck doesn't have to be complete, that eight cards could mean something apart from a card game. She played with the new penguin hand puppet, turning its head to her son, speaking through the penguin: 'I am a funny bird. I am black and I am white. I am two things. But I am also one thing. A bird that loves water. And I live in a colony, which is like a playpen for penguins. Sometimes we play, sometimes we fight. But we never play cards.' She glanced at the cards side by side on her desk. She tried to get inside Nongluck's mind. What had she wanted?

By then, Casey was on the other side of the partition talking to her boss. She could hear them arguing. Casey's bluster and temper echoed around the small office. Then it hit her, the way Thai women feel when under threat. They need to get to a safe haven, to someone who will protect them. Who would Nongluck have phoned if she had been in a life-and-death situation? She stared at the cards and then dialed the sequence of numbers they corresponded to, 1–866–7659, and waited. On the other side of the partition Ratana heard a cell phone ringing.

On the third ring, Casey looked at his cell phone and stared at the caller ID. He recognized the number.

He hesitated, the blood draining from his face, and punched the reject button. Ratana dialed the number again. On the third attempt, with Calvino watching him, he looked like a cornered Doberman and answered. 'Can I speak to Vincent Calvino?' Ratana said.

Casey, like a good soldier, handed the phone to Calvino.

'Vinny,' said Ratana, 'Do you mind if I bring in some playing cards?'

Calvino stared at Casey, who rubbed his three-day growth of beard like a man trying to start a fire in a rainstorm. 'Bring them in.'

'What are you trying to pull, Calvino?'

Ratana came into the office and laid the cards on her boss's desk. 'Khun Nongluck had eight cards in her handbag the night she died. The police found them. I wondered if they might be a phone number of someone close to her, in case she got in trouble.'

'With a secretary like Ratana, I don't need any qualifications,' Calvino said. 'You might want to explain how she got your cellphone number.'

Casey shook his head and sighed like a race-horse kicked in the guts by a jockey bringing him around the back stretch. 'Yeah, Nongluck had my number. I gave it to her. She had it in case of an emergency.'

'You lied to me about her.'

'She had a thing with my son. They had lived together for a while. Then broke up, got back together, broke up. She wasn't living with him when he was murdered. But that didn't stop her from coming to his cremation. She came with a friend and stood in the back crying. There weren't a lot of people shedding tears over Joel's death. It got to me. She said she had really loved Joel and she wanted me to know that he was a good man. And I told her if she ever needed anything to call me on this number. It's a private number. Not many people have it. She was one of them.'

Casey was so convincing, it was nearly impossible

not to believe him, though everything about the man said such an attitude was an essential part of his prison job.

'You're saying she would have called you if she were in trouble.'

'That's exactly what I am saying.'

'Only this time, when you expected her to call, she didn't get around to it.'

He shook his head. 'I said, she didn't call.'

'Any idea who'd have used her to get me a hotel-room upgrade? Not just any upgrade but one for a suite straight below hers? That takes some planning.'

'There must be someone who doesn't like you,' said Casey. 'My guess is that there's a pretty long list of people.' He got up from his chair. 'You're right. We shouldn't be working together.'

'I get the feeling we were never working together, Casey.'

The only fact to support Casey's story was Nongluck's actions. She'd carried around eight cards that spelled out his private cell-phone number. She must have had some high degree of confidence that this man was someone she could rely on if things ever came to a flashpoint. Assuming she could reach for the phone before getting pushed off the balcony. She left behind a private code for the rainy day when Casey would ride to the rescue. It rained; Casey didn't rescue her. There was another possibility that had nothing to do with a backup rescue plan. Nongluck had left the cards in the hotel room as a way to identify her killer.

CHAPTER 28

J arrett sat behind the rifle, elbows on the table, listening to a blues song about women, guns, and Baton Rouge. Tracer sat on the edge of the pool table, slowly rolled the cue ball down the length of the table, waited until it rolled back, and started over again. When he listened to the blues he could go on playing catch with himself for hours. Jarrett had no complaints about staying hunkered down waiting out the time until the job was finished. Slipping into Soi Cowboy had been a mistake. The lure of a quiet drink, a platform of yings, and the blues had proved too much. Jarrett had put his money where his mouth was. He couldn't resist having a last look at his investment. It was the kind of thing any man would understand.

The two of them had gone fishing only to find they'd been hooked. It was a hazard in Bangkok, but knowing that was one thing and not falling into the open manhole was another. Harry had always taught him that the major decisions in life were about how and where a man chooses to take a stand and enter the game, whether it was love, pool, or an ambush. The stakes were never the same.

A man needed to know those stakes before playing the game. 'Choose carefully, son,' Harry had said. 'In your line of work you don't get to choose wrong more than once.' The odds always favored the house; that was a given. But on Cowboy the odds favored the punters by a wide margin. Cowboy was one of the few places on the planet where even a habitual sexual loser couldn't lose. The pull of the place had sucked them out of the condo. Jarrett had rationalized going out, forgetting what his daddy had taught him, and Tracer had showed himself to be the true friend he'd always been by not calling him on it. They'd both known Jarrett had been determined to see Wan one last time, and they had gotten tired of playing pool, so Tracer had no serious argument. They hadn't so much abandoned their position as taken a small side diversion to stretch their legs and let Jarrett make his final play in the game with Wan.

'You had to see her,' said Tracer, breaking the silence. He caught the cue ball, flipping it in the air behind his back, and making a one-handed catch. 'So it had to be done.'

'How do you do that?'

Tracer grinned. 'Do what?'

'Catch the ball behind your back?'

'I got eyes in the back of my head.'

Jarrett grinned, watching as Tracer repeated the trick. 'Rack 'em up.'

Tracer tossed him the cue ball. 'You go first.'

No question going to Reno's bar had been a

fuck-up, and Jarrett appreciated that Tracer had let it slide. Jarrett pushed back from his chair and walked over to the pool table, picked up his cue and made a good break. He had a look of satisfaction as he chalked his cue stick.

'Man, not being a hedonist in Bangkok is like not being a gambler in Las Vegas,' said Tracer, watching as Jarrett concentrated on his next shot. 'There just isn't much else to do.' Waters had come up with that piece of wisdom the day before they'd flown to Bangkok.

Jarrett smiled, sinking the yellow number-one ball in the corner pocket right as Tracer pursed his lips and whistled, 'When you're hot, you're hot.'

'This guy Somporn, you think he's famous?' asked Jarrett. 'Because I never heard of him.'

'Your not hearing of him isn't the definition of famous. There's probably a lot of famous people you never heard of. Think about it.'

'I am thinking about it. And I don't think anyone in America's ever heard of him. Unless they can spell your name in Fargo, North Dakota, then you ain't famous. You're just a wannabe.'

Tracer lined up on the red-striped eleven ball and nudged it into the side pocket. He'd never known anyone from North Dakota. It made him think about what kind of people lived there with all the responsibility for determining fame. He twirled the blue chalk cube between his fingers, then caught Jarrett's eye. 'We gotta concentrate on the facts that make this a Jack kinda of case.'

Jarrett nodded.

'The man ordered Casey's son to be murdered. He left a trail of evidence right to his doorstep, and what happened? The authorities said they had insufficient evidence to charge him. You follow a trail of white feathers to an old hound's doghouse, find him inside grinning with feathers all around his mouth, but you don't believe that old Rex eats chickens. It must've been some other dog that got into the chicken house. You gotta be a famous dog to have that kind of influence.'

'Money's enough. Fame don't have nothing to do with it.'

'Paying for an election takes money,' said Tracer. 'Your shot.'

Jarrett smiled, surveying the lay of the balls on the pool table. Tomorrow it would be his shot all right, the shot that would settle the accounts. 'You're my spotter, do you think that I can sink the three ball?' He pointed with his cue at the far corner pocket.

Tracer frowned, seeing it was a difficult bank shot. 'You sink that shot, you should turn pro.'

Jarrett stretched over the table, one foot on the floor, brought the cue stick back, sending the cue ball off the cushion, hitting the three ball, which rolled toward the pocket.

'That has a nice ring to it.'

The ball stopped short of falling in. 'Semipro,' said Tracer. It was his shot.

Tracer's eyes cut across the room to the sliding doors.

'I thought you wanted to play?'

Tracer shrugged, putting down his cue stick. Jarrett's almost-in-the-pocket shot rattled him; he didn't like thinking about his man missing a shot, even a difficult shot. It got him wound up. 'I need some air, that's all.' He opened the sliding door and walked out onto the balcony. He drew in a deep breath. Nothing like fresh air, he said to himself. His chest expanded, making him look like the football player he'd once been.

He stood next to the railing fingering his mojo bag, looking across the road. Power wasn't just carrying a gun or having someone whacked. There was invisible power too. Spirits had their say. There'd been a general once who ordered all of his troops in the south of Thailand to wear amulets. He thought they would work better than bulletproof vests. Everyone had laughed at him. Except for Tracer, who understood the General's way of looking at life and death. The way things worked in Louisiana wasn't all that different from Thailand. The man who controlled the invisible forces could stop people from getting water, food, clothing, and a place to sleep. He could shut down just about anyone if he was so inclined. All he had to do was draw on his mojo. Power was the way to resolve access to the things a man needed to stay alive. When someone had that kind of power, and they wanted something from you, then you had two choices: yield or die.

Jarrett, holding his cue stick, walked to the door. 'I ain't gonna miss tomorrow. It's a straight shot.'

'I know you won't.' Tracer looked around at the buildings, wondering if any of the thousands of eyes inside had spotted him. It wasn't a good idea to stick around on the balcony. He ducked back inside, closed the sliding door, and pulled back the curtains. He walked back to the pool table and took his turn.

'Casey had a problem in one of the prisons in Baghdad,' said Tracer. 'One of those shithole village insurgents died during an interrogation.'

'That was the guy who ambushed a unit,' said Jarrett. 'They lost three men. I'd say Casey was doing his job.'

'They say the guy wasn't an insurgent. He was a civilian.'

'He shouldn't have been in a war zone,' said Jarrett. 'That's askin' for shit to come down on you.'

Tracer picked the eight ball off the table. With a sloping underhand toss, he threw it to Jarrett who caught it in his right hand. 'Sometimes you get eight-balled and you can't figure out why it happened. In Baghdad there wasn't any inquiry,' said Tracer. 'No charges, no reprimand. No nothing.'

Jarrett put the eight ball back on the table. 'You saying Casey's situation is like Somporn's? Because if you are, I'd be saying that's bullshit.'

'You know what bothers me about pool?'

Jarrett shrugged. 'Enlighten me.'

'There's no gray ball. In life there's a lot of gray. That's a fact.'

'We weren't there. So how can we judge what happened in the village?'

No way that Tracer was backing down. His mojo told him that it wasn't so much a judgment on Casey's involvement in the death of an insurgent, but the question of why the man had paid them to do what he could do himself. 'You're right. I wasn't there. I don't know. Casey's got a green badge and top security clearance, so somebody must trust him. And I wasn't there when Casey's kid got capped either. All I'm saying is there is something called karma. I just can't figure out his game.'

Jarrett looked up from the pool table. 'Maybe there's no game. It's straight up.'

'You make my point.' Tracer's hands were wrapped around his cue stick, the end balanced on the floor. 'It's no better than a maybe. Not like our friend from Spain.'

There was no maybe about the foreign woman with the private detective in Reno's bar. It was the same woman who'd been on the beach in Gijón.

CHAPTER 29

After he'd left Marisa's condo, Calvino had returned to his office. The neon One Hand Clapping sign over the massage parlor cast shadows from a thick clot of telephone and electric lines. The sign was on but there was no activity. No yings, no customers, no plastic stools outside. The translation service on the ground floor was dark. At three in the morning, it was quiet on the soi. In the distance a dog barked.

Calvino walked a couple more feet before he was jumped from behind. The attacker, a fireplug of a man, had moved out with a grunt from his hiding position behind a vendor's cart covered in canvas. Calvino had heard the fall of a footstep and immediately turned, crouching down and reaching for his handgun. The attacker held a steel rod like a baseball bat and took a wild, loping swing at Calvino. Strike one, thought Calvino. He half lost his balance as he fanned the night air. A second attacker ran out of the shadows holding a long knife. Not long enough to be a sword, but long enough to close a man's accounts in this life. The man with the knife ran straight at him.

Calvino held his .38 service revolver with both hands, counted to five, rose up, and swung, catching the attacker chin-high. The crack of bone echoed down the small soi, and the attacker fell headfirst onto the pavement. Home run, thought Calvino. The first attacker, having regained his balance, came back for a second round with the steel rod raised like a samurai sword. Calvino, holding the .38 service revolver with both hands, aimed at the spot between the man's eyes.

'You probably don't want to do that,' he said.

The Thai man froze, staring at the gun, and then glanced down at his fallen comrade. His hair was long and oily, like it hadn't been washed for a few days. Nothing about him looked like a cop.

'Put it down,' Calvino said. 'Now lean up against the car, hands stretched out.'

Calvino removed the attacker's wallet and stuffed it in his pocket.

'Who sent you?'

'Don't understand,' said the man, spitting on the pavement.

Calvino hit him a sharp, hard rabbit punch to the kidneys. 'Try harder.'

The attacker, a man in his late twenties, cried out in pain.

'Who sent you and your friend?'

The friend who had been face-down managed to stagger to his feet. The man on the ground was shorter and fatter. Those extra pounds had made him one step too slow to get the job done. No one

370

goes to work with a steel rod and a knife unless they're intending to inflict some major damage. He moaned, holding his broken chin with both hands.

'You want more?'

He shook his head.

'Who sent you? Was it Apichart?'

'Big boss.'

'What's his name?'

'Boss.'

Calvino hit him hard enough to draw blood.

'Apichart. His name Mr. Apichart.' In Thai the name translated as 'the great one in this life,' a man of destiny.

Calvino backed away, thinking the man's parents should have chosen a different name. The long-haired attacker eased away from the car, slowly turned, and made a cautious circle around where Calvino stood his ground, never taking his eye off the handgun. He helped his fallen friend to his feet, wrapping the fat man's arm around his shoulder, and they walked down the dark soi.

'You and your friend did better than the last two he sent.'

'I not forget you,' said the man, brushing the long unwashed hair from his eyes.

'I not forget you, too,' said Calvino. 'You tell Mr. Apichart, I remember him, too.'

'Fuck you,' shouted the attacker as they reached the top of the soi.

The world was riddled like a machine-gunned corpse with such insane hatred.

Watching them limp off, Calvino thought to himself, The thing about Thais not speaking English was once again exposed as a lie. Then it struck him. They hadn't spoken that many words to him in any language. They hadn't been sent to find out anything. The two thugs were the message. The messengers wanted to bust me up, and let that filter down. Maybe Apichart was holding Calvino responsible, coming after him.

He climbed the stairs to his office, turned on the lights, and sat down at his desk. Rotating in his chair, he looked out the window at the neon signs below. There was no point in calling the police. He thought about how Marisa had been repulsed not so much by his resort to violence as by his absence of any residue of introspection. He hadn't broken into a sweat. He looked at his hands in the light, rotating them from knuckles to palms and back. Out in the night were the men who had attacked him. They'd been injured, broken up enough to communicate to their boss what he was up against. Predators underestimated their prey – overshot, undershot, missed altogether, then licked their wounds before circling him again. His message had been clear: he wasn't one of the weak, vulnerable farangs who could be easily pulled down; if they wanted him, he was going to make it costly and difficult. There was always the chance that these predators would move on to a weaker target. But Calvino knew that he was kidding himself; that the attack had been the first wave, others would be sent to finish the job, and if they failed, they'd be replaced. Somewhere in the city would be a man determined to use whatever force was necessary to secure his objective.

He thought about calling Marisa and talking to her about how without the promise of violence such forces could never be contained. He had an idea of what he wanted to explain to her. The proper response was never a prayer, an extended hand, or a friendly smile; it was a fist, knife, iron pipe, gun, or any available weapon. There is no time to sweat, to argue, to plan, or to reason. You take him down on his own terms or he owns you. Marginalize the role of violence. That's what you UN people talk about. But when it comes to the street, violence marginalizes people. There are rules for the playing field, rules for the killing field, and you stay alive by knowing which field you are on.

He looked at the phone, then at his watch. After three in the morning there was no way he'd phone her. It could wait until tomorrow. Or it could wait forever. He thought also about phoning Colonel Pratt. But there was nothing he could do, and that also covered going back to sleep. He wondered about the men who had run off. He had fed them Apichart's name; they would have said anything to get out of the situation. It was like Casey and his torture buddies; inflicting pain meant the person on the receiving end would tell you whatever you wanted to hear. Gangsters on Cowboy might have sent them around. He wasn't known on the street.

Roughing him up would have sent a powerful message for him to give up the kid. Or they could have been muggers, drug addicts looking for some quick cash. The underbelly of the night in Bangkok produced many plausible explanations. Listing the possible motives of thugs attacking a private eye at three in the morning could fill a notebook the size of the Manhattan phone directory.

Reaching inside his jacket, Calvino pulled out his microrecorder and set it on the desk. He plugged in a set of earphones. Her voice, a honeyed, smoky tone etched from cigarettes and scotch, came through loud and clear as Marisa told the story about the killing on the beach in Spain. He'd taped her in stereo and her rich, accented sound, the one from her bedroom, filled his head. There wasn't any background static. The recording conditions had been perfect. He fast-forwarded through the sound of their lovemaking.

The Colombian who'd been popped on the beach had met his destiny around the same time that Bakhita had been in another explosion a few thousand miles away in Baghdad. She had survived, but at a huge personal cost. She'd parted with her real leg that day at the Canal Hotel in Baghdad when a cement truck exploded at the front entrance. But when the dust settled, Bakhita realized she'd lost much more than a leg.

They'd first met in a therapy session, a UN-sponsored group session for those suffering from post-traumatic stress. Misery made for a friendship.

Calvino rewound the tape and listened as Marisa talked about the importance of the anniversary of the day a UN official named Sergio had been killed in Baghdad. There was a moment when it seemed the talk would end as the mind fogged with the possibility of sex. But the moment passed and Marisa kept talking, and Calvino kept listening, encouraging her to reveal a scene from her past that played on an endless loop.

'Unless you've lost someone through violence, you don't know how important the anniversary of a death is for the family,' Marisa had said.

Calvino flipped through Casey's file. He had gone underground two days before the anniversary of his son's death. Something Marisa had said that evening had stayed with him: 'Either you remember or you let the memory die. Such a thing can fall so deep inside you that it bounces around in places where you can lose yourself. You may think what happened is gone, finished, buried in the past . . . but of course that's impossible. It will always be there, waiting for you. That's why every twentieth of August, Bakhita and I have dinner. We light a candle and we say a prayer.'

He turned off the recorder, leaned back in his chair, and rotated around to face the window. He dumped the contents of the thug's wallet on his desk. Three crisp one-thousand-baht notes; the man's fee made Calvino reflect on how little it cost to have someone beaten-up or killed. He read the Thai ID card, looking at the picture of the man who'd attacked him. He stuffed the cash and the ID card back into the wallet and switched off his office lights. He looked out onto the soi. The neon light reflected off the windows across the way. Red, green, blue, and yellow, as the hand moved through the clapping-itself gesture.

In the mean streets people from another world moved through the night. Daytime people rarely saw them; if they did, they would know what it was these people did at night. Calvino considered whether he would have helped Fon if she hadn't been with Marisa, or if he hadn't bumped into Marisa at the Skytrain. The world moved that way, in a series of small interconnected gestures, events, and strivings that merged together. He wanted to think he would have helped the kid if Marisa hadn't been part of the package. But he wasn't all that sure about it. He'd been on Cowboy before and had likely walked right past Fon without seeing her. That was foresight looking in the mirror of hindsight, and neither one standing aside. He didn't know at that moment if a man could ever know who he really was. Except maybe Casey, who was too sure, someone who had an ego gorged with self-importance until it had swollen like a tick's belly bloated with the blood. Like most shallow men, Casey thought most people could be handled, broken, kicked into submission. Calvino asked himself if any truth could be pulled out of such a wreckage of man who lived in a world where truth was associated with primal screams of pain.

CHAPTER 30

Calvino had been putting on his shoes at the door of Marisa's condo, Juan Carlos holding it open, when Fon had walked out of the bedroom holding Wan's hand. She had heard him at the door and wanted to say goodbye. The side of the kid's face had creases from the pillow. She'd been sleeping but she no longer looked tired. Fon wasn't wearing her dress and makeup. She had changed into a fake Manchester City T-shirt and red shorts she'd borrowed from Wan. Shirt and shorts were both two sizes too large. The effect was to make her look even younger. She had wanted to tell him that she was sorry that she had been frightened earlier.

Fon blinked and rubbed her sad, empty eyes. Juan Carlos saw a flash of fear in there, as if that emotion had been repeated enough that in the end it had hollowed out and dumped some basic innocence into a streetside bin.

'My sister says that you speak Thai. Is that true?' he asked her.

She laughed and rattled off a sentence in Burmese, switched to Thai, finished that sentence in Shan dialect, and in English asked if he had ever bought flowers from kids on Soi Cowboy. Her performance impressed Juan Carlos. He applauded.

'You have a talent for words.'

She hung her head. 'Thais say, "I am khaya sangkom."'

'I am certain that's very good,' said Juan Carlos. It was the kind of street slang he didn't know.

Wan shuddered at hearing the phrase, her smile fading. 'It's very bad. It means society's garbage. Like drug addicts, small-time dealers, kids selling stuff at streetlights. Or women who work in bars.'

'Don't buy into that, kid,' said Calvino, looking at Wan and then at Fon. From their expressions Calvino saw that the sting of the phrase cut deep. It was a widespread attitude that made it next to impossible for them not to feel rejected by everyone except for the handful of people who exploited them.

He looked at Marisa's wounded reaction as a simple question about language had turned into a dark, nasty cultural corner. 'Do you know whom to call?' he asked.

She nodded, grateful that he'd broken the silence. 'I can handle it.'

Wan, who had recovered her smile, put a hand on Fon's shoulder, giving her a gentle squeeze. 'I speak the language of bees.' That made Fon giggle and squirm as if a bee had landed on her shoulder. Wan smiled at Juan Carlos, who returned her smile.

Hands open at his sides and looking highly

amused, Juan Carlos asked, 'And what language do bees speak?'

She moved her head to the side. It was her way of thinking through a question. She almost never answered straight out, a quality that her mother had criticized. 'It's not a word language like ours. For bees, it's more like a dance. They dance to tell each other stories. They understand each movement the way we understand words,' she said.

Juan Carlos was oblivious to his sister, and Calvino was intrigued. 'Bees dance to make language?' he asked Wan.

'To tell other bees, they dance to show where flowers are blooming and they dance to point other bees toward home.'

Juan Carlos nodded. He liked the idea of a dance that was an arrow pointing to home. He knew the word for home in many languages, but here was a language he hadn't learned, one he'd never thought about. 'When I danced in the bar,' she said, watching his eyes as she revealed her occupation, 'I always tried to face toward home.'

Juan Carlos had snapped a series of digital photos of Fon that night after Calvino had gone out the door. They showed her in Wan's baggy clothes, sitting on the red velvet sofa. He tossed and turned through the night, excited over the outpouring of sympathy that would naturally arise once he showed Kalya the photograph. The following morning he was up early and out the door.

But her reaction wasn't what he had expected.

'We need to help this child. Her father works at one of your father's factories on the Burmese border. Or if he doesn't own it, he knows who does and can help.'

Her response was indignation and anger. 'Why are you doing this, Juan?'

What kind of question was she asking him? It was perfectly obvious what needed to be done. Wasn't his English sufficient to express the urgency, the emotion, the danger, and his promise to help a child find her family? He changed tactics. 'I'm doing this for my sister. She witnessed a terrible murder years ago.'

'I'm sorry, but what's that got to do with the child?'

'The anniversary is coming soon.'

'I still don't understand,' said Kalya.

'After the murder, she changed. Who wouldn't? It could have destroyed her. But it made her stronger, wanting to help people who suffer. That's why she does the kind of work she does. She would never say to you what I am saying. But I know her. To rescue a child is everything for her. It is her way of making – what is the right word? – atonement. But it's nothing to do with religion. Marisa saw how invaluable a life is. How easily a life can be ended. And to save one life says I refuse to get knocked down and accept the world as a place that's ugly, selfish and hostile. I will make a stand for life. That's her way of retrieving some part of herself she lost that day.'

For all of his gifts of language, he hadn't found the right words to convey how important it was for Marisa to make amends for the damage caused that day on the beach. Fon had been adopted for his sister's annual recovery program.

Kalya looked at the digital image on Juan Carlos's cell phone. 'You must be careful that by helping someone you don't cause more damage to others.'

That afternoon, they went to see Somporn in his office the size of an airplane hangar. He smiled as he stared at Fon's photographs. 'She's a beautiful child.'

'The gang that held her has found a buyer for her virginity.'

Somporn cleared his throat as if to dislodge a small fish bone. He rose and walked around his desk and stood in the window looking out at the skyline of Bangkok. Thousands of high-rises as far as the eye could see. He turned back and looked at Juan Carlos. 'Of course, that is regrettable. But the best solution is for the authorities to handle the child.'

'They won't help. That's the point. But if she could return to her father, that would solve the problem. You could rescue her. That would help you win votes. You would become the man who fights for the rights of children. Helping Fon will help your campaign.'

Somporn thought about the implications for several minutes, looking down at the paperwork on his desk. He sighed and shook his head. 'I would be seen as interfering with the authorities. Grandstanding, I think the Americans call it. Something like this could backfire. To be seen helping the Burmese could be very bad for the campaign. In Thailand, they are our historic enemy, like Catalonia is in Spain.'

'According to you, her father sent her to Bangkok,' said Kalya.

Juan Carlos had expected more support from her. He swallowed his disappointment, telling himself it was a minor point that could be overcome. 'He certainly didn't sell her to become a prostitute.'

'You don't know how Shan people think, Juan Carlos,' said Somporn. 'Some of them have been known to sell their daughters. It is sad. I do not like it any more than you. Now I must return to work. You will excuse me.' He showed them out the door.

In the corridor, Kalya, upset and near tears, turned away from Juan Carlos. He put his arm around her but she pushed it away. 'You made my father very unhappy. You were unfair to him.'

'How was I unfair?'

'Using your relationship with me to put him in an impossible situation. I can't believe you did that.' She pulled away and walked down the hall without waiting for him.

Juan Carlos wasn't one to give up, and his last resort was Kalya's mother. When he left Somporn's office, he made no mention to Kalya that he intended to see her mother. Kalya had been less than helpful with her father, and he saw no reason to believe that her support would be forthcoming with her mother. He drove out to the riding school where she was putting one of her prized horses through his paces. When she saw him, she smiled and waved. A few minutes later she rode over to him and dismounted.

'What a pleasant surprise to see you, Juan Carlos.'

While they walked together, he showed her the digital photos of Fon and explained her situation. 'I know that you can help. One phone call and her father will be on his way to pick up his daughter.'

'What I like about you, Juan Carlos, is your absolute passion. You breathe passion like a kind of fire. It suits you. It makes you attractive to men and women. But there is a downside to all great passions. That fire burns the reason away and leaves pure emotion. That can lead to reckless behavior. But, then, you are Spanish, and this is your nature.'

'Why can't we help her? I don't understand.'

It was a challenge, and she was accustomed to being deferred to by everyone. 'A reason is what you wish to hear? Here's one. I find a loose thread on your jacket. It seems that the right thing is to pull it out. If I do that, how do I know the whole jacket won't unravel and fall apart? The girl isn't alone in the world. You don't know and can't know who is behind her and what they are capable of doing. Being the knight in shining armor riding in on your handsome steed is all right for the movies. In real life, knights are easily slaughtered, their horses taken, their families brutalized and murdered. The people in this line of business guard their assets. To them you aren't a savior; you are a robber.'

'The girl's father may be working at one of your toy factories.'

The argument didn't move her. 'The girl's father could be brushing down my horse in the stables. That doesn't matter, Juan Carlos. I know from Kalya that you wish to help your sister, and that is a tribute to your loyalty and love of family. I told Kalya not to be too upset with you, that you were to be congratulated for this display of honor. It is rare among men these days. As much as I admire what you are doing, your honor is misplaced in this case. You will need to find another way to give back to your sister what she wishes to recover.'

Kalya had phoned her mother with the entire story of what had happened in her father's office. He should have expected as much, and he felt foolish for not realizing the earlier conversation would have immediately reached the mother's ears.

Juan Carlos searched his mind for the right word. 'If you won't help a child, then who will you help?'

She gave him a hard, calculated stare. 'That's simple to answer, Juan Carlos. My family. And you are about to become part of that family.'

'By helping Fon, you will help my sister, who is my family.'

Her smile reminded him of one Kalya used when she wanted to express her disapproval. 'I feel you are not listening when I say this can cause danger.'

CHAPTER 31

McPhail was walking into Washington Square with his arm bandaged and in a sling. The sound of a distant ocean tide rang in his ears. He stopped and slowly turned. The roar of the Sukhumvit Road traffic had fooled him into thinking for a moment that he was at the beach. The attack in Cowboy had left him bloodied and disoriented. His head hadn't stopped ringing like a phone lost inside a house, with no way to find it, no way to turn it off. Mistaking traffic noise for the pounding sea worried him. He sighed and adjusted his arm inside the sling. Below the elbow, his arm was the color of a day-old burrito. He backtracked a couple of steps and squatted down on his haunches to look at a five-baht coin. He turned it over between the finger and thumb of his good hand and then, slipping it into his pocket, slowly rose to his feet.

'This is going to be my lucky day,' he said. Then he reminded himself that yesterday was supposed to have been his lucky day too, according to his horoscope. Some days were luckier than others. He remembered what Calvino had once told him:

'The future used to be Bangkok, until it moved on to some other place that was luckier.'

McPhail had been thinking about the attack. If his arm had been a few inches lower, the blade would have severed a major blood vessel and he'd be dead. If he'd held the curtain a few inches higher, the knife would have missed his arm altogether. The nineteen stitches were a compromise decision marking the boundary between certain death and a clean getaway. He was satisfied with the hand he'd been dealt. It could have been a lot worse.

He walked past Mambo – an old cinema that had been converted into a katoey theater mainly for Chinese tourists – and a half-dozen motor-cycle-taxi drivers who lounged on the stairs like lizards sunning themselves on a tropical morning. They wore orange vests that looked like those emergency vests stored under the seat of a budget airline. They smoked, slept, read newspapers, and watched people coming and going in the soi. The cops used them as eyes and ears, though they understood that sometimes the drivers saw things that weren't there, heard things that weren't said. Tensions were rising as the election campaign was coming to a close. People were at each other's throats, and the police wanted to know who was planning trouble. The love affair with surveillance cameras had sidestepped Washington Square, so the taxi boys still played their old role.

They clocked McPhail, a regular they recognized,

and immediately noticed his sling. A farang with a busted-up arm, head, or leg gave them a certain pleasure. They laughed and nodded, as if it was about the funniest thing they'd seen all morning. McPhail had lived in Thailand long enough to know they didn't mean anything bad by it. If one of their own fell off his bike and broke his leg, they'd all be roaring with laughter.

'No, I didn't fall off a motorcycle. No, my girl-friend didn't get jealous. No, a giant lizard wearing an orange vest didn't attack me. A forest dwarf jumped me.'

The drivers shrugged, grinned, and whispered to each other. They hadn't understood a thing he'd said in English. For McPhail that was the whole point. They would never understand how a man like McPhail had come to live among them and how some men of their background had cut him with a knife. He wondered how many of the drivers leaning back on the steps were armed, and what it would take to have one of them plunge a knife into someone's body. He continued past them, thinking how it was less a language problem than a compre-hension issue. Why, they wondered, would any man want to leave his homeland? Seeing a farang bruised or cut-up, from their point of view, seemed like a fit punishment for having abandoned his family.

In the Lonesome Hawk, heads twisted around as McPhail walked in. Stories about his fight had circulated around the Square since early morning. The fact that McPhail had been the source of the stories wasn't something anyone talked about. He waved and smiled before pushing his stomach against the bar. 'Honey buns, bring me a large vodka and tonic with two slices of lime. I need to take a pill.' He looked pale as his hand shoved deep into his pocket and emerged with a screw-top container filled with painkillers. He popped two into his mouth as the bartender slipped the vodka and tonic into his hand. He drank from the glass and then threw his head back and swallowed.

By the time Calvino entered the bar, McPhail had mellowed out. 'You should have stayed in the hospital,' said Calvino. 'You look terrible.'

'Vinny, you don't exactly look like Brad Pitt yourself.' He raised his glass in a mock toast. 'To a couple of beat-up old guys. But we won. Tell George that we won.'

Old George frowned and shook his head. 'What the fuck did you win? All I see are serious injuries. If that's winning, what the fuck do you call losing?'

'We rescued a kid, you old fart.'

Calvino stood close to the bar; he still hadn't got a drink. He raised his hand, pretending he had a glass. Old George looked pale, his eyes cloudy. All the years had accumulated and were pushing him from behind. He had started to feel his eighty-four years.

Old George sneered. 'I've got socks older than you, McPhail.'

'That's because you haven't changed them since I was born.'

Old George hummed and waved him off like he was one of the lottery ticket sellers trying to get into his bar. 'How many stitches did they put in?'

McPhail looked at his arm, 'A hundred and ten.'

'Fuck off,' said Old George. He leaned out of the booth and looked down the bar until he spotted Calvino. He waved his cane to draw his attention. 'Vinny. That's right, it's you I'm talking to. What's this about you staying overnight with some Spanish princess?'

'Where did that come from?' asked Calvino, staring at McPhail.

'How would I know? But it's all over the Square.'

'You believe rumors on the Square?'

Old George looked sheepish, leaning forward on his cane. 'Don't bite my head off. I thought I'd ask. After the war I was in Spain and, ooh la la, those Spanish women were something. I thought maybe you got lucky. That's all.'

'Come on, man, you left Cowboy with her, a kid, and a hooker,' said McPhail, pulling a cigarette out of his mouth and gesturing with it.

'And a kid and a hooker,' said Old George, his eyebrows shooting up. 'The story's getting a lot better. A tag team. That's my boy.'

The half-a-dozen people at the bar stared at Calvino, waiting for somebody to say something. 'It wasn't that way, George,' said Calvino.

Baby Bear, the waitress, dressed in tight jeans and a T-shirt, appeared and put a Mehkong and Coke in his hand. She gave him a wide grin and nodded at Old George. He looked at the drink and then caught Old George's idea.

'It's on the house,' said Old George. 'You helped some people out last night. That's what I heard. It's your buddy here who said you bagged a Spanish princess. What the fuck does he know about Spanish?'

'I speak better Spanish than you speak English,' said McPhail.

Old George's face knotted up as if he'd got a whiff of something dead behind the kitchen fridge. 'I was speaking English to Nazis waving white flags before you were born. "Drop your rifle or I'll blow your fucking head off." That's all the English you needed to know during the war.'

Calvino flashed an easy smile at Old George, whose heavily lidded eyes squeezed shut. The old man went still as if he was reliving some moment when German soldiers had refused to come out of a farmhouse.

Calvino walked to his usual booth in the back of the bar. The plastic placemat, the spoon and fork, and the bottle of expensive ground pepper had already been laid out for him. McPhail followed with a fresh glass of vodka and tonic.

'You phoned and asked about Casey. That's why I'm here,' said McPhail, sucking on his cigarette.

Baby Bear climbed into the booth behind McPhail and began to rub his shoulders and neck. 'Don't stop,' he said, eyes closed. 'That feels good.'

'What's this about a Spanish princess?' asked Calvino.

McPhail's eyes half-opened. 'I was joking with George. You know how he takes things literally. I know and you know the mem-farang wasn't gonna get anywhere close to you. But do these guys want to hear that she brushed you off after you saved her ass?'

'Why do you think she brushed me off?' asked Calvino.

'After years bar-fining yings, you don't have the skill that it takes for a mem-farang. They want a young guy and they want to be wooed. When's the last time you ever wooed a woman? Sometime last century would be my guess.'

Calvino shook his head and pulled his wallet out. 'How much did the hospital set you back last night?'

He saw that McPhail was looking past him, his brow furrowed. Calvino half-turned and saw the small corner shelf with the ceremonial plastic lotus painted gold, augmented with real flowers and a plate of bananas. A family of geckos had attacked the bananas. Calvino turned back around to find that Baby Bear, now kneeling, had both hands massaging McPhail's skull. As she dug her nails in, he made tiny whimpering noises.

'McPhail. Money. Hospital bill. Hello?'

'Sorry, man, I'm still on painkillers,' he said, finishing off the rest of his vodka tonic.

Putting down his empty glass, McPhail took out

the envelope from inside the sling and passed it across the table. Calvino opened it, looked at the bill, and put it back in the envelope along with five thousand baht. He slid it across the table. McPhail stuffed it back into his sling without looking inside.

'That fucker with the knife last night wanted blood. And he got blood. If I ever see that asshole, he'll wish he'd never been born.'

'Did you get a look at him?' asked Calvino.

McPhail shook his head. Only a few of the white skulls on McPhail's black T-shirt were visible around the edges of the sling. It was his I-almost-died shirt that he wore whenever he had a near-death experience. 'But I can find out.'

'There's no point doing that unless you plan on taking things to another level.'

McPhail's face deflated. He lit another cigarette. With his arm in a sling, there was no other level to which McPhail intended to take the matter. He just wanted to drink and smoke and talk – and get sympathy from the yings over his damaged arm. 'What happened with you and the Spanish princess last night? Come on, something must have happened.'

'Let's talk about Casey,' said Calvino. The waitress, a grandmother to two children, brought a chicken potpie to their booth, dumping it, steaming hot, out of the aluminum pan and onto Calvino's plate. She smiled like he was one of her grandkids.

'Casey? You wanna talk about Casey?' said McPhail. 'Let's get it out of the way.'

'You see the newspaper?' Calvino asked McPhail.

Sipping his drink, McPhail shook his head.

Calvino continued. 'There's a story about a secret CIA prison in Thailand, and it looks like Casey's got some information. They want to pull him in to ask some questions.'

'What kind of questions?' asked McPhail.

'Why he destroyed the tapes of the interrogations,' said Calvino.

'Casey knocking heads and smiling into the camera. That would be in character,' said McPhail. 'That'll have them talking at JUSMAG bingo night.'

Earlier in the morning, Colonel Pratt had phoned Calvino, asking if he knew where Casey had gone. Calvino had had no idea. Casey was a client; he wasn't babysitting the guy. He could be anywhere.

'He's making himself scarce.'

McPhail exhaled a cloud of smoke and coughed. 'Who in the fuck wouldn't?'

The Colonel had been around to Casey's apartment and had been told Casey had left town. A lot of other people had been in and out of Casey's apartment as well. Last time anyone had seen him, he'd shown up at the security desk with two suitcases and asked the guard to call a taxi for the airport. He must have been tipped that the storm was coming and slipped out of the country while he could.

The security guard said he'd watched Casey climb into the back of a taxi, and that was the last anyone had seen of him.

'He may have left the country,' said Calvino. 'If Interpol's after him, he's on the run.'

'What does Pratt think?' asked McPhail.

'That he's here in Thailand somewhere.' The Colonel had said it was doubtful that Casey had left the country. Immigration had a computer record of all foreigners who entered and left; Casey wasn't one of the foreigners who'd left. Calvino's reaction was that someone at immigration had fucked up – put in the wrong spelling of the name, lost the card, or misfiled it. Or maybe Casey had managed to get through without the card getting processed or had used a fake passport. Or maybe he'd gone to the airport but hadn't left the country.

There were private ways of entering and exiting the airport, and a special-ops guy like Casey would have been familiar with how to come and go like a ghost, leaving no trail. 'But why would he want to do that?' Colonel Pratt had asked. With someone like Casey there could have been a dozen good reasons bubbling under the surface. Colonel Pratt thought it most interesting that Casey would have told everyone he was going to the airport without saying exactly where he was going.

The point the Colonel had made was that a military man like Casey didn't go missing in action.

Men like him knew exactly where they were going and the purpose for going there. Colonel Pratt thought it was more than a coincidence that Casey had left for the airport shortly after Ratana had come up with his phone number as the reason for Nongluck's bundle of playing cards.

After Calvino finished explaining to McPhail the Colonel's failed attempts to track down Casey, he cut open his chicken pie.

'Colonel Pratt found the taxi driver who took Casey to the airport. He'd dropped Casey and his two suitcases on the departure level. Casey gave him a hundred-baht tip.'

'And he went inside, took the escalator up to arrivals, and took another taxi back to the city,' said McPhail.

'Maybe, or maybe he just kept on going. If he doubled back, do you have any idea where he'd be hiding?'

McPhail sipped his drink and got Baby Bear to light his cigarette. Worry lines appeared on his forehead. He shook his head side to side, as if to dislodge the little box holding all the ideas he had about Casey. 'I followed him for three days. JUSMAG, Siam Paragon, Chinatown, the Nana Hotel coffee shop, an outdoor restaurant on Soi 4, a short-time hotel on Soi 40, and an eye clinic on Thong Lo. The man had a full schedule. I don't see how he'd have time to draw the water for a waterboarding interrogation. Or rob banks or whatever other crimes they want him for.'

Calvino had gone over the list with Colonel Pratt that morning. 'You said you lost him in Chinatown.'

'He fucking disappeared,' said McPhail. 'Like a rat up a drainpipe.'

Old George looked down the aisle from his perch. He pounded his cane on the floor a couple of times until he caught Calvino's eye. 'Does medical coverage come with McPhail's assignments?'

'Blue Cross all the way, George.'

'Don't talk to me about crosses. Are you paying his bill?'

'He's fully covered.' Calvino counted out the amount of the bill all over again, folded the notes, and handed them to McPhail.

McPhail flipped through the notes and turned around. 'He's paid it, George. Twice over.'

Old George leaned over his cane and smiled. 'Don't give him so much money, Vinny. He'll slit his other arm himself. Now order some more goddamn food. Think of it as rent. I can't make any money if all you do is come in here and use my place as your second office.'

'Two specials. Will that do it, George?'

'That's more like it,' Old George shouted.

Old George grimaced as he looked at the TV. He murmured under his breath, 'I hate this cut-'em-up shit. But the girls love it. Go figure.'

'How's the arm by the way?' Calvino had forgotten to ask McPhail.

'It looks like Godzilla chewed on it, mistaking it for a Happy Meal.'

Calvino pushed the potatoes and carrots around his plate. He put down the knife and fork and leaned back, arms stretched out. Baby Bear worked her fingers into the knotted muscles along the sides of McPhail's neck. He might have been cut up, but he didn't look like he was suffering much.

'What was Casey doing at an eye clinic on Thong Lo?' asked Calvino.

'Getting glasses or his eyes checked.'

'You don't know? You didn't take two minutes to go inside and ask?'

'I didn't have fucking time. This guy is running around like an Olympic sprinter. Did you want me to go in the clinic and yap about whether Casey is twenty-twenty or to follow circus boy to where he was flying to next?'

'You did the right thing.'

'Of course he did the right thing, Calvino.' Old George was eavesdropping while pretending to listen to the music. He couldn't help himself from making editorial comments.

'We all know that, George. I'm trying to have a conversation here.'

'Have your conversation. Go ahead. Get your specials and talk. What do I care if some punk goes into some high-priced eye clinic in Thong Lo? It's no skin off my nose. I know Casey. He's been in my bar. He seems to have no eye problems. A man who goes to an eye clinic who doesn't have an eye problem is looking at some other problem to solve. I'm eighty-four years old and don't wear glasses. You see this black hair? That ain't dyed black; it's natural. And my kishkes are as good as when I was twenty-one years old. Ask any of these girls if I've got a problem with my kishkes. Just ask them.'

Calvino thought sometimes he should put Old George on the payroll.

'How many times can you use your kishkes? One day they're gonna blow out like cheap tires on the expressway,' said McPhail.

'Don't you start with me, McPhail. I just got you full medical coverage and you're threatening my kishkes. They'll be bumping and grinding long after you're gone.'

CHAPTER 32

Tracer was parading around the condo in black boxer shorts and an undershirt, side-stepping the pool table with the balls racked. The previous night hadn't changed anything. They'd awoken in Bangkok to another hot day, a day of work in progress. A bank of clouds closed in on the distant horizon. He opened the balcony door and stepped outside. The air was heavy. Squatting down, he read the dial on the wind meter he'd clipped to the metal railing. The readout gave direction and speed. He glanced over his shoulder at Jarrett sitting at the table and nodded. Wind was down. That was good news. One factor in the calculation of targeting over distance was wind. Ignore it and the chances increased that the sniper would miss the target. Back inside, Tracer picked up a notebook and made notes.

'Wind check?' asked Jarrett.

'Five kilometers an hour, some gusting. Wind coming from the east.'

'The weather report predicts rain. It shouldn't be raining this time of year, should it?' asked Jarrett. He hated rain on the job. Shooting in a rainstorm not only knocked visibility down to twenty meters, it interfered with the flight pattern of the round. Bullets did funny things in the rain, and funny things weren't what a sniper wanted a bullet to do. It wasn't a standup comedy act; it was a closing act.

'It's been raining most afternoons,' said Tracer, looking up from his notebook.

During the preparation for a job, Jarrett sometimes thought of himself as something like a professional golfer. His assistant, the spotter, was like a combination coach and caddy, a man whose wisdom, experience, and knowledge were indispensable on the course. But there was an important difference between the two games. A professional golfer who shot eight under par would go on to win nearly every tournament he played in and walk away with fat promotion contracts, a busload of groupies, and of course the prize money. Shooting the equivalent of eight under par for a sniper was failure. The expectation was a hole in one every time he teed off. Not even Tiger Woods could do that. Jarrett rotated his left arm in a wide arc, then his right arm. After that he dropped to the floor and did fifty push-ups.

Waiting for the shot caused Jarrett's muscles to stiffen up. The total focus and concentration made him feel edgy. He stayed alert and depended on the blues to pull him into the psychological zone he needed to occupy before pulling the trigger. Every sniper had his trick for finding that zone. Jarrett found it with Tracer's help and the blues.

So far it had been a normal job and normal conditions. The aborted shot came with the territory; Jarrett could deal with it. Sometimes they would set up in the field and wait three or four days for the target to appear. Then they got one shot, what in the trade they called the JFK special, the headshot that seals the deal. Pack up and leave the scene. In a few seconds the downtime is logged into the past as forgotten history.

Something different was playing in Tracer's mind. Jarrett looked up from his position at his friend. Tracer's restlessness, his constant high-alert mode, was obvious, for instance in the way small things like a noise in the outside corridor spooked him.

'Something's bothering you, Tracer. It ain't the wind. It ain't the possibility of rain.'

Tracer slowly moved his binoculars clockwise, scanning the buildings and the road below. 'The first time we set up, the target didn't show. An abort makes me uneasy. An abort is a whisper from deeper voices that somethin's wrong.'

'What else is the whisper saying, Tracer?'

'They never tell you straight out. But they give little hints. Like, Tracer, you keep your eye out for what's out of place. Look for what doesn't fit in the picture. Is there anything or anyone who breaks the pattern of what you should be finding?' Tracer scanned the scene, finding vans, police cars, and a chopper that flew overhead; people in the windows of apartments, offices, and shops.

'Anything stick out that shouldn't?' asked Jarrett.

Despite the long hours of waiting, a mission could roll faster than a dog with a back full of fleas. It made them both uneasy.

Tracer lowered the binoculars; he had a ritual to perform. He touched them with his mojo bag, gently rubbing it down the barrel of the lens in neat, measured strokes. He muttered some words his father had taught him. Ever since Jarrett had known him, Tracer had had his touch of magic, a pinch of good-luck thing, and Jarrett never complained or made fun of it. Only this time, the ritual had gone on longer than before. That troubled Jarrett, who liked everything to be in place exactly as it always had been.

'Not yet,' said Tracer. 'But I'm lookin' hard. What you look for is partly inside your head and partly something on the ground.'

'I'm looking, too, but I don't see anything different,' said Jarrett.

Tracer shook his head, his back turned to Jarrett. 'Finding a needle before a needle finds you takes more than just looking. You have to feel where a needle might hide.' The binoculars dangled from a string around his neck, resting solidly against his mojo bag.

'A needle can hide wherever it wants,' said Jarrett.

Tracer had gone out early in the morning to jog, stopped at Starbucks, and read the papers. 'I saw something in the paper about how Casey's disappeared. He's part of some big investigation in

Washington. I'd thought Waters would've called and said something. He phone you?' asked Tracer.

Jarrett shook his head. 'What'd the newspaper say they were investigating?'

'Stuff happened in one of the prisons.'

'We've been paid for the job. Nothing from Waters to say stand down.'

'I don't like it,' said Tracer.

'It's just another day, Tracer. I beat your sorry ass at pool and you're in a bad mood. That's all. We've done jobs like this one before. Sorry to hear about Casey's problem. But it's got nothing to do with us.'

Tracer shook his head; jaw clenched, binoculars hanging around his neck, he walked around the large room. He'd gone into his thinking mode, observed Jarrett.

'You remember Mark?'

'One of the suits who fetches for the CEO.'

'That's him. The paper quotes him as saying Casey could've been involved in activities outside the scope of his authority. You ever think about the name?'

Jarrett blinked at him and shrugged.

'I am talking about Logistic Risk Assessment Services. It seems they've done an assessment on the risk of Casey's hurting them. From the paper, I'd say it sounds like the company's gonna cut him loose. Hang him out to dry.'

'That's fucked,' said Jarrett.

'That's what I've been trying to say.'

Tracer looked back, nodded, then bent over his computer, feeding in and adjusting the formula for sighting Cat's condo balcony. Wind, distance, the velocity of the round, temperature, and humidity would play a role on the drop rate of the .308 caliber soft-nosed slug from the end of the rifle barrel to the impact point on Somporn's body.

Tracer looked up from the computer screen. 'Technical analysis gets us to the target. But what we do isn't mechanical. Otherwise, Colonel Waters could send along a robot to do the job. We ain't robots. I look for things in the field of vision that no formula could predict.'

Jarrett nodded, upper teeth biting into his lip. Tracer working the mojo bag overtime wasn't like him. He was part of a no-nonsense, straight-ahead, focused killing machine. It was normal to feel nervous as the anticipation of the moment came closer. But they were still hours away from the time the target would appear.

'Talk to me. This could turn into some seriously bad shit.'

Jarrett ran his hand through his hair and breathed out. 'Where do you think Casey's gone?'

Tracer punched his forefinger against his own chest. 'Me? I think he's on the run from Congress. They want him to testify. They might as well kill Casey as make him a scapegoat for their secret prisons. The man's had nothing but a streak of bad luck. Was Casey dragged into his bad luck? You gotta think about that.'

Jarrett rose from his chair, walked over to the pool table, picked up his cue stick and sent the balls scattering across the table. 'Okay, I've thought about it.'

'What if our first day to do the job wasn't really a screw-up over Somporn's schedule? What if someone wanted to put us through a trial run? They wanted to see how we'd set up. What if we were told he'd be on the balcony so our location could be compromised? It could have been intentional.'

Tracer's pushback was always the same; after a succession of belly jabs from the voodoo hand-book, he countered with an unexpected uppercut to the jaw by appealing to reason.

Jarrett hadn't seen that one coming.

Jarrett aimed at the one ball and missed; the white cue ball rolled into the side pocket. He put the cue down on the table and leaned back, his arms folded over his chest.

'Talk to me about why someone would set us up,' said Jarrett.

'I've been thinking about a couple of things. You were supposed to meet Jack Malone with your dad in Hua Hin. What do we find in this condo? A newspaper from Hua Hin. Man, come on, this is fucking Bangkok. And this pool table. You tell me what was the color of the felt on the table you played on in Hua Hin?'

'Blue.'

Tracer nodded. 'That's right. It was blue. Same as this.'

'What're you saying?'

Tracer threw up his hands, a look of anguish on his face. 'Fuck if I know. But, I don't like that we gave away our position on the first day. We've done that. If it wasn't a real abort, someone's locked to us right now, watching us. The other thing I already told you, but you think it's some voodoo bullshit. The money Casey gave to Colonel Waters had the smell of earth. That money had been buried. And when I said something to Colonel Waters about it, he said not to worry.'

'And you're saying it has something to do with what happened in Hua Hin with my dad?'

'I don't know,' Tracer said, rubbing the back of his neck with his right hand. 'All I'm saying is the Hua Hin newspaper and that pool table gotta mean something. Like that night you walked into the bar in Hua Hin and found that guy with red hair and it wasn't Jack. You told me it gave you a bad feeling. But you couldn't say why.'

Prior experience strongly suggested to Jarrett that when Tracer had a bad feeling, it was time to listen carefully. A couple of times Tracer's sixth sense had saved them from getting shot. When a team sets up an ambush, the way they stay alive is to appreciate that on the other side there are sniper teams just like them, hunting for them, looking to ambush them before they can carry out their mission. In every hellhole they'd been sent to on a job, there had always been another side. And the men on the other side shot back. Jarrett and Tracer had friends who'd been killed because either the sniper or the spotter hadn't had that extra feature beyond the formula for getting to the target. Tracer had an ability to put dates, smells, tones, and tiny wrinkles in the fabric of a mission into a larger frame and then focus and adjust until the danger around the target revealed itself.

'You're saying maybe we've been targeted?' The hair stood up on the back of Jarrett's neck. He slapped his neck as if a black fly had landed on his skin and started racking the balls.

Tracer closed the lid on his laptop and stretched out on the sofa, facing the balcony. Standard operating procedure in an urban firezone was to set up a clear line of fire to the target and to shelter against any countersniper team deployed inside that zone of fire. It was a little insurance policy against being ambushed. It had become a habit, even though it had been years since another sniper had taken a shot at them.

'Somethin's telling my mojo that someone's out there,' said Tracer, one eye opening, as he twisted his finger around the string of the mojo bag. 'I haven't found him, but I ain't stoppin' until I do.' The same determination had made Tracer a top prospect for professional football. But back then, the thing that had been out there had caught him by surprise, dragged him down, put him in court, and shot him out the mouth of a cannon straight into the Marine Corps. By the time he'd picked himself up and dusted himself off, he was in the field spotting skinnies for Jarrett to pick off in Mogadishu. He wasn't ever going to let that happen again.

Jarrett walked back to the table, sat behind the sniper rifle, and looked down the barrel and silencer. He had a clear view of the balcony where Somporn would appear.

'Are you saying we pack it in?' asked Jarrett.

'I ain't there yet.'

Tracer rose from the sofa, using his binoculars to scan the horizon. He looked back over his shoulder at Jarrett who stood at the table, running his hand over the blue felt. Tracer knew he was thinking about that night years before in Hua Hin when Jack Malone had been a no-show. But the man had a good reason. He was dead.

'You think your darling is on her way to the beehives in Surin? She was looking at that private investigator like she might be more interested in him than in bees.'

Jarrett smiled, relieved for a moment to be thinking about the ying holding her backpack. 'Her family lost all of their hives. That was how they'd made their living. I figure she's on her way back home.'

Tracer laughed, watching Jarrett leaning over the pool table, stroking it as if under the surface he'd find an answer to some larger question of loss. 'Man, you are such a dreamer. That girl ain't ever gonna stay put and raise bees. It's not the nature of life.'

CHAPTER 33

The day before Casey had vanished, McPhail had followed him to an eye clinic in Soi Thong Lo. The following morning, Calvino had retraced Casey's trail. Located in a rich section of Sukhumvit Road, the district had more than its share of inhabitants with bad eyes, and Chinese merchants seized the chance to make fast money by opening dozens of eye clinics. They competed for business in the collision of residential and commercial buildings, beauty parlors, fast-food restaurants, shopping malls, offices, nightclubs, taverns, and car dealerships. Casey had chosen a clinic set back from the main drag, meaning that the business didn't depend on foot traffic. They had a higher class of clientele, the kind of people who would learn of it by word-of-mouth and then go to the trouble of finding it inside a high-rise. The first shop these clients would find there wasn't an eye clinic but a flower shop for the well-heeled – girlfriends and hot dates, with weddings and funerals more of a sideline. A person would need a major head cold to visit the ground floor without noticing the scent of roses, geranium, and evergreens, with a whiff of tom yam gung from the staff's leftover lunch. A woman might get a little heady from the fragrance; a man might think he'd stumbled into the women's restroom by mistake.

Above the commercial level rose a residential high-rise: floor after floor of ultra-modern serviced apartments and offices, devoted to the comfort of the well-off who wanted a barrier between themselves and ordinary Thais. It had been built for foreigners – European kitchen, American sitting room, Chinese ancestor-worship room. Teeming with different nationalities, the building was a beehive with all kinds of species living side by side. It was every place and no place. Arches and pillars and fountains and high ceilings combined Gothic, Delphic, and Victorian flourishes – touches randomly plucked from design magazines to carry the branded prestige associated with farang elites. The interiors could've been borrowed from the blueprints of a high-class whorehouse multiplied by twenty-nine floors.

Following McPhail's directions, Calvino had passed many high-rise buildings. One of them had been grand and elegant, with a uniformed security guard stationed at the front door. He'd recognized it. Cat's condo was on the ninth floor. He remembered it from his stakeout. Her building, like the other luxury buildings in Thong Lo, was a universe away from the seedy beauty salon with the old crones playing mah-jongg and stapling bribes to Somporn campaign cards. He wondered if the sister who had worked in that dump had ever seen Cat's place. This was more than just an average upgrade from the sea-level of a beauty salon stuck amid lower-middle-class shop-houses. Cat had come a long way; he gave her that much.

He figured the sister would have been impressed. Living in such a building guaranteed a face so large that the occupant would have to turn sideways to get in and out of doors. But could Cat hold on to what she had? That was always the question with a mia noi. Lack of job security made a mia noi a little crazy except on a really hot day, when she might accelerate from mildly paranoid to barking-dog mad.

Calvino headed inside to look for the eye clinic. The two buildings were on the same side of the road. What was Casey doing in Cat's neighborhood? Why hire him to follow a woman whom he already knew where to find? He couldn't have expected McPhail to have the answers; Calvino was still working through the possibilities arising from the proximity of the eye clinic to Cat's condo.

Calvino entered the heavily scented main lobby. Shops lined one wall. Elevators to the upper floors were on the other. A uniformed security guard sitting behind the reception desk was gazing into a compact mirror, pulling hairs out of his chin and occasionally looking up to check out someone walking to the elevators.

A blast of cold air hit Calvino the way those icy

fronts from Canada blow through New York, giving Upper East Side poodles and their matronly owners a shiver that cuts deep inside. Calvino stopped outside the eye clinic and looked through the window. Behind the counter was a ying in her early thirties in a nurselike uniform and cap. She looked all right if a man liked the doctor-and-nurse game. The presentation of the clinic fell between a hospital and a boutique spa. He picked up a brochure on the counter and opened it.

'Do you have an appointment?' The nurse, receptionist, or whatever she called herself looked up from a game of solitaire on her computer screen. She looked bored, her eyes heavy, the line of her mouth dipping into the depression zone.

Calvino shook his head. She stared at his eyes as if to determine the nature of his problem. 'My friend Mr Casey said this was a good place to have my eyes checked.'

'Fill out the form, please.' She slid a piece of paper across the counter.

'Do you remember Mr Casey?'

It was clear from her expression that she did not. He took out a photograph of Casey and handed it to her. 'That's Casey.'

She slipped on her glasses and looked.

She nodded. 'Yes, I remember him. We fitted him with contact lenses.'

Now he was getting somewhere. They had established a mutual acquaintance and that always made a woman relax. The life came back into her face and she managed a smile. The fact they both knew Casey had washed away the utter strangeness of an unknown farang coming in off the street. 'Has he picked them up?'

She checked her records. 'Yesterday he came down to get them.'

'Right, he lives upstairs.'

She seemed happy that he knew about Casey. 'Yes, he lives upstairs.'

He slipped Casey's record around. He had given his address as being on the ninth floor. 'When was the last time you saw him?'

She thought for a minute, growing suspicious of Calvino. 'I don't remember.'

That was good enough for Vincent Calvino. He'd gone as far as he could with her, then the cold front had once again rolled across her face, freezing him out.

'You can see the doctor now,' she said.

He glanced at his watch. 'Let me think about it. I need lunch. I wouldn't do an eye test without eating. I can't see right without food.'

The food-injection argument nearly always won over the Thais. The common greeting. 'Have you eaten rice yet?' came from this abiding, deep concern that hunger might overcome a person at any moment. No one ever would think of interfering with someone's need to eat immediately. And that's how it worked. The Thais didn't work up an appetite; something happened in their gut that triggered a starvation reaction. Calvino saw

414

what might just pass as sympathy in her eyes as he repeated his need to eat.

'You'll come back?'

'After I eat a bowl of noodles,' he said, taking a namecard from the plastic box on the counter. He hadn't filled in the form. He hadn't really done anything that people coming into a clinic were supposed to do – nothing at all, really, except ask a bunch of questions. As he left, he knew she would remember him. She might phone Casey and tell him that someone had been looking for him. A farang who'd come into the clinic shivering from the air-conditioning, a man hungry to dive into a bowl of noodles. But he hadn't let his hunger get in the way of asking a lot of awkward personal questions. She was in awe that the questions in this farang's head had assumed priority over the immediate demands of his stomach; that was one thing a Thai rarely witnessed.

He stopped in the door, turned around. 'You like jazz?'

She smiled.

'Ever hear of a guitar player named Ball?'

Her head tilted down, as if trying to recall a memory. 'Is he Thai?'

'He was last night when my friend and I had a talk with him.'

CHAPTER 34

Colonel Pratt and Calvino waited until Ball got out of his red sports car. He'd parked it in the same spot as before, in front of Saxophone. When Ball spotted Colonel Pratt, he fumbled with his keys, trying to get back into his car, but his reaction came too late. Calvino grabbed the keys and slammed Ball against the car.

'You're going to let a farang do that to a Thai?' Ball asked, his eyes filled with rage, his lower lip quivering.

Colonel Pratt's expression remained calm. 'We have some unfinished business.'

'I have nothing more to say,' said Ball, folding his arms around his chest. 'I want to call my lawyer.'

The request was fallout from too much American TV. Americans were cowed by lawyers. Thais had no fear of them. There were forces more powerful than the law, and lawyers who went against those forces disappeared. Fear resided elsewhere, and Ball was staring straight in the face of his worst nightmare. Calvino touched the tip of the car key against the side of the car. 'A car like this, people remember. You have to be careful or it can get scratched. Of course, you could sue me.' He ran the key against the side, leaving a sluglike trail across the front door.

'Nothing to say? Never mind, I've just got started.' Calvino touched the key on the hood. He might as well have driven a fist between Ball's legs.

Ball went wild, grabbing Calvino's arm. 'Wait! Don't do that!'

Calvino pushed him against the car. 'Don't fuck with me, Ball.'

'Let's have a talk,' said Colonel Pratt.

Ball looked at Calvino. 'Can I have my key?'

'After we have a little talk,' said Calvino.

'It won't take long,' said Colonel Pratt.

Calvino moved back, standing level with Pratt. Ball looked from one man to the other, trying to figure out his best play – who was going to cut him the best deal. He went with the standard default: trust the Thai to help you.

'Our band is on soon,' he said. His plea was intended to appeal to the musician in Colonel Pratt. 'If I'm not inside, they'll start looking for me.'

'We aren't going anywhere,' said Colonel Pratt. 'A few minutes, Ball. You can do that, can't you?'

Ball nodded. Sighing and head-down, he followed Colonel Pratt to a Volvo parked a few feet away. Ball climbed into the back and Colonel Pratt followed. Calvino got in the front and turned on the ignition. Cool air circulated as Ball sat

417

against the far door, crunched up like a child waiting for punishment. Calvino had suggested the idea of a private interrogation, and Colonel Pratt had decided that going back to Saxophone and inviting Ball to have a talk wouldn't be a problem.

Just then a ying walked past the Volvo. She stopped when she saw Calvino sitting behind the wheel. Smiling, she knocked on the window. It was Amy, the ying who'd ordered a bottle of Johnnie Walker Black for her friends and then ignored him. She was coming back for another tap on the money machine.

He rolled down the window and said, 'See you inside.'

She looked at the men in the backseat. 'Hi, Ball,' she said, smiling. 'You playing tonight?'

'Yeah, I'm playing. See you inside,' Ball said, flashing her a big smile.

She looked at the three men. Calvino remembered that she'd given her phone number to Ball on a coaster. None of them said anything.

'I guess I'll see you inside later.'

Calvino rolled up the window, and after a few seconds she turned and walked into the club. He leaned over the seat and stared hard at Ball. He was suddenly alone with two men he definitely hadn't wanted to see again. Ball shrank against the door, his shoulder folding like an umbrella. He looked like a bat that had dropped off a cave ceiling, blinking, nervous, and scared.

Colonel Pratt laid the trap. 'Casey's dropped the dime on you, Ball. He says you killed Nongluck in Pattaya. It could go bad for you.'

'Casey says it was your idea. You wanted to help Cat,' said Calvino.

'If you want us to help you, then you better tell us what happened.'

Ball's face showed nothing other than fear. He was wondering to himself if the cop and his farang friend were setting him up. Ball might not have known the game called prisoner's dilemma, but he didn't have to know the game to know the rules. Do you rat out your accomplice before he rats you out, or do you both stick to your mutual pact to stay silent, no matter what the police say? When the police insist that the other guy dropped the dime on you, the correct response is to call their bluff. But fear and doubt tend to knock intellectual game rules apart.

'I don't know anyone named Casey,' said Ball.

'That's a lie,' said Calvino. 'The manager at the club has seen you talking to him.'

'I talk to a lot of people. That doesn't mean I know their names,' said Ball.

'This farang is ex-military. Tough, wiry, strong, wears aviator glasses. After the sun sets, he keeps his sunglasses on. You get the picture. He's someone you'd remember,' said Colonel Pratt. He'd half turned in the seat, facing Ball.

Ball thought for a moment. 'Yeah, I may have seen a guy like that. So what?'

Calvino exchanged a look with Colonel Pratt. The oyster shell had cracked open, and it was time for the Colonel to spoon out the fleshy bits and see if he'd find a pearl.

Calvino opened the glove compartment. He took out a notebook, tore out a page, and wrote down Casey's cell-phone number. Handing it to Ball, he said, 'He gave me this. It's a secret number. He said Nongluck had this number. He said you also had it. Casey said you'd understand. Maybe it's in your phone book.'

'When is the last time you saw Casey?' asked Colonel Pratt.

Ball looked up from the paper with Casey's private number on it.

'A couple of days ago,' said Ball.

'Before he left town?'

'I didn't know he left town.'

'Some say he did,' said Calvino.

'But I think he might still be in Bangkok,' said Colonel Pratt. The Colonel showed no emotion. It was a matter-of-fact statement.

'I don't know if he's in Bangkok.' Ball looked at Colonel Pratt, thinking the Colonel might take his side. 'It's true. How would I know?'

'I think that's bullshit,' said Calvino.

'Any idea why he'd tell us you killed Nongluck?' asked Colonel Pratt.

Ball crumpled up the paper.

'Tell us your side of the story, Ball,' said Calvino. 'The farang got you in over your head. We know that. It wasn't your fault. Casey's a dangerous man. I know it, and you know it. Of course you're scared.'

The smell drifted from the bad odor of a possible trap baited by his interrogators to something even more rancid: a setup by Casey, and Ball suddenly couldn't wait to set the record straight. Casey had come around to Saxophone and gotten to know Ball. He'd bought him drinks, gotten friendly with him. Casey had asked if Ball would like to work for him. Ball needed the cash and agreed to sign on to Casey's payroll.

'He offered you money?' asked Colonel Pratt.

'After he followed me.'

'Why was he following you?'

Ball shrugged, tossing his head side to side, like he was playing his guitar. 'It had something to do with Meow. I teach her nephews the guitar.'

'How much is he paying you?' asked Calvino.

'Twenty thousand baht.'

'A month, a year?' asked Colonel Pratt.

'A week.'

Calvino raised an eyebrow. That was big-time money for a guitar player like Ball. Keeping up the monthly installments on the Mazda meant a few compromises. The question was what Ball had brought to Casey's table to justify the expense.

Casey must have found out about the guitar player and Cat being a number, not of the musical variety but in the nature of a gig – the Thai version of a no-strings sexual relationship. Cat was no

421

different from other minor wives who needed a personal diversion to relieve their cabin fever waiting for the phone to ring, alternating between boredom and hostility in the long periods between the infrequent visits by her patron. She liked Ball. He made her laugh and played love songs for her. They danced together on the balcony of her condo. It wasn't a strictly genuine gig because Cat was paying him money. And with that plus the money from his guitar playing and teaching and this new source of revenue he'd found in Casey, Ball was riding high on the hog wagon, forgetting that the wagon always ended up at the slaughterhouse.

'What did you do for Casey?' asked Calvino.

Ball's lips tightened and his eyes looked wild with hate and fear.

'He didn't give you money for nothing, Ball. What did he want?'

'Was the money to kill Nongluck?' asked Colonel Pratt.

Ball's attitude changed, and he shifted position in his seat, arms folded tight like someone in a straightjacket. When a mug like Ball opened up, it was the shower going full-blast, and everyone was going to get wet. Ball said that Casey's deal was simple. His job was to report on Cat's relationship with Somporn. That was the way it had started. But soon after Ball took the money, Casey tapped him for gossip and found it a convenient two-way street, passing along gossip to Ball about

422

the affair between Nongluck and Somporn. He knew it would get back to her.

Cat didn't take the gossip well. She exploded, broke a vase, screamed, cried, and railed. Like most minor wives, her whole life was threatened. And she'd watched enough Thai soap operas to understand that Ball expected, as she expected of herself, the need for a dramatic outburst, if only to get the shock out of her system. The bottom line was that Somporn wasn't someone she wanted to let go; she didn't want to share him with another woman. The major wife was enough of a headache, but that was an established way of structuring the man's needs.

But an arrangement like a resort time-share with a string of yings was playing fast and easy with the unwritten rules. Casey, according to Ball, had him drill into Cat's spinning, revenge-seeking head that as long as Nongluck was alive, she was at risk of losing her ticket to the big buffet. She obsessed about the possibility of losing her man and had nightmares of Somporn throwing her and her two nephews out into the street. Cat decided that Ball, if he really loved her, had to help her eliminate the risk. The way it came down was exactly what Casey said would happen. Ball had been Casey's backdoor into Somporn's secret life. Ball liked his well-paid side job with Casey and parted freely with his newly acquired information after each visit with Cat.

'To help Meow, you killed Nongluck,' said Calvino.

'I didn't kill her.'

'Casey says you did,' said Colonel Pratt.

'I didn't do it.'

'Then who did?' asked Calvino.

'Casey,' Ball said. 'I drove him to Pattaya. I told him that I wouldn't do it. He said never mind, he'd find another way.'

'Why did Casey want Nongluck dead?'

Nongluck had been with Casey's son when he was grabbed in a half-lit soi. Casey never quite got over the fact that she'd waited over an hour before calling the police. She said she'd been scared; the men who took Joel away threatened to kill her if she went to the cops. It had taken her a good hour to overcome her anxiety. Another woman in her place might have waited a lifetime. Ultimately Casey excused her delay. She was young, a woman; the men had guns. She had drawn a pass. But that hadn't ended the matter. Casey had nagging doubts about her role in the abduction. Had it been a coincidence that she'd been the one who'd suggested dinner earlier in the evening on the Thornburi side of the Chao Phraya River, at a hole-in-the-wall restaurant?

The restaurant was in the middle of nowhere. How would Somporn's thugs have known to find him on that soi at that time unless they had inside information? And who better than Joel's squeeze to pass the information along? John Dillinger's ying had worn a red dress that fingered him. The police opened fire and cut him down. That would have been a better ending than the one Joel faced. He'd been taken sixty kilometers outside the city, tied up, beaten, tortured, and shot. Casey's boy had suffered the worst kind of death at the hands of thugs who'd been hired to send a message: don't send people who cause a problem. As Casey was in the torture business himself, he'd assumed the photographs of his son's body were intended to cause maximum suffering.

The late night Calvino had walked back to his office, he had a taste of that don't-cause-a-problem message. He nodded as Ball spoke, and glanced at the Colonel, who acknowledged the bingo moment.

'Were you with Nongluck at the hotel when she paid for my upgrade?'

Ball looked genuinely puzzled.

'Upgrade? I don't understand.'

Calvino had the sense that Ball was telling the truth.

For Casey, the verdict had been out on Nongluck until he found out that she had been involved with Somporn. He had the idea in his head that their involvement had happened before Joel died. As far as Casey was concerned, it looked like Nongluck had no more good excuses. She was implicated in his son's murder.

So why involve me? Calvino asked himself. It was a question for Casey.

He needed a foolproof plan to nail Somporn. Pinning Nongluck's death on him would never have worked. Even in a case where all ten fingers pointed to Somporn's guilt in the murder of Casey's son, Somporn had walked on insufficient evidence. He was slippery. If Casey were going down that road, he'd wanted to make certain that all ten fingers pointed at Somporn as the killer. Killing Nongluck had its own rationale. Maybe the best reason was settling accounts for his dead son. And if compromising the private eye he'd hired could be folded into the transaction, he'd get two for one. But the question Calvino continued to ask himself was why Casey would bother tying him to Nongluck's death?

Colonel Pratt reached over and opened the door. 'You can go, Ball.' said Colonel Pratt. 'But remember, if Casey's story is right, and you are lying, you will be in more trouble than you ever thought possible.'

'I told you. I didn't kill Khun Nongluck.'

'You saw Casey do it?' asked Calvino.

'I didn't see anything,' he said.

Ball climbed out of the car. Walking around the front, he slipped into the door of Saxophone.

'What do you think, Pratt?'

The Colonel leaned back in his seat. 'Ball's lying.'

Calvino had felt Ball had stitched together enough real information to paint a plausible explanation that let him off the hook. 'And Casey doesn't want to be found,' said Calvino. 'But he's got me wanting to find him.'

'He thought that you'd be in a Pattaya jail and out of his hair,' said Colonel Pratt.

'You think he's that smart?' asked Calvino.

Colonel Pratt glanced at a couple passing on the street. He waited until they passed. 'Don't know. But I wouldn't underestimate him. Think, Vincent, you must have some idea where we can pick him up.'

Calvino closed his eyes and sighed. 'He was trained to hide without leaving any clues. His history is black-bag operations. How do you find a guy like that?'

'That doesn't answer my question, Vincent.'

'I don't know where he is,' answered Calvino.

Colonel Pratt got out of the backseat and waited until Calvino shifted over to the passenger seat. 'If you find him, you'll let me know.'

Calvino pursed his lips, his upper lip disappearing below the teeth line. He was thinking that in some ways he'd been no different from Ball. He'd taken money from Casey, knowing that something about the whole assignment had the smell of three-day-old fish. 'Yeah, if I see him, I'll tell him you're looking for him.'

'You're going after him,' said Colonel Pratt. The matter-of-fact tone of his voice meant that he hadn't expected any confirmation.

But Calvino provided one nonetheless. 'He killed a woman and tried to make it look like I was involved. Of course I'm going after him.'

Colonel Pratt reversed the Volvo. He understood

427

that for Calvino it wasn't about money. Calvino had been drawn into a situation by a professional who had been using him, someone who had arranged to throw a woman off the balcony above his room in Pattaya. It was personal. Casey had used him for gathering information and then implicated him in a murder case. 'Vincent, as your friend, I want you to listen.'

'I always listen,' Calvino said.

Whenever the Colonel prefaced his remarks with 'Vincent, as your friend,' what followed was in the way of a warning, a stop sign – hazard ahead.

'You said it yourself. Casey was trained to operate in a world you can't begin to comprehend. He worked in a secret CIA prison here. He worked at another prison in Baghdad. If you try taking Casey on your own, he will kill you.'

Calvino glanced over and caught the Colonel's eye.

'I'll keep that in mind,' said Calvino.

Frustration seeped into Colonel Pratt's voice. 'You're underestimating the advantage his training gives him.'

'He set me up. I take that personally.'

'When you make it personal, you make mistakes,' said Colonel Pratt. 'So far Casey hasn't made one.'

'Believe me, he will.'

CHAPTER 35

A halo circled the sun. Dabs of brilliant colors painted a rainbow on it. Marisa stood on the sidewalk staring directly at the halo, with her right hand shading her eyes from the sun. The sky was a polished gray glazed with slivers of white, like crystals of frost on a dirty window. Marisa couldn't take her eyes off the rainbow. She phoned Juan Carlos and told him to go outside and look. They agreed it was an unusual sky. Marisa said it was a sign. Centuries ago, peasants would have fallen on their knees and prayed. It was an end-of-the-world sky.

Somporn had turned Juan Carlos down. Somporn's wife hadn't been any help either.

'It's such a small thing to ask, Juan Carlos.' She'd been thinking of a Catalan proverb – 'Who has a daughter has bread; who has sons goes begging.' Marisa bit her tongue and waited for his reply.

'He said, "You don't understand how Thai people think."'

'I remember at lunch he said that you did understand the Thais.'

'He's changed his mind.'

'What does that mean?' A sense of bitterness mixed with sadness colored his voice. Juan Carlos, the forever-optimistic brother, had crashed.

Juan Carlos stepped back, feeling the flow of the air-conditioning. 'In the West, Somporn told me, the top people at a company or in politics are replaceable, like light bulbs. They get thrown out the moment someone brighter, smarter, better-looking comes along. For the Thais,' he said, 'the big people are indispensable. They are not challenged. They are not replaced. The military might overthrow the government. A company head might be shot. But those are extreme cases. I asked Somporn what that had to do with finding Fon's father. And he said, "You don't get involved in a business that is not yours. It is an unwritten rule." I said, "Her father works for one of your companies. You are involved." And he said, "That is Western logic."'

There had been no changing Somporn's mind. Fon's father wasn't Somporn's business. He worked in one factory out of many factories, with thousands of other employees, and most of them had some kind of trouble. That was their business, not his.

'Fon and her father are dispensable, but he's not?' Marisa asked. 'That's what he's saying?'

'He said to move on.'

'Is that what you want to do? Move on and forget Fon?'

'He's a politician.'

'And what are you?'

Somporn had been clear with his friends – protect community values while promoting fairness abroad. His friends in the business community understood how to decode his message – support local cartels while demanding free trade in foreign markets. The message played the music that those contributing to his campaign wanted to hear.

Saying goodbye, she could picture her brother standing before her, crying, as she held her hand above her eyes and stared at the halo with the shimmering rainbow colors.

She dialed Calvino's number.

'I'm on a stakeout,' he said. 'That would be difficult.'

She thought he sounded distant, almost cold and calculated, as if she were just another caller. Her feelings were hurt.

'I need to see you. It's urgent.'

Marisa was someone Calvino liked to think of as being in his debt. They'd been through the thunder and lightning in her bedroom. 'I want to see you too.'

That was what she'd wanted to hear.

He gave her directions to a restaurant on Thong Lo, opposite the building with the eye clinic and Casey's condo. Twenty minutes later, slightly shaken and stirred, her hair wind-blown, she climbed off the back of a motorcycle taxi, paid the driver, and entered the restaurant. She'd walked past Calvino without seeing him. A waitress brought her to his table. He sat at an out-of-the-way window table. It was easy to walk past; that was why he'd chosen it.

Marisa sat facing Calvino with her back to the window. The halo around the sun, the conversation with her twin brother, the motorcycle ride, and her anguish over Fon made her appear rattled and suspicious. Her frustration increased as she sought eye contact with Calvino and failed. From where he sat with a pair of binoculars, he had a good view of the entrance to Casey's building. When she tried again to find his eyes, he was looking straight past her.

'You don't seem very happy to see me,' she said.

He smiled, thinking of the old Mae West line, delivered looking at the pistol in the man's pocket: '. . . or are you just happy to see me?' But there was no humor in Marisa's delivery. When a woman has slept with a man, she loses that mystery, a prize she holds back, and the first meeting afterwards she is looking for some sign of attachment, a recognition that the man is under her charm. Or had she slept with a man who felt no attachment after sex? She searched Calvino's face, looking for evidence of the kind of man he was.

'It's good to see you,' he said. He lowered his binoculars, leaned forward, and kissed her on one cheek, then the other. He tilted his head to the side. In his family everyone greeted each other with an exchange of kisses on both cheeks. It was the same thing in Catalan culture. It was one of the comforting, common rituals that made people feel like they'd known each other for a lifetime.

'Yeah, it's good to see you too. About the other night: I didn't thank you properly. Thanks again.' She held his hands in hers.

'Sorry, but I'm on a stakeout. I'm working. What I'm trying to say is I'm not ignoring you. But I have to keep an eye out for someone across the street.'

She turned around and looked out the window.

'Don't do that,' he said. 'It draws attention.'

She slumped in her seat, dropping her bag with a thud, sulking.

'Anyone looking in the window would see you with the binoculars. Now that would draw attention,' she said, the smile coming back.

Being with a really smart woman was a bit like running a car into a wall at full speed; there might be enough juice to back up and drive away, but most likely the car would stall and shoot gray steam from its busted radiator. He put down the binoculars.

'Did you see them when you were outside?'

'No, I wasn't looking,' she said.

'The glass is tinted.'

'No one can see in. So it doesn't matter.' She had the last word.

She hadn't decided how much she cared about him. But she knew that she could care if she let herself. He'd snapped at her, and all she'd wanted to do was see what he was looking at across the street.

A cold, unsettling feeling swept over her. She hated herself for the tears that welled up in her eyes. She wanted to leave. Calvino stretched his hand forward, touching her hand. 'I didn't mean to get on your case, but the guy I'm looking for knows I want to find him. He's jumpy, I'm jumpy.'

'I understand,' she said, meaning it.

Reaching across the table, he took her hand and squeezed it. He said, 'I'm watching the condo across the road. On the phone you said you wanted to talk about Fon and that it was important.' He inhaled the faint scent of her perfume, a subtle, soft smell of roses, like the roses in the lobby of Casey's building. She wore a light blue dress that flattered her figure, and silver-and-gold earrings that moved like tiny windchimes every time she brushed back her hair. He looked away. An image of her in bed flashed back. He sighed, exhaling slowly, as if doing a breathing meditation. She'd had this thing that she wasn't pretty; that her brother robbed all the looks in the womb. But he didn't buy it. She was the kind of woman who made concentration on work impossible. He found himself glancing back at her face, her dress, her breasts, and her hands.

'What's happening with the kid?'

Her hands folded nervously on the table. She watched as a waitress brought a glass of water. 'Nothing.'

Calvino looked away from the window, a look of surprise in his eyes. 'Yeah?'

She nodded. 'What can I do when everyone tells me that what is right can't be done?'

'You congratulate yourself and relax. Because you finally understand how the world works,' he said. 'Or . . .'

'I don't believe that,' she said, cutting him off. He'd gotten under her skin but she wasn't sure how far, or how far she was prepared to let him go.

'You didn't let me finish,' said Calvino. 'You push back. That's what you have to do, or the right thing never gets done.'

'There's a way to help this child,' she said. Fon's face had looked so worried as she'd left her at the condo for the UN meeting. She had grabbed Marisa's arm and asked her not to leave. Marisa had leaned down and brushed Fon's hair. 'It'll be okay. I won't be long.' Fon stared at her, looking for some sign of truth overpowering her doubt. What would it take to destroy that look of pure terror on Fon's face? she'd wondered.

Calvino brushed a tear rolling down her cheek with the back of his hand. 'I don't see any good option for the kid. Or for you,' said Calvino. 'You keep her and then get arrested, lose your job, get deported from the country, and they take the kid back. Or you give back the kid and cut out the drama in between.'

Marisa fought back tears. 'Look at me, just for a second.' He looked at her face, which was clouded with emotion. 'Please don't tell me there is no way.'

There are people who believe that limits can be exceeded, and then there are those who believe that we are on the planet because our ancestors stuck to the limits. Calvino walked around to her side of the table, pulled up a chair, and held her. She took in a deep breath, her head on his shoulder. She had pumped the blood through his system at a rate that made him want to loosen his collar. He patted her back softly. Another time, another place, he might have gone for her; but when he stared into his own future, he saw himself walking alone. He admitted there was a moment when Marisa had gone below the skin and entered his bloodstream. But so did the common cold. Five days in bed usually cured what ailed him. Call it a chemical reaction, a biological imperative that hit all the right switches in his brain; sure the desire had coiled up inside, and he was having a hard time focusing on the building across the road, but he knew, and assumed she did as well, they had no real future.

'What about Juan Carlos? Wasn't he going to handle it?'

She shrugged her shoulders. 'He tried.'

'But Somporn said no,' said Calvino. 'No votes in helping a Burmese kid.'

Her eyes widened. 'That's what he told Juan Carlos.' Marisa moved like a fox with full concentration on its prey nibbling a piece of cheese. 'They only care about their money and power. Like the people in Madrid.'

'In Thailand, money buys a yes.'

'That's true of every country,' she said.

'Except that here most everything is for sale.'

'You're saying I should buy Fon?'

Leaning forward in his chair, he found the entrance to Casey's building in his binoculars. She had pretty much nailed it. In his mind, he hadn't been thinking it all the way through, but he guessed that if he had thought it through, that would have been exactly what he would have said.

He put it another way. 'Auntie has made an investment in the kid. Auntie's a businessperson. She looks at profit as a good thing. But she hates a loss. She'd as soon cut someone's throat to stop someone from taking what was hers. There's nothing personal between the girl and Auntie. They have a commercial relationship. She owns the girl. She wants to get paid. The price may be high. It's got to cover loss of face, too, not just the value of the girl.'

'Can you do this?' She searched his face.

He thought for a moment about what he was getting himself into. 'It takes time to make such arrangements.'

'I don't have time. Tomorrow at noon she goes back.'

Calvino drank from his coffee cup. 'She goes to Auntie. At least we know where to find her. We can negotiate later.'

Marisa shook her head. 'The guy from Taiwan will take her.'

He admitted that she had a point. Auntie had already sold her. The only thing missing was delivery of the goods. That wasn't usual. The habit of selling someone a couple of times remained widespread. A pimp like Auntie would have had a long history of taking money from more than one buyer and delivering, in the end, to the highest bidder. That was business. Fon was a seller's delight: she promised a rich reward, and Auntie liked pocketing the profits from a prime asset.

'It's probably what happened between us the other night. I've been thinking about it, and I don't know why, but I trust you. You didn't have to help on Cowboy. But you did. It proves at least that you can do the right thing.'

'When a man's got too many outstanding markers, it means he's been trading good and bad for a living. What happened on Cowboy happened before I could think about it. I'm no saint. You just caught me on a good night. Sometimes I get lucky and slip into doing something right. But I don't make a habit of hopeless rescue operations. It burns through a lot of good chits, and you still come out empty-handed.'

She reached out and touched his hand. 'You have a close friend on the police force. Could he do something?'

'There are limits to friendship and even greater limits on the power your friends have.'

She winced. It wasn't the answer she'd wanted to hear. He'd mentioned Colonel Pratt when he was at her condo. The perceived wisdom in Thailand that most farangs believed was that if you had a friend inside the police force, then he automatically protected you as if you possessed an unofficial immunity.

'Let me explain it this way,' Calvino said. 'Not too long ago in an upcountry town, a godfather and his goons stormed into a police station and, in front of the brass, beat an officer unconscious. The word was the cop might have slapped the son of the godfather. The cop said he hadn't hit the son. But it doesn't much matter if he did or didn't slap the kid. The father believed his kid.

'You get the picture? That's the kind of people you're dealing with. Godfathers who've got influence. What I'm saying is that not even the police are safe from assault in their stationhouse. You've got ranking officers who are afraid to help one of their own who's getting the shit kicked out of him right before their eyes. They freeze. When someone powerful decides to take revenge, it means that you are truly alone. There is no life raft in my friendship with the Colonel. If Auntie's people want to hurt you, or the kid, or me, there's no one who is going to stop them.'

'I don't believe that your friend would stand by while that happened to you.'

'No, he wouldn't. And that might get him killed.'

'Then you won't help me.'

'I didn't say that. All I'm saying is it isn't going to be easy. It's going to be very expensive.'

'Whatever you want to charge, I'll pay you.'

'Don't ever say that to anyone. Or if you do, make certain it's someone you love. And who loves you.'

'I like you, Vincent.' She was about to say something more but changed her mind. She touched his cheek. 'I'll go now. And thanks.'

'Never thank anyone until you've got what you want.'

She started to smile. 'I always get what I want.'

He watched her leave the restaurant. At the door, she looked back and smiled. Then she was gone. She was in the wrong country if she thought getting her way was the default setting. As he turned back with the binoculars, watching Casey's building, he thought of all the things he should have said, the sorts of things that immediately pop into mind once it's too late. What he'd wanted to say before she left was that when you fall off the edge in Thailand, just assume there will be no one to break your fall. It brought to mind the image of Nongluck falling past his balcony – as he'd sat, book open, drink in hand, looking out at the beach and the sea. He'd wanted to tell Marisa to remember that once the descent started, there was nothing between you and the street below.

CHAPTER 36

Casey's phone rang until an automatic message played. Calvino stood in the corridor outside Casey's unit. He switched his cell phone to a second SIM card and dialed again. He had his ear against the door and could hear Casey's phone ringing. It had one of those standard, default rings that people with no sensitivity about sound left on because it never occurred to them that they could change it.

Casey answered on the third ring from the second SIM card. The ringing on the other side of the door stopped.

'Open the door, Casey.' Calvino unbuttoned his jacket and reached inside, his hand resting on his .38 caliber police service revolver.

'Calvino, I'm not dressed. Nor is the girl next to me. Come back in an hour and we can talk.'

That constricted catch in the male voice that identifies he's a sexual bunny thumping inside the rabbit hole wasn't in Casey's voice. Instead, the voice was deliberate and measured; a soldier's voice.

'Ball's told the police what happened with

441

Nongluck. I could call them now if you want. Five minutes tops and they're here. Or you can open the door and we can have a talk.'

'You want money?'

Calvino drew his weapon and held it barrel-down with both hands as he stood away from the door, his back to the wall. He looked up and down the empty corridor. That time of the morning, most people were at work, or if they were the type who didn't hold down a job, they were still in bed.

'Read the newspapers, Casey. You've got the American Congress, the American military, and the Thai police all looking to talk to you.'

'And the CIA, the FBI, and the DEA,' said Casey.

'The whole alphabet.' Calvino listened for movement. It had gone quiet inside Casey's unit. 'Or I could make a call and let the Thai police know where they can find you.'

The cylinders in the deadbolt lock clicked with the solemn brevity of a hanged man's last dance. The door slowly swung open. When no one appeared, Calvino moved forward and looked around the corner, both of his hands gripping the .38. It was no more than a side glance into an empty doorway. He pulled back, thought about Casey's special-operations training.

'Casey, let's talk.' He hesitated before stepping further inside. From the corner of his eye, he registered something moving, like a bat flying down from a rafter.

Casey, his right hand coming out of nowhere,

smashed against Calvino's hands in one swift move. No words, nothing but the physical blow. The force of it dislodged Calvino's .38, which scuttled across the hardwood floor till it struck a chrome leg of the coffee table and started spinning like a top in front of the TV. Before Calvino reacted, Casey slammed his boot into his chest. The kick caught him with sufficient momentum to briefly lift him off the floor, knocking him against the doorjamb and drawing blood from the back of his head. Casey dragged Calvino half-conscious across the floor and dropped him in the middle of the room. He retrieved the .38 and stuck it in his belt. Then he stood over Calvino, looking down, holding a nine-millimeter Colt handgun a couple of inches from Calvino's head.

Calvino looked at the barrel of the gun; there was no silencer. 'That's gonna make a lot of noise,' said Calvino.

Casey smiled, his finger on the trigger, his eyes hidden by sunglasses. Lifting the gun away, he walked across the room and closed the door, locking it. 'You think I am going to shoot you?' he said. 'Why would I do that? That'd be a crime, wouldn't it?'

Calvino didn't like the tone in Casey's voice. Whatever the idea was, Casey made it sound positively lethal. With his free hand, Casey removed a pair of handcuffs from a leather pouch clipped to the side of his belt. 'Roll over, put your hands behind your back, and stay very still.'

'Is this part of your job description?'

'I've seen a lot of guys like you full of wise-cracks. They're the ones who usually cry out for their mother to come and rescue them.'

He cuffed Calvino's hands behind his back and wrapped duct tape around his ankles tight enough that the bones crunched together. Then he tore off more duct tape, using it to wrap Calvino's upper arms close to his body. He lifted him from the floor and pushed him into a sofa chair next to a bank of windows. The blinds were drawn shut.

As Calvino looked around the room, he spotted the rifle and telescopic scope on the table, the barrel pointed at the balcony window. Casey sat in a chair behind the sniper's rifle, hands folded behind his head, grinning like he'd heard a joke or won a poker jackpot. He picked up Calvino's .38 from the table and pointed it at him.

'Bang,' said Casey. He laughed as he examined the .38. 'No one uses a thirty-eight except in the movies. It's a good number if you're talking bra size, but as a weapon for stopping someone from drawing down on you? Nah, you wouldn't want to take it into a den of lions.'

'What's with the rifle?'

'Big game hunting,' Casey said. He closed his left eye and, with his right against the telescopic scope, sat with the silence of a cat watching its prey.

'You've got a lot of people looking for you,' said Calvino.

'I'm not in the country.'

Calvino looked around the condo. It was neat and clean. Not a shirt or a pair of underwear on the floor. No magazines, dishes, food or bottles, empty or full, in sight. The furniture polished, the floor swept, the smell of pine cleaner.

'Who you planning to kill? Anyone I know?'

Casey sighed, rose up from the rifle. His smile reappeared as he looked past Calvino. 'That's the wrong question, Calvino. You should be asking me who is going to kill you, if it ain't gonna be me.'

Calvino moved his head slowly. His chest felt like a stampede of buffalo had just passed over it, leaving the pain of hundreds of thundering hooves. He glimpsed another scoped rifle on a table no more than a foot away. He reminded himself of one of his laws: You are never as safe as you think you are.

'Your beef is with Somporn,' said Calvino. 'Maybe you special-forces guys specialize in trick shots, but I know that even you can't hit him from this window.'

'You're the guy who followed Cat. So you have inside information.'

'What's the game, Casey?'

'Shut the fuck up.'

'I thought your job was to get people talking. Or are you going through a career change?'

Casey sat straight in his chair, arched his back, and stretched his arms over his head. 'You had McPhail follow me. What underground school did

445

that boy attend to learn surveillance one-oh-one? I'd like to see McPhail's report card. Let me guess. Straight Fs, for fuck-up. He keeps on my tail across town. Not once does he lose me. Shouldn't that have rung a bell? I'm following a guy who has spent a lifetime following people and would pick up a tail in a minute. But no, of course he thinks it's his skill. He's convinced that old Casey wouldn't ever spot a tail. He thinks he's Sherlock fucking Holmes, and he reports to you about seeing me go into an eye clinic. Jet, the girl behind the counter, she gives you my address. What did you think, it was your charm? No, you thought, I have the element of surprise. Casey's not expecting me. What third-world detective training manual have you been reading?

'Let's play it the other way. I invite you to come here. And you think to yourself, Casey's planning something nasty. I'd better ask my friend the Colonel to come along.' He stopped as if a silent bell had rung and looked through the scope again. 'Not yet,' he says. 'Modern society has forgotten the distinction between a predator and a voyeur. The doer and the watcher. To be a successful sniper requires that you must be both.'

'Why kill Nongluck?'

'Did she wave when she dropped past?'

Calvino tried working the handcuffs behind his back. This pair wasn't bought off a vendor's table in Patpong. 'Why not just kill her? Why go to all the trouble with a room upgrade so you could frame me for her murder?'

446

'What would you do if your dead son's girlfriend was screwing his killer for money?' Then his mood changed.

'That doesn't really answer my question,' said Calvino. 'Why make me take the fall for Nongluck?'

Casey had another look through the scope. The sniper's rifle smelled of fresh oil, and the shiny barrel caught the light. When he looked up at Calvino, he rolled his head from side to side and exercised his jaw as if the air pressure inside an airplane cabin had suddenly changed.

'Operational convenience,' said Casey.

'But Somporn is the mission objective.'

Casey smiled and lowered his sunglasses. 'You're not so stupid. I needed to settle some accounts. Nongluck's account is settled. You know how bookkeeping works. Assets and liabilities have to balance. You were part of the accounting.'

'There's more accounting,' said Calvino.

Casey grunted. 'Ain't that the truth. A couple of more books get balanced. I can never turn down killing two birds with one stone. It's what I like to call a special bonus. But it's not easy to make happen. You got to plan and anticipate what your enemy will do. What he's thinking. You can't underestimate his capability. In my line of work, you search through another man's secret life, find out the things he can't admit to himself. That's the place where he's most easily killed.'

'And you passed these little pieces of wisdom along to your son, Joel. You tortured people in a secret prison. Did he know about your day job? Did you teach him your Chinese-fortune-cookie wisdom about how to interrogate people? Maybe that only works inside a secret prison. Maybe when he applied that wisdom in a Thai family business, it got him killed. He found the secrets. He demanded answers. But you didn't teach him that unless you keep the man in a cell, he could come after you. You forgot that lesson. And it eats you up. So what do you do? You blame Nongluck. That lets you off the hook. Nice play, Casey. After you killed the ying did you feel better?'

Calvino could see from the tension in Casey's arms and neck that he was exercising every power of restraint to stop from crossing over and killing him. Casey inhaled loudly. 'The first lesson is to understand your enemy, and a man who has this knowledge will never be defeated.'

'That's Sun Tzu,' said Calvino. 'Only you left out an important part. A man has to first define his enemy and not confuse him with his friend. I get the feeling you got an F on your report card for not being able to pick out bad guys from good ones in the underground school the military sent you to.'

'For a guy who has about ten minutes to live, you should be praying and not worrying about what Sun Tzu said.'

Calvino saw what had been near him the entire time, but he hadn't registered the meaning of until now. It was a second sniper's rifle positioned behind his chair. He strained to look over his shoulder, twisting the best he could on the chair. For the first time, he saw the role that Casey had planned for him. One he walked right into without seeing.

'I'm the decoy.' He turned back and looked over at Casey, the man who had been nicknamed the Ghost.

'Give the man a cigar and a hundred dollars,' said Casey, removing his sunglasses and turning his baseball cap backwards so he could slip on a pair of night-vision goggles. A sloppy grin crossed his face as he examined the .38 in the light, turning it over and laying it on the table. 'A hundred dollars for your secretary to give you the funeral you deserve.'

'You know about Apichart and the coffin,' said Calvino, resigned to Casey's ability to unearth the details from his personal and business life. Casey didn't bother to reply. Calvino looked at Casey's profile as he sat behind the sniper's rifle. Fearmakers were what insurgents supposedly called guys like Casey. They have a carte-blanche license to be creative in producing real fear. 'They've sucker-punched you, Casey. You're going to be the poster boy for torture. Your face is gonna be on every newspaper, TV, and website as the man who inflicts pain and gets a regular paycheck for it.'

'You ought to spend your last moments on this earth asking your creator for forgiveness,' said Casey. 'Leave me to worry about my problems.'

The masters of fear had cut Casey loose, tagging him as the fall guy. Leaving him isolated and with no possibility of escape, they were giving him his own taste of terror. Every man is a hero in his own story. Casey was no exception. Everyone he'd killed had deserved to die. There had been no innocent deaths on his watch. His service and company record, in his mind, had been perfect ones. He had only one regret, one blemish on his personal record, and that was his son's death. A few hundred dollars had been paid to have Joel killed. Nothing in his life would ever deliver the satisfaction of seeing that stain removed.

CHAPTER 37

Tracer's eyes cut across the night skyline, window after window, swinging the binoculars back into focus on the balcony of Cat's condo. The definition was perfect enough to see the petals on a potted orchid. It was half an hour from the appointed time when the target would appear; every one of those remaining thirty minutes threatened to stretch out into long and thin dimensions, making a one-minute segment into a unit that went on and on. He felt the thump of his pulse in his neck, the blood pumping as he worked buildings outside. He was looking for an infrared scope, which would identify itself with a telltale signature. Tracer knew that signature; he thought of an infrared marker as a squiggly line of thread that blurred into fuzziness. If someone out there had targeted them, Tracer would find him from that infrared signature. He turned up nothing except for the ghostly outlines rising off bodies and objects like steam. But Tracer didn't give up, thinking somewhere in that landscape of heat-generated movement, a signature was waiting to write its name in blood.

'In New Orleans, I knew a guy who had gone to Korea with the army,' he said. 'Everyone should live for four years in a country where people eat rats and wash them down with rice wine. Then they'd understand the meaning of hunger, when empty plays the blues inside the guts. All other desires fall away when the belly wails.'

Jarrett knew that the intel had troubled Tracer. It was no different in the marines. Intel was like women: some of them were good, a lot of them bad, and the man who survived had an instinct for navigating the switchbacks in the field and had planned his exit. No father, mother, doctor, brother, brilliant sister, or friend mattered on the job – nothing but the crosshairs and the feel of the rifle against his shoulder. Nor his Muslim heritage from Istanbul, the same background that had made him so valuable an asset on the ground. But at the moment of truth, it had to be submerged like all other distractions.

He'd been trained to see the target as a math-and-physics problem. Depersonalize it, turn the killing into an equation. He'd learned to take the curvature of the earth into account, to measure wind and distance, and to calculate the velocity of the round. Like all snipers, Jarrett had the formula tables imprinted. In his dreams he saw them tumbling out of a hat with a white feather. The numbers wrote themselves on a whiteboard inside his sleeping mind. He dreamed of rows and rows of numbers, and at the end of each row was a picture of a dead man. Sometimes an error crept into the calculation and the shot splashed. The margin of error was unforgiving. It could be that the wind gusted, or the bullet had to travel through a pane of glass, or the target moved. When that happened, the target knew the score. All the formulas, tables, and calculations went out the window.

'It don't feel right,' said Tracer. 'Can't tell you exactly what's wrong. But it's a feeling in my bones that something's gone sideways. Something we should see. Something right in front of us.'

'For instance?' said Jarrett.

'We were told to set up for a daytime shot. Now it's a nighttime deal. Did anyone sight the infrared? I don't know. Mooney took the scope out early in the morning and sighted the day scope. But we ain't using that scope. And what if there's a counter-surveillance team? They now know our exact location.'

'You picking up any infrared out there? I'm not.'

'They don't need to turn on their infrared until the last second. They know we're here. You can ignore what I'm saying.'

'I never ignore what you say.' He was thinking about what had happened on their mission in Gijón. And he was thinking about how Casey had matched the pool table from a bar in Hua Hin – not any bar, the one where Jarrett and his father had arranged to meet Jack years before – and just so the point of Casey's inside information had not been overlooked, he'd gone to the trouble of leaving behind a news-paper from Hua Hin. Through the infrared scope Jarrett couldn't find the signature either.

'Don't get all superstitious on me,' he said. 'Today is just another day. It's nothing special. We do the job. The assignment is a matter of honor. It's paying back Jack. It's a good thing we're doing.'

The word 'honor' hung like a mantra as they fell quiet and concentrated on their work. It was a word Harry'd used that night as they had dumped two bodies over the side of a boat and watched them sink into the Andaman Sea. Honor was also the word that had taken them to the room in Gijón. For centuries, it had been a reason to kill. Nothing much had changed since the beginning of time when someone first discovered that honor ranked above a life degraded into a state of disgrace.

Honor had once been one of the most important virtues. Some said it had been knocked down the list by big new money. Others said honor only worked alongside the mystical. Just as superstition was on the retreat in the West, so was honor, and people had forgotten that everywhere else, relations were secured by a code of honor. Tracer loved Jarrett because he was one of the few men he knew who still believed in the original idea of honor. Though it might have fled from the lives of most people, it had stuck in Jarrett's heart ever since he and his daddy had nearly died learning that lesson years before in a beach house outside of Hua Hin.

Both Tracer and Jarrett had been briefed about Casey, and each step leading up to the mission had been given the green light. Waters told Jarrett that at first the case to help Casey had been a stretch for a paying-back-Jack assignment. Joel Casey hadn't been a soldier. But his father had been, and a highly decorated one. He'd been green-badged by the CIA. Colonel Waters said Casey's assignment had rolled around the rim a couple of times before it had fallen into the basket. The son had been tortured and then murdered. His father had been ex-special forces and had served his country, even though he fucked up on a mission. The fuck-up had caused another officer to die. Waters said that Casey had been to see him a couple of times, asking for the special-ops team from the company. Casey's security clearance meant he had knowledge of the team. Waters had told him that nothing was going to happen until the Thais refused to act. Casey had waited. When the local authorities had refused to bring charges, claiming insufficient evidence, he'd asked Waters again. Waters went around company protocol and took the assignment directly to his team.

Jarrett remembered the newspaper clipping Waters had given them of Joel Casey's murder in Thailand. It occurred to him that if that had happened to someone in his family, he wouldn't have gone asking for help. But then he didn't need to ask; it was what he did.

Tracer reached behind, picked up the remote,

and pressed the off button. The blues gave way to the faint buzz of the air-conditioning compressor.

Tracer stood to Jarrett's right, holding the binoculars and rotating left to right. He started at Cat's balcony – Zapper three-nine – and worked a ninety-degree sweep across the landscape of the other buildings – Ripper, Papa Bear, Grizzly, Scorpion, Firebird, Rooks, and Black Sheep – taking a close look at the ninth floor of each one, and then sweeping back on the tenth floor. After each sweep he raised his binoculars to get the next row of windows and balconies. Office or residence, Tracer gave them equal attention. It was possible that an ambush team had been set up nearby. Shooting up or down in a city wasn't difficult; it was nearly impossible.

'Check out Scorpion. Four degrees right, two degrees above current position.'

At the midway point between their location and Cat's balcony, Tracer saw something that stopped him cold. Jarrett moved his telescopic sight, bringing the crosshairs to the windows of the residential building. Lights turned off and on in hundreds of windows, and there was movement as people crossed their rooms in front of the window. 'What do you see?' asked Jarrett.

'I'm picking up light bouncing off something. Like a lens.'

Jarrett looked again but couldn't find any glint. The clutter of lights created a noise of flashpoints – flickering TV screens, lamps being switched on or off, digital cameras flashing, small-but-bright reading lamps in bedroom windows, candles. Jarrett adjusted the focus on the lens and swept across a bank of buildings until he found Scorpion again.

Tracer clicked his tongue, stretching out to brush the edge of the telescope. 'If you're seeing what I am seeing, that's not good.'

'If it's a sniper, he could have shot me thirty minutes ago,' said Jarrett. 'I'd have taken my shot.'

'Maybe he's waiting for something.'

'Like what?'

'Waiting until we've finished the job.' He rubbed his mojo bag. 'Then he takes his shot.'

Jarrett sat up, looking away from the rifle. 'What are you saying. Tracer? Who's going to shoot? Where are you looking?' He pushed his hat back on and pulled it forward on his forehead. 'This is crazy.'

Tracer shook his head. 'Man, it's not crazy. Think about it. What if it's Casey? Did you know he was state-champion marksman in high school? He could have passed snipers' school. He likes close-up contact. So he let it pass. He has the skills. The guy's on the run. He's got himself in a deep hole, one he ain't never climbing out of.'

'He checked out with Waters,' said Jarrett. 'And he's a tough son of a bitch.' The bedrock of Jarrett's training was to follow his orders without question. A senior officer's authority was unquestioned. It was disturbing for him to think that Tracer could even suggest such a thing was possible. Casey was part of their community, one of them, like Waters and the others they'd served with. They were a band of brothers who understood each other in a way no outsider could begin to understand. And they understood the inner workings of the field. Small things like knowing drug dealers buried mountains of money. All those wrinkled tens, twenties, and fifties; hundreds counted and wrapped. Every day there was more. No way that flow could be spent; no way the dealers would risk putting it in a bank, and because there was so much of it, the only way to hide it was to bury it. The rich loam smell of the earth took up home in such money. Like the smell of death, once it entered the nostrils, the scent could never be confused with anything else.

'What if Casey paid for the job with money that'd been buried? It's not the way you do things. People who use buried money do bad, evil things. You need special mojo against that kind of thing.'

'I need more than that, Tracer. Give me something that shows Casey's not one of us. That glare could be from anything. From an old hooker's glass eye to a piece of crystal. Are you trying to get me spooked?'

Tracer trained his binoculars on the light source. A light went on at five-nine Firebird. A woman stood behind an astronomer's telescope looking at the stars. The lens was clear. The woman was joined by a man who gave her a glass of red wine. They kissed, and a moment later the light in the room went out and the balcony light was switched on.

Jarrett looked up from his scope. 'There are two of them, Tracer. They're lovers. Star-gazers.' They were ghostly images in the crosshairs, heat vapors rising from their bodies.

Tracer let out a long sigh, rubbing his thigh with the flat palm of his hand.

Jarrett leaned forward, eye to the scope. 'It's time to go to work.'

Somporn had stepped out onto the balcony with an arm wrapped around Cat's waist, drawing her close to him. She wore a low-cut evening gown and a small tiara with glittering stones in her hair. Smiling and laughing, in her high heels she was eye-level with Somporn as they kissed. He looked like a man about to win an election, a man confident enough to leave the campaign trail for time with his mia noi.

Jarrett had been at that precise moment before; the narrow lane between life and death. The target appeared on time. Jarrett's finger touched the trigger. There weren't many moments to compare with it; this presented a slice of time just before the final moment ran out.

She danced with Somporn like she'd danced with Ball. This woman, Cat, had blues flowing through her soul, thought Tracer. But she also kept the target in motion, and Jarrett waited for the dancing to pause. All he needed was one brief moment.

CHAPTER 38

In the darkness of Casey's living room, Calvino worked his hands behind his back to unhook the small laser pen from one of the pockets sewn into the hem of his sports jacket. He thought of how Fon had held out the laser pen, insisting he take it as a gift. The pocket had a Velcro strip that he wedged his fingers into to open it. He slipped the laser pen out, pointed it toward the window, pressed the button with his thumb, quickly released it, and repeated the sequence of three short bursts, followed by three long ones, and then three more short bursts.

'With all of their resources, they'll find you, Casey. Wherever you go, they'll have some connection who'll let them know your precise location.'

'You chase around after cheating husbands. You don't know fuck.'

Calvino sent Morse code for SOS with the laser pen again.

'What don't I know?'

'That'd be a long list.'

'You're settling the score for your son. Somporn's enemy number one.' Casey coughed up phlegm and spat across the room, missing Calvino by a couple of feet. 'How are you going to settle that score?'

'If your crooked friend the Colonel hadn't paid off the Pattaya police, you'd be in jail, but at least you'd be alive. That was the idea, Calvino. But having you here works out just fine.'

'Pratt's never paid or taken a bribe,' said Calvino.

'This place is a Mafia state. You think your colonel friend is an exception?'

'Fuck you, Casey.'

Casey laughed and pushed back his baseball cap. The anger rising off Calvino had given him some satisfaction. He had experience in knowing which buttons to push. It seemed to relax him in a strange way. He believed that an enemy is defeated with a combination of violence, fear, and surprise. Calvino, as far as Casey was concerned, was no different; his being a civilian made everything much simpler.

Calvino had no way of knowing if whomever Casey had targeted would see the flash of light, and if they did, whether it would stand out and mean something. He punched out the Morse code for SOS. A man in uniform, or a mee see in Thai, would immediately recognize an SOS message. Judging from Casey's position, he had the target in a direct line of vision. One way to be sure the laser message was delivered was to get on the outside and on to the balcony. The first principle of communication is to eliminate the noise. With

461

all of the lights shooting from the building, seeing one point of light wouldn't be easy, unless someone with training was looking. Calvino decided he had to get on the other side. Calvino thought about the glass in the windows. His fingers pressed through the blind, touching the glass. There was only one way through. He started to rock back and forth in his chair.

'I've got to take a piss,' said Calvino. He squirmed in his chair. After a lull he started rocking the chair again.

Casey lay flat on a bench behind the rifle with his right eye pressed against the scope, waiting for the muzzle flash from Jarrett's rifle. He hadn't turned on the infrared scope. He'd fixed the location of Jarrett's rifle and scope and was locked in.

Calvino thought that without the night-vision goggles, Casey looked much as he had the day he'd barged into the Lonesome Hawk for lunch and gotten under Old George's skin.

'Stop that fucking rocking.' Casey glanced up long enough to see that Calvino had reached a critical mass in the movement of the chair. Calvino, who had been positioned beside the ceiling-to-floor window in near darkness, was outlined in a soft ray of light that streaked over his shoulder. A few feet behind where he sat, the light faded and finally disappeared.

Calvino waited until Casey had positioned himself behind the rifle again, his concentration focused as he stared through the nightscope, watching Jarrett through the crosshairs. Calvino pressed the laser pen to signal his SOS. He prayed that somewhere in the universe that mattered, someone would spot the speck of red light. Whether anyone had seen it against the backdrop of a street of high-rise buildings, Calvino had no idea. He could only hope. Because hope was all he had left. 'Then let me go take a piss.'

Calvino started rocking the chair and the front legs rose slightly from the floor. Casey trained his eye on the scope. 'No time, friend. It's rock 'n' roll time.'

Calvino had been gift-wrapped by an expert. He examined the balcony window. He had a couple of choices. He could go headfirst and risk his brain getting damaged on the way through the shards of glass, or he could do a skateboard flip and go through feet first, risking his genitals against jagged pieces of broken glass. Calvino thought about the two possibilities for a moment and then, as most men would do, decided to go through the window headfirst. He prayed that a crooked glass contractor had gone with an unauthorized cheap sheet for the window.

Calvino inhaled, held his breath, and with all of his strength rocked the chair forward and then back as hard as he could push, flipping his feet through the curtains and shattering the glass window into a million pieces. The glass had been paper thin. But glass was glass, and going through a window clean only happened in the movies. He rolled onto the balcony with cuts biting deep into his legs and arms. An inch to the right and a shard of glass would have severed an artery. The curtain had come through the window with him and for a split second Casey's head rose from the rifle.

Tracer had been the first to spot the dot of light coming from Calvino's laser pen. The beam was tiny but distinctive against the wall of steel, chrome, and glass closing out the night sky. Tracer had frowned, looked again. This wasn't any signature from an infrared scope. Whatever it was, it had come from a window on the opposite side of Thong Lo. His elbows fixed on a table, Tracer had seen the pattern in the light. Everyone in special ops knew the Morse code for SOS. He read it through his binoculars, and then someone had exploded through the window and onto the balcony. 'Rooks. Alpha-side, four-nine. Are you seeing what I'm seeing?'

Jarrett raised a pair of night-vision binoculars to the ninth floor of Rooks and scanned from left to right, stopping at the fourth unit. He saw the glowing white outline of a person in the fetal position, legs curled up, lying on the balcony in a debris of broken glass, blinds, and a rifle.

'Sniper's rifle,' said Tracer.

'Got it,' said Jarrett.

The man continued sending an SOS with the laser pen. Jarrett laid down the binoculars and looked through the infrared nightscope. He'd picked up the scope of a rifle and knew that he had only a couple of seconds to decide on a course of action.

Jarrett repositioned the rifle, lining up with the new coordinates. He was eyeball-to-eyeball with Casey's nightscope when he squeezed off a .308 caliber round. The silencer largely muffled the explosion. It sounded like an old car backfiring, a car with a rusty muffler that still absorbed most of the noise.

Tracer swung the rifle around and had another look at the activity on Cat's balcony. They were oblivious to the shot that had slammed into a building down the road. Cat continued to dance with Somporn, framed by the lights from the condo living room. She had positioned her man so that Jarrett had his choice of any number of perfect targets. Like a bullfighter with a red cape, she danced so as to remain in control of his advances.

Over on the ninth floor of Rooks, a neighbor's light had come on. The light illuminated the smashed window, a man bloodied and struggling. Tracer switched to a normal pair of binoculars.

'Holy shit,' he said, passing them to Jarrett. 'Have a look.'

'Yeah, I've got him. A guy on the balcony,' said Jarrett. 'Am I seeing what you're seeing?'

'Our favorite private investigator.'

'What the fuck's he doing?'

'Looks like he's tied up.'

'Saved our ass. That's what he did.'

'Who's the guy inside?'

'Who was the guy inside? Whoever it was, you were right, Tracer.'

'Casey?'

'Fuck if I know.'

'I have a visual on the target,' said Tracer. His binoculars had picked up Somporn on the balcony. Cat had kept him dancing, though he looked like he was losing steam. They'd go inside soon.

'Jack's gonna be paid back. But shooting Somporn isn't the way we're gonna do it. We're standing down.'

Tracer nodded.

They exchanged a high five. Jarrett removed the earplugs and his hat, put on a jacket, and slipped on a necktie. Tracer stored away his earplugs, rubbed his ears good and hard, and then pulled his jacket off a chair and put it on. Together they broke down Kate and loaded it into the Pelican case. In less than five minutes they'd walked into the parking lot, opened the truck of the Benz, and put the case inside.

Jarrett drove. Tracer sat in the backseat, assuming his cover as an ambassador in an embassy car.

'We're not going to Pattaya,' said Jarrett.

'Mooney's going to be very pissed off.'

'You don't know whether Mooney knew what was going down.'

Tracer wrinkled his nose, shook his head. Jarrett caught sight of him in the rearview mirror. 'It don't matter much one way or another.'

They pulled out of the condo building and onto Thong Lo, heading for Petchaburi Road, where they'd turn onto the motorway for the international airport.

The lyrics of a blues song accompanied by piano, sax, and harmonica filled the silence as Jarrett drove: 'You stole my soul when you left me. You buried it where I'll never find it. 'Cos I know you ain't ever comin' back. Leavin' me on the street walkin' around like I was dead.'

CHAPTER 39

On the balcony of Rooks four-nine, the lights from the neighboring residential high-rises and from the street threw a tangled web of long, dark shadows across the balcony where Calvino struggled. He had just enough light to see through the window. On the floor the body of Casey lay motionless.

Calvino lay with his face resting against the tiles, his head swimming with the smell of blood. He worked his body to the side and, dragging the chair like a marooned shell creature, he crawled and slid across the balcony, the broken glass cutting into his shoulder and arm. Halfway up the wall, he saw the light switch for the balcony and managed to turn it on. He examined his hands. He'd been cut. He saw a large shard of glass protruding from the slider and he edged himself close enough so he could cut the duct tape around his ankles. With his feet free, he kicked out the remaining glass panel and dragged himself still taped to the chair through the opening and into the sitting room.

He felt his knees wobble as he walked over and sat down beside Casey's body. The anatomy had been transformed. There was a body, but no discernible head was attached. The stump of ragged flesh around the neck, half a jaw with some teeth, hung among the loose flaps of skin in the region where a head had once looked out on the world. The remains of a skull, flesh, and brains had splattered against the back wall in a grotesque graffiti. The brain parts, glossy and soft, shined as if some soft-bellied creature had colonized the wall. The force of the .308 soft-tipped slug had expanded on impact, tumbling at great velocity, ripping away Casey's bully-like smile, shredding cheek, nose, forehead, and everything that had gone with it. Steam rose from the gaping wound where the head should have been. The body had landed face up – if there had been a face – with arms and legs flopping over a teak wood table.

It was a chek bin moment. Payback. Someone had pushed back, and all that was left of Casey had become part of the décor.

Calvino banged the chair against the wall until the duct tape around his torso loosened. He kept banging it until the chair fell free. For the first time, he was able to stand. He turned so that his back faced the wall and pushed his cuffed hands up far enough to hit an interior light switch.

Light flooded the room. He moved to the table where Casey's rifle had been mounted. He lowered himself into the chair and looked at a fresh stain of his own blood on his sports jacket. This time his jacket was soaked in it. He sat, breathing, feeling the air go in and out of his body. Feeling light-headed, knowing that he had to tap into a fresh reservoir of energy, he let the exhaustion pass before he moved over to Casey's body. He used his shoulder to turn the body over. Dead weight had a great amount of resistance. Finally he leaned back and used his feet to finish the job.

Calvino sat beside the body. Working blind, his hands cuffed, he fished through Casey's pockets. After he found the keys, he dropped the key ring a half-a-dozen times before he could get the right key to fit the handcuffs. With his cuffs off, he searched all of Casey's pockets, looked through the contents of his wallet, found more keys, and grabbed hold of the dead man's cell phone. Calvino stuffed the handcuffs in one of Casey's pockets. He opened Casey's phone and scrolled through the list of calls dialed, calls received, and calls missed. Calvino saw the two numbers from Nongluck's phone, the ones that he had used to call Casey. Scrolling through the address book, he found his own number listed under 'Private Investigator.' Most of the addresses had generic descriptions, a combination of numbers and names: .308, Spotter, Private Eye. Impersonal and cold military codes and the kind of civilian shorthand labels a soldier might use.

Looking at Casey's phone, he had a second thought. Why not call .308? See who answered the phone. When he hit the auto dial, he listened to the ring. A man came onto the line. 'You the one who fired that shot?'

'Who the fuck . . .' and the line went dead.

Calvino smiled, putting down the phone. He thought about phoning again. But he had what he wanted. He was glad he'd likely let the right person know that someone had a firsthand account of the accuracy of his shot. Assuming .308 in Casey's cell-phone address book was the sniper who'd fired the shot.

Calvino's law: In case of doubt, always make the phone call.

He walked down the corridor, pushed open the door to Casey's bedroom, switched on the light, and looked around. He sat on the bed next to a carry-on case, which was still open. He pulled out the contents – DVDs, passport, tickets, files, a notebook computer, and a change of clothes. Casey had packed light. Calvino took out one of the DVDs and put it into a DVD player below the TV in the sitting room. In the dark, with Casey's body a few feet away, he played the video. Casey had a naked hooded suspect tied to a board, with water being poured down his throat. The man's legs and feet were elevated, and his face was covered with a white muslin cloth. He struggled against his restraints as water was slowly poured into his mouth through a funnel forced between the lips. The gasping and gurgling were disturbing to hear as the sounds of pure terror filled the soundtrack. It looked like Casey had copied the contents of the destroyed secret-prison tapes. He watched the tape twice and then squatted down beside Casey. Calvino stared at the body before stepping back onto the balcony.

The noise had caused someone to switch on a line. But below there were no sirens, no flashing red or blue police lights in the street. Excessive noise was something people accepted in Bangkok. They must have listened for a repeat but what they heard instead was a perfectly ordinary evening. The tiny rupture in the night had soon disappeared. He leaned forward at the railing. Nothing unusual in terms of movement or sound came from the neighboring units. It had started to occur to Calvino that the single shot hadn't been detected over the general noise of traffic, TVs, stereos, and voices. There had been the moment of impact when the glass shattered. But it was over in an instant. For a sound to rise above the din of the nightly dragon dance of noise in a Bangkok street, it had to be not just loud but sustained. Whoever had fired the killing round, Calvino was sure, had already escaped. It had been a professional job, and Calvino understood that someone in that line of business would be gone as if carried on the wind. He decided that it was also time for him to leave.

Calvino switched off the light and let himself out of the room, using Casey's keys to lock the deadbolts. He walked down the corridor and took the stairs down to the lobby. Opening the door cautiously, he saw no one. How long would it be until the police were notified and burst into the room? Entering the hallway, he closed the door behind him, walked to the emergency exit, and took the stairs to the underground parking garage. Casey's key ring had a fancy electronic security gadget and a BMW key attached. The last time he had phoned Pratt, there had been a long pause as if Pratt had been waiting in dread to discover what trouble his friend had gotten himself into. This time Calvino would steer him to a body that looked like a mango caught in a lawnmower. Pratt had wanted to find Casey, but the condition Casey was in now was not what Pratt had in mind. Calvino eased off the idea, thinking there had to be a better way. Pratt didn't need this. Calling him wouldn't be doing him a favor.

Calvino walked through the first floor of the underground parking, looking for Beemers, pointing the key ring at a row of cars. Nothing happened. He turned and pointed in the other direction, and the lights of a BMW flashed. He opened the door of a new black BMW and climbed in. It had the new-car smell and a 747 flight deck of instruments. Tinted windows made the interior seem like the cockpit of a plane too. Calvino inserted the key and drove out of the parking garage. Two other cars were ahead of him. There was no evidence of police in the parking garage or at the ground level as he pulled out. Other than him and the sniper, he thought, no one knew yet that Casey was dead.

CHAPTER 40

'He's gonna call back,' said Jarrett. 'Bet on it.'

'You shouldn't've hung up on him.'

'I don't know who it was.'

Tracer growled. 'If the man hadn't signaled us, you'd be dead. I'd probably be dead, too,' he said from the back. 'What the fuck was he doing on that balcony? Why'd he do that?'

'He got lucky, too. Otherwise, Casey would have killed him,' said Jarrett. 'Or I'd have shot him.'

'Yeah?'

'We saved his ass. That's what I am saying. So we're even.'

It looked like Calvino would never know exactly how close he'd been to kissing the soft lips of a military-issued .308 round. But Tracer had a point: the private eye had given away Casey's position just as Casey had him in the crosshairs. Jarrett shivered as both hands held the wheel. The feeling passed quickly, but he took note. There's close, and then there's very close. Like an orgasm, death edges to a boundary and flounders, falling forward or gripping the edge and pulling back. It was never a sure thing, and Jarrett still had a bitter taste in his mouth. The bile had crept up, and as much as he tried to swallow it back, it clung in his throat.

Jarrett's cell phone rang but he made no attempt to answer it. A moment later Tracer's phone rang, and he exchanged a look with Jarrett.

'Answer it,' said Jarrett. In the dim dashboard light he could see it was the same number as before.

Tracer pressed the answer call button but remained silent.

'This is Vincent Calvino. I've got a question for .308. Why did you hang up on me?' asked Calvino.

Tracer covered the phone. 'It's Calvino.'

'Ask him what he wants.'

'Man, I don't know what game you're playing. But you should be way the fuck away from that condo and us. You understand what I'm saying?'

Calvino sighed. 'Let's meet.'

'Impossible.'

The sound of traffic filtered through the phone. 'Let me make an educated guess. You're going to the airport. I could make a call and they'd lock it down. Or we could talk.'

'I'll call you back,' said Tracer, ending the call.

A moment later Jarrett's phone rang again. This time he answered. 'Calvino, you have no idea what this is about. Go back to your office and tail expat husbands with bar girls.'

'I'd rather have a talk with the two of you. I'm on my way to the airport. Half an hour won't make any difference. The police aren't involved. When I left Casey's condo, it was quiet. They've got no idea he's dead. You've got time.'

'Casey?' Tracer caught the expression on Jarrett's face as he said the man's name. 'Am I hearing you right? You said something about Casey?'

'Who do you think you killed?' asked Calvino. He had a feeling that Tracer already knew they'd killed Casey and was playing him along. If that was their attempt at diversion, Calvino decided to let them have it.

Calvino had set in motion a paying-back-Jack moment. Tracer had been right about one thing: Calvino had saved his life.

'Arrivals. Phone again in thirty minutes.'

Jarrett handed him the cell phone on the passenger's seat. 'You agreed to meet him?' asked Tracer.

'As you said, I'd be dead without his SOS.'

The international airport, a mammoth structure that had enriched politician clans, was a perfect place for the meeting Calvino had in mind. Built under a cloud of corruption, the runways had cracked in places, and the surrounding neighborhoods threatened to release balloons in the flight pathway to stop aircraft from taking of and landing. The constant noise of jet engines had driven them crazy. The attempts to pay kah pit pak, or money to shut them up, had failed. They wanted silence, not money. As a quasicriminal enterprise, the airport had all the grandeur of a greenhouse lowered over an ultracool shopping mall.

Jarrett parked the car in a long-term lot and they walked into the departures level of the terminal. They saw a row of empty seats, walked over, and sat down. They had been sitting for more than a minute when Tracer rose and walked over to check the big board listing the departure schedule. Flights to London, New York, Frankfurt, Hanoi, Phnom Penh, and Jakarta scrolled up with times for departure and gate numbers. They had a lot of cities to choose from. Tracer detached himself from a crowd of package tourists and sat next to Jarrett.

'Casey. Fucking Casey. He nearly pulled it off,' said Tracer. 'I told you something wasn't right. I smelled it. When the papers said he was on the run, I said to myself, "Tracer, that man's a walking time bomb, and when he goes off, there's gonna be a lot of collateral damage."' He fished his mojo bag out of his pocket and rubbed it against his cheek. 'But we got him. We had the mojo working for us tonight. Mr Mojo saw what was coming and sent us an assistant.'

'London is good in August,' said Jarrett. 'I know a place in Bayswater. That's my suggestion, for what it's worth.' All around them hundreds of people passed, pulling or carrying their luggage, pushing trolleys, and drinking or eating on the run.

Tracer grinned, made a fist, and tapped Jarrett's

477

shoulder. 'You and me, we're gettin' soft. You asked me once if we'd ever make it to forty. That's a hundred-and-eight years old in sniper-team years. And I said, man, we don't want to live that long. It almost happened tonight. We almost got our early checkout. And we didn't survive just to go to London. Fucking Casey, he had some plan. He sees the muzzle flash, and bam, he shoots you, and before I can react, bam, he hits me.'

'Why would Casey wanna shoot us?'

'Fuck if I know. Why'd he put that blue pool table in the condo? Was that some kind of an accident? Or was he trying to tell us something?'

'About Jack?'

Tracer fingered his mojo bag as if some genie would pop out and grant him three wishes. 'Jack? The Colombians? There's a long list if you think about it. You can't forget we aren't the only ones in the pay-back business.'

'Casey knew about our job in Gijón.'

'He knew from Waters what Harry and you did in Hua Hin. He knew about half-a-dozen other assignments.'

Jarrett scratched his nose. 'Think for a moment. Casey had his back channels with the Colombians. Those guys bury money, right? You said yourself the forty grand had that smell. But that business guy in Perth, the guy whose thugs killed Jack, he could have buried money, too. So I don't know. It's making my head hurt.'

Tracer leaned forward, folding his hands around

the mojo bag, as if studying it for inspiration. 'Concentrate on Casey, man. He had heat coming down on him in Bangkok. He must have known it was just a matter of time before they dragged his ass kicking and screaming to Washington to tell them what he was doing in Bangkok. Why didn't Waters see this coming? He should've put Casey in the risk category, taken away his clearance, and taken away the green badge. That was stupid to leave him in the field. But that's what Waters did. He didn't wanna hurt a man's pride.'

'You win an all-expenses-paid trip to Las Vegas,' said Jarrett. That was his backup city after London.

'How much you figure someone was willing to pay Casey to kill us?'

'Whoever it was, they knew Casey could be turned for a price. Our company was about to throw him to the wolves. Someone inside had to know Casey was in trouble and open to a business proposition.' Jarrett shook his head, balled his right hand into a fist and slammed it into his open hand.

Tracer swallowed hard, shaking his head as he looked at Jarrett. 'This is gonna fuck them up. When they find their boy didn't deliver, they'll find someone else to finish the job.' Tracer sighed and watched the faces of strangers passing by: young women, old people, a man in a wheelchair, a Singapore flight crew in scooped-top uniforms, looking like movie stars on their way to a sound stage. He preferred waiting outside under the starless sky. Darkness was a man's friend; a man could shelter in the dark.

'Someone paid Casey for the job,' said Jarrett. 'Only he didn't get it done.'

'That means whoever set this up will send someone else to finish the job.'

Jarrett raised his hand like he wanted to ask a question. 'Casey had to have help on this,' he said. 'And I wanna know who that is.'

'Maybe someone high in the company chain of command.'

'One of the suits?' asked Jarrett, thinking of a connection to the Perth businessman.

'What about Waters?' Tracer's eyes grew large.

'Can't be Waters.'

'Because he's close to your dad?' Tracer had the expression of a man suffering from an acute case of sensitive-bowel syndrome.

Jarrett glanced at him. Tracer had been talking about Waters for days, worrying and twisting his mojo bag like it was a string of worry beads. He'd had a hunch all along, feeling something in the equation hadn't added up.

'Waters is the only one who had the operational details,' said Jarrett.

'You think Casey hired a private eye to track us?' asked Tracer.

'He hired a private eye to cover his ass, you mean.'

'Looks like Colonel Waters and Casey went into a business deal together.' Tracer shook his head, exhaling a long, low whistle. 'We have a long history with that man. Harry recruited him, supported him, saw he got promoted, and recommended him to the company after he left the service. He owes Harry. That means he owes you.'

There was a boarding call for a flight to Paris. Men in blue uniforms and sidearms walked German shepherd dogs along the corridor. They passed Tracer and Jarrett without stopping.

'We can talk about possibilities all night but we ain't getting any closer to the truth. More than one person had enough money to have turned him, just like they did Casey. All it takes is to find a man's price, and he'll pull up anchor and sail away. Don't matter all the things Harry did to help. That was the past. This is today.'

A second detail of police, this time in brown uniforms, walked past, and Jarrett put his hands behind his head, yawned, and stretched out his legs, waiting for the police to move on. Tracer and Jarrett looked like a couple of passengers waiting for a flight: nothing special or out of the ordinary, just a couple of faces no different from thousands of others.

Tracer exhaled, put his head back against the seat, and closed his eyes. 'Money does funny things to people. But the smell of money didn't bother Waters. It smelled of clay. Buried money.' He tried to remember the smell of dirt in a dozen different places. He'd never been able to come up with a place he remembered that had that smell.

Jarrett nudged him and he looked up. 'You were right about the money. You said that before. The point is, we had no direct proof. We were just talking it through. We didn't know.'

'How we ever gonna know? That's the question.'

'You can't say Waters was working with Casey. It's just words. We need to find some evidence. Otherwise, we got ourselves a real problem.'

'Roger that,' said Tracer. 'Like the infertile man who gets himself a vasectomy.'

'Because a man can never be too careful.'

'But where are we going to find that evidence?' He saw Jarrett look away, knowing that they both knew the answer to that question. 'You could always phone your father. You know, run it past him.'

Jarrett shook his head. 'I don't know if I should get my dad involved. This is going to blow big, and when it does it's gonna knock down a lot of big trees.' Harry had taught him there was a category of basic doubts that no man could ever resolve.

'I'm thinking that maybe they were working on a success fee. What's Waters gonna do? Who's he gonna send to finish what Casey screwed up? Is he gonna do it himself? Harry would have some ideas that might be useful.'

Jarrett didn't have an answer. Those were the kinds of doubts a man had to learn to live with. Sitting in the airport departure area with nothing but the clothes on his back, he saw no other choice

482

but to move on and do what needed to be done. Go to ground, stay low, wait out the other side, at least until he and Tracer could figure out who was playing on the other side. Whether Waters had known about Casey's plan from the beginning or had been tricked by Casey didn't matter much. He didn't want to think that it could be Waters. But he kept going back to the reality that Waters knew – and more than his knowing, had been instrumental in setting the mission in motion. Had Waters the team player decided to start his own league with Casey? A lot of cash had appeared from somewhere, and had bought an act of revenge. The idea that sex was the ultimate pull on mankind might have had the ring of truth, but revenge followed one step behind and in a footrace beat sex to the finish line every time.

Jarrett pulled out his cell phone and scrolled down to the last call. He stared at the number. The private investigator had phoned from a number Jarrett didn't recognize. He thought about the number of people who had that phone number. The SIM card had been reserved for operational purposes only. Tracer had the number, so did Waters. Harry had the number. But no one else, as far as he knew, had the number. Not even Mooney, who'd lent them the weapons. There would have been some people at company head-quarters who had access to the number. That was standard procedure.

'Who you calling?' asked Tracer.

'My fortune-teller. I want to ask him for an auspicious time to leave Bangkok.'

'Any time is good, Jarrett.'

'We've got some lead time,' said Jarrett. It would still be a while before the police found what was left of Casey.

'Anyone else you wanna call?' asked Tracer, looking at his own cell phone.

Jarrett thought about the beekeeper's daughter. He smiled to himself. It would have been good to hear her voice again. And he thought about the Western woman in the bar with the little kid, wishing he could phone her and say that he was sorry that she had witnessed a man being shot. 'There's no one I want to call,' said Jarrett.

'That was some crazy shit Casey tried.'

Jarrett eased the cell phone back into his pocket.

'Change of plan,' said Jarrett. 'We're leaving the country.' He got up from the chair and looked at Tracer.

'I like that idea.'

Together they walked toward a Thai International sales counter.

'Fuck Mooney.'

'Fuck Waters and the Colombians.'

'The car's in long-term storage. In a couple of months they'll find it.'

Each of them carried, strapped around their bodies, a pouch with credit cards, cash, and passports. They had enough cash to buy business-class tickets and fly out in style. Training had taught them that where they were going the first order of business would be to acquire new passports, new identities; that would take some money and time, maybe forty-eight hours. Making a new life, that would take a lot longer. They would be cut off from the company, friends, and family. It wasn't clear how long they'd have to stay in the shadows.

'Waters will come looking for us. He has to. You know that,' said Tracer.

Jarrett smiled, head to the side, looking at the departure schedule. 'We'll find him before the cops find the car.'

Tracer liked that. 'It reminds me of a blues song: "Take me down the road where I've done wrong. Take me back to a place we used to go. I don't blame you, baby, 'cause I had it coming."'

Jarrett's phone rang as they reached the counter. It rang until the ying behind the counter asked why he didn't answer the phone. She wondered if he might be hard of hearing. When he finally took out the phone he heard a voice with a familiar Brooklyn accent.

'I'm at the airport. Where are you?' the voice asked.

CHAPTER 41

C alvino found the two men inside an airport coffee shop, sitting far back in a sea of untidy passengers and even untidier tables. The self-service restaurant served greasy half-cold noodles prepared by a staffer with that startled, unsettled look of someone who'd been stabbed. The two passed for average tourists killing time until their flight was called, their hands wrapped around large cups of coffee. Tracer drank it black, stirring it with a spoon as if something inside hadn't dissolved. Jarrett dropped two sugar-loads from tiny paper pouches into his cup. He was, after all, a man with a sweet tooth and a love of honey. At the tables around them were Thais and foreign travelers sitting with their carry-on bags in clusters of twos or threes, the cattle-class passengers who had no access to the VIP lounge.

Jarrett and Tracer sat in silence, blending into the crowd. What set them apart was a degree of alertness that people waiting for planes don't usually possess. From the tension in their bodies and the way they scanned everyone around them, Calvino could see they were still pumped up – on full-alert and looking for another shoe to fall. A couple of young farangs, one white, one black, looking like the weight of the world was perched on their shoulders. Calvino lowered Casey's carry-on suitcase onto the table and eased himself into the chair next to Tracer.

Calvino's face was puffy and discolored from Casey's beating and nicked here and there. There were small tears in his clothes, and his knuckles were raw from crawling on the balcony. He might have passed as a farang who looked the wrong way before crossing the street. Or he could pass as a geezer who had been mugged by a katoey in the shadows of a walkover.

'How did you get through the front door?' asked Jarrett.

'I told them I had a fight with my Thai wife. She won. I'm leaving the country. They waved me through. I think they get a lot of that,' said Calvino.

'What do you want?' asked Tracer.

Calvino searched his right pocket and then, shifting his weight, searched the left one. Digging deep, he pulled out the laser pen and pointed it at Tracer's head and depressed the button on top. Then he laid it on the table. 'Funny what kinds of gadgets can end up saving your ass,' said Calvino. Then he opened the carry-on case, pulled out Casey's cell phone, and laid it on the table. 'Casey had your numbers in his cell phone.'

Jarrett picked up the phone.

'He had you listed under Sniper and Spotter,'

said Calvino, watching him scroll down the list of names and numbers.

Jarrett found Waters at the very end. That was the name he wanted. He showed the phone to Tracer. 'Lots of numbers,' he said.

'He had me listed under PI, but I didn't take it personally,' said Calvino. He didn't mention that Casey had Nongluck's buried under Whore #3 and Cat as Whore #2. That had left him guessing who Whore #1 was.

Casey had a reputation for planning his missions meticulously. There was nothing half-cocked about the man. His training included counter-surveillance teamwork where he watched over high-value friendlies. That required an eye for detail. Hunting for a high-value target required one set of skills; another set was needed to find that one person in a crowd, an assassin, whose sole mission was to take out the person you'd been assigned to protect. Anyone in the crowd might pull a gun. Casey had the advantage, but this time it had failed him. If you did the numbers, you could see it was bound to happen. While talent and preparation minimized the risk, it didn't eliminate it. In Casey's case, he had been undone by a private investigator with no training but who came up, when it was needed, with one lucky move. Both Jarrett and Tracer marveled at how Casey had made the mistake of thinking he had it all figured out, that he was in control of the situation.

'Take down all the numbers you want,' said Calvino. He watched Jarrett erase his number and Tracer's from the address book.

'What else you got inside that case?' asked Tracer.

'Casey's passport, showing immigration had stamped him out two days earlier, and a return ticket to London. The Bangkok-to-London leg has been used.'

He'd booked the same flight that Jarrett and Tracer had bought tickets on. Tracer smiled as he looked at Casey's ticket.

'He planned it well,' said Calvino. 'If you look at the whole package, Casey isn't in Thailand. He's somewhere in London. One more thing, I parked his car in the long-term parking with a ticket issued two days ago.'

Tracer and Jarrett looked at each other. 'How'd you do that?' asked Jarrett.

'I switched tickets with another car I found one level up.'

'So Casey's in a pub drinking warm beer,' said Tracer, sipping his coffee.

'Although there is a mess to clean up.' Calvino held out the keys to Casey's apartment. 'I don't do housework.'

Both men stared at the keys. 'What's in this for you?' asked Jarrett.

'I don't like being set up. And I don't like cleaning up someone else's mess.'

Calvino dropped the keys on the table and pushed them across to Jarrett.

'You're not listening to what I'm asking. What do you want?'

Calvino nodded, grinned, and put a hand on Jarrett's shoulder. 'Someone fucked with me. I'd like some payback. And I'd like some help.'

Jarrett smiled and Calvino removed his hand.

'You got your payback. Casey's dead,' said Tracer.

'He's right,' said Jarrett. It was a moment that reminded him of MacDonald blinking back tears as he stared at the two dead men on the floor. The absurdity of standing and breathing flooded over MacDonald. Jarrett saw something similar in Calvino.

Rumpled, bruised, with cuts on his face and hands, Calvino looked like a supervisor at a glass factory whom angry workers had fed through a machine. 'It's not finished. Casey was no lone gunman. He had to be working for someone. Maybe you've figured out who that is. And that's why you're leaving in a hurry. You know they aren't going to let this go. I don't see why I should take the blowback alone. You hear what I'm saying?'

'Roger that,' said Tracer.

Jarrett pressed his lips together; he still wasn't convinced. 'Why don't you tell us what you were doing hanging out with Casey?'

Calvino shrugged, looked down at the blood-matted sleeve of his sports jacket, thinking there was no way the dry cleaner was going to get that out. 'He came to my office with a job to do.' A tone of unease entered his voice. 'Well, it seemed like a normal investigation at the time. He paid me to follow a Thai businessman's mia noi and report her movements. His son had been killed in Thailand. The businessman was implicated in the murder. Casey had a legit beef. But it seemed his beef was with you guys. And as hard as I try, I can't understand the connection.'

A smile crept across Jarrett's lips. 'I hear you loud and clear, but there's a problem.' He said it in a way that a Thai might say it, meaning a mountain stood in the way of getting across the road. 'We're not sure why he had a beef with us.'

'I don't see that as a problem. I see it as an opportunity.'

'You don't want to get involved in this,' said Tracer.

Calvino cocked his head, nodded his head for a moment. 'I am already involved. And I've got a bad feeling none of this ends with Casey. Tell me I'm wrong.'

Jarrett tapped a finger on the set of keys. 'Casey's condo might be a problem.' He looked around and, in a half-whisper, continued: 'You have to understand that a .308 may have gone through the wall and hit something else. Maybe it hit someone across the hall. Someone may have called the cops, and they might be crawling all over Casey's place now. We walk in and the first thing the cops are gonna say is, welcome boys, thought you might like to explain what you're doing here and how Casey's head isn't where it should be, and his neighbor next door has a gaping hole in his chest.'

'Except it was a soft-nosed round,' said Tracer. 'That doesn't keep on going for a mile and a half.'

Calvino, hands on the table, looked at the two men. 'The round didn't go through the wall. Once it hit his head, it must've gone into ten thousand pieces.' Casey had just taken his eye away from the scope and looked up when the .308 slug passed through his skull at a point just above his ear.

Jarrett and Tracer exchanged a look, with Jarrett leaning over and whispering something to Tracer.

'If you're fucking with us, understand that that is a mistake,' said Jarrett.

'I've made mistakes with Casey. I don't intend to repeat them,' said Calvino. 'And from your situation, I'd say you two made a couple of mistakes along the line, too.' Jarrett and Tracer exchanged an uneasy look, part alienation mixed up with some serious anxiety. Calvino later told Colonel Pratt that at that moment, he saw something in Jarrett; something that convinced him, this was a man who wanted to go back and deal with the problem. Tracer had been the one who'd have been happy to close the books on Casey, but he did what Jarrett wanted. The three of them shared a bond: Casey had carefully worked to put them in a position to kill them and someone had paid him for the job.

'How do we know that you aren't a fuck-up?' asked Tracer.

'You don't. I suggest we start by going to Thong Lo. You stay in the car a soi away,' said Calvino. 'If the cops are there, you won't get a call. If the floor is clear and Casey's room is the same as I left it, I'll phone and we'll deal with it.'

Jarrett exchanged a glance with Tracer, who nodded. There'd been something else, something from Reno's bar, that had been bothering Jarrett. He decided it was best to get it out in the open. 'What's your connection with Wan?' asked Jarrett.

Somehow it always came down to a ying. 'I don't have one. If it's sex you're thinking about, forget it. She helped us get that kid out of Cowboy. Wan knew the backdoor escape and led us out. I never saw her before that night. You see this?' He'd opened the palm of his hand and showed them the laser pen. 'You saw the kid. Later, she gave it to me. One of those things you don't think too much about. Maybe going through the window would've been enough to draw your attention. Or, again, maybe you'd have missed it. Somehow I have the feeling if she hadn't given it to me, then you'd both be dead. I'd be dead, too. Does that answer your question?'

The men waited, heads down, thinking, hands around their coffee cups. Then they looked up to study the private investigator sitting on the opposite side of the table. What did they know about this guy? Going back to town was taking one huge risk. Everything they knew told them to go straight through immigration and into the busi-

493

nessclass lounge and forget this had happened. Calvino had run into their car in Washington Square, he'd run away with Jarrett's ying, and he'd used a laser pen and a back flip through a balcony window to save their lives. But who was he?

'Give us an hour. If we decide to board the plane, thanks for the signal. If we don't get on the plane, we'll meet you outside the arrivals terminal. And we can take a taxi back into town.'

Calvino nodded, got up, and left the table. Jarrett checked the time and then dialed Harry Jarrett. He had a few questions about Casey that he wanted to ask his father. When the old man picked up the phone, Jarrett said, 'I'm in a situation.'

Harry knew exactly what that meant. He had about one hour.

CHAPTER 42

Forty-eight hours were required to fluff the premises; precision slicing, cutting, and cleaning left Casey's condo clean – on the surface, that is. If a forensic team had gone through the place, they'd have still found all kinds of evidence. But the work was good enough for a condo with the rent paid up for three months and a tenant who'd punched out of the country, according to immigration records.

As they'd worked, removing glass fragments from the balcony, stuffing the shards into a large black plastic bag lined with newspapers, Calvino had held up a mango-shaped piece of glass, turned it over, and dropped it in the bag. 'You did the right thing,' he said. 'Not shooting Somporn.'

Jarrett caught Tracer's eye. A glint of resignation passed between them.

'Then I'm glad it worked out the way it did,' said Jarrett.

'That would have been a shame. Hitting the wrong person,' said Tracer.

'We never should've been sent to do this job,' said Jarrett.

Calvino looked at the two men. 'You know what? I want to believe you.'

Two weeks later, Calvino received a plain envelope with a clipping from a New Jersey newspaper inside. No return address appeared on the envelope; it was postmarked from Newark. Waters's body had been found by police, curled up inside the trunk of a car outside Port Elizabeth, New Jersey. He had been shot at close range, execution-style, into the back of his head. The killers had mutilated the body, removing the male package and placing it in a ziplock bag next to the body. The New Jersey authorities had no suspects or leads, and the murder was a professional hit. Calvino had to decide whether to pass the clipping on to Colonel Pratt. His friend had been patient, as well as distracted, as the election campaign had come to an end. Everyone in the department had been holding their breath, reading tea leaves to find evidence of their future under the new government. Somporn had been elected and was rumored to be in consideration for a cabinet position.

Calvino had had some news of his own. Wan had gone home. Fon's father hadn't wanted her, so Wan had taken the kid with her. Juan Carlos had spent the money set aside for sinsor, the bride price, and cut a deal with Auntie, who was happy to count the money and hand over the girl. The Taiwanese customer wasn't willing to match the one-million-baht price that Juan Carlos had offered. Juan Carlos and Wan had taken Fon upcountry, buying new hives and bees. He still hadn't come back to Bangkok. Marisa had said, 'He's helping her with the bees.'

Calvino understood and backed off.

Marisa laughed. 'Of course, you should go see Juan Carlos. But I'm returning to Spain. It's where I belong. Not in this place.'

The shock wore off as he recalled no one from the outside belonged in this place. The fortunate ones discovered that early enough to cut their losses.

'When do you leave?'

'Tomorrow.'

'You weren't going to tell me?'

'I think you knew,' she said. 'This is your world, Vinny. These people are you and you are them. I know you tell everyone that you're from New York. But that isn't true anymore. You're from here. I can never be from this place.'

'Thailand, home? I'm a New Yorker.'

She grinned. 'It doesn't matter, does it? One day you must come and visit, and then we can talk about it,' she said. 'We need some time.'

'You might find me on your doorstep.' His crooked smile drew a smile from her as well.

Her answer had been vague, open-ended, as their relationship had been. She'd chosen to be polite and he had chosen to let her slender thread of dignity and hope stretch to beyond the horizon.

CHAPTER 43

You can't kill people without being haunted by them. Words to that effect crept into the conversation Jarrett had with his father. Harry Jarrett sat forward on the deck chair, slapping sunblock onto his neck. His son opened a beer and drank straight from the bottle. Behind them was the outline of Hua Hin, a fishing village that had become a small city hugging the shoreline. Casey had been dead for more than a week when Harry flew into Thailand. His son waited at the airport with a hired car and they'd driven to Hua Hin.

'Looks different,' said Alan, nodding at the city.

Harry rubbed sunblock on his arm, smoothing it forward toward his wrist. 'We look different, too. So does the world once you let enough years accumulate.' He rubbed his hands together, stretched them back behind his head. 'That feels better.'

'You think it was a mistake to let MacDonald go?' he asked his father. It had been his idea at the time.

'You said he was as much a victim as Jack. I thought at the time that that was a pretty good argument. After we'd saved his ass. I thought that a man's not gonna forget that fact anytime soon.'

The boat rocked softly as they sat together, watching for some movement of their fishing poles. The last couple of hours, Harry had been talking about a lot of people, places, incidents, but MacDonald had been one of the people who'd most interested Alan.

Harry had classified clearance. But better than access to secret files, he had work experience with and personal knowledge of both Waters and Casey. But it came as a surprise to Harry that these two would betray everything they'd stood for. He phoned his son back on a secure line once and they talked about the possibilities. Included on Harry's short-list were the Colombians, a Bosnian, and an Australian businessman. They all had their reasons and sufficient funds for such an operation. But the Bosnian general was appealing a war-crimes conviction and that made it unlikely he'd risk getting involved in something that might prejudice his case. That left the clan running drugs out of Cali and the crooked businessman from Perth.

He had done some deep soul-searching and following-up with people he'd not been in contact with for many years before he was confident about why things had happened the way they had in Bangkok.

Harry reeled in the line, checked the bait before making a perfect overhead cast. The hook, line, and sinker broke the surface with a splash. 'I've got a few ideas, but you've got to understand that a lot of what I'm saying is conjecture.'

Jarrett stared at the empty sea, feeling the movement of the boat.

'What's your take?'

'Casey was under pressure. Things went sideways on his last tour at a secret prison in Baghdad. I know the guy who got him the assignment in Bangkok and fixed his problems in Baghdad. A report got passed down the line along with a death certificate or two, stapled to a medical affidavit that the men had died of natural causes.'

Jarrett looked at his father, who'd stopped to take a sip of beer. The old man was still in pretty good shape, he thought. It had been Harry's idea to hire the boat in Hua Hin.

'What was the deal he had with Waters?'

Harry showed his teeth, pulled his baseball hat forward over his forehead. 'Damn, I forget how hot it gets here.'

'Waters,' said Jarrett.

'Casey had accumulated a lot of chits, knowing one day he might need them. It seems one of his major debtors was Waters. You already know they were buddies in the marines. Waters first met Casey in Beirut. Terrorists had blown up a building, killing a lot of our men. Waters should have been in that building, but he wasn't. Casey had insisted he stay behind and help him close the bar late. So Casey had saved his life. A few years later, Casey was best man at Waters's wedding. Waters and Casey stayed in touch. After the first Gulf War, Waters joined Logistic Risk Assessment Services as a private contractor. I always liked that name; it could have been an insurance company. They sent him to Iraq. I'd known Waters for a long time. It seemed kind of natural he'd continue helping out as he had in the past. He was good at finding the right men for a freelance job. He'd done a payback job before, and I'd briefed him on the background. Maybe I talked a little too much about Jack Malone and what happened to him.' Harry Jarrett sighed like a man with a regret rising to the surface.

'You're saying Waters and Casey worked on special ops before?' asked Jarrett. He finished the beer and threw the bottle in a long arc, watching as it skittered over the surface and then sunk.

'We're not gonna catch any fish if you keep doing that.' Harry wrinkled his nose, feeling the sunburn tightening the skin.

'We're just pretending to fish.'

'Speak for yourself,' said Harry, tugging on his line.

He told his son about how Casey and Waters had had an annual reunion, one that coincided with Waters's wedding anniversary. It didn't matter where they were stationed or living, they always met outside MacDill Air Force Base in Florida. There was a seafood restaurant there that Casey loved. During the most recent reunion, they'd cracked crab legs there and drunk beer as they caught up with each other's lives. Only it hadn't been all that happy of a meeting. The secret prison in Thailand had been blown; a military lawyer had cautioned Casey to cooperate in the investigation, to tell the truth. There had been videotapes of the torture but they'd been destroyed, the lawyer told Casey. After a lifetime of doing his duty for his country, it looked like his country was going to reward him with a prison cell. Casey knew how the system worked; it was just a matter of time before he was reeled in and put through an inquisition.

Harry stood up, stretched his legs, walked over to the bait bucket, looked inside, and spat over the side. 'Now comes the conjecture part.'

Jarrett nodded, opening another beer, sweat pouring down his neck. He touched the cold beer bottle against his cheek and waited until Harry sat down. He came back with a chunk of tuna and slipped the hook into the center of the flesh before casting the line back. Harry wasn't the kind of man who rushed into judgment. 'It could've happened like this. Casey and Waters met and discussed life over a few drinks. Let's say they met in a bar near the base, a classy place – not the usual place they drank, but Waters was paying the bill. Casey had been uneasy, looking over his shoulder. The upscale nature of the place made him feel uncomfortable. Waters got him to relax with a couple of accents and jokes. Then Waters said something about how the government hadn't really given a shit about looking after veterans, how their company was no better than the government, and the real men of honor were being fucked around. I suspect that would've scored points with Casey, who'd thought he'd been lucky to not get busted in Baghdad and to get an assignment in Bangkok. His luck ran out when he got an appointment to testify before Congress. They discussed the unfinished business of his son's death. During dinner, they considered how to put things right, including avenging the death of Casey's son. When Waters came to me, using me as a sounding board, I told him frankly that I had reservations. But I let him talk me into it.'

'How'd he do that?'

His father looked at him for a full half-minute.

'He said, what if that had been your son? I am afraid he got to me.'

'Where'd they get the money?'

Harry smiled and said, 'Offer a man a million dollars and he'll become indignant; offer him a couple of million and his point of view shifts from north to south on the moral compass.' Harry had a nibble on his line and picked up the pole and started reeling in the line, but was getting resistance. He definitely had something on the other end. Jarrett helped him with the pole, and reached down with a net and brought on deck a thirty-pound grouper, gills heaving in and out, body and tail flopping around on deck. The huge mouth gasped for air. Conscious and half-paralyzed, the fish struggled until Harry lifted the club, stopped, looked at it.

'You ever wonder why they call one of these a "priest"?' he asked.

'Because it's used for last rites?'

Harry rewarded his son with a smile as he brought down the club on the grouper's head. The body went still, and Harry dropped the club on the deck, knelt down beside the large fish and examined it. Death stalked them in the Gulf of Thailand. Neither man said anything as Jarrett gutted the fish, drawing in the seagulls as he flung the guts into the sea.

'As I was saying, someone threw a sizeable amount of money at Casey,' he said. 'I did a little checking, and found money had gone into an offshore account in Casey's name. It's not apparent who had transferred the money or why. These guys were pros, and catching them wasn't an easy thing.'

'How much money?'

'Two million,' said Harry.

'That's enough.'

'Seems so,' said Harry, looking over at the cleaned fish. 'Looks like we caught supper.'

'You caught it.'

'I figure Casey and Waters hammered out a deal. They'd bring Tracer and you in and make a forty-thousand-dollar contribution to the Jack Malone Foundation. They had me on their side. It looked pretty solid in their eyes. Casey had the perfect cover for a paying-back-Jack mission; his son had been murdered in Thailand, the police force didn't have a reputation for solving crimes without the perp making a confession and reenacting the crime in front of TV cameras and the press. Casey was someone both of us had known in the past. Waters had vouched for him. There was nothing to raise a suspicion.'

'Tracer kept talking about how Casey's money had a funny smell. Like it'd been buried.'

'We don't know that all of the money paid went into that account. There was probably cash. When you're talking about criminal activity, you're talkin' billions of dollars a year. One of these days, the government's gonna find there's more money buried in the ground than stuffed in bank vaults. Most of it illegal.'

Harry didn't bother baiting his line. He left the pole on the deck.

'You wanna go back, dad?'

'Not a bad idea. The sun's getting to me. And we got what we came for.'

Jarrett moved to start up the engine, then turned, bent down on the deck, facing his father. 'If we'd have killed Somporn, and Casey had killed us, the Thai police would have been left with an unsolved crime, a mystery with no clues. He made it appear that he'd left the country.'

'I think Casey gave his ticket to Waters, who used it to board the flight to London. Gate security had been shown a phony passport in Casey's name, along with the boarding card.'

'Conjecture. But seems reasonable.'

'Who paid them the money?'

'That's where it gets real complicated,' said Harry, seeing his son had no intention of returning to shore without a few more answers. 'I've been thinking about the newspaper from Hua Hin he put in the condo, and the pool table. So I did some checking. It could be that Casey was making it appear that your death was connected to Cleary who was still running scam deals out of Perth.'

'Why would he go to the trouble?'

Harry smiled much the way Tracer had. 'He wanted to fuck with us. It could be as simple as that. Look what he did for a living. And that was certainly part of his stock in trade.'

'You're saying we don't know?'

Harry nodded. 'It comes down to that. We've got a gap in our information big enough to fly a C-130 through. We don't know if MacDonald ever told Cleary what happened that night.'

Jarrett thought his old man had lost it. 'That's crazy. MacDonald was scared shitless. They'd burned him with cigarettes.'

'What if I told you I had information that they were back in business? Another thing, you remember the guy with the gold earring?'

Varley. Jarrett would never forget killing him.

'Seems that he was Cleary's nephew. We thought at the time that those two guys weren't professionals. We got that part right.' Harry stared at the dead fish, tapping the gaping mouth with his toe. He looked up, not smiling, not frowning, but with his worried look. 'Maybe they got loaded on

Perth bud and MacDonald said, 'What if I told you I know who did your nephew and his friend?' Cleary would have been all ears, don't you think?'

'That's conjecture?'

'Varley was his nephew. That's a fact.'

'I can't believe MacDonald would do that.' Jarrett sat back hard on the deck chair.

Harry shrugged, opened the sunblock-lotion bottle and started applying lotion to his face. 'What about this guy Calvino?'

'What about him?'

'Another MacDonald? Another loose end to deal with in the future?'

Jarrett cracked a smile. 'You said it was conjecture about MacDonald.'

'I did.'

'Calvino saved our ass.'

'Like we saved MacDonald's?' Harry wasn't smiling. He missed sunblock on his left shoulder and the skin was already turning red.

Jarrett watched as several seagulls swooped down, following the boat, looking for more guts and blood. 'It's about the odds.'

His father made a face as he touched the sunburnt shoulder. 'It's always about the odds. You got to figure him right. Even then, you got to ask yourself. "Am I willing to lose the bet?"'

Jarrett fired up the engines and headed back to Hua Hin. The boat smelled of fish. He looked up and saw the seagulls following behind. They were also playing the odds.

CHAPTER 44

C huck Beckwith, the cheating husband Calvino had photographed at Washington Square – a few seconds after his first encounter with Jarrett and Tracer – barged into Calvino's office and threatened him. The man didn't understand he was in the wrong weight class the moment he'd stepped into Calvino's ring.

Calvino sifted through all the Bangkoks within Bangkok that he knew and couldn't come up with anything as lame as Beckwith. The man was a loser, one of the emotional cripples that yings learned had one essential function – they were reliable cash machines. Calvino had seen the spouses of clients like this before, bullies with American wives whose attack folded at the first sign of resistance. Pale, shaking with rage, Beckwith rushed him, throwing a sloppy, loopy punch. The fist flew out like it was the first time the man had ever tried to hit another man. Calvino deflected it with his forearm and swung hard, hitting Beckwith in the mouth and then again, hard, in the flabby midsection. Instead of a brick wall, Calvino's fist hit a pillow. There was no need to hit him again. Beckwith emitted a sound like air escaping from a puncture. His eyes bulged like an insect with its guts run through by a long, sharp pin. Calvino pushed him over and onto the floor with his foot. Beckwith doubled over and vomited on the floor. What came out was scrambled molten lava of bacon and eggs that smelled worse than the diapers of Ratana's kid.

'That's a bad diet for someone looking to pick a fight,' said Calvino.

The outraged husband tried to raise himself up but failed and sat down hard on his ass with his legs sprawled out. His intention to be a tough guy was there inside his head. He'd seen it all in movies and television, but in reality nothing ever worked so smoothly. His right hook was pathetic. He was an out-of-shape, middle-aged farang who'd forgotten he was no longer in high school or beating up on his wife.

'Don't come around with threats, Mr Beckwith. I don't like threats. You can understand that. Your wife hired me. I did the job. You take the consequences. Don't come along and try and lay your problems with your wife on me. Now get the fuck out of my office. I'm meeting my tailor.'

Calvino helped him to his feet and escorted him through the reception area and out the door.

'What time is my appointment?'

Ratana looked at her diary. 'After your lunch with Colonel Pratt.'

She handed him a computer printout. There

were several pages, and the color printer made the sports jackets as attractive as a full-page ad in *Vanity Fair*.

'I recommend Armani.'

Calvino sifted through the printouts and liked what he saw. 'Armani?'

'The Brioni didn't last long,' she said. 'It's time for a change.'

'The problem has been the fabric. This time I want the right material. Something that's easy to dry clean.'

Baby clothes hung along the side of the playpen. 'Blood's hard to get out unless you rinse it right away in cold water.'

'I'll remember that.' He folded up the prints and put them inside his jacket.

Colonel Pratt arrived for lunch a few minutes after Calvino had sat down. The Italian restaurant off Asoke had only been open for a few months. The décor was suitable for a colonel, and the homemade lasagna was worth the visit. Calvino was studying the Armani sports jackets in the printouts when Colonel Pratt pulled back a chair and sat down.

'Nice-looking jacket,' he said.

Calvino had a mellow smile. 'Ratana showed you these pictures of the Armani?' He knew the answer to the question. The two of them had conspired to upgrade his tailoring, but so far they'd been faced with unforeseen challenges that would test the limits of any brand.

'I liked the Brioni, but it wasn't all that durable,' the Colonel said.

Calvino liked it when the Colonel tried his hand at farang humor.

'Speaking of durability. Apichart's now an adviser to the new government.'

'It's his advertising background they want.'

'He's also not bad at shuffling up a makeshift hit team,' said Calvino.

'Isn't that what advertising agencies do?'

Calvino took out the newspaper clipping from New Jersey. There was a photograph of Waters's body wrapped in a tarpaulin in the trunk of a Buick. 'Here's a present,' Calvino said, handing the Colonel the clipping.

As Colonel Pratt sat back in his chair, he put on his reading glasses, and read the article. When the Colonel looked up, removing his reading glasses at the same time, Calvino said, 'Remember that Thai proverb, the one about the fish with the big mouth? Here's one who should have kept his mouth shut.'

'I thought you might have some news about Casey.'

'I recommend the lasagna,' Calvino said. 'And the rocket salad. And half-a-liter of house red. That should do it.'

'No one seems to know where to look for Casey. With all the resources of the American government, I find that strange,' said Colonel Pratt.

Calvino smiled and folded the clipping, putting

it back in his jacket. 'What if I told you the Colombians and the Americans were wasting their money looking for him?'

'They wouldn't believe you.'

Calvino had a broad grin. 'Exactly right. They'd just keep on looking.'

'If he's alive, they'll find him sooner or later. These people don't give up.'

'That would be good,' said Calvino. 'I hope they can put the pieces together.'

The waitress came to the table, and the Colonel ordered the lamb chops and pumpkin soup. Calvino wavered for a second before sticking with the lasagna and salad.

'Some people think Casey might have copied the video of some interrogations. That could prove embarrassing for the government,' said Colonel Pratt. 'I had a strange dream last night. Casey was in it. Only he was in the distance, lying still on a raised platform. From a side door a man appeared and came straight up to where I stood. He pointed at Casey and said, "I spoke with someone who saw him die, and he said that Casey openly confessed his treasons, begged for forgiveness, and repented deeply. He never did anything in his whole life that looked as good as the way he died."'

'Isn't that Shakespeare?'

'Macbeth,' said Colonel Pratt.

'Pratt, sometimes dreams are real.'

'You think my dream about Casey is a sign?'

Calvino shrugged as his salad arrived. 'Casey's

like a picture that fell out of the frame and disappeared.' Pratt had some idea that Calvino was holding back.

'Out of the frame as in dead, or on the run?'

Calvino shifted his weight as their main courses arrived. Calvino eyed the lamb chops as he inhaled hot steam rising from his own plate. 'Maybe. But there's a whole range of possibilities. Take the Chinese deity, Guan Yu. He's the god of war and literature. In Singapore and Hong Kong the locals have shrines to him. Guan Yu's the god of the police brotherhood. And the Triad and other Chinese gangsters, he's their god too. The gangsters, cops, and poets all put their faith in the same god.'

'Guan Yu isn't going to find Casey.'

Calvino tasted the lasagna, wishing he'd ordered the lamb chops. 'This is a little salty. But it's good.' He wiped his face with the cloth napkin, took a sip of wine. 'Of course Guan Yu won't find Casey. That's okay. The people who are looking would be better off hunting for Santa Claus.'

A grin came across Colonel Pratt's face. 'He's dead.'

Calvino held his fork suspended over his plate. 'He's dead.'

'Next time you should try the lamb chops,' said Colonel Pratt.

'Did you really have that dream about Casey with a ghost who channeled Shakespeare?'

'You're starting to sound like a wife,' said Colonel Pratt, cutting into the lamb chop.

Calvino stared at the lasagna going cold on the end of his fork, still suspended midair. He thought about Marisa and how, for a moment, he'd asked himself if she could be a wife, could be his wife. They'd sat across a table in a restaurant, and she'd told him that what she wanted more than anything was to go home. She knew he was already home.

Colonel Pratt raised his wine glass. Getting no reaction from Calvino, he reached across the table and clinked the rim of Calvino's glass where it stood.

'I'd like to make a toast.'

Calvino lowered his fork with the cold pasta and raised his glass.

'To the Java Jazz Festival,' said Colonel Pratt, grinning.

Calvino's jaw dropped. 'You got an invitation?'

The Colonel nodded. 'Yesterday.'

'Why didn't you phone me?'

The waiter refilled the wine glasses. Calvino sat back in his chair at a loss for words. Witnessing a friend's dream come true is a rare event.

'To the bonds of brotherhood and honor,' said Colonel Pratt, raising his glass and touching the rim on Calvino's. 'May those bonds never stop running in our blood.'

'Shakespeare?'

'Guan Yu.'

After lunch, Colonel Pratt dropped Calvino at his office. He walked up the stairs, unlocked the door, and closed the door behind him. Downstairs at One Hand Clapping, clients slipped in and out of the door, clients with their neckties unknotted, staggering down the small sub-soi. Calvino closed the blinds on his window, turned around, and used a key to unlock his desk drawer. Casey's DVDs were inside an envelope. He slipped one into his computer and waited until it loaded. Resting back in his chair, he watched Casey and a hooded man in a small room. Casey appeared on the screen wearing his sunglasses and baseball cap, circling the man like an animal closing in on helpless prey. The feeling of absolute power and absolute power-lessness coalesced in the frame. Hope had gone out of the frame, and in the emptiness was raw, unrestrained terror.

He'd asked himself what the right thing to do was with the DVDs. Hand them over to Colonel Pratt, and suddenly his friend's life would be turned upside down. Send them in an unmarked envelope to *The New York Times*? Or send them to a congressman on the committee looking into illegal CIA prisons? He'd been through all the possibilities.

He understood how the world worked if you were small-time with a big story; it worked against you. And how no matter whom he sent the DVDs to, in a matter of days or weeks the authorities would trace them back to the point of origin. The DVDs, like homing pigeons, would fly back to their roost above One Hand Clapping. Then what would happen? That was all too predictable. His life would never be the same; it would be forever turned upside down. Not even Pratt could help him if it were found out he had something to do with the DVDs. He tried to imagine the loss of face, the officials who would call for an inquiry. Men like Apichart and Somporn pointing a finger at the bad farang. With no Casey at hand, someone else would have to take the fall. A farang whistle-blower would fit the bill.

He played the video again, watching Casey take the bearded man, who couldn't have been more than in his mid-twenties, through a brutal interrogation. The man was around the same age as Casey's son. In the background were a couple of Thai officers. That would have been enough to cause an entire government to lose face, and disclosure could end only one way: bad for them, bad for him. There had just been an election. They'd have to start over. The bad publicity coming from a thousand lead editorials around the world would shift the spotlight from murderous thugs who happily strapped on a suicide vest to blow up innocent civilians to the American government and the secret prisons. But what was to be done with the killers in suicide vests? No one had the answer, but everyone had an opinion. Warehousing them was one thing, torture another. There was no simple solution. No matter what he did with the DVDs, something like Guan Yu had been unleashed across all lands, and those wanting jihad had fallen in love with death and blood.

He looked away from the screen to Colonel Pratt's drawing of the fish on the wall and thought about the Thai proverb, pla moh taay praw pak – or in English, the fish is dead because of its own mouth. Being a quiet American wasn't such a bad thing.

He turned up the volume on the computer, listening to the screams of the man who thought he was drowning. It was that kind of world. Men like Casey were the last line of defense against men whose basic wiring was not that different from Casey's.

Calvino had a rich Thai friend who had a starscape on his bedroom ceiling. It showed the exact configuration of stars and planets in the sky at the hour and minute of his birth. Calvino had once seen the ceiling and imagined what it would be like to lie in a bed under the sky of the night of your birth. He turned down the volume on the computer. The screams became muted and distant. And he wondered, in the world of men under that huge, infinite sky, how the influence of stars had ever resulted in secret prisons, sniper teams, drug dealers, and crooked politicians. He checked his email before closing down for the day. There was a message from Jarrett, asking if he were interested in hiring a boat and going out fishing next week.

Calvino leaned back in his chair. He glanced at

the open-mouthed fish drawing on the wall. He saw something he'd not seen before. The fish wasn't dead because of its big mouth; it died because it lived in a world that dreaded the truth. Calvino emailed back, saying he'd think about the invitation.

Calvino's tailor had promised that the Armani jacket would be ready next Wednesday. He'd sworn the new material had been treated to be resilient to all elements. He'd demonstrated by smearing ketchup on a piece of fabric, and it had wiped off neatly. It was durable enough to wrap the Shuttle as a heat shield. Only time would prove how it would handle the first splash of blood splashed off the mean Bangkok streets.